Witches BE CRAZY

A Tale That Happened Once Upon a Time in the Middle of Nowhere

LOGAN J. HUNDER

Night Shade Books
NEW YORK

Night Shade books may be purchased in bulk at special discounts for sales promotion, corporate gifts, fund-raising, or educational purposes. Special editions can also be created to specifications. For details, contact the Special Sales Department, Night Shade Books, 307 West 36th Street, 11th Floor, New York, NY 10018 or info@skyhorsepublishing.com.

Night Shade Books® is a registered trademark of Skyhorse Publishing, Inc.®, a Delaware corporation.

Visit our website at www.nightshadebooks.com.

10 9 8 7 6 5 4 3 2

Library of Congress Cataloging-in-Publication Data

Hunder, Logan J.
    Witches be crazy / Logan J. Hunder.
        pages cm.
    ISBN 978-1-59780-820-0 (paperback)
    1. Imaginary creatures—Fiction. 2. Imaginary wars and battles—Fiction. I. Title.
    PS3608.U53W58 2015
    813'.6—dc23

                                        2015006848

Print ISBN: 978-1-59780-820-0

Cover design by Jason Snair

Printed in the United States of America

Special thanks to Rachel: For supporting me even when this book was just a collection of semi-coherent ramblings about wizards and lesbians.

DRAMATIS PERSONAE

DUNGAR.. Angry ex-ironworker

JIMMINY... Whimsical wanderer

ROSE .... Studious young miss

GILLY... Devout guardswoman

KOEY... New queen of Jenair

RAINCHILD............................... Diamond making dickhead

HERROW... Local business owner

DRITUNGO .... Project manager

SIR LEE ....Former defender of the crown

SIR PENT .... Current defender of the crown

NOBEARD.................... Sailor with name-defining facial hair

STRANGER .... Foreigner

The kingdom of Jenair
Imposing and grand.
Was very well-known
All throughout the land.
Fortified by walls
Wrapped around its towers,
It was the peak of pristine
From its spires to its flowers.
This jewel of the country
Where the winds of change blow
Will soon shift its power
To whoever's got the dough.
For the king's only daughter
Must soon be wed
To a suited young man
Who can rule in his stead.
He's been forced to retire
As he's fallen quite ill
So he must find his heir
And put him in the will.
Thus this marriage will not be
For love, affection, or fate.
You don't even have to be
Friendly, good-looking, or straight.
It is in this search for suitors
Where our story will start,
Yes it's another tale involving
A quest for a lady's heart.
But don't shut this story yet
For drawing on paradigms.
A lot of stuff is going to happen
Once I stop writing in rhymes.

PROLOGUE

Dying flames chewed hungrily on the remaining morsels of a once mighty city. The final traces of the thick smoke had finally begun to dissipate, leaving a clear view to gauge the destruction. Not a structure still stood in the piles of ash and wreckage. That sort of thing tended to happen when every building was made out of wood. All that once was now was no longer, and all that would be was now a mystery. In order to solve that mystery, someone was going to need a really big broom.

Despite the heat of the razing, the empty streets were cold and lifeless. The only movement they saw now were the scorched embers that were blown away with each light breeze. So many had walked them just the day before, completely unaware that they would never walk them again. Not that they would want to anyway, as the only things they would find were remains of homes, livelihoods, and memories. Not to mention the truly awful smell.

There was but one man seen departing the devastation alive, the only one to escape the fatal fate of his former fellows. No one knew his name or face, nor did they know his relation to the city. He was simply a lone man stained with soot from head to foot that wore a tattered cloak which fluttered behind him as he hurried away. If there were anyone who could explain what happened, it would probably have been him. But the world was a big place, and a man with nothing had nowhere he couldn't go. Except for country clubs, they tended to only allow access to people who possessed things.

As for the mysterious man himself, he was last seen heading eastward into the lands of a kingdom called Jenair.

**

The pride of the kingdom of Jenair was its capital city, which was senselessly also named Jenair. Strategically placed on the center hill overlooking the lush yet manicured countryside, it marked the perfect focal point for the numerous winding cross-roads and the nomadic souls that routinely traversed them.

Like any societal epicenter where travelers from faraway lands would congregate, the kingdom was always teeming with the usual products of these people: foreign goods, innovative inventions, venereal diseases, and the most common of all: stories, rumors, and information. Each new temporary resi-dent to the city contributed to and perpetuated the influx of tales of every topic one could imagine. The cobblestone streets were reliably rife with stories of gallant warriors saving prin-cesses, dragon caves that lay just over the next mountain, or this week's underground group of revolutionaries that were "totally gonna topple the fascist regime this time!"

Normally in the wake of a disaster like the one that befell their neighbor, no one in the kingdom would find themselves discussing anything else. However, before any theories even had a chance to develop, the health of their beloved King Ik found itself taking a sharp turn for the worse. The illness's rapid progression left the king with little time to set his affairs in order, particularly the most pressing matter of finding a suitable heir to marry his daughter and assume the throne.

The shocking and saddening news spread among the res-idents of the city and kingdom like a plague. Ik's decaying health on its own may not have been enough to phase out the neighboring kingdom's capital's destruction, but the gossip was given an enhanced allure due to the fact that nobody was aware that the king even had a daughter.

Relatively little personal information was known about their beloved monarch. Formally known as King Ik Theik V, he assumed the throne at the young age of seventeen after the horrific affair many years ago when a pack of rabid redbears that just happened to be in the area stormed the royal lunch-eon that was foolishly being held outside the castle walls. King Ik IV was among the casualties as well as several of his advisors.

As a result, Ik V's first official act as king was the instruc-tion of the royal detective detachment to investigate the inci-dent and produce a blameworthy individual. The investigation lasted well over a year and never produced such an individual, likely because it was pretty obvious they were mauled by wild animals.

When he received this news, Ik decided to have the atroc-ity blamed on the other neighboring kingdom of Nonamay. In the long run it proved to be a very smart decision because when the people were coaxed into hating something else they became less likely to aim their hate at their overlords.

During his tenure as king, Ik V only instigated one other official act. Today it is still known as "Everyone Go Out Into the Forest and Kill Redbears Day," and it takes place on the anniversary of Ik IV's death every year. The holiday is named as such because it is an accurate description of the events that take place and because the king's minister of propaganda, who was also in charge of naming things, was one of the advisors ground up by redbear jowls on that fateful day.

After the implementation of this classic holiday, King Ik retired into his castle and outsourced the vast majority of kingdom management to his remaining advisors. Little had been heard from King Ik in the years that followed and he had been largely forgotten. However now the word of his illness and daughter's existence were the talk of the town and the news was being spread far and wide prompting men and even women to journey from all over the land to compete for the hand of the princess, or foot, if they were into that sort of thing.

As word spread, tales regarding the origins of the royal heir evolved at an equal pace. It was said her mother was an angel who descended from the skies many years ago during the celebration of what was thought at the time to be the official genocide of the redbears. The princess was then allegedly kept secret from the public for the purposes of receiving proper instruction on princess etiquette. This instruction supposedly included numerous lessons based around mastering skills such as diplomacy, proper manners, feigning convincing empathy, keeping one's opinions to one's self, and sandwich making.

There were also alternative theories surrounding the princess. One postulated she was not a descendent of the Theik lineage at all, but was instead an apocryphal daughter that Ik V had smuggled in for the purposes of concealing his impotence and thus preserving his status as a dominant male figure. This theory was fishy at best as it would be nonsensical to devote effort to faking an heir only for that heir to be a female bastard, but there were always some who would believe anything that would allow them to laugh at their leader.

Irrespective of her questionable origins, the one unmistakable quality of the princess was her undeniable beauty. She was known to have left the castle and made a public appearance only once. It is said that during this appearance her skin, which was oddly tanned for someone who had apparently never been outside, emitted a light more radiant than that of the sun and her smile was so alluring that a flock of birds splattered themselves all over a tower because they were physically unable to watch where they were going.

She had long blonde hair that cascaded downward, flowing over her shoulders and encompassing her in a sheen of gold down to her hips. Her eyes were a brilliant blue and conveyed a sense of magic and wonder as they gleamed in the daylight like sapphires. Her cheekbones were high and wide, etching a faithful lingering smile and air of friendliness into her visage. Her lips were an ideal color and proportion to adequately convey the notion that she was a healthy and viable individual with which to conduct reproduction activities. Her body also reflected a similar notion. It was insisted by all that no maiden embodied the concepts of beauty, grace, and refinement than the unfairly fair Princess Koey.

Needless to say, women wanted to be her and men wanted to own her. And so it was that nobles, knights, and generally important individuals began to make the trek from far and wide, across treacherous volcanic landscapes, dark forests, and giant chicken infested steppes to make her acquaintance and participate in the bidding war. As a result, the numerous small towns and tiny villages hidden along the main routes began to receive a massive influx of traffic consisting of royal hopefuls, tourists, traders, circus folk, and shady characters who would inform unlikely heroes that all was not as it seemed in the kingdom of Jenair.

ONE

ONCE UPON A TIME IN THE MIDDLE OF NOWHERE

Far to the south, across the Dagger Mountains in the lone oasis of the Snake Eye Desert, there lay a small village by the name of Woodwall. The town's nonsensical positioning in the middle of a barren desert had left it largely isolated from the rest of the country. Traversing the arid landscape to reach the town was a perilous journey on its own. However the danger was worsened by local legends of a giant python that was said to lull travelers into complacency with its adorable big doughy eyes before head butting them into the distance with all its might for no other apparent reason than its own personal enjoyment.

As a result of its isolation the town had been forced to adapt itself into a relatively self-sustaining community, but was not completely devoid of a tourism market. Occasionally visitors would brave the barrens and visit the town with one specific delicacy in mind.

A unique quality of this oasis was that it possessed the only source in all the country of the coveted emdeema fungus; a rare mushroom that was only ever found growing on oasis trees. Upon ingestion, emdeema induced euphoria, vivid hallucinations, and an overwhelming feeling of joy in an individual. The effect was so intense that it made addicts willing to put themselves through the side effects of dysentery, itchy eyeballs, and left-side-only weight gain. However those with the tendency to partake in such narcotics and those who were willing to make long and treacherous journeys did not overlap much, so most of the emdeema users were permanent residents.

As a result of its isolation and drug-addled demographic, the town of Woodwall found itself in a stage of suspended growth. Fortunately, the members of the community who still considered themselves to be working class had been enough to keep the town afloat. From the butchers and bakers to the candlestick makers, they were content to live their lives of modest means and even took pride in their rural community. But with every community there will always be those who don't quite fit in.

In the heart of the dilapidated building on the south side of the oasis, obscured by the broad palm fronds and his generally unkempt yard, there was a faint glow of the local blacksmith's forge. Dungar Loloth and every Loloth before him had lived there producing all of the ironware in the town of Woodwall since its inception many generations ago.

Despite their legacy, the Loloths never quite properly meshed into the fabric of the tiny hamlet. Their inherently gruff nature combined with their unabashed contempt for junkies rendered them unable to properly connect with their neighbors. Luckily for them, all denizens of the desert had a need for iron tools whether or not they were fond of their supplier. Since no one else in town even knew a vise from a pair of tongs, they remained captive customers to the monopolized market.

After the death of his father, Gundar, a few years ago, Dungar became the only remaining member of the Loloth bloodline; thereupon at the ripe old age of thirty-four he also became the sole heir to the family business. Like his father, he had a mane of dull curly carmine hair and matching beard which he had to keep short due to it constantly catching fire from the forge.

What he lacked in height was compensated for by his broad shoulders and stocky build, but his most prominent feature was what were referred to as his "crazy eyes." They were a pale blue which seemed to capture the light in any room and vibrantly stand out against his weather-beaten skin. They always had a look that could strike a feeling of unease in whoever peered into them, which gave him the impression of someone who could snap at any moment. This notion was further supported by his resting facial expression being perceived as one of perpetual disdain.

He bore the other classic Loloth features as well, particularly the broad flattened nose and thin lips which were frequently curled upward to reveal teeth during his many moments of agitation. Whatever business the Loloths lost due to their intimidating visage, however, was regained by their quality iron products and lack of competitors.

Unfortunately, despite upholding his family's reputation for superior craftsmanship business had been at an all-time low for the blacksmith in recent years. The steadily waning Woodwall ironware market then all but dissolved when that hippie wizard showed up in town flaunting his drug-addled discovery of how to transmute wood into diamond, leaving Dungar hopelessly unable to compete with the diamondware's aesthetic appeal and ease of production.

Consequently, Dungar was forced to begin relying on the makeshift inn he converted his home into when business first began to decline. Originally meant to merely supplement his income, it became his fulltime profession while he looked forward to the day Rainchild Earthumper the Wise inevitably died from an overdose or ramifications of trying to "connect with nature." Or if he just simply left, but that's not as gratifying.

The inn's business, albeit not substantial, was still a defini-tive improvement on the small income of his remaining black-smithing business. Dungar quickly came to find no customer was more loyal and reliable than an alcoholic once he had liquor on his menu. As long as he kept the booze flowing there would always be food on his table.

Despite it still not being his ideal trade, the blacksmith fit quite well into the role of an innkeeper. His years working the forge had tempered his body into a condition as hardy as the very iron he folded. And although he was not a particularly sociable fellow, his inherently honorable nature coupled with his sturdy physique allowed him to foster his inn's reputation for fair prices, safety from theft, and swift defenestration of any who opted to not follow the rules or keep the peace.

With the recent business of a potential true love and/or meal ticket up for grabs, the many travelers making the journey to the kingdom created a marked increase in guests to his inn. As they came and went, he found himself actually beginning to mildly enjoy their company. The newfound public interest in politics and current events was a breath of fresh air com-pared to the usual sanctimonious ramblings of Rainchild that everyone would otherwise be eating up.

Since this marriage business began, many guests of all walks of life had shown up at his door. One was a man of wealthy means who clearly believed he was the best candidate for royal ascension. He traveled with a caravan of several vehi-cles holding many different exotic goods as well as his own personal detachment of archers. He also had a man covered in leaves whose only duty was apparently to stand very still and pretend to be a potted plant.

Another guest was a mild mannered little old man in shabby clothes who had been making his way up from the val-ley in the south. He presented himself as a chauffeur and was working his way towards the kingdom, stopping off at any little town he came across in search of someone who would commission a ride from him, a venture that was not going well since he didn't seem to understand that chauffeurs were generally expected to provide the cart as well as drive it.

Dungar had virtually no regard for trivial traits like ambition and social status. All guests received an equal amount of apathy and disinterest from him. He would consent to idle chit chat with any who graced his tavern with their coin, but primarily felt compelled to keep to himself and pay no interest to whatever their intent and wherever they intended it. So long as tabs were paid and disturbances were not caused, he was willing to accommodate any and all. That being said, the odd forcible removal was something he discerned an occasional pleasure from providing.

However today would not be business as usual for the pub proprietor, for yet another soon-to-be guest lay on the horizon and friendliness was not in the aura he was projecting. Quite the opposite in fact; this man had clearly seen some shit.

TWO

GET OFF MY PORCH

After opening the inn and administering a size thirteen boot suppository to the child drawing graffiti on his front door, Dungar began to carry out his daily ritual of setting up his practice. This practice of setting up practice consisted of little more than unlatching the saloon doors of his entrance and then setting out the stools in front of his bar.

The bar was the only area within the inn for which he had any pride or affection. The walls were kept completely free of any paintings, lamps, or windows. Instead, every square inch was covered in intricate designs he hand carved by himself. Often they took the form of patterns tracing the grains of the wood, but some portions of the wall almost appeared to be murals of sorts. With a trained eye one could spot pictures here and there such as dragons or knights. The royal crest of the Theik royal family was also very plain to see carved right above the liquor cabinet, particularly the firefin piranha on the shield. One could also not help but notice many carvings of what appeared to be wizards hanging from trees and being burned at stakes hidden within the patterns.

Shortly after he had set out all the barstools a tell-tale shrill squeak of the door alerted him to his first, and often only, customer of the day. Ever so slowly the wizened old man shambled his way into the bar, leaning heavily on a cane that looked even older than he was.

"Mister Jitters, my friend. How are you this fine morning?" Dungar greeted enthusiastically.

Mister Jitters raised his non-cane hand and smiled a toothless grin before replying with an equally enthusiastic "Mrgrrglrglrlllrblr!"

For as long as Dungar had known Mister Jitters he had never heard the man make any noise that sounded like a coherent language. He had no idea what the man's name was, or anything about him really. The name "Jitters" was merely derived from the fact that every single limb on the man's body shook with violent tremors on a relatively constant basis, provoking the assumption that he was likely very ill or incredibly cold. The former seemed to be the most likely explanation, as Mister Jitters appeared to be at a very advanced age to the point that it's questionable how he was even still alive.

However, irrespective of his appearance or conditions, Jitters had been coming to the inn regularly since the day it opened and, after much trial and error trying to figure out what the man was ordering, he became a steady consumer of every drop of aquavit that the innkeeper could produce. After that, the innkeeper began to genuinely cherish the company of the curious old man.

Jitters would patiently listen to anything he had to say, occasionally even responding with one of his usual guttural croaks. Occasionally Dungar found himself questioning the man's sanity or lucidity, wondering if the man even was aware of himself or understood anything said to him, but those thoughts were usually quickly dismissed once he remembered how much money Jitters has dropped in his bar. Of course then that thought would lead him to question where a seemingly senile centenarian is getting all this money from, but he doubted he would receive an intelligible answer if he asked.

Unfortunately, Dungar's soft spot for Mister Jitters was not usually shared by other patrons. For starters, his shaking condition caused his tankard to clang loudly against the table and often spill its contents on nearby bar dwellers. Secondly, while personal hygiene was not very well maintained by most people in these times, Jitters' sanitary shortfalls were second to none. The stench that emanated from his pores was foul to say the least and deadly to say the most. Usually he would take it upon himself to simply retire into a corner away from the vicinity of the other bar dwellers. However on this day he opted not to move a muscle when the latest traveler graced the inn with his presence.

Dungar just happened to be out behind the inn fetching a rum barrel when the saloon doors swung open revealing a disheveled looking man wrapped in a tattered and soot-stained green cloak with the hood up. A shady looking character if there ever was one. Under the hood you could see his pronounced chin adorned with a thick bushy soul patch jutting out. He had a severe underbite which caused his lower lip to protrude noticeably farther than the upper which did wonders to pronounce the sneer on his face. He surveyed the inside of the bar, tracing the wood carvings with his eyes until they fell on the shaky old grey-haired man sitting at the bar, his tankard jingling loudly against the table.

The stranger removed his hood to reveal the face of a middle aged man with narrow eyes and a receding hairline. He had a noticeable scar underneath his left eyebrow which followed along the outline of his eye socket. Slowly he made his way to the bar, calmly and deliberately putting a little extra effort into each step as if to enhance the sound of his heavy boots banging against the floor.

As he reached the bar he took the stool next to Jitters, taking a moment to size the man up before his eyes made their way back to the tankard which continued to clank against the counter in rhythm with Jitters' tremors. After a brief twinge of disgust crossed his face he turned his attention to the other side of the counter, which was still empty.

"Oi!" he bellowed at the empty space behind the bar, "I'm thirsty!"

His voice echoed in the silence of the empty tavern. It was hoarse with a faint rumble, he probably smoked a lot. The man scanned the bar once again but nothing had changed. He saw no shadows moving in the back nor did he hear anything except for the continued oscillating clashing of Jitters' mug against the counter.

His patience finally worn, the man raised his hand and slammed Jitters' clanging container against the table. Head still facing forward, Jitters' quivering continued but the room was now completely silent.

The stranger's eyes were now transfixed on the sheepish old man with a look of extreme antipathy. Narrowing his eyes he drew a breath to speak but stopped short when he felt a monstrous hand roughly clasp his shoulder. As he turned his head the stranger found himself face to face with the crazy eyes of the bearded brute looming over him. Seeing the man frozen in a wide-eyed expression before him, Dungar's hostile gaze softened and he chuckled to himself as he walked around to the other side of the bar.

By the time Dungar had made his way back over to the liquor side, the stranger's anxiety had decreased and he appeared comfortable again; which is why it came as a huge surprise to him when the innkeeper reached over the bar, grabbed a handful of his shirt, and jerked him out of his seat and halfway over the counter. Once again the stranger found himself staring into the pair of crazy eyes as they stared back at him. As their eyes locked and their noses touched a slight grin formed on Dungar's face, and with audible amusement he growled at the man.

"Listen to me very carefully there, stranger. If you touch Mister Jitters's mug again then I will pin your head against the bar, patiently wait for Mister Jitters to finish his beverage, then

I'm gonna take that tankard and I'm gonna drive it through your skull. Do I make myself clear?"

"Crystal." The stranger sputtered, staring at the ceiling.

Casually, Dungar tossed him backwards onto his seat. Despite the brief ordeal that just ensued, the stranger's resolve did not appear to have weakened. He continued to eye his bartender curiously with a look of slight disesteem.

"You folks don't have much law around here do you?" The stranger mused.

"Within these walls I am the law." Dungar decreed. "Now I suggest you order a drink."

The stranger grumbled something incoherent under his breath. "Fine then. I'll take the strongest, most potent, and cheapest drink you've got."

Eyes gleaming, Dungar smirked at him. "Unless you want a tall glass of my piss, I suggest you order something else."

At this, his guest sighed briefly before smirking up at the bartender. Nodding his head towards Jitters he then mumbled "I'll have what he's having then, just give me a damned drink."

Tensions rapidly decreased within the inn as the alcohol began to flow. Soon the initial contention between Dungar and his guests had been all but forgotten.

"Anyone ever tell you you're a real shady lookin' character?" Dungar asked, as he slid yet another freshly filled tankard towards the cloaked man.

"More than you might think."

"So do you have a name, stranger?"

"Seems you already know it." He retorted, with an inebriated chortle.

Dungar paused cleaning a glass and gave him a puzzled look. "Stranger?"

Stranger chuckled again.

"Your name is Stranger . . . ?" Dungar repeated with skepticism as he set the glass down.

"Where I come from children are named based off of the impression their parents have of them." Stranger explained nonchalantly. "My father didn't want any kids." He added with a sigh, still not looking up from his mug.

After a silent and awkward pause, he looked up expectantly. Dungar pondered the information provided to him briefly before he shrugged and resumed cleaning his glass.

"Ah I've heard worse." He dismissed. "So Daddy didn't love ya, it's not as if you . . . I dunno . . . Watched an evil wizard destroy your home and murder your family or something."

Stranger sat silently giving him a blank stare.

". . . Did you?" Dungar asked awkwardly, detecting the tension in the room.

"No, no, certainly not." Stranger admitted, eyes returning to his beverage. "I didn't sit around and watch as it happened."

Once again Dungar ceased polishing his glass and looked at Stranger, this time visibly agitated. Stranger met his look with his own defiant one.

"Come again?"

"You heard me."

Dungar frowned at the offended man before him. His eyes then moved to the clasp on Stranger's cloak. It was made of cheap iron, but bore the shape of a kingdom's crest. Twin daggers crossed beneath a panther.

"You're from the city of Farrawee?"

"Maybe. Might be better to call it the remains of the city of Farrawee now." Stranger grumbled mournfully.

"Quit being such a pity whore and either tell me what happened or don't!"

"I thought innkeepers were supposed to be wise and compassionate."

"My job is simply to get you as drunk as your coin purse will allow." Dungar informed him firmly. "Sympathy is not a service I sell. Either drink until you forget your problems or maybe go send word to King Ik pleading for assistance against whatever your problem is."

"HAH." Stranger scoffed loudly into the inn. "As if King Ik could possibly help my home."

At this, Dungar grabbed hold of his cloak again. "I may not be the most patriotic guy around these parts, but if you come into my bar and start belittling my monarch then you're gonna have a bad time."

Stranger stared back into Dungar's crazy eyes, but they no longer had any effect on him.

"Your king can't even save his own kingdom!" he snapped.

Dungar's pique briefly subsided in favor of amazement. Brazenness in the face of immediate physical danger was not something he witnessed in his clientele very often, so intimidation was a tactic that was usually effective. He glanced at Jitters but as usual the fidgety old man seemed completely oblivious to everything happening around him. Dungar turned his attention back towards the stranger.

"Well then, it's been a while since we had a customer choose to leave through the window."

With that, he wrapped a steely arm around Stranger's neck and proceeded to drag him up the stairs to the second floor. Stranger kicked his feet against the floor and clawed at the arm but it was to no avail.

"No you don't understand!" He choked.

"Perhaps you should help me understand then." Dungar quipped, not slowing his pace.

Stranger continued to pull at his arm. Between wheezes and assorted choking sounds the only words caught were "can't breathe!"

As they reached the landing at the top of the stairs, he kicked open the nearest door and hurled the now barely conscious man into it, causing him to land in a pile of dust. From floor to ceiling the room was filled with broken furniture and other assorted junk that Dungar had collected. Carved into the heap of debris there was a path leading across the room to a lone window frame on the far wall.

This was no ordinary window. This was his favorite window in all the land. It was from this window that he tossed cheats, troublemakers, and other various miscreants who evoked his instinct to impose his own brand of order. The glass was long missing and the frame had seen much abuse from previous incidents wherein the victim was too fat to fit or Dungar was too drunk to aim his tosses properly.

Looking out the window filled one's eyes with a wonderful hilltop view of the edge of the oasis as the bank sharply turned downward before meeting with the sands of the desert. There was also a noticeable indent in the long grass which had been worn into it over time by the various perpetrators of incidents past. One glance out the window and, even after downing many drinks, Stranger was able to deduce what was going to happen next.

As Dungar's colossal paw gripped his clothing again, Stranger managed to sputter "Your king cannot help because he's likely already dead!"

Dungar, who had been winding up, stopped short. "What?"

"He has been sick, really sick," Stranger sputtered. "The same thing that did in my king has already set upon yours!"

Dungar remained frozen, processing the information.

Stranger gripped Dungar's wrist. "Don't do this!"

Dungar looked back at him, staring into his eyes with anguish. "But I have to."

Stranger's expression of fear changed to bewilderment. "What?"

"Everyone's expecting a window toss." Dungar explained, stepping to the side to reveal a crowd of people that had formed in the doorway.

"It's really one of the few forms of entertainment we get around here." He amended.

Stranger began to stammer incoherently, trying and failing to convey his competing fear, surprise, and confusion.

"We'll pick this up again in a moment, just close your eyes and relax the body." Dungar comforted.

Suddenly everything turned to slow motion for Stranger, and the only sound he was able to make as he flew through the air was a drawn out "Noooooooo" which was effectively drowned out by the cheer of the crowd.

THREE

WITCHES BE CRAZY

After the event had finished, Dungar wasted no time ushering the crowd that had formed in his bar out the door. It was rather uncanny how they seemed to have advanced warning every time he was to throw somebody out the window and would always gather to watch the spectacle. However after the first few times his amazement began to wear off and he simply resigned himself to his audience.

Unlike his many previous victims, this patron was no ordinary troublemaker and that was what worried him. Their conversation had transcended beyond typical bar chat and Dungar was compelled to get to the bottom of his claims one way or another. Quickly as his stubby legs could take him, he strode out the back door past the forge and into the field where Stranger now lay.

"Stranger. Stranger. Wake up."

Stranger opened his eyes to reveal the big blue ones of Dungar staring back with a look of judgment.

"You're fine. Get up." He asserted as he picked Stranger off the ground. "We need to talk."

"You threw me out a window . . ." Stranger grumbled, still adjusting to consciousness.

"Don't worry, nothing is broken. And you were being a jackass anyway." The blacksmith dismissed. "Besides, nothing sobers you up faster than fear."

Still carrying Stranger, he strolled back to the bar and casually dropped him back into his stool beside Jitters, who had been regularly sipping at his long empty tankard the entire time. Snatching Jitters' mug for a refill, Dungar addressed Stranger again.

"So what is going on in Jenair?"

Stranger gaped at him, incredulous towards his nonchalance. "You threw me out a window!"

"I also let you back in afterwards, and that's unprecedented. Have some scotch and you'll feel fine. Now I won't ask you again. What happened to King Ik?"

Stranger sighed as he accepted the whiskey. "It happened a few months ago . . ." Stranger began, as he proceeded to recount the story of the fall of Farrawee. The tale goes something like this:

In a land fairly close by lay Jenair's sister kingdom of Farrawee. Like most entitled younger siblings, it tended to rip off the things its older siblings did, and as such also senselessly named its capital the same name as the kingdom itself. Farrawee's capital city of Farrawee was presided over by a charming, handsome, and truly benevolent king. To those who could overlook the fact that he was an unabashed manwhore, he was the perfect ruler. He was incredibly fond of the ladies of his kingdom, and the ladies of his kingdom were incredibly fond of his money, and permissive of his bedroom skills. His marriage to the queen of his fair kingdom was never negatively affected by his infidelity either because the queen was blessed with the mindset of being totally into that sort of thing.

One day while the king was making his rounds through the kingdom looking for his next plaything he came across the most exquisite creature. She had spectacular golden hair stretching down to the small of her back, smoother than silk and reflected light so brilliantly it was amazing she didn't start fires everywhere she went. Her eyes cast an enveloping feeling of warmth upon you as they sparkled in the afternoon sunshine more dazzling than the most perfectly cut aquamarine crystal; and her lips and body perfectly conveyed to the king the notion that she was a healthy and viable individual with which to conduct reproduction activities. Needless to say, the king wasted no time before picking her up and whisking her away to the chamber of unspeakable happenings within his castle.

Unbeknownst to the king, this fraternization fuelled a fiendish fate for his city. The following morning she was not dismissed with the usual fruit basket and slap on the ass, but was rather escorted in a tour around the castle privately led by the king himself. She was treated to banquets and tournaments as the king's special guest, and was quickly welcomed as a permanent resident into the castle. Much speculation was had as to exactly what she was doing to the king, but the results were indisputable. The king thoroughly besotted. When the king was completely wrapped around her fingers the drama would *really* begin.

The first step down the kingdom's road to ruin came when the king had a very public and messy divorce with the queen followed by a hasty drive-thru wedding where leech and lecher tied the knot. In addition to being stripped of all her royal ties, the former queen was also inexplicably banished from the kingdom. But even more suspicious than her nonsensical banishment was the fact she had disappeared without a trace and even those most loyal to her were unable to locate her.

Only after she had firmly become the only woman in the king's life did the new queen's true colors begin to show through. She hoarded extravagant treasures, exclusively ate exotic and expensive foods, and regularly staged festivals; none of these things could have ever been afforded if she had not hiked the taxes up to extortionate levels.

During all of this turmoil the king, who up until this point had been a truly benevolent and caring monarch, remained uncharacteristically apathetic and dejected. The mysterious woman began to seize more and more kingdom control from him until eventually he had relinquished nearly all his power.

Over time the kingdom gradually began to buckle under this new regime, and talk of revolt began to circulate the streets. At the first hint of it, the queen enacted martial law. Peasants and general lower class individuals began to be swept off the streets in droves and made to disappear. After capture, one's death was all but certain; but it always took place inside the castle away from the eyes of the masses. During all of this time, the gates were barred and under constant watch. No one was permitted to leave; only to suffer and stand helplessly by as their fair kingdom collapsed around them.

Finally came the most fateful day of them all. The remaining citizens who still drew breath cowered within the decrepit walls of what remained of their homes when they heard the marching of a thousand feet. The entire king's guard patrolled the streets, searching every building for whoever would dwell within. Men women and children were torn from their homes and herded towards the castle where the mysterious woman and her pet king lay within. As per their orders, the guards ensured that every last soul within that city was herded into the bowels of the castle. However, after the doors closed behind them, not a single person emerged from that intricate pile of stones ever again. No peasant, guard, whore, noble, king, nor even the mysterious woman herself have been seen since.

By the time Stranger had finished even Jitters appeared to have been absorbed by his story.

"How did you escape?" Asked an unfamiliar voice.

Everyone turned to see a little old man had entered the room during the story without anyone noticing.

"Oi!" Dungar bellowed. "Buy a drink, buy a room, or get out!"

"B-But I've already bought a room." The old man stammered.

"Then go to it!" Dungar ordered.

Muttering something about poor customer service, the man departed. When he had cleared the room, Dungar turned back to Stranger.

"I remember him." Dungar chuckled. "Chauffeur by trade. Nice guy. He did have a point though, if everyone disappeared to never be seen again then how are you here to tell me all this?"

"I managed to leap from a window of my bedroom shortly before the guards stormed my house."

"Ohhhhh. It all makes sense now."

Stranger cocked his head to the side, looking at him confusedly.

"Well that's clearly why you're so terrified of being thrown out windows."

At a loss for words, Stranger just gaped at him.

Slamming his hand on the table, Dungar began to cackle a deep throaty laugh. "Ah lighten up! I'm just kiddin' ya!"

Seeing that the man was clearly not amused, he continued his inquiry. "So before I threw you out the window you were saying the same thing that did in your king was coming here."

Stranger snorted loudly at the notion. "Coming here? She's already here, you oaf. I've heard the talk of your king's new 'daughter,' strange how she fits the exact description of my former queen."

"Oh is that right." The innkeeper responded with only slight interest, peering into Jitters's mug. "So is that why you're here then? Some good old fashioned revenge?"

"Nothing of the sort!" His guest huffed sanctimoniously. "Now that she has made her way here I'm headed eastward to Nonamay. You lot would be wise to do the same. It's the only way to temporarily escape your doom!"

Dungar's blissful mood evaporated immediately at this, partially because he'd rather die than go to Nonamay, but mostly due to the other implications. "You mean to tell me that you are the only one aware of a force that means to see us all destroyed, and you are going to simply carry on your way without so much as a warning?"

"Consider this your warning." Stranger scoffed, draining the contents of his tankard. "I already tried waiting around to see how things turned out and I nearly paid for it with my own life, and missed out on getting to drink this rotgut oil you serve. You lot are responsible for yourselves, my hide is more important to me than yours."

Without even a pause he got up to leave, but did not manage to make it far before he felt the familiar iron-grip of Dungar's hairy bicep and forearm wrapped around him. The blacksmith was pretty quick for his size.

"Well I'll be." Stranger heard the bearded man growl into his ear. Although he couldn't see them, he could feel the crazy eyes boring holes into his skull. "I don't reckon we've ever had the same man volunteer for the window twice in one night."

This time Stranger hardly struggled as he was hauled up the stairs.

"I am not the one who seeks to do you harm, innkeeper." Stranger tried to reason.

"Perhaps not." Dungar acknowledged as he placed Stranger before the familiar window frame which now over-looked the same landscape as before only this time under a blanket of the darkness of the night.

"But you are fine to just walk away without even trying to prevent countless others from facing the fate you yourself barely escaped. That makes me not very fond of you, and this is what I do to people I'm not very fond of."

Without missing a beat, Dungar then drove his heel into the cloaked man's midsection, propelling him a good five or six feet horizontally ass-first out the window before falling to the ground below and producing the satisfactory "Thud" that

Dungar had come to grow very fond of over the last few years. He paused briefly to catch any last words that may be called out, but none came. As he made his way back down the stairs he surmised the man had likely been knocked out cold.

Upon returning to the bar, Dungar couldn't help feeling a twinge of guilt for his newly departed patron.

"Don't suppose you think I was a bit rough on him?" He asked Jitters.

For the first time since Stranger had arrived, Jitters looked up from his mug and into Dungar's eyes. His tremors had noticeably diminished now that Stranger had been removed from his side.

"Ah you're right." Dungar rationalized, shaking his head. "That man was nothing but trouble. Likely wasn't even speaking the truth."

But as he did his nightly rounds clearing the clutter, he couldn't shake the conversation that had just transpired. After all, the king's health was never spotty before the arrival of this princess. He also had to consider the fact that no one was even aware of her existence before now. No matter which way he looked at it, considering Stranger's story or not, the situation was certainly suspicious.

"I hate to say it, Mr. Jitters, but we've got ourselves a problem." Dungar mused.

When he turned to face the old man he found the seat to be empty, Jitters having silently got up and left for the night.

"Boy he's a quiet old bugger." Dungar soliloquized. "But I suppose his days are numbered no matter what danger is lurking up north. It's the rest of us that need worry about it."

fOUR

cakING accion

Dungar awoke the next morning with a strong sense of purpose. He had slept like a baby the night beforehand, that is to say in sporadic sessions between repeatedly waking up in a state of distress. He had no evidence of his kingdom's imminent danger, aside from the mildly suspicious rumors regarding the royalty and the unreliable ramblings of a random traveler. However there was still an overpowering feeling in his gut that such notions were true and that danger indeed lay brooding beyond the horizon. Therefore when he awoke that morning he decided that he was going to hijack the town meeting that just happened to be being held that afternoon.

With a goal in his mind and confidence in his step, he started down the overgrown alley that was the path to town whilst trying to formulate his pitch in his mind. He had never been to one of these meetings in his entire life. As such, he was unsure just how they were carried out. He briefly entertained the notion of simply storming the stage, but in practice it would probably just make him look like a crazy person.

As the wooden shacks in the distance began to creep closer, his steps began to slow and his confidence began to wane. No matter how he attempted to approach the subject it still sounded crazy. How was he going to pitch a far-fetched notion like an evil, perhaps even magical princess to a village full of people, most of whom hated his guts, and had no reason to believe him even if they didn't? He began to mildly regret throwing Stranger out the window.

The words to express his concerns had still not come by the time he had reached the crowd. He gazed around at his neighbors and other fellow residents, none of whom had even acknowledged his presence. All eyes in the crowd were trans-fixed on the short, fat, and bald man with a hilarious patchy moustache and lazy eye who stood behind a podium address-ing them all.

Town leader Walph Dooble, or Dooble Walph, no one actually knew which was his first and last name, was unanimously elected town leader fifteen years ago due to being the only resident to apply for the job. Despite being a rather simple man, he has continued to hold the position unopposed in the years since; primarily because the village leader had absolutely no authority and would probably be the only person to be killed in the event a foreign party tried to annex the town. However that is not to say he has brought nothing to the village since his appointment.

Attendance at meetings has steadily increased since he took office because he has a bizarrely high pitched and melodic voice that did not fit his ridiculous appearance at all. The combination of those two aspects made every speech given by the man an entertaining affair indeed, no matter what the topic.

"Onto our next order of business then." The stout man chirped. "Has anyone yet come up with any ideas to deal with the troll problem?"

He glanced up from his podium to stare into the sea of blank faces which offered nothing more than the distant sound of a throat clearing.

"Anyone? Anyone at all? Come on, folks, they have preyed upon at least three people's mothers this month!"

The crowd still remained silent.

"No suggestions on that one either. Alrighty then. That concludes our tri-weekly review of current events."

As the crowd began to shuffle in their own directions Dungar realized that this would be his final moment to seize an opportunity and he had to either capture it or let it slip. He drew a breath to call out. Then he changed his mind and exhaled because he didn't want to look like a lunatic.

"However, before you all leave, we have one last order of business on the docket." Walph added hastily. "We have received word from governmental functionaries in the castle that King Ik has officially become living-impaired." There was an awkward pause, perhaps out of respect for his passing, perhaps because it took some people a second to figure out what "living-impaired" meant. "And as such they have requested all settlements within the kingdom to send their most high standing citizens as suitors for the purpose of hastening the matrimony of his sole daughter, our new Queen Koey, so that the monarchy may be restored."

He paused briefly to gauge the reactions of his audience, which had become no less tepid. "Do we have any volunteers?"

Dungar immediately realized this was about as perfect an opportunity as he was going to get. He stiffened up straight, put his shoulders back, and called as authoritatively as he could muster out of the crowd: "I volunteer as a tribute."

Immediately he began glancing around, waiting for the scoffs and challenges from the inevitable folks who would contest him, but none came. A few heads within his vicinity turned and glanced at him, but his proclamation was largely ignored by the masses.

"Hey!" Dungar called out again.

A few more heads started to turn. He gestured around at the denizens of the crowd, commanding their attention and grimacing at the amount of half-humanoid blobs that surrounded him. He was astounded these junkies could even walk with such unbalanced bodies. But he now had their attention and was committed to his quarter-baked scheme.

"I'm a member of one of the deepest rooted families of this town. I own and run two businesses that have provided services to all of the lazy freaks that I'm forced to share my home with. Frankly I'm also a damn fine looking man too. Given all that, where would you find a more suited candidate than me in this dump?"

The now incredibly uncomfortable group of onlookers exchanged awkward glances, but none offered any rebuttal.

"Sorry I'm late, friends!" An all-too-familiar voice called out from a distance.

All heads now turned in the direction just in time to see Rainchild step out from the patch of trees. He had long scraggly brown hair that was perfectly parted down the middle to frame his face which constantly flashed his intoxicating smile that made most of the ladies and some of the men swoon each time they saw it.

His face bore the closest of shaves that Woodwall barbers had to offer so nothing would obscure his perfectly sculpted jaw line, and his glorious face was rounded off by his deep brown eyes that could permeate the core of your being and stare right on through into your soul. It was those eyes from which Dungar derived his true loathing of the man.

Rainchild had everyone else fooled, but not him. Behind those seemingly kind eyes Dungar knew lay the man's true nature of being little more than an arrogant and entitled pissant.

"I am terribly sorry I couldn't have been in attendance sooner, but I was making the final touches on the diamond adornments for our town's wedding gift while I sang lullabies to the orphaned grouchawks I rescued this morning and fed them helpings of my organic honey root soup." Rainchild explained to the crowd, smiling wide as he did.

Dungar rolled his eyes amidst the cooing of the congrega-tion. Rainchild's voice was smooth and articulate with just the slightest hint of an exotic accent. It offered significant contri-bution to his already infectious charm, and every word that slithered off of his silver tongue made Dungar's eyes twitch and fists clench.

Mayor Dooble was incredibly relieved to see Rainchild, primarily because it meant he didn't have to be the one to confront Dungar.

"Mister Earthumper I am so glad to see you! We had just finished discussing who we were going to send to the kingdom as a suitor. Naturally you are everyone's unanimous choice. Isn't that right, gang?"

"Aye!" The entire crowd erupted in unison.

"Hey!" Dungar bellowed yet again, but everyone resumed ignoring him.

"This is a true honor you have requested of me!" Rainchild gushed. "It will be so hard for me to leave behind my beloved kinsmen of my humble home, but if my presence is sought by royal decree then I owe it to everyone to participate!"

He continued to spout his saccharine speech but none of it was relevant. Dungar had to get out of there before he could no longer resist the urge to choke him out with his own hair. Defeated, he slowly began the trek back to his inn. He couldn't bring himself to be particularly surprised by the out-come though; it would have been way more surprising if his scheme had actually worked.

By the time he returned to the bar everything had begun to sink in. He poured himself a drink and sat down in front of the Jenair coat of arms he had carved into his wall. It was official now, his king, King Ik of Jenair, was dead. He had never even left his humble home of Woodwall, let alone met the man, but in spite of that information he still had liked him a lot.

By all accounts the king had been a reclusive gentleman not unlike himself, but he had also served as a symbol of order and unity throughout the kingdom. He kept everyone under the same banner and served to remind the citizens of the kingdom that, irrespective of their differences, they were all on the same side. A side that hated everyone from the kingdom of Nonamay.

If there were two things he felt he needed from his home in order to lead a happy lifestyle, they would be freedom and homeostasis. King Ik's general disinterest in governing resulted in a lack of royal intervention in nearly all sectors. However by merely existing he kept the government intact, preventing the kingdom from becoming ruled by anarchy. Dungar couldn't have asked for a better person in charge, and now he was gone and the kingdom's fate was unclear.

As he lamented the state of his state, he heard the doors to the inn open. He rose from his chair expecting to see the familiar face of Jitters, only to lock eyes with none other than Rainchild Earthumper.

FIVE

TIME TO GET A PARTNER IN CRIME

Dungar stood, eyes transfixed on his unwelcome guest.

"Hello, blacksmith." Rainchild greeted sweetly, his smooth and confident voice filling the room.

He remained immune to the infectious charm of the prattle.

"What are you doing here?"

"This is a lovely quaint little establishment you have here." Rainchild mused as his eyes traced the inside of the bar. "I quite like the artwork." Glancing back around, he could see that the perpetual look of agitation on the innkeeper's face had not waned.

"Look, blacksmith," the wizard continued. "I just came over here because I wanted to say I think what you did at the meeting today was very brave. And I couldn't help but be a little curious as to what motivated you to do it."

Dungar was slightly taken aback by this explanation, but left his guard up and brow furled.

"It's a shot at being king, why wouldn't I try?"

"Oh come now." Rainchild scoffed, resuming his pacing. "You are clearly a man of simple means. What allure could the extravagance of royalty possibly have to you?"

Dungar found himself made rather uncomfortable by these questions. Clearly his guest had to have some ulterior motive. A man like Rainchild who had never before given him the time of day wouldn't pay a simple social visit out of nowhere.

"Maybe the simple life has gotten too dull for my tastes." He reasoned.

Rainchild halted mid-pace.

"Is that so?"

Dungar was positive he could hear blatant disbelief in his voice, but Rainchild seemed to accept his reasoning.

The wizard leaned back, a slight frown on his face. "Well, my friend, it causes me great sorrow to be put in a position which will result in the deprivation of your dreams." He spread his arms wide, motioning for a hug. "But I have much faith in your ability to make the best of your circumstances."

Dungar shuddered at the idea of hugging him, but he was a guest in his inn and he was at least being polite. So, begrudgingly, Dungar opted not to put the wizard through the wall when he moved in for the embrace. As he tried to pull away he felt Rainchild's grip tighten and head raise to speak into his ear.

"So enjoy your pathetic life of squalor because you are going to die alone in this desert." With that, Rainchild ended the hug with a shove backwards.

Dungar gaped at the long-haired man that stood grinning before him.

"What did you just say to me?" he tried to growl through his surprise.

Rainchild maintained his cocky smile. "I honestly don't know what you thought would happen at the meeting today, as if the town would consent to sending a lowly disheveled blacksmith like yourself to represent them."

His voice still bore its usual charm and charisma, but there was palpable malice exuding from every word. Dungar swiped to grab at him but the wizard was too quick, gracefully stepping backwards.

"I don't know if you have shared your true intentions with me or not, blacksmith; but if you interfere with my play for the queen then I will not hesitate to destroy you. I would hope that you are not too stupid to know you should fear me." With that he darted out the door, the innkeeper hot on his heels brandishing an iron mug.

"Come back here and say that to my face, you gutless coward!" He bellowed as he gave chase into the forest surrounding the inn. "I'll grind you up and make you truly one with nature!"

As Rainchild disappeared into the forest ahead of him, he paused to listen and locate the wizard's footsteps. The frantic rustling of bushes being crushed underfoot was unmistakable, and soon he was back on the trail. However another sound began to interfere with the rustling, slowly growing louder and louder. This was no natural sound of the forest, it was high pitched and rhythmic, the unmistakable notes of a song being played. As the noise grew louder the rustling of Rainchild making his escape became more and more difficult to track. Frustrated and still angry, Dungar began to slow to a stop. Opting to turn his agitation on whatever was producing that racket, he began to scan around wildly for the culprit. He didn't have to look long.

He watched with mild trepidation as the bushes a few paces in front of him began to rustle briefly until a tall disheveled looking man came bounding out of them. At his mouth he held a wooden flute from which he produced the distracting melody.

Every aspect of the man was about as unkempt as possible. From his long, bushy black hair to his matching furry eyebrows and patchy goatee to his tattered green tunic to his filthy faded trousers, this man clearly was not looking to impress anyone. If anything, he looked like a homeless jester.

"Oh hello there, mate!" He greeted with the utmost enthusiasm.

His voice was rather high and optimistic sounding. There was also a distinct accent present; it was uncharacteristically posh and articulate for what one would have expected from him.

"It's such lovely weather I figured I fancied me a stroll through the wood with me flute!"

Dungar studied the skinny man with mild amusement before he calmly walked up to him, snatched the flute from his hand, and snapped it in half before walking away.

The man froze briefly, trying to process what just happened. "Hey, me flute!" He called after him.

Ignoring him, Dungar continued trekking back towards home whilst considering possible means of vengeance against Rainchild. His to-do list was really starting to load up.

Suddenly the shaggy man came bounding into his path.

"Excuse me, good sir, but I can't help but notice you appear to have obliterated my method of making melodies."

Dungar stopped and considered the statement for a moment. "Hm. I suppose I did . . ." He said as he looked back at the fellow. Then he shrugged and pushed past the man to continue on his way.

"Oh so that's how it's gonna be, is it?" Dungar heard the man call again, but he couldn't be bothered to deal with him. As he previously established, there are many more important matters to attend to.

By the time he'd returned to the bar, his mindset had shifted from legitimate brainstorming to fantasizing about exotic ways in which to murder Rainchild. Shaking his head, he mentally wrangled himself back on track. Even Rainchild had to be put on hold. Dealing with the new queen was the central matter, and if he couldn't gain access as a suitor, he would need another way into the castle.

It was at that point that Dungar remembered he had a chauffeur staying in his very inn. A chauffeur specifically offering rides to Jenair. The answer had been under his nose the entire time. Quickly, he made his way up the stairs and knocked on the gentleman's door. No answer.

"No no no" Dungar muttered to himself as he knocked again, hoping against hope that he hadn't taken off. Still no answer. Dungar decided to try the handle and found the door to be unlocked. As he stepped into the room he found it empty, all trace of inhabitant having been removed. All that remained was a scrap of paper with the words "I'd ask for a refund, but you're probably crazy" written on it.

Just his luck, he thought. He hadn't considered the idea that terrorizing his guests may have consequences. Defeated, he headed back for the door. As he opened it he was greeted with the sound of music for the second time that day. This time it was no instrumental melody, but rather excruciatingly off-key singing from a very familiar, very annoying voice. As he rounded the corner and peered down the stairs Dungar was met with the unfortunate sight of the musician from the woods belting out a song with everything he had; all the while slamming his palm against the bar to the beat.

Way hey and away we go
A long hard trek, through the snow
When can we stop? We don't know
A way hey and away we go!
EVERYBODY!

He seemed to be unaware that the bar area was completely empty except for himself. When he heard the creak of the stairs, the man turned and beamed at the sight of Dungar.

"Oh why hello there, mate! Fancy seeing you again today. This here is me favorite pub in all the land!"

Grumbling to himself, he walked down the stairs and made his way behind the bar. As he did, the gentleman's facial expression changed from his big grin to a feigned look of immense surprise.

"Whaaaaaat? You work here? No way, mate!"

Dungar furled his brow. "If you've come here to rob me for money to replace your flute you're welcome to try, but it probably won't end well for you." He stated, putting his fists on the counter.

"Rob you? Wot do you take me for!" The incredulous man bellowed into the bar, every word leaving his mouth roughly three times as loud as it needed to be. "I am merely a weary traveler who has come seeking a hospitality provider such as yourself, in order to obtain some water!"

Upon saying those words, he produced a large water skin from his pack.

"Fill up me cup if you would, kind sir!"

Dungar glanced contemptuously at the skin, pondering for a moment if the man knew what a cup was. Beneath the whimsy and childishness, he was sure this fellow was no stranger to pulling cons. Also he did break the man's flute after all. So, eager to be rid of his unwelcome guest as quickly as possible, he took the skin and began to fill it with water without complaint.

"As for the funds required to replace my beloved instrument . . ." The man began, waiting for Dungar to turn towards him before he finished. "I am certain that you'll be providing me with adequate reparations by your own free will. No robbing required."

He grinned and winked at the end of his prediction. Dungar handed him his now full water skin.

"No dice. Enjoy your water, and off with you."

As Dungar began ushering him towards the door, the man stopped in the doorway.

"So just so we're clear, you are refusing to reimburse me?"

"Correct." The blacksmith grunted before closing the door.

Turning back towards the bar, he made it maybe 5 paces before the singing piped up again, louder and shriller than before.

Way hey and away I sit
Lovely music I do emit
Sooner or later he'll submit
A way hey and away I sit
EVERYBODY!

Dungar came flying out of the inn brandishing a black-smith hammer and looking for someone to swing it at. Only there were no targets in sight. Bewildered, he lowered his hammer and began scanning the tree line.

"Oh hey look who it is!" A familiar voice called from the top of a nearby palm tree. "Fancy seeing you yet again, mate! This here is me favorite singing spot in all the land!"

"Get outta that tree right now!" Dungar bellowed.

The man cocked his head to the side as he looked at Dungar quizzically.

"Does that really work for you that often? Just ordering people to do stuff?"

"Yes."

"Oh really? Well in that case:" He began bouncing up and down waving his arms parodying Dungar. "Give me me money right now!"

Growling to himself, Dungar headed around the back of the inn to his workshop where he then swapped out his hammer for an axe. By the time he made it back out front though, his new friend was nowhere to be found. His frustration reaching its peak, he drove the axe into a nearby tree so it would be ready if needed before stomping back inside.

Slowly and carefully Dungar made his way back to the bar, keeping his eyes and ears perked so as to detect any movement. Reaching the counter, he proceeded to pull out a cloth and began polishing it.

"I spy with my little eye . . ."

Enraged, but with one smooth movement, Dungar turned, grabbed a nearby bottle and flung it across the room towards the noise. The intruder had to duck to avoid being hit and the bottle instead shattered against the wall.

"Blimey, mate. Good shot!" The grinning man complimented. "You didn't even look first!"

Shoulders rising and falling with every heaving breath, Dungar glared at the man with a seething hatred. The stranger, on the other hand, continued to beam at Dungar.

"I spy with my little eye . . ." He began again.

"If I guess correctly. . . . Will you leave and never, *ever,* come back?" Dungar asked.

Clapping his hands, the man became rather giddy. "Now you're getting into the swing of things, mate! Ten guesses! If you're wrong you give me a new flute!"

Dungar knew the inside of his bar better than a parent knew its own child. Nothing could get past him.

"Deal."

Clapping his hands again, the man began studying the room. "Oh how fun! Now let's see here . . . I spy with my little eye . . . Something that begins with an 'S'!"

Shrugging, Dungar gestured towards his seat. "Stool."

"Incorrect!" The man exclaimed eagerly.

Dungar began looking around his bar. He studied his wall carvings, kinds of alcohol, his glassware, cups, pitchers, every adornment his bar had acquired over the years. He came to the realization there weren't actually many things in there that began with an 'S'.

". . . Sword?" He finally inquired, gesturing towards his carving of a knight.

"Incorrect again! Uh oh. Methinks someone is having a spot of trouble." The shaggy man taunted.

Dungar shook his head. No, he won't lose at this in his own bar. Hastily he scanned around the room, listing any 'S' items that came to mind.

"Shield."

"Nope."

"Sack."

"Wrong."

"Shirts, shoes, socks."

"Wrong, wrong wrong!"

"Scissors."

"Really?"

"Stones."

"Oh come on mate, you're not even trying!"

"Strings!"

"You have strings in here?"

"Spices."

"Nuh uh."

"Soap."

"You're outta guesses, mate."

"Gaaaaaaahhhh!!!!"

Dungar slammed his fists against the counter. His opponent looked at him with mild concern.

"You okay, mate?"

"What was it?"

"What?"

Dungar raised his head and stared his confused guest in the face. "What was it? The thing you were looking at, what in the blazes were you possibly looking at!?"

The man started laughing. "Circle!" He guffawed, picking up his coaster and brandishing it triumphantly.

Dungar was struck dumb. He had to review that statement in his head several times just to establish that he wasn't going crazy.

"THAT DOESN'T EVEN BEGIN WITH AN 'S'!!"

"Really? You sure about that, mate?"

"GAAAAAHHHH!"

Dungar screamed a guttural war cry before he leapt across the counter, hands outstretched for the man's neck. They rolled around on the floor, Dungar's screams of rage harmonizing with the other fellow's girlish shrieks of fear. They traded blows, Dungar's massive fists leaving holes in the floor while his victim writhed around slapping him in the face repeatedly. Finally one of Dungar's swings connected right in the side of his head and the man went limp beneath him. Exhausted, the blacksmith lifted himself off of his opponent and dragged himself to the counter to grab a drink and slump into a stool.

Within a moment his adversary had pried himself off of the floor and collapsed into the stool beside him, upper body draped over the counter.

"Ah. . ." He began, between labored breathing. "Blimey, that kinda hurt."

The two men eyed each other as they worked to regain their breath. There was nothing quite like a physical altercation as a method for bringing a relationship to a head. Finally the man opened his mouth. Before he could speak the booming rumble of Dungar's growl cut him off.

Eyes remaining facing forward, he sternly, but articulately spoke. "I swear by all that is just, if you say another word I'm going to hit you again." At that the man closed his mouth and returned his eyes facing forward.

But after a brief moment he defiantly turned back and said "You're one of them guys that just always gotta be mista gruff all the time, ain't ya?"

At the sound of his voice, Dungar immediately tensed up and turned towards him but the man did not budge, his composure did not break, and his trusting smile did not fade. Dungar couldn't help it, his body relaxed and he began to just chuckle to himself as he turned back to his drink. His visitor joined him in his chuckling too, and after a brief moment of that he casually reached over, grabbed the blacksmith's beverage, and shamelessly took a long drink out of it. As he did so, Dungar stared at him incredulously, but still took no action towards him. Taking his time, calm as ever, the man finished the drink, put it on the counter, and exhaled with an audible "ahh."

He remained staring at the bizarre individual unblinkingly. He had no words, no idea how to react and no notion what to make of this bizarrely brash musician. Not that it mattered of course, for when this odd newcomer made his mind up about something he would clearly stick to it with an unbeatable, undying enthusiasm. So whether or not the blacksmith realized it, his fate became sealed when the man looked thoughtfully into the distance wearing his cheeky smile and said "I think you and me are gonna be good friends, mate."

SIX

IF YOU CAN'T BEAT 'EM
OR DID AND IT DIDN'T WORK

It was a dark and stormy night. Somewhere. However back at the bar the day was still bright and the sky cloudless. Dungar remained where he sat, nursing his brew between sideways glances at the intriguing interloper. He still could not decide what to make of the man. This silly stranger who had called him friend so brazenly now sat wordlessly sharing his company. He had always heard the best of friends often meet in odd circumstances, but if this man was to be his best friend then he shed an internal tear for his future. Savage beat-downs on the first day did not usually bode well for relationship longevity. Although, perhaps the burden fell on himself to stop issuing them so readily.

With a tremendous belch and long, drawn out exhale, the glorious silence was once again broken as his guest polished off his drink and decided it had been too long since he had last spoken.

"I don't believe I've, *hic,* caught your name yet, mate!" he declared, clasping his hand on the blacksmith's shoulder.

"Dungar," he growled, swatting the arm away.

"Dungar . . ." the man repeated to himself, and then again in a dramatized deep voice. "Dungar! Blimey, that's a manly name. Makes you sound like you have a giant beard and fight marbalts!"

Realizing the man's gibbering had finally stopped, and that he had no idea what a marbalt was, Dungar felt compelled to draw the attention away from himself.

"And your name?"

"Oh pish, where are me manners?" The man replied, flustered. Straightening up in his seat, putting on his most charming grin, and raising an outstretched hand, he offered his introduction.

"The name's Jimminy Appaya! How do you do, good sir?"

As they rolled off Jimminy's tongue, the syllables resounded throughout Dungar's mind as the culmination of all the characteristics put forth by this clownish individual. His comical appearance, care-free attitude, and whimsical nature all became summed up by those two words. As such, Dungar concluded there was only one appropriate way to respond when someone introduced themselves as Jimminy Appaya.

"My god, what a ridiculous name."

"Perhaps!" Jimminy replied enthusiastically. "I prefer to think of it as being distinguished! Not unlike myself, mind you."

Dungar pondered the statement for a moment before returning back to his drink. Distinguished was not in the list of words he would have used to describe Jimminy, but he'd rather not contest the man on the notion because it would cause him to keep talking.

Unfortunately for him, contested or not, Jimminy was not one to let a silence last for too long and was more than happy to individually keep the conversation alive.

"Just so you know, us being best pals now has no bearing on the flute debt a certain mista Dungar still owes."

At mention of this, Dungar perked up. Depending on how bad mister Appaya wanted his flute, there could perhaps be some use for him after all.

"Have you ever been to Jenair, Jimmy?"

"My name's actually Jimminy. It's similar to Jimmy, but with more 'ins.'"

"I'll pretend to try and remember that; but have you or not?"

"Well of course I've been to Jenair! I have traversed all over this fine land! I have surveyed its acreage from the peak of the Demon's Kettle! I have traipsed through the teeming vegetation of the Lotsotri forest! I have braved the beast-riddled grounds of the Notasmochtri Forest! I have—"

"Do you ever stop talking!?!!"

At that, Jimminy clammed right up prompting Dungar to take the opportunity to continue.

"As all of my beloved neighbors are now very much aware, I wish to put myself forward as a potential suitor for the queen. However, I have absolutely no idea how to get to Jenair. Do you see where I am going with this?"

Jimminy pondered the question briefly. Casually leaning on the bar, he stared blankly ahead whilst twiddling his moustache thoughtfully. Suddenly his eyes lit up and he turned back to Dungar, sporting his trademarked cheeky grin.

"I believe I do see where you're going with this, friend!" Jimminy paused briefly to sip from his mug. "And I assure you that you will not have to fear competing with me dashing good looks and irresistible charms for the queen's hand. Frankly she's not even really me type anyway. Of course I've never seen her before, but even simply based off of the tales regarding her physical appearance I feel I can conclude—"

"CAN YOU TAKE ME TO JENAIR OR NOT?!!"

"Oh yeah, sure, mate! Why didn't you just ask?"

Dungar sighed. Although he had never been to Jenair, he was well aware of the fair amount of distance between his humble home and the core of the country. He was in for a long walk with this man; therefore it would be in his best interest to hone his patience for puerility. Still, he couldn't help but wonder why Jimminy would so readily help him; he hadn't even offered a replacement flute when requesting assistance.

"By the way, mate, naturally when you marry the queen lady and live happily ever after you are going to reward me with a flute so expensive that I will fear for my life each time I play it in public."

On the other hand, Dungar also couldn't help but feel his skepticism of Jimminy was unjustified when it was he himself with the ulterior motives. It was of utmost importance that the nature of his mission remain a secret though; especially when forced to partner up with a cannon as loose as Jimminy.

Stealth and surprise were going to be his most important tools on this venture. Unfortunately those were two tactics that Dungar would wager Jimminy was not particularly adept in. Therefore, the less Jimminy knew the better. As far as everyone shall remain concerned, he is just another hopeful commoner who is deluded enough to think he had a shot with a queen.

"DUNGAR LOLOTH!" an unknown voice roared from outside.

The two heroes jumped; both startled by the call.

"You expecting company, mate?" Jimminy asked nonchalantly.

Dungar turned in his seat to face the direction from which the sound had come. He was certainly not expecting company. He also theorized, given the manner in which he was addressed, that this was likely not a social call.

"That didn't sound particularly friendly." He expressed with mild concern.

"The missionaries here really don't mess around eh?" Jimminy said, laughing.

They remained where they were seated. Both eyed the door tentatively, unsure how to proceed. Sure enough, the unknown voice piped up again.

"Dungar Loloth! As a charged knight of the crown I am ordering you to exit the building, unarmed."

The voice was firm, authoritative, and clearly used to bellowing commands. Dungar wasn't entirely sure what a knight sounded like, but if he were to wager a guess it probably would have sounded something like the voice currently calling to him. He rose from his seat and began to proceed to the door before the voice of Jimminy cut him off.

"Wot are you doing, mate!? You're going surrender just like that?"

"I am being summoned by a knight, Jimmy. Last thing I need is to establish bad blood with the queen's guard. The sooner I get whatever he wants sorted out, the sooner we can be on our way."

Jimminy opened his mouth to protest, but Dungar had already strolled out the door. Looking down as he grumbled to himself, he closed the door behind him and began to traipse his way over to the knight whilst addressing him back.

"Alright, what's this all about?"

He stopped short when he looked up. Before him stood a hardened looking man completely clad in armor which was polished to a mirror shine. He had short and greyed hair which was neatly parted right down the middle and his face, though bearing the marks of aging, was tough and resilient looking.

The man's eyes were transfixed on him. They were dark and unforgiving, and generated a stare cold enough to freeze a forge. However it was not the intimidating knight that halted Dungar's advance, but rather the smug looking hippy wizard pompously standing next to him. Rainchild stood calmly, hands behind his back, wearing a smile so self-satisfied that Dungar would happily trade his entire livelihood just to smack it off of him.

"Mister Loloth, you are under arrest for the attempted murder of a royal suitor." The knight stated. He then tossed a pair of shackles at Dungar's feet. "I am ordering you to put those on and surrender yourself into my custody."

Dungar contemptuously inspected the shackles and the knight who produced them.

"Do you have any proof of this?" He demanded, kicking the shackles aside. "And since when do royal suitors have special rights? Anyone can call themselves one. In fact I too am one."

"MISTER LOLOTH." The knight yelled, drawing a strange diamond sword from his scabbard. "I am not a man who repeats himself. Do as I command you."

Begrudgingly he picked up the shackles that he had so brazenly discarded. As they locked around his wrists, so too did his fate become sealed. Suddenly the idea of a trip with Jimminy began to seem so appealing in comparison to being helplessly placed in the hands of his worst enemy and his corrupt caretaker. As Dungar affixed his restraints, the knight sheathed his sword and proceeded towards him.

"I'll deal with you once we reach the capital." He said flatly, shoving him towards the center of town. "The main priority currently is making sure Mister Earthumper here reaches the queen in a timely manner."

At the mention of the queen the wheels in Dungar's head began to turn once more. Perhaps his situation wasn't as hopeless as he thought. Provided he could devise a way to escape upon arrival, he could potentially swing this as an all-expenses paid escorted trip to the capital. However, given what he had heard about the castle dungeons, escape was a rather rare feat and it was unlikely he would be able to manage it, let alone manage it in a manner of time before it was too late. No sooner had he began plotting his new plan than did the next surprise of the day happen upon the party.

"I'LL SAVE YOU, DUNGAR!" A very shrill, very familiar voice shouted from above.

The three turned their eyes skyward just in time to see a hairy and pale blur leap from the rooftop brandishing a large rum barrel. The open end of the barrel landed on top of the knight with Jimminy right on top of it, his weight temporarily sealing Dungar's captor inside.

Immediately the barrel began to violently pound and shake while emitting the muffled yells of the agitated individual trapped inside. Jimminy, doing everything in his power to remain on top of it, called out to Dungar again.

"FLEE, YOU GREAT STUPID MAN! USE YOUR STUBBY LITTLE LEGS!"

At Jimminy's decree, Dungar bolted. Running was difficult with his hands awkwardly shackled in front of him, but with his only chance at freedom lying beyond the dunes of the Snake Eye desert, he persevered through the awkwardness and discomfort. A hasty backward glance over his shoulder granted him the visual of Jimminy hot on his heels, having been thrown from the barrel. Rainchild and the knight were also in pursuit.

Despite being weighed down by his armor, the knight was making up ground on the two fugitives. Even though Dungar couldn't decipher his incoherent shouting, he knew that, no matter what it was, it was certainly bad news for him.

As he made his way out of the oasis, his feet hit the smooth powder-like desert sand and his pace significantly slowed on the uneven and ever-shifting ground. Although he had spent his whole life in this place, he had never actually tried running on the sand. He had always enjoyed the feel of it beneath his feet and would often drag them through it, but maintaining a quick pace was not something he had ever felt compelled to practice.

His unpreparedness for the terrain coupled with the stress of the situation only served to further hinder his flight. The blazing sun beat down on his body as his throat grew raw from huffing the parching desert air. Still he persevered, forcing each foot in front of the other as his boots began to fill with the gritty sand. In addition to his own heavy breathing, Dungar could hear the frantic respiration of Jimminy who had now caught up to him.

"Keep moving, mate!" He panted. "Blimey. He's fast for an old bloke."

The two finally reached the crest of the dune they were scaling. The heat was intense. Even in the short distance they had traveled they were already nearing exhaustion, but the angered grunts of the pursuing knight creeping ever closer urged them on. After a quick scan of his surroundings, Jimminy shouted "Head for the Lotsotri forest!" before he picked the steepest looking side of the dune and threw himself down it expecting to gracefully slide down like a snow bank. Dungar then watched with bewilderment as Jimminy gracelessly faceplanted and tumbled down the hill before setting off after him.

"Get up, you hairy klutz." He barked, hoisting Jimminy to his feet.

Before he could get the man fully upright though, Dungar found himself being hindered by the weight of a steel-clad partisan tackling him to the ground. Not one to give up without a fight, he fruitlessly tried to grapple with the knight from below. However his bound hands presented an insurmountable disadvantage and before long he found the knight looming over him, sword drawn.

"Give me one good reason why I shouldn't gut you right here." The knight snarled.

"Well. My body will probably stink something fierce by the time you get it back to Jenair if you kill me here." Dungar offered.

The knight narrowed his eyes, his lips curled into a sneer. "You assaulted and fled from one of the crown's own elite. There is no trip and trial for you."

"To be fair:" Jimminy interjected. "It was actually me who assaulted you, mate."

Ignoring him, the knight raised his sword high in the air. The blade shined brightly in the sweltering midday sun. As he drew breath for the final blow, Jimminy rang out again, this time in protest.

"WAIT!!"

Dungar had no idea why, but for some reason the knight actually did wait, and turned towards Jimminy.

"You can't kill him yet!" Jimminy insisted. "The adventure has only just begun!"

Every second felt like an eternity. Then Dungar and the knight both answered in unison.

"What?!"

The knight did not wait for a response. He immediately turned back to Dungar and went for the kill. His sword lunged downward. Moments before it met flesh, both the weapon and its wielder were thrown to the side by the wake of an immense creature erupting from the sand.

Time slowed to a crawl for Dungar as he watched the monstrous being continue to emerge from the sand and surround the three men with its long slender body. His eyes traced along the smooth faded green scales of the serpent as it passed over him. Sand smoothly flowed off of its body as it elegantly slid along the terrain sizing up the new prey that lay before it.

As they followed along the body of the beast, his eyes inevitably met the creature's. They were amazing. They were so . . . Captivating. They were so large and innocent looking that he couldn't help but become lost in them as he felt a wave of docility wash over him. Staring into those eyes made all of his cares fade away, removing any desire to do anything besides keep gazing into those big, beautiful, glistening eyes. The sweeping, fluffy eyelashes were a very odd and out of place sight to see on a reptile, but with every bat they served to strengthen the victim's transfixion.

As the animal circled around to the rear of the party, eye contact between Dungar and the snake was broken and he was relieved of his hypnotic trans. Immediately he collected his thoughts and memories of the local legends came flooding back to him. As he turned around, he found Jimminy and the knight both entranced by the beast's ocular magic.

"JIMMY!" Dungar bellowed. "DON'T LOOK INTO ITS EYES!"

Jimminy, not moving a muscle or breaking eye contact, called back to him. "BUT . . . LOOK AT HIM . . . MATE! HE'S SO ADORABLE!"

Satisfied with its target's submission, the serpent reared its colossal head. Knowing what was coming next, reasoning took passenger to action for Dungar and he lunged at Jimminy. When he collided with his mesmerized ally, he used every bit of his strength to pull him to the ground. The snake's massive head careened towards them like a scaly pendulum of death. They hit the soft terrain not a moment too soon as the sudden rush of wind generated by the reptilian projectile blowing past them covered them in sand.

The knight, however, was not so lucky.

When beast collided with man there was a sickening crescendo of pulverized metal and shattered bones. As Dungar looked up from the ground he caught only a mere glimpse of the limp body of his pursuer flying off into the distance before disappearing from sight. As the knight vanished beyond the horizon, the snake emitted rhythmic breathy noise that sounded eerily like laughter before taking off in the same direction like a fetching hound.

The ordeal had ended as quickly as it had begun. As Dungar began to collect himself, he turned back towards Jimminy just in time for the man to throw his arms him.

"Oh Dungar, you marvelous soul, I could kiss you!"

"You'd only get to do it once." He growled back, prying Jimminy off of him.

They remained seated in the sand for some time; partially out of exhaustion and partially out of amazement at the circumstances. Jimminy summed it up the most eloquently.

"Wow! We almost died. This is a real adventure already!"

Dungar couldn't help but laugh. Not even a narrowly averted scrape with death could undermine Jimminy's unparalleled optimism and misplaced confidence. Oddly enough, he couldn't help but start to feel that a mindset like that was exactly what their little quest needed. He still had no plan, no supplies, and was now stranded in the middle of a desert in with a gigantic, vicious, and oddly dreamy snake who could return at any moment and devour them. His mission was not off to a flying start.

"It's kind of ironic when you think about it, mate." Jimminy chuckled.

"What's that?"

"I knew that knight. Sir Pent was his name. He was always a crooked one, a real hard-ass too. Folks took to calling him 'The Snake.'" Jimminy grinned. "I guess there really is always a bigger badder wolf, eh?"

At that, they both let loose a hearty laugh as they rose to their feet.

"Sir Pent the snake. Boy, that's creative." Dungar sardonically quipped.

They laughed again as they began to shuffle northward over the dunes at a much more comfortable pace than initially. Jimminy was right about one thing. The adventure had certainly begun.

SEVEN

WHERE ARE WE?

It was only after the mirth had died down that the gravity of the situation began to set in. They were walking aimlessly through the desert with no food, no water, and no plan whatsoever. Dungar's hands also remained shackled in front of him, and Jimminy had been singing "Way hey and away we go" songs ever since they started walking.

"Do you have a crippling fear of silences or something, Jimmy?" Dungar sarcastically asked.

"Me mum was killed by a silence." Jimminy joked back, not missing a beat.

Dungar shook his head.

"Wot about you, mista Dungar? Whereabouts do mista and missus Dungar senior reside?"

"Rainchild will be able to answer that once I'm through with him."

"So they're in a dispensary?"

"They're dead, you dunce."

"Oh. Did you beat them to death?"

Dungar shook his head again. All the turmoil of today had made him physically exhausted enough as is without having to deal with the mental stresses of satiating Jimminy's incessant need for banter.

"I'll make you a deal, Jimmy." Dungar offered. "If you agree to stop talking to me, then I'll agree to not have you beheaded when I'm running the kingdom."

"I'll make YOU a deal, Dungar." Jimminy countered. "If you agree to sing a song with me, then I will get those cuffs off your hands."

Dungar gaped at him. He looked down at his wrists and the shackles that had worn into them. The repeated friction and heat had caused them to become raw and blistered as the metal continued to dig into his skin. He deeply regretted putting them on so tight. His eyes returned to Jimminy. The man's usual cheeky smile still present, peppered with the smugness of knowing the corner he was in. Grimacing, he looked away. Much as he didn't like it, he knew what he had to do. The mere thought of what he was about to willingly put himself through pained him, but the pain was slightly lesser than that of the alternative.

He looked back at Jimminy. "No deal, jackass." He defiantly grunted as he continued walking, shackles remaining firmly in place.

Even though Jimminy hadn't explicitly accepted Dungar's proposal, he remained quiet for the next few hours of walking. Occasionally he would mumble something to himself, but ultimately the majority of sound was generated by the soft, rhythmic squishing sound of their feet hitting the sand harmonizing with their scratchy breaths. Dungar was no stranger to the arid environment, and as such his throat and lungs were less bothered by it than Jimminy. However both men felt the pangs of dehydration taking hold as they continued to slog through the sand.

As their hike through the desert neared its conclusion, Jimminy shattered the silence with his first exclamation in hours.

"Hark, mista Dungar! Look alive, mate! I see me some trees! Soon we'll be in the shade!"

Dungar looked in the direction where Jimminy was pointing. He had no idea why his companion was just pointing it out now though; it had been visible for quite some time and was now less than fifty feet in front of them. If the forest hadn't been visible then it would have been certain that they had been walking in the wrong bloody direction. He opted to remain silent anyway. Decoding Jimminy's convoluted thought process was unquestioningly of secondary importance compared to reaching the lush, green, fertile embodiment of relief.

As his feet touched grass and the shade swept over him, he immediately slumped against a tree. Jimminy, taking it one step further, collapsed to the ground and proceeded to roll in the grass making satisfied moaning noises. Nothing should have been said; a rest as required as this needed no words. But this type of thought naturally did not occur to Jimminy.

"Blimey. I have no idea how this ecosystem is even possible, but I'll be burned if I really care right now." He mused indifferently whilst rubbing the moist leaves of some foliage on his face.

All Dungar wanted to do was collapse to the ground right next to him. But making it into the woods did not mean that they were out of the woods. He pinched at his skin. Overheated as he was, it was virtually devoid of sweat and elasticity.

"We have to keep moving, Jimmy." He sighed. "We need to find a town or at least a water source before we can stop."

Impressively, Jimminy bounded to his feet when he said that. "Well slap me flap, mista Dungar, I do believe you're right!" He proclaimed enthusiastically before confidently picking a direction into the forest to walk towards.

Dungar, having no idea what to make of any of that, quickly set out after him.

"Is there a town in this direction?"

"How should I know? I'm crazy!"

As the two trudged through the trees, Dungar constantly kept his ears open for any indication of a nearby water source. With Jimminy even loopier than usual, he felt the weight of their survival falling solely to his shoulders.

Fortunately, not long after they entered the forest, Dungar caught the sounds of flowing water somewhere nearby. Maybe Jimminy actually did have an inkling that he neglected to mention. Probably not, though, because his dehydration appeared to have deteriorated his mental state into bouts of delirium. He seemed far more interested in feeling up a nearby tree and burying his head between its branches than anything else at the moment. Dungar wasn't entirely sure what Jimminy was whispering to it; but, given the few words he had caught, he was relatively certain he didn't want to know.

Exasperated, he peeled his partner off of the tree amid the frail man's fruitless attempts to resist and proceeded to carry him in the direction of the water source.

"Mista Dungar, you blockheaded buffoon, you are the worst wingman ever. She had a friend, you know!" The deranged man hollered. "Say, when's lunch?"

The stream was definitely close now; he could hear it very clearly even over the maniacal cackling of the lunatic slung over his shoulder. Finally they emerged from the thick tree cover into a small clearing and there it was. It was a small and shallow stream roughly three feet wide, but to Dungar it may as well have been its own prominent oasis not unlike the one he called home. He dropped Jimminy like a sack of potatoes and plunged his face into the water. The cold and refreshing feeling of satiating his ferocious thirst was sweeter than any beverage he had ever brewed in all his years as an innkeeper. When his head emerged from the water he felt like a new man. He turned back to Jimminy, who remained lying exactly where he had been dropped, gibbering something to himself about how he wished his beard was as soft as this grass.

"Jimmy!" He barked. "There's water here. Drink it before you die."

Jimminy perked up as soon as he was addressed. "You can lead a horse to water, mista Dungar! But you can't make him drink!" He declared, giggling to himself. "And I, my dear friend, am a stallion!" At that, he began rolling on the ground chortling loudly.

Dungar rolled his eyes. Irrespective of whatever mythical creature his guide purported to be, he wasn't about to let it die of thirst before it had carried out his mandate. Casually, he grabbed a fist full of Jimminy's long, scraggly black hair, plunged him face first into the water, and held him there until he felt the man had likely ingested a sufficient amount of liquid down one pipe or the other.

Jimminy seemed mildly more lucid after he emerged from the water, spluttering. He surveyed his surroundings as if trying to orient himself.

"Do you have any idea where we are, Jimmy?"

"Well, I would imagine my most educated of hypotheses would dictate we're currently in a forest, likely near a water source of some kind judging by the moistness of me face!"

He sighed. The sun was in the midst of setting and the stresses of the day had worn him thin. He would walk no more that day; so instead he began to settle in for a long awaited rest. A soft snoring sound indicated Jimminy had already passed out right where he lay.

Dungar wasn't an experienced survivalist in any capacity, but he figured sleeping exposed in the middle of an unfamiliar land populated by unfamiliar creatures was likely a bad idea. He attempted to survey his surroundings, looking for some sort of cover, but his mind was fuzzy and unfocused as the irresistible temptress of sleep beckoned to him. Some nearby bushes would have to do; it at least made sense to him at the time. Slowly, he dragged Jimminy's unconscious body over to them before flopping into the bushes himself. The discomfort of being slumped over a clump of foliage was of no consequence, as the moment Dungar became horizontal his whole world started to drift away.

When he awoke in the morning it was to the sound of his rumbling stomach. The mental refreshing that resulted from his slumber allowed him to more adequately take stock of his situation. They were still a significant distance away from Jenair, so particular directions were not required yet. The main priority for the time being would be to procure some supplies and simply head northward.

"Get up, Jimmy." He said, nudging the fellow with his foot.

Jimminy awoke with a start.

"I didn't order the continental breakfast!"

Ignoring him, Dungar began scanning the sky for his bearings. From the clearing he currently stood in he had a relatively unimpeded view of the horizon. The sun was only just beginning to creep out from behind it. Using that information, he deduced which direction would take him northward. Covering distance was very important to him, but he also hoped they would come across a town soon as well. Having been maliciously chased from his home before he got to eat lunch the day before, he was starting to feel quite peckish.

Jimminy rose to his feet and appeared to try and gather his bearings in the same manner. His attention was diverted by another violent rumble from Dungar's stomach.

"Blimey." Jimminy laughed. "You keepin' a bear in your belly, mate?"

Dungar grumbled. "Ah what do you expect, I'm really bloody hungry."

"Well hi there, Really Bloody Hungry." Jimminy joked, grinning and outstretching a hand. "They call me Jimminy!"

And so it was that mere moments after being roused into consciousness by Dungar's foot, Jimminy found himself returned to unconsciousness by Dungar's fist.

As he looked down at Jimminy's crumpled body, Dungar felt a mild pang of regret for his response. Not because he felt bad for Jimminy, for anyone who makes that joke deserves such treatment, but rather because he was now going to have to carry the bastard along the way until he finally wakes up. He looked down at his wrists which still bore the shackles as a metallic manifestation of the memories of yesterday. Even though Jimminy's lack of size would make carrying him easier, having constrained limbs would still make it awkward.

Grabbing two handfuls of ragged shirt, he attempted to pick his friend up. Jimminy's mouth was wide open with his tongue comically hanging out of it, and his head flopped side to side with each lateral movement. As he studied his accomplice's limp and lifeless body, an alternative idea to getting the walking underway popped into Dungar's head.

Jimminy awoke with a start for the second time that day. Rather than the familiar surly face of Dungar looming over him though, he instead woke face to face with the sharp beak of a vulture.

"GAAAAAAAAAAH!" He shrieked, the penetrating shrillness of his cry of terror echoing through the clearing he lay in.

The vulture answered with a loud squawk of fear itself before the sound was sharply cut off by a large rock colliding with the bird creating an audible "thud" and cloud of feathers.

Perplexed beyond belief, Jimminy looked at the lifeless bird that now lay on the ground next to him. Then, as he began to survey his surroundings, he noticed there were rocks and feathers littering the field all around him. As he turned back facing forward, Jimminy saw Dungar casually step over him and retrieve the battered bird.

"Morning, sunshine." He quipped. "Hungry?"

Upon being extended the offer, Jimminy traded his look of confusion for one of a more blithe nature. "I suppose I am feeling a bit peckish." He mused.

Dungar smiled as he lifted the man to his feet. "More than you even know, it seems." He intoned in his usual manner, smirking.

Jimminy followed him out of the clearing to a small outcrop sheltered by trees. There, he found a fire complete with spit and a rather impressive looking pile of bird carcasses, all of which were plucked of feathers. As Dungar sat on a nearby log by the fire, he looked up at Jimminy, who still remained standing. Things appeared to be falling into place in his mind.

"You used me as live bait to attract vultures didn't ya?"

"Whatever could have given you that idea?" Dungar gibed, nonchalantly picking at his breakfast.

"I made me deductions!"

"Did any of those deductions involve the fact you're currently bleeding from the face?"

"Aw! Not the face! This is me favorite face!"

Jimminy dashed back to the stream, followed only by the sound of Dungar's laughter. From the opposite side of the outcrop from which Jimminy exited, someone else could be heard rustling in the foliage. Dungar hopped to his feet just in time for a petite, attractive woman to step out of the woods. She had long dark brown hair neatly swept to the side so as not to hinder the view of her delicate features. As she turned to face him, her kind looking brown eyes met with his crazy looking blue ones.

"Hello there, fellow traveler!" She called to him, raising a hand. "May I share your fire?"

Her voice was silvery and feminine; it hit the ears very pleasantly.

Dungar's eyes remained on her for a moment before he shook his head back into the present. "Be my guest." He stated dismissively as he sat back down.

Shyly, the lady clasped her hands in front of her and slowly walked towards him. As she sat down, she looked back over to study him. Her cute button nose sat perfectly between her pronounced cheekbones just as her dimples aligned with her thin lips, which were curled into a bashful smile.

"Hello." She greeted again with a small wave and nervous laugh. "Why are you in shackles?" She asked after noticing his wrists.

"Trust me, it's a long story."

The lady laughed. "I'll take your word for it."

Dungar offered a short, awkward smile in response.

"So where are you from, stranger?"

"Oh, uh. Woodwall." He mumbled disinterestedly.

"I've heard of Woodwall, actually." She acknowledged. "It's that drug town in the middle of the desert right?"

Dungar perked up, ready to defend his home. But after mulling it over for a moment, he realized he didn't have much of a leg to stand on.

"More or less actually, now that you mention it." He admitted with a slight nod. "But not me though." He added quickly.

She smiled at him again as he said that, and the two sat in silence for a moment before she spoke again.

"So where are you headed?"

"Oh, uh. Jenair."

"Oooh, the big city! What's your business there?"

At that, he clammed up. He found himself very conflicted as to how to answer that question. The secrecy of the true nature of his mission was of paramount importance to him. However, for reasons he chose not to analyze, he found himself reluctant to claim himself as a suitor for the queen either.

Fortunately he found himself let off the hook from answering any more questions as Jimminy came noisily tromping through the brush back into the campsite. He had removed his shirt to reveal his pale frail chest which was pockmarked with lesions matching those on his face. As he held up his shirt to reveal a plethora of holes that had been poked in it, he addressed Dungar.

"I just got your 'feeling peckish' joke, mate. Real cute." After that, Jimminy turned his attention to the strange woman. "Oh

63

look, you made a friend. Hello, my darling, what's your name?" He greeted, bending down and extending his hand to her.

"Herrow." The woman acknowledged, shaking his hand.

"Hello there." Jimminy repeated, continuing to shake her hand.

"Hi."

"What's your name, my dear?"

"Herrow." She repeated again.

"Yes, hello!" Jimminy exclaimed. "Do you have a bloody name?"

"Who . . . ?" Herrow asked whilst looking around, puzzled.

"You!"

"Me?"

"Yes!"

"Herrow."

"HELLO."

Herrow just stared at him blankly.

"She seems nice!" Jimminy cheerily informed Dungar whilst patting Herrow on the head. "If things don't work out between you and the queen maybe you two might have something!"

"Oh, you're a royal suitor?" Herrow interjected, looking at Dungar.

"He sure is!" Jimminy answered before Dungar could say anything. "And I'm his trusty guide!"

"So the two of you are attempting a trip to Jenair all by your lonesome . . ." Herrow clarified.

Dungar raised a skeptical eyebrow at her, but Jimminy carried on candidly.

"We sure are! We're on an adventure! A quest if you will."

At that, Herrow stood up. "Alright, I've heard enough." She announced in a much colder and firmer voice as she strode several quick steps away from the men. As she turned back to them, all kindness had vanished from her eyes and her cute smile had been replaced with an emotionless glower. "Clearly no one is going to miss you two naïve fools. Grab em, boys!"

Mere moments after the words escaped her mouth, no less than ten thugs came bounding out of the brush and set upon them. Still seated and confined by cuffs, Dungar found himself quickly overpowered by the goons as they pinned him down and put a sack over his head.

Though deprived of his vision, he surmised from the sounds he was hearing that quite a struggle was taking place between Jimminy and the ruffians. Jimminy's classic girlish screams were still present. However, also present were thuds, groans of pain, and occasional shrieks of "AHHHH HE BIT ME." Inevitably the scuffle came to an end, though, at the sound of a metallic clang followed by the familiar thud of Jimminy's unconscious body. Dungar found himself somewhat ashamed to realize he was now familiar with the unique sound of his friend's body in particular crumpling to the ground lifelessly.

As he felt himself being hoisted off the ground and carried away by his new captors, he couldn't help but feel that the only lesson he's derived from his adventure so far is the fact he is apparently not a very lucky man. Maybe, just maybe, his kidnappers were at least carrying him northward.

EIGHT

DETOUR

During his days working as an innkeeper, Dungar had been subjected to all matter of tales regarding all matter of circumstances. From the mundane to the fantastic and the blatant fabrications to the undisputable truths, he was convinced he had heard it all. Among those stories, tales involving kidnappings were hardly scarce. But as he felt himself being manhandled along his current route by his captors, he found himself realizing that no one ever took the time to really illustrate the actual journey itself between the spot at which one was kidnapped and the spot they were taken to.

He lay draped over the shoulders of two of the goons who snatched Jimminy and himself. The shackles on his hands remained firmly in place and his vision was plunged into complete darkness due to the sack fastened around his head. The surge of adrenaline induced by the kidnapping itself coupled with the overwhelming conflicting emotions of fear, anger, and frustration served to deprive him of his situational focus and clarity of mind. All of these elements of the event were to be expected, given what he had heard from stories of similar situations.

What the aforementioned stories always failed to address was the time period of the trip itself. The time period in which the stress began to ease, focus began to return, and the adrenaline began to dissipate. In their place began to surface feelings such as helplessness, mounting discomfort, and mind-numbing boredom. To kick or even wriggle around was fruitless. Every movement which served to hinder the hired help from doing their jobs would quickly warrant a sharp blow to the ribs and harsh warning. As such, he was forced to simply stay as still as he could in the uncomfortable position he lay draped in. With every bump in the terrain he could feel the shoulders digging more and more into his chest and thighs.

Dungar had no concept of how long they walked for. His eyesight was completely revoked and his hearing was quite obstructed by the bag over his head, the air inside which was slowly becoming heavier and moister due to his sweat and vulture-meat breath. Due to a complete lack of all other kinds of stimuli, he found himself counting the steps of the man charged with carrying his upper body. He estimated the man's stride to be roughly two feet. Using that information, he felt he could calculate the rough distance they traveled in whatever direction they were going.

After 150 feet or so he decided that was a stupid idea and instead opted to distract himself with fantasies of bludgeoning the man carrying his torso to death with the body of the man carrying his legs.

Somewhere up ahead of him, Dungar could hear the sounds of Jimminy just being himself. It appeared that his tactic for preserving what little sanity he still had left involved simply annoying the traffickers as much as possible. The pain tolerance in the man was remarkable. Even over the exasperated orders and threats from the kidnapping crew commanding Jimminy to shut up, Dungar could hear the repeated thuds of them working his friend's body over. But bless the man and his stalwart defiance; he kept right on ringing out his ridiculous songs in as shrill and tone-deaf a voice he could muster.

> *Way hey and away we're dragged*
> *To an unknown place since we got snagged*

I'm gonna keep singin' until I'm gagged
A way hey and away we're dragged
EVERYBODY!

Groans and complaints continued to echo from the company, but most of them found themselves resigned into acceptance of the aggravation. Periodically Jimminy would cease his repetition and instead be bothersome in other ways while he came up with new lyrics. Repeatedly inquiring "Are we there yet?" usually elicited the most grief, followed by the classic "I spy with my little eye: something black." It took the goons forever to finally guess what it was since the bag covering Jimminy's head was actually brown and just looked black from the inside.

Eventually a hush fell over the fellowship as the tell-tale sound of heavy boots stomping on wooden floors indicated they had entered a building. After a short jaunt through the building and down some stairs, and a short grunt and groan from his escorts, Dungar found himself roughly dropped onto a hard floor of packed dirt. Soon he felt the bag removed from his face and he found himself blinking in the dim light of the room. His eyesight returned just in time to see a large wooden gate slowly being lowered over the exit of the cell he appeared to be in.

Dungar surveyed the cell that now housed Jimminy and himself. The air in the room was stuffy and dusty; it reeked of sweat and, for some reason, old cheese. The room itself appeared to be carved entirely into hard, dry dirt; likely indicating that they were underground. It was rather large too. It was currently populated by only Jimminy and himself, but appeared to have been built to accommodate significantly more people. Off in one of the corners there was a small amount of bread and water. The dirt walls were all lined with iron bars that disappeared through both the floor and ceiling, likely to prevent any attempts at digging one's way out. The only way in and out of the room was blocked by a thick wooden gate which lowered from above.

Dungar's first inclination was to attempt to lift it. As he strained his muscles he could only feel the gate give ever so slightly; no more than an inch. Dropping it, he peered between the wooden slats the gate was comprised of. He could just make out a large iron turnstile that was likely used for the raising and lowering of the door. His view was largely obstructed, but he surmised the most likely explanation was a locking mechanism on the turnstile that prevented it from rotating when not in use.

With a sigh, he sank into a sitting position. At that moment he realized Jimminy had been being oddly quiet this whole time. It wasn't a far-fetched notion that maybe the man had finally worn his voice out, but, even if only in lieu of having anything else to do, Dungar figured he may as well investigate. Slowly he approached Jimminy's limp body, which was bound with ropes on his wrists and ankles, and pulled the sack off of his head. Even though the only light in the room emanated from the spaces in between the thick wooden slats of the gate, Jimminy too required a few moments to adjust from the total darkness he had been subjected to for an indeterminate amount of time.

"Never thought I'd say this." Dungar grunted. "But talk to me, Jimmy."

"Mglnph." Jimminy responded.

Dungar cocked his head to the side curiously then grabbed Jimminy by the jaw and turned the man's head towards the door to shed some more light on his face. There appeared to be something balled up inside his mouth; perhaps the kidnappers took his song a little too literally. The object was a dark grey color, and stood out quite well when contrasted against the pearly white teeth of Jimminy's mouth. With a slight amount of apprehension, Dungar reached between the man's lips, which seemed oddly full for a face as gaunt as his, and pinched a small corner of the item between his fingers before pulling it out.

Jimminy immediately began hacking and spitting out of his newly vacated mouth.

"Much obliged, mista Dungar." He thanked as he spit stray fibers out of his mouth.

Dungar held the object up to the light. It was a sock; a dirty one at that. He immediately let it go causing it to drop to the floor where it made a faint squelching sound due to the copious amounts of saliva and sweat that it had been marinated in. Grimacing, he turned back to Jimminy who, having wriggled out of his restraints, had taken to surveying the cell himself. He still appeared to be chipper as ever as he turned back to Dungar and studied the grimace on his face.

"Ah don't be so mortified, mate. Believe it or not, I've had worse in me mouth."

Dungar shuddered and returned to sitting. Looking at the walls he considered perhaps trying to dig his way out. However he had no idea how deep into the floor the bars went. Also, depending how often they were checked on, he likely wouldn't make it very far with only his hands to work with.

He scratched at the ground. Even though it was completely dirt it was packed down very hard and would only come off in thin layers. With a glance back at Jimminy, Dungar found him to have removed his pants and casually reclined himself against a wall looking relaxed without a care in the world. Catching Dungar's glance, Jimminy opted to address him.

"Aw whatsamatter, mate? Never been in a cell before?"

"I've felt like a prisoner ever since you came into my life; does that count?"

Jimminy opted to ignore the remark and instead resumed with his musing.

"Out in the land of Farrawee they like to line the floors of their cells with broken glass. Blimey, you had to be bloody tired to get any sleep in that place."

After he finished his thought, Jimminy turned back towards his cellmate. "I'm sorry, mate, where are my manners?"

Dungar glanced back at him with a confused look. Before he could speak though, Jimminy had already removed a small metal object from his shoe and began fumbling around with Dungar's handcuffs. Soon after he began, they popped right off.

Dungar examined his now freed wrists. They were red and raw; the skin on them had been significantly worn down from the sweat and friction. They smelled awful too.

Jimminy flicked his metal utensil in the air and deftly caught it. "Good as new!"

"Well aren't you talented." He acknowledged sarcastically, rubbing at his wrists.

"In more ways than you know, mate." Jimminy said with a wink.

Dungar raised an eyebrow.

Taking that as a prompt to carry on, Jimminy continued. "Nah this was just a little hobby I picked up in the service. I joined up right around the time that whole chastity belt fad was just becoming popular." He exhaled a nostalgic sigh as his eyes began to drift off in favor of the memories being recollected in his mind. "I saved so many from oppression. Those were the days."

"Disturbing implications of your story aside," Dungar interrupted. "What is this service that you were apparently a part of?"

"The Jenair Foreign Legion!" He boasted proudly. "The fearless troops who keep this land and you lot within it safe from impending outside threats! And sometimes drugs."

"You were a soldier . . . ?" Dungar inquired with disbelief.

"You better believe it, boyo! Those were some times! All of us handsome strapping young lads boldly going into unknown territory to face foreign foes! Memories to last a lifetime."

Dungar was quite intrigued by this sudden shift in conversation. Up until this point he hadn't taken much time to really consider the contents of Jimminy's past. However he was certain that, even if he had given it some thought, the notion of a former military career would certainly not have crossed his mind. Jimminy didn't exactly exude a persona of someone with any measurable amount of discipline.

"Did you ever actually do any battle?" he asked.

At that, Jimminy's eyes glazed over and his head cocked slightly to the side while all traces of previous facial expressions melted away to be replaced with an unmistakable thousand yard stare.

"I did the battliest of all the battles . . ." he whispered painfully.

Dungar's crazy blue eyes were locked in on Jimminy's beady brown ones. While their gazes appeared to meet, Jimminy's stare offered no connection whatsoever; his focus was clearly elsewhere.

But with a quick blink and shake of his head, the veteran's eyes regained their usual life and his persona returned to its status quo. With his usual chipper nonchalance, he began to regale his tale.

"I was but a wee wide-eyed young lad with a spring in me step and a sword in me scabbard. We were all well out of general training which allowed us to practice swordplay by day and get drunk off our asses at night! But one day we received word of an uprising."

Jimminy stopped talking and looked at Dungar, who gazed back at him, completely absorbed in the story. The room remained totally silent as the two men continued to just stare at each other. Finally Dungar spoke.

"Are you gonna finish the story or . . . ?"

"I'm pausing for effect, mate! It's the key to any good story."

With that he stopped talking again; his hands frozen in an expressive position in front of him.

"Just tell me what happened!"

"Far to the east!" Jimminy began. "There is a jungle-y area with a bunch of farmers and general modest folk who simply live their lives as simply as simple men do. But one day they came. Sharleys, thousands of them. They're great cannibal monstrosities with row upon row of razor sharp three-inch teeth protruding from their gaping maws."

While he didn't let it show on his face, Dungar was quite taken aback by what he was hearing. He was well aware of the conflict that Jimminy was beginning to describe. Everyone was. It was one of the most famous and controversial wars Jenair had ever been involved in. During his days as bartender he had even come across someone who had seen it with their own eyes and graciously provided him with a sketch of a Sharley.

They were humanoid creatures, not much larger than the average man. They were completely hairless and had a deeper pink hue in their skin though. But as Jimminy had described, their most prominent feature had to be the two rows of fangs that stuck out of their mouths like long, sharp snaggleteeth. Their hands had two large fingers each with an attached foot long talon-like object that was strong enough to stand up to a sword. Their many sharp parts and general bloodlust caused them to be terrifying and dangerous adversaries.

". . . and on their hands they had these claw things . . ."

"I know what a Sharley is, skip to the next part."

"Well fine then, mista Knowitall!" Jimminy grumbled flippantly. "The Sharleys had ransacked the entire countryside. By the time we had arrived there was only fire and death as far as the eye could see. Adjusting to that stink of destruction, that was the easy part. When we encountered the beasts was when the true testing of one's might began. They weren't very nice fellows. Me penchant for diplomacy was all but lost on them. Wouldn't you know it; the first time we met they tried to eat me. I wasn't a particularly educated lad so I wasn't exactly aware that's what the term cannibal meant. Despite a few brief nibbles, I managed to finish me tour mostly intact. 'Twas the longest tour of me life. It was the only one too, but I'd reckon even if I did others this one would have still seemed like the longest. I'll never forget the time I spent in Nom."

"I never would have figured you for a Nom veteran." Dungar admitted.

"I never would have figured you for a homosexual." Jimminy replied.

"What?!"

"Goodnight!"

And just like that Jimminy flopped over onto his side and fell right to sleep. It was the most bizarre talent Dungar had ever seen, the ability to just turn it off and on like that. He looked around again at the dim room that currently housed him. There was no indication as to what time of day it currently was. For all he knew they had only walked for about an hour and it was still day time.

But as he looked back at Jimminy, laying on the ground snoring his ridiculous "hort hort hort hort" snore, he felt a familiar tired sentiment. A nap to refresh his mind and body wouldn't be remiss. Perhaps afterwards he would find himself better equipped for the clearing up of the complication he was currently confronted by. Or maybe he'd wake up to find this has all been a dream and he could continue his life of serving drinks and throwing people out windows. Or maybe Sharleys will ransack the kingdom and eat the queen alive for him. So many possibilities and so little bearing he had right now. As he lay slumped against the wall considering them all, Dungar eventually drifted off to sleep.

He had no idea how long him and Jimminy slept for due to time being impossible to track whilst in their cell. However their rouse to consciousness came in the form of an angry booming voice reverberating through their chamber.

"Get up!"

He awoke with a jump to see the silhouette of an incredibly burly man in the entranceway who appeared to have been sent to fetch them. The characteristics of the man were difficult to make out in the dim light of the room, but Dungar could see he had long and oily black hair which he kept in a ponytail behind him. He wore no shirt leaving his enormous, scarred up body in full view.

He was a short man, but his shoulders were immense, like two boulders jutting out of his neck. Farther down his torso there was a noticeable bulge of a belly, but it did nothing to impede his menacing physique. His arms may well have been carved out of the same iron as Dungar's, and the colossal hands on the ends of them looked to be no stranger to crushing bones into dust.

When he turned his head towards Dungar the light caught it, offering a glimpse of his face. It was caked with deep creases indicative of a man who was battle-hardened and tougher than nails. His eyes were cold and primal, emanating an animalistic rage. The bushy eyebrows above them matched the thick, bushy handlebar moustache framing his pursed lips.

"Rise and shine, murtos." He ordered matter-of-factly.

His voice was gravelly and had a very dangerous air to it.

"What in the blazes is a murto?" Dungar grumbled, rubbing his eyes and defiantly remaining in place.

The man turned and faced Dungar.

"It means you're fresh meat." He grinned threateningly.

A soft "hort hort hort hort"ing from the far corner indicated his message of impending doom hadn't reached Jimminy yet. Realizing this, the man wordlessly marched over to him and stood beside the sleeping man's body. Then, with one hand, he casually reached down, grasped a fist full of Jimminy's shirt, and hoisted him off the ground with so much force that Jimminy flew into the ten foot high ceiling before crashing back to the ground.

Sufficiently woken up, Jimminy looked around wildly before his eyes settled on his caller.

"Oh hello, Dritungo, fancy meeting you here, mate."

"Do I know you, little man?" Growled the goon.

"Apparently not." Jimminy pointed out, mildly put off.

There was a brief silence due to the mild confusion caused by the brief exchange. Then, opting to return to business, Dritungo addressed both of them.

"Out the door, both of you. It's almost show time."

As he walked towards the door, Dungar moved at a deliberately slow pace, taking the extra time to size up this Dritungo person.

"I recognize that look, tough guy. Don't even think about it." Dritungo warned.

"Your fists are indeed mighty, mista Dungar, but even if you could take him there would be plenty of other hired helpers upon us before we made it out of here." Jimminy chimed in.

"What is going on, Jimmy?" Dungar insisted.

"Well, assuming mista Dritungo here is under the same employment as he was when we last crossed paths, we are currently underneath the Vthnnqouayey arena."

"The fight arena? What a boring name."

"It's a foreign word, that's just how it's pronounced, it's spelled nothing like how it sounds."

"So what does this mean for us?"

"Well, most likely that we're either going to be fed to exotic beasts, or beaten to death by gladiators. Personally I myself am hoping for the former, what a way to go that would be eh?"

Dungar shook his head. He never ceased to be amazed by Jimminy's idiosyncrasies. Here he was calmly explaining their impending death as nonchalantly as if he were discussing the weather.

"You're not right in the head, are you?" He asked rhetorically.

"Dungar, me friend . . ." Jimminy began, as he put an arm around his mate's shoulder. "Take it from me. Wrong is the best kind of right."

They walked for a few moments like that, Dungar contemplating his situation and Jimminy's words while Dritungo continued to usher them down the narrow hallway towards a staircase.

"That doesn't make any bloody sense, Jimmy." He finally stated.

"Well what do you expect from me, mista Dungar?" Jimminy asked. "We just established I'm not right in the head." He added with a laugh.

As they made it up the staircase and exited through the door, the two heroes found themselves walking into the bright daylight of the outdoors. After his eyes adjusted, Dungar found himself in the middle of a large coliseum filled with spectators all presumably there to watch him die. He gaped at the spectacle of it, amazed that such a thing was allowed to exist in the kingdom he had held so dear.

The doorway from which they had come was now sealed behind them, Dritungo presumably behind it. Even amid the screaming crowd, Dungar and Jimminy were entirely alone. Alone to face whatever lay behind the ominous gate on the other side of the arena. There were no weapons in sight, no escapes available, and no one to rely on but the shaggy loose cannon who was waving and blowing kisses to the crowd. Dungar swallowed nervously, hoping it wasn't too much to ask for to be kidnapped again right about now.

nine

put up your dukes

The sun shone brightly as it rose higher into the midday sky. A warm breeze swept over the arena, the only respite available from the heat of the day. The weather was ideal for viewing a sporting event, it's a shame they couldn't have picked a sport that didn't revolve around him brutally dying, Dungar thought.

A hush fell over the crowd. The gate on the far side of the arena slowly began to creep upward. Dungar wasn't sure if his heart had stopped or was simply beating so fast he could no longer feel it. Even Jimminy appeared to be mildly absorbed in the anticipation. The gate continued to open until finally it revealed a dark entranceway. Dungar began to wonder to himself what he would prefer to deal with. He had never actually seen a redbear in the flesh before; so perhaps if it was his time to go he could at least mark that milestone beforehand.

Finally, at the sound of a tremendous cheer from a crowd, a figure walked through the gate. It was a man, a mountain of a man, several inches taller than Jimminy and roughly three times as wide. His entire body was covered by chain mail except for his head, which was free from any armor whatsoever. His wavy golden hair blew gently in the afternoon breeze as he flashed a winning smile to the crowd making several ladies as well as a few men swoon. Given the confidence with which he wielded his monstrous battle axe, he had clearly done this before; making his feat of an unscathed face all the more impressive for the crowd and ominous for Dungar and Jimminy.

He smirked at Dungar and Jimminy with condescension; clearly he was unimpressed by his opponents. Dungar surmised that could perhaps be used to his advantage. Soldier or not, Dungar still wasn't entirely sure how much use Jimminy would be in a fight. But perhaps, even if Jimminy were to simply serve as a distraction while Dungar tried to get the jump on the gladiator, they may be able to win this.

"Ladies and gentleman!" A familiar feminine voice rang out from above.

Dungar turned towards the source of it to see Herrow looming over the arena addressing the crowd. The volume of her voice was quite impressive for someone who seemed to be so soft spoken, it was almost inhuman. Her long, wavy brown hair flowed down elegantly past her shoulders, contrasting nicely with the flowing formal white dress she was wearing. As much as Dungar hated her, he had to admit she was quite beautiful.

A hush fell over the crowd as all eyes began to turn to her.

"Thank you again for coming to the preliminary events for the biannual Vthnnqouayey arena blood bath!" Herrow announced triumphantly.

Another loud cheer erupted from the crowd before she continued.

"Ah we're still in the prelims!" Jimminy pointed out.

"What does that mean?" Dungar asked.

"These are just the battles to warm up the gladiators, mate. We're just here to be fodder for the handsome gent over there before he does the real competition tomorrow!" Jimminy explained.

Herrow's voice rang out again in the arena. "In our current match-up we have another returning favorite. He has survived not one, not two, but five Vthnnqouayey arena bloodbaths! And he's still as handsome as ever. Give it up for Pretty Boy Panin!"

With a smug smile, the man gestured with both arms towards the crowd as they enthusiastically screamed their thunderous approval.

"And here to help him stretch his legs," Herrow continued, flashing a cold smile towards Dungar and Jimminy, "are two convicts generously donated to us from the infamous dungeons of Jenair. Both were found guilty of trafficking women and children. Let us see how they fare when confronted by an opponent who can fight back!"

Jeers and boos erupted from the crowd. Dungar felt a seething hatred rising in his chest.

"Mista Dungar!" Jimminy exclaimed incredulously. "You never told me you were a trafficker! I never would have agreed to this quest if I knew—"

Jimminy's spiel was cut short by Dungar backhanding him.

"Shut up, Jimmy." Dungar said with disgust. "She's obviously lying."

"Oh, right." Jimminy acknowledged as he rubbed his face.

"Are you ready to get this fight started!?" The triumphant voice of Herrow rang out one last time, followed by a final tremendous cheer from the crowd.

Dungar was fuming. If pretty boy over there was looking for a fight then Dungar felt happy to oblige in his current state. But Jimminy tapped him on the shoulder to get his attention.

"Relax, mate." Jimminy mumbled as he leaned in close to Dungar. "I got this!"

Thoroughly confused, but also curious, Dungar decided to see what Jimminy had in mind.

Putting on his signature grin, Jimminy confidently strode towards Pretty Boy Panin as calm as the hush that had settled over the crowd. Dungar wasn't surprised by his audacity, and was instead surprised at his own lack of surprise at Jimminy's audacity.

"Hello there, you great brute of a combatant, you!" Jimminy greeted the large man as he continued to walk closer.

Panin tentatively stared Jimminy down as he continued to walk closer, clearly confused. Before long Jimminy was just a few paces away, still confidently strolling towards Panin. Then suddenly, and without warning, Panin drew a deep breath, raised his axe, and moved to lunge at Jimminy.

"Whoa whoa whoa there!" Jimminy admonished his opponent with impressive conviction. "Just what do you think you're doing, mista gladiator!"

Panin froze.

"Uhh . . ."

"Don't you 'uhh' me!" Jimminy continued to chastise. "You were actually about to strike an official referee! Why I oughtta disqualify you from the tournament!"

"What are you talking about?!" The gladiator demanded.

"You see that burly gent over there?" Jimminy asked, pointing at Dungar. "He is your opponent, not me!"

"There ain't no referees . . ." Panin grunted unsurely.

"Did you not read the official rulebook update that was issued for this tournament!?"

Panin did not respond. Instead he just looked around helplessly.

"Of course you didn't." Jimminy exclaimed, exasperated. "I bet you can't even read!"

Panin still continued to stare at him, stone faced. It was unclear if Jimminy's words were even registering.

"Blimey . . ." Jimminy sighed, smacking his palm to his face. "Mista Dungar! Come face your opponent!"

Dungar cautiously began to walk towards them. He had no idea what Jimminy was planning, but if the man was really shoving the burden of fighting this guy entirely onto his shoulders then Jimminy better hope he doesn't survive.

"'Twas an honest mistake, mate." Jimminy comforted Panin, slapping him on the back. "Just go do your thing, we'll chat about this later."

Confidence regained, Panin lumbered towards Dungar. His shoulders were hunched and his arms were flexed into attack position. Dungar, on the other hand, stood straight and stoically. Even standing up straight he still didn't come close to matching Pretty Boy's hunched over height. Nonetheless, Dungar defiantly stared him down. Regardless of whatever conflicting feelings were flying through his mind, his eyes were unfaltering.

"Alright boys!" Jimminy cut in. "I want to see a nice clean fight between ya! No scratching, biting, eye gouging, hooking, facemasking, throwing sand in the face, insensitive slurs regarding your opponent's mother, or hitting below the belt!"

Dungar continued to stare Panin down. Even in spite of the height difference, he could spot the twinge of trepidation on the pretty boy's face.

"Let's get it on!" Jimminy bellowed, clapping his hands and ducking out of the way.

Pretty Boy Panin straightened up and raised his axe high above his head, going for the killing blow early.

Dungar immediately lunged for him, his hands grasping the chain mail, intent on turning this fight into a grappling match.

Then, out of nowhere, there was a sickening thwacking sound. Dungar looked down to see the limp body of Pretty Boy Panin bleeding profusely from the right side of his face and being supported by nothing but Dungar's firm grip on his chain mail. Dungar then looked up at Jimminy, who was staring down at Panin's face. He had a large, bloody rock in his hand.

"Hah! He ain't pretty no more!" Jimminy gleefully exclaimed.

"Jimmy!" Dungar shouted with surprise. "Where did you get that rock?"

"I always keep a large rock on me." Jimminy said with a shrug, before stuffing the rock down the front of his pants. "Never know when ya might need one!"

Dungar laughed heartily before casually dropping the limp body of Panin to the ground.

"Well that was . . . Interesting." The voice of Herrow rang out through the stadium. "In a stunning upset, the child rapists from Jenair managed to pull a fast one on our honorable hero and defeat him using deceit and deception!"

The crowd rang out in more boos and angry yells. As loose objects began to be hurled towards them, Dungar and Jimminy made a dash for the gate they came from. It opened up to reveal several armed guards and Dritungo, the latter having a very sour look on his face. The guards all grabbed Dungar to take him back to his cell while Dritungo stayed behind to pin Jimminy to the wall.

"Alright, wise guy." Dritungo snarled. "Give me the rock."

Jimminy laughed at him. "How about you reach in and get it, mate?"

"Unless you want to lose more than the rock, I suggest you hand it over now"

"Here you go, friend!" Jimminy grinned, immediately producing the rock for him.

After that brief exchange, they were led back to their cell. As he walked towards it, Dungar took the opportunity to study the turnstile. Contrary to his suspicions, there was no locking mechanism. The turnstile simply rotated normally. Puzzled as to what kept the gate shut, Dungar looked at the gate itself and that was when he saw it. Affixed to the top of the gate was an enormous rock, the weight of which was surely enough to keep the gate down. It took the efforts of three guards to rotate the turnstile and lift the gate.

Secure in the cell once again, Dungar and Jimminy settled in. Dungar took to pacing while once again Jimminy removed his pants and reclined against a wall.

"You knew Dritungo." Dungar stated, halting his pacing and turning to Jimminy. "And you knew where we were. Have you been to a one of these before?"

"Before I left the service, me battalion was in these parts during this season one year." Jimminy explained. "'Tis quite the spectacle. They import great creatures of exotic ferociousness and sic 'em on a big group of folks. If today was the prelims then tomorrow will probably be the blood bath!"

"What about the gladiators?"

"Oh they have a tournament for them too. It's a daylong event, mate; can't expect the lemmings to outrun the beasties all day now."

Dungar grumbled to himself. It'll take more than a rock in Jimminy's pants to save them against whatever monsters awaited them tomorrow. He walked over to the gate and looked through it. Soon as he did, he heard footsteps and saw faint movement far down the dimness of the hallway. Then out of the darkness emerged a detachment of armed guards followed by a large group of assorted individuals in varying forms of restraints. The gate to the cell opened and in stepped Dritungo.

"Get in there, all of ya!"

One by one each prisoner filed into the cell. By the time they had all made it inside, everyone had to rub shoulders in order for everyone to fit. As the gate slammed behind him, Dritungo sneered through the gate at them.

"Hope you lot are comfortable. You have a big day tomorrow."

A few sharp glances at those within his immediate vicinity allowed Dungar a small buffer zone between him and the crowd. Jimminy, on the other hand, had proceeded to make his way up to everyone to introduce himself and shake each of their hands.

Soon the room was filled with the dull roar of pockets of people talking amongst themselves. Dungar could hear Jimminy interviewing people as he made his rounds.

"Good whatever-time-of-day-it-is, kind sir!" Jimminy greeted a particularly terrified looking man. "No need to be afraid now, we're all friends in here."

"I don't belong here!" The trembling man insisted. "Please! There has been some kind of mistake. I'm just a farmer; I'm not whoever they were after!"

Hearing this, other prisoners began to weigh in.

"I'm a farmer too!" Another man exclaimed. "I was just minding my own business out in the field when I was attacked."

"I was at the market with my kids." A small, frail man standing to the side sobbed. "They threatened to harm my children if I called for help."

A nearby prisoner put his hand on his shoulder to try and console him. At mention of children, other people in the cell began to break down.

"My boys are probably wondering where I am right now." A woman choked through tears. "My husband was killed in battle; I'm all they have left."

As he sat secluded in his corner, Dungar spent the next few hours catching snippets of conversations. People's names, back-stories, and how they came to be stuck in this situation. Nearly every one of them was a normal, simple individual not unlike himself. Most were snatched from their homes, their businesses, their families; all doomed to die screaming and hopelessly trying to escape. He had no doubt that Herrow probably fabricated similar incriminating backstories for all of these people as she had for Jimminy and himself to justify their bloodshed.

As he sat seething in the corner for hours, eavesdropping on one heartbreaking story after another, Dungar found himself at the end of his rope. Silently, he rose from the spot where he had remained motionless. Slowly, deliberately, and unstoppably, he moved towards the gate. Anyone who did not step out of his way was thrown aside. He reached the ominous wooden gate that obstructed his freedom. The loathsome gate that was the catalyst to their captivity. Worn and warped by age, but nonetheless imposing and unbreakable still.

With a grip strong enough to slightly conform the wood to the shape of his massive hands, he grabbed a hold of it and heaved. The rebellious door would not give, but Dungar continued to pull. The room had quieted as each pair of eyes began to move in his direction, studying the seemingly delusional man who sought to overpower their instrument of oppression.

Dungar's mind was focused entirely on his body. He could feel every facet of the pressure of the eyes, the gravity of the situation, and the strain of his muscles. With a guttural and animalistic yell he heaved again. But this time slowly, surely, the gate began to rise. Small gasps and sounds of disbelief could be heard from the group as more light began to creep into the cell from the doorway.

Dungar's hands were in agony, his arms felt like they may rip right from their sockets, but he could not stop now. He continued his inhuman feat of strength until he was finally standing up straight. The impossibly heavy gate was now almost two feet off the ground, supported by nothing but Dungar's white fingertips and his unshakeable mental and physical fortitude.

Quickly the residents of the room began to see this for the opportunity this was. They dashed to the gate and began to slide themselves through the opening. Dungar's face was red. His ears pounded from the sound of blood rushing through his body. He had no idea if he was being thanked or not, he could hear nothing. But still he held on, despite every fiber of his body screaming in protest.

Eventually only Jimminy remained. Every other prisoner had taken off in search of their freedom with nary a backwards glance or attempt to aid Dungar in holding the gate.

"Get out of here, Jimmy!" Dungar ordered.

"But mista Dungar! What about—"

"I DON'T HAVE TIME TO ARGUE WITH YOU!" Dungar screamed into the room. The pain was excruciating. "I can't hang on!" He spit out in between heavy breaths. "Go! NOW!"

Without a word Jimminy sprinted towards the gate and dove underneath it. As soon as he cleared the room Dungar's hands gave out sending the gate plummeting to the ground resulting in a thunderous crash. His arms, legs, hands, and back, every muscle that he could have possibly engaged to hold that door, burned like fire. As soon as he let go he collapsed to the ground in crippled heap.

Outside the room Jimminy was trying fruitlessly to work the turnstile. No matter how he heaved or kicked at it, the gate did not so much as shudder.

"Go before they catch you and throw you back in here, Jimmy!" Dungar yelled from his spot on the floor.

"But mate . . ." Jimminy began. He stood at the gate looking through at Dungar laying on the ground. Even in the dim light the pain on Jimminy's face was visible. ". . . Wot are you going to do?"

Using whatever remained of his strength, Dungar got off the floor and met Jimminy at the gate.

"I'm going to marry a princess and live happily ever after."

Jimminy smiled sheepishly at him, and the two simply stayed where they were for a moment.

"Okay seriously, what in the blazes do you think you're doing?" Dungar demanded incredulously. "I just freed you, how dare you insult my efforts by sticking around. Get out of here. Go go go go go go." He continued to repeat go whilst slamming his hand against the gate in rhythm with his demands until Jimminy disappeared into the darkness. As soon as he was alone, Dungar again crumpled to the floor in a wreck.

"Kidnap me, will ya?" Dungar soliloquized from the floor. "Fine, I'll just ruin your livelihood." He chuckled to himself for a few moments where he lay before his tiredness overtook him and he nodded off.

His second wake-up call in the cell was very similar to his first one. Only it wasn't just Dritungo's voice rousing him this time, but also the feeling of a fist roughly the size of a cannonball being drove into his stomach. Dungar's eyes opened to the sight of the angriest face he had ever seen nose to nose with his own.

"YOU ARE A DEAD MAN!" Dritungo bellowed at him whilst laying more murderous punches into his midsection.

"Enough, Dritungo." Herrow's voice chimed in.

The petite lady entered the room wearing a long black cloak with the hood up. Dritungo dropped his fist, but remained holding Dungar up by the collar of his shirt.

"I'm not entirely sure how you managed it, Dungar." She addressed him, giving him a cold stare. "But you've sabotaged my main event for tomorrow and now you're going to have to find a way to make it up to me."

"Well send the ogre outside and I'll make it up to ya right here." Dungar sneered, earning him another punch in the face from Dritungo.

Herrow strode over to where Dungar lay and pressed the sharp heel of her boot deep into his neck.

"Not on your life, you disgusting, hairy animal." She snarled at him. "No, I already have other plans for you. We'll find more people for the main event before it happens, and until then you are going to entertain the crowd."

She stepped off of his neck and strode out of the room. Dritungo stayed behind.

"You're lucky we need you for tomorrow." Dritungo growled. "Or I'd break you right now."

Dungar lay where Dritungo dropped him as the henchman stormed out of the room, locking him in there once more. He thought about his aching ribs and the feeling of the sharp boot heel pressed against his neck.

"Totally worth it." He grunted to himself with a chuckle.

ten

ARE YOU NOT ENTERTAINED!?

Being alone in the cell started to grate on Dungar after a short while. He would occasionally nibble on his provisions and take short naps periodically due to boredom and lack of stimuli. Before long he sense of time was all but obliterated. He had no idea how long he had been confined there alone by the time the gate opened up again.

"I thought we were supposed to take blood bath people to the other cell?"

"It's totally full. It's no big deal to leave him here, he only has to last the night."

Dungar watched as a tied up man was tossed into the cell with him. As the gate closed and the room turned to dimness, Dungar made his way over to the individual. He was an older gentleman with long greying hair, most of which was swept back behind his head. His face was old and weathered, but still tough looking. It was a similar toughness to that of Sir Pent's face, battle-hardened and unapologetic.

"You plan on staring at me all day, or are you gonna help me up, son?" The man groaned exasperatedly.

Like many of the men Dungar had encountered on his journey, this man's voice too had a bit of drag to it. But it was slightly higher than what he had been becoming accustomed to, and there was a noticeable drawl to it. He bent down and undid the binds on the man's hands before helping him to his feet.

"Appreciate that, boy." The man thanked, dusting himself off.

"No problem, sir." Dungar responded.

"Sir? How did you know I was a knight?"

"You're a knight?"

"You just called me sir."

"Is that not a typical way of addressing an older man?"

"Older man!? Just who do you think you are, son?"

"How about you stop calling me son and I won't refer to you as an old man."

"How about I feed you my fist, son!?"

At that, the man wound up and took a very uncoordinated swing at Dungar. Effortlessly, he sidestepped the punch which caused the man to lose his balance and stagger before falling to the floor. Dungar gaped at him as the man gracelessly rolled around trying to get back up before settling into a sitting position.

"Alright son, I'll let ya beat around the stump . . . This time!"

"Are you drunk?" Dungar bluntly asked.

"Well that depends on what you mean by . . . You." The man slurred while looking around.

Sighing, Dungar slumped against the wall into a sitting position as well. They sat for a long time, neither speaking to the other. Dungar eyed the older fellow suspiciously as he sat in the middle of the floor gibbering to himself before finally going silent.

"Is that blood event tomorrow?" The man finally spoke

"Yes." Dungar replied matter-of-factly

"Well that sucks." He stated. "How'd y'all get holed up in this calaboose?"

". . . Uh. What?"

". . . Where did they snag you from?"

"Lotsotri forest."

"Lotsotri forest? What were you doing there?"

"I was on my way to Jenair."

Upon hearing that, the man sighed to himself.

"Aw flaming piss buckets. You weren't intending to marry the queen were ye? Because if you were then I got bad news for ya."

Dungar perked up at the mention of her. It's only been a few days; surely she couldn't have gotten married already. If she ended up with Rainchild then he's really going to kill her.

"What do you mean?"

"The queen, son." The man repeated. "The fishy wench ain't who ya think she is. She's a witch and a killer. And I'll have her head on a spike even if I gotta see every last one of you suitors knocked galley west."

The multitude of questions roiling around in Dungar's mind left him with a very odd look on his face. The man, however, assumed his odd look was surprise resulting from the information he was just presented with.

"Hope this doesn't foster no bad blood between us, son."

"I think we'll be okay, sir."

Dungar wasn't sure what to make of the strange man he found himself locked in a room with. Did he actually know about the queen, or was he just a crazy conspiracy theorist? Questions like those forced Dungar to question his own stance on the matter. If he were to write off this old fellow as a crazy conspiracy theorist, how could he justify his own quest? On the other hand, perhaps this man could be the ally he needed.

"What do you know?" Dungar asked.

"What do I know!? I know she's a witch and a murderer!" The man responded defensively.

"I'm asking how you know that, you crazy old goat." Dungar countered, irritated.

"You watch your tongue or I'll take it from you, boy!" The cellmate growled.

Dungar stared at him with a bored expression of contempt. He was imprisoned, starved, and beaten. Petty threats of violence from an old man weren't about to faze him now. Something about Dungar's scrutinizing stare must have tipped the man off to that notion, because he opted to carry on.

"I saw it with my own eyes. I was stationed outside the king's private chambers to superintend his slumber that night, and I had barely even been drinking before this shift! Then the princess came, so naturally I let her inside. I figured if there was anyone on whom his highness could rely it would be his own dang daughter. But after she went in I watched her. She went right up to his bed and knelt by him."

"Why were you spying on the princess when she thought she was alone with the king?"

"THAT'S NONE O' YER GODDAMN BUSINESS, BOY!"

". . . Alrighty then."

"Ahem now where was I? Ah yes. She began to work some sorta witchery on my dear king. There were flashes of red and purple and all them other colors and before I knew it King Ik was lookin' all gone up the flume in his bed. When she left his chambers, the harlot tried to convince me the king was resting and not to be disturbed, BUT I KNEW BETTER! I rushed to his side only to feel the touch of the king's cold carcass. Naturally, as any of us knights would do, I rushed to our betrayer to beef her where she stood! But wouldn't you know it, son, she knew I would come for her. I was arrested by my own brothers, my cries of treason falling on deaf ears. But mark my words, boy. I'm gonna track down yer bride-to-be, and she's gonna die."

"So wait." Dungar replied. "You mean to tell me that you were actually a knight?"

"Still am, boy!" The man declared. "A true knight serves his king! And even stripped of my position I still am and will always be Sir Lee of Castle Jenair!"

"Dungar Loloth." He introduced himself, stretching out one of his giant bear paws of a hand. Lee took it in one of his and they had themselves a nice manly handshake with just the right amount of firmness.

"Did you perhaps know a Sir Pent?" Dungar asked.

"DID I!?" Lee exclaimed. "Why that wretched scumbag is one of the traitorous lowlifes who arrested me. He's so crooked he'd swallow a nail and shat out a corkscrew. I wouldn't piss on him if he was on fire!"

"I think he's dead." Dungar added nonchalantly.

"Don't be so sure, boy." Lee warned. "He's a wall-eyed, lippy bastard, but he's also one tough son of a whore. If you didn't hear no death rattle from em, then don't bet all yer chips just yet."

They sat in silence for a little while after that. Dungar couldn't figure out whether to be amused or annoyed by the man's idiomatic jargon. He had no idea what most of the phrases the man was saying meant, and yet still found himself able to understand the bulk of it. He was still convinced the man was at least a little bit loopy, but he couldn't help but like him anyway. He was a stand up fellow with a chip on his shoulder and a burning vengeance for the queen. Just the kind of guy Dungar needed.

"I have it in for the queen too." Dungar finally spoke.

Lee, who had been ventriloquizing to himself with his hand, paused and looked at Dungar.

"I met a man from the Kingdom of Farrawee . . ." Dungar began, and proceeded to fill Sir Lee in on the details of his encounter with Stranger.

When Dungar finished recounting the story, Lee spoke again.

"Why that no-good squirrelly mudsill of a woman, soon as we find her she's getting nailed to the wall, son."

"Agreed," Dungar nodded.

"BUT UNTIL THEN!" Lee yelled for some reason. "I suggest we find a way to survive our current predicament. Once that blood bath starts that whole arena is gonna get hotter than a whorehouse on copper night. Best get some shut-eye, son. Yer gonna need to have yer wits about ya when that place starts turnin' into a bone orchard."

And without another word, the two men rolled over to go to sleep. Not that it was that easy to drift off with the threat of death looming at any moment. Dungar's mind drifted back to what Herrow said to him earlier that day about how he was apparently going to entertain the crowd while they rounded up more people to replace the ones he released. He doubted she knew that he knew how to juggle, so she probably had something more sinister in mind. All the more reason for him to get some sleep, he knew he was going to need his strength tomorrow.

When Dungar woke up the next morning it was not to the sound of Dritungo yelling; nor was it to the feeling of fists being driven into his body. Instead, it was to the feeling of being picked up and gagged by four guards while they carried him out of his cell, probably to avoid waking Sir Lee.

As he was dropped in front of the familiar arena gate, Dritungo came up to him and clasped a hand onto Dungar's shoulder.

"How're the ribs, murto?"

"Better than yours will be when I'm done with ya."

Dritungo laughed a deep belly laugh.

"Well here's hopin' you get to find out, tough guy." Dritungo foreshadowed as the hand of his on Dungar's shoulder grasped the back of his tunic. "If you live through today then I'll let ya go toe to toe with me."

Before Dungar could respond, he felt himself thrown through the door and out into the arena. The familiar dull roar of a large audience surrounded him as he blinked in the harsh sunlight. When his vision adjusted, Dungar looked around. He was truly alone in the arena this time. No Jimminy, no rock stuffed down his pants, just his own weary body to rely on.

"Gentleman and ladies!" Herrow's voice rang out through the stadium. "Welcome to the biannual Vthnnqouayey arena blood bath!"

As usual, a tremendous cheer reverberated from the crowd.

"Before we reach our prestigious main event though, we have a special treat for you this year! Down in the arena before you there is your first round of entertainment! He is one of the most elite members of the infamous Bare Knuckle Bandits."

The usual jeers and boos then erupted from the crowd. Dungar just rolled his eyes. Were the Bare Knuckle Bandits even a thing, or did she just make that up too?

"The bandit you see before you," Herrow continued, "Was caught and tried for his numerous counts of theft, arson, vandalism, rape, and of course, murders. Rather than seeing him simply executed for his heinous crimes though, we here at the arena petitioned to have his cowardly presence here for his final hours, so he could at least see what it's like to fight with real men before he dies!"

As she finished speaking, the gate on the far side of the arena opened to reveal Dungar's opponent. It was a tall individual with incredibly long arms and of average build, but it did not appear to be human. Its skin was a brilliant white color and had an odd layered texture to it like papier-mâché. It was completely hairless and had beady black eyes and no lips or nose, just an opening that Dungar assumed was its mouth. It wore nothing but a loincloth and a ring of fur around its neck, and it was armed with several spears as well as a small, circular wooden shield.

"Our gladiator this fine morning is Chocky of the Weib Tribe. He may not be the burliest of our gladiators but he is fast with a spear and has quite a reach!"

The crowd was clearly as used to seeing a member of the Weib tribe as Dungar was. There were cheers for the gladiator, but they were quieter and more unsure sounding than usual.

"His village was also burned down by the Bare Knuckle Bandits!" Herrow added, hoping to add some drama and sympathy. "Here is his chance for revenge! Let the fight begin!"

Immediately Dungar found himself being forced to dive out of the way as a spear was thrown at him. As he hopped back to his feet, he found his opponent bearing down on him with a second spear in hand. He frantically had to dodge side to side as the spear was repeatedly thrust towards him. As the barrage of attacks continued, Dungar felt himself rapidly losing control of the fight. He started to back away while continuing to dodge the wild swings and thrusts of the savage white man.

Soon enough, Dungar felt his back against the wall of the coliseum as his opponent moved to corner him. Chocky wound up and thrust forward the intended killing blow. Dungar felt the cool breeze created by the weapon on his face as he barely managed to duck out of the way. Just as Dungar had hoped, the spear became embedded in the wooden wall of the arena right where his neck was a second earlier. As the gladiator grasped his weapon, frantically trying to pull it from the wall, Dungar ball up his fist and delivered a massive uppercut right into his opponent's chin.

The force of the blow was so tremendous that not only did the Weib Tribe representative's hands leave his spear, but his feet also left the ground as he careened backwards towards the center of the stadium. With impressive resilience, the gladiator managed to get back on his feet just as Dungar reached him. As Dungar grabbed him by his fur necklace, the gladiator delivered a return blow to the side of Dungar's face. When knuckle met cheekbone a faint cracking sound could be heard. It was the sound of Chocky shattering his hand. He hardly had time to make a pained facial expression before a storm of enraged swings from Dungar sent him back to the ground.

Dungar loomed over his battered opponent, who was bleeding from the face and gasping for air, before he looked up at Herrow. She was seated comfortably in a large throne overlooking the fight. Seeing that it had come to a close, she got up from her chair and raised a hand towards the arena; her thumb protruding downward from that hand.

Dungar looked at her with her odd hand expression, before making one back to her with a different lone finger protruding from his. Then he kicked Chocky in the ribs one more time for good measure before strolling back to his gate.

"Not so fast, convict!" Herrow's voice rang out through the stadium. "Your term here in Vthnnqouayey arena is only just beginning!"

As if on cue, the gate at the other end of the coliseum opened up to reveal another gladiator.

"So that's how it's gonna be, huh?" Dungar growled through gritted teeth. She kidnapped him against his will, slandered him and painted him as a convict, subjected him to beatings and solitary confinement, and then sentenced him to die like an animal. No more. Dungar was going to tear her limb from limb even if he had to go through every gladiator north of the Great Fall.

He wasted no time with this new challenger. He bowed his shoulders and took off towards his opponent at an all-out sprint. The new gladiator, a shorter man in gold armor and a matching gold helmet, froze in awe of the barbarous blacksmith bearing down on him. Once he reached about five paces away from his target Dungar leaped an epic leap into the sky, winding back his fist as he rose. As he came back towards the ground, he drove his fist into the gladiator's face with an impact so thunderous that the man's helmet and shoes were thrown from his body as he hurtled backwards at breakneck speed into the wall. The gladiator's face was gone; all that remained was a solution of pulverized bones, teeth, and blood.

Adrenaline coursing through his veins, and thoughts of vengeance coursing through his mind, Dungar paced in front of the gate like a rabid redbear just begging for someone to come through. When someone did, Dungar lunged for them just the same. However this time Dungar watched in horror as this opponent deftly ducked under his wild haymaker and delivered a counter crushing blow to Dungar's foot with his mace.

The momentum of the fight took a serious turn as Dungar felt his body go crashing to the ground; his foot in implacable pain. As he tried to get up, the imbalance of his body made his movements slow and predictable and he quickly received another mace blow to his chest sending him right back to the ground. His mind was disoriented and his lungs were breathless, it was all he could do to roll out of the way of the crushing blows of his opponent's mace.

As he dodged another swing and the mace crashed into the ground, Dungar took his opportunity to retaliate. He grabbed the handle of the mace just below the head as the gladiator went to pull it back. Using his opponent's own strength to get him back in his feet, as well as net him a bit of forward momentum, Dungar used his good leg to support himself while using his other leg to drive his knee into the gladiator's gut. The man recoiled backwards, hunched over forward with his hands clutching his stomach. The mace now in his hands, Dungar finished his adversary off with an upwards swing of it right into the man's jaw.

Three bodies now littered the arena. It was far from a bath of blood, but Dungar certainly had enough of the stuff on him. His chest ached from the blow, and he leaned heavily to his left side due to inability to put much weight on his right foot. His confidence and ferocity had waned, but his life was on the line, and he was not going to let Herrow beat him regardless of how many henchmen she had to hide herself behind. At least that's what he thought before his next opponent came out.

The next gladiator that walked out of that gate was nothing that Dungar could have possibly expected. It was a tall thin creature, at least nine feet high at the head, but the strangest part of it was how thin it was. Its chest had to have been almost four feet long, but it was only about as big around as Dungar's leg. The limbs that protruded from it offered a matching description; long and skinny. The face was the strangest of all though. Its eyes consisted of thin glowing red slits and its nose was long and sharp not unlike a beak. Its lips were all but non-existent, simply thin folds of skin curled into a deep, ingrained frown where the mouth would be. The unnerving visage was capped off by patches of long strands of silky white hair that flowed shabbily down all sides of the creature's head.

Slowly and gracefully it walked towards him, it's incredibly long legs taking enormous strides, before coming to a halt in front of him.

Clouded by pain, adrenaline, anger, and desperation, Dungar looked the creature up and down with contempt.

"You think you're tough, skinny?" Dungar bellowed. "Let's see what you're made of!"

He reared the mace back, but before he could swing it forward he was knocked off his feet and several paces to his right by a punishing right hook from the creature. Dungar sat up from the ground rubbing his face just in time to see the creature effortlessly pick up the body of the gold-clad gladiator with one hand and begin swinging it around like a mace. It was truly horrifying.

It was all he could do to dive and roll and limp and do any movement within his power to avoid the constant slamming of the 180 pound body against the ground all around him. However, a man of Dungar's size and in Dungar's condition could only be so agile. The beatings he had endured over the last few days coupled with the physical exhaustion of pushing his body in the ways that he had been today and the night before had heavily sapped at his once tremendous vigor. A half step too short or a half second too late and he would inevitably find the battered remains of his former opponent crashing down upon him. And surely that is what happened.

Reality slowed to a crawl for Dungar as the full force of a fully grown adult male being swung by an even larger creature impacted his body. He felt the impact, but there was no instantly registered pain. Just the feeling of his body involuntarily seizing up as his legs continued to move in one direction while his body moved in the other. He could not cry out in pain, he could not reach out to brace his fall; he could only experience the ride as if he were simply a passenger in his own body as it experienced the physical punishment completely separately.

When Dungar's body impacted the ground was when time sped up to its normal rate for him. It was as if pain were a white hot molten liquid that had suddenly washed over his entire body. He could not articulate where he hurt, he could not even articulate what kind of hurt it was, all he knew was that he was in pain and all he had the physical capacity to do was to lay there and pray for the molten agony that currently enveloped him to cool.

His animal of an opponent now loomed over him menacingly before delivering a crushing punch into the side of his face. But Dungar didn't even react. The blow of the punch was simply a small extra bubble on the surface of his molten lake of misery.

Satisfied with his decimation of Dungar, the creature reached down and picked him up, holding him high for the arena to see. Dungar wasn't sure if it was the bright sunlight shining on his face that reignited his burning desire for life, or if it was the roar of that crowd of horrible people that he hated so much, but at that very moment he decided he'd be burned if he was going to let some twiggy bird thing be the instrument of his undoing.

He grabbed the gladiator by the hand it held him with and sunk his teeth as far as they would go into the meaty area just below the thumb. His opponent jerked and screeched but his teeth held firm until the chunk of flesh his teeth were latched onto was torn loose from the creature's hand.

Dungar spit out the chunk of meat he'd just bitten off before he grabbed the closest item he could find, which was the small round shield from his first opponent, and smashed it as hard as he could against the tall thing's knee.

With a chunk torn from its hand, and a thoroughly shattered patella, the gladiator fell to its one good knee leaving it eye level with Dungar. In a last ditch effort, the gladiator threw a final swing at Dungar's face, but Dungar effortlessly caught the fist in his hand.

His blood was pounding, his muscles were all but completely exerted, and his legs were about to give, but Dungar stood strong and firm with his opponent at his mercy. With his free hand, cool as can be, Dungar reached over and seized a massive fist full of the creature's patchy, silky hair, and catapulted the creature's head towards his own so fast that the resulting head-butt echoed throughout the stadium.

The long beak of a nose on his opponent was utterly obliterated and the eye socket where impact was made was completely shattered, the eye totally liquidized. As the creature's limp body fell to the ground, several teeth could be seen spilling out of its mouth.

Dungar stood stoically in the center of the coliseum. His clothes were ripped and torn to shreds; his hands and face were coated in the blood of his enemies. His chest heaved up and down as he struggled to satiate his body's heavy desire for oxygen. He knew that as soon as he moved a single muscle, his body was going to give underneath him.

"Bring out the next challenger." The bored voice of Herrow rang out.

Dungar strained against his body's desire to give up, but it was no good. He fell to his knees. His vision was blurry and the world was spinning. He couldn't even make out the cheering of the crowd anymore, everything sounded like it was underwater. He closed his eyes trying to regain his senses, but his equilibrium was shot and he keeled over backwards as a result.

When Dungar opened his eyes again he saw the figure of his opponent looming over him. But for some reason he looked vaguely familiar. As Dungar struggled to focus his eyes, his opponent leaned in closer to his face. That's when Dungar clued in.

He was face to face with the yellow cat-like eyes and long, sharp snaggleteeth of a Sharley.

ELEVEN

OUT OF THE FIRE
AND BACK INTO THE PAN

Dungar's life never flashed before his eyes. He made no final pleas to a god he never acknowledged. He couldn't even say what his final thoughts were. He just lay there in the dirt and the blood focusing on each new breath as it came. The Sharley's breath carried a uniquely sickening combination of old eggs and flatulence. He couldn't help but wonder if his body would have any kind of impact on the vile halitosis when the Sharley consumes him. He then thought maybe having ridiculous thoughts like that about his own demise indicated he was ready to die. It was irrelevant either way though; because as the rascally children of Woodwall used to say: ready or not, here it comes.

Dungar waited impatiently, hoping the beast hadn't decided to start at his feet and work its way up. Nothing came though. Dungar peeled his eyes open so he could see just what was going on. His body still hadn't really come back online, so getting to an upright position was excruciatingly difficult. As he struggled to get up, he heard the Sharley speak in a deep, raspy voice.

"What are you doing here, pathetic human?" The creature demanded.

"What?" Dungar spat. "Now what kind of stupid question is tha—"

But his response was cut off by an even louder, more incredulous response by a voice so ingrained in Dungar's mind that he sometimes hears it when he's trying to sleep.

"Wot am I doing here?!?!"

Dungar immediately sat bolt upright. His eyes could see clearly now, but he still did not believe them. Jimminy was boldly standing in the middle of the stadium facing down the Sharley; he appeared to be totally unarmed.

In as grandiose a gesture as he could muster, Jimminy clenched one fist and used his other hand to dramatically point at the Sharley.

"My name is Jimminy Appaya . . . And I'm here to kick your ass!"

With a vicious snarl, the Sharley did not so much as hesitate before setting off at a run towards Jimminy. Its long talons were raised and its gaping maw was open wide as it set in for the kill.

Jimminy stood fast as the beast rapidly closed ground. One of his hands disappeared deep into his pocket. Once the Sharley was within a close enough range, Jimminy loudly proclaimed "POCKET SAND!!" and threw a large hand full of the grit into the fiend's face.

The Sharley, now thoroughly blinded and coughing up clouds of sand, began to violently thrash around, its long talons menacingly swinging to and fro. Jimminy, who was quite agile for a tall and lanky man, did a quick shoulder roll underneath a pair of the swinging claws and ended up behind his opponent. Without missing a beat, he took a run at the creature and delivered a mighty kick right between the humanoid monster's legs and square into its groin.

With a gurgling groan, the entire body of the Sharley seized up and it crumpled to the ground in a heap, rolling around and clutching its stomach.

"Nothin' wins brawls like a kick in the balls!" Jimminy declared triumphantly, before stomping on them once more which elicited a pained wail from the downed creature. Satisfied that his opponent was out of commission, Jimminy made his way over to Dungar.

"Good afternoon, mista Dungar! How are you today?"

"Jimmy, what in the bloody blazes—"

"Me too! Come on; let's get you out of here!"

As Jimminy hauled him to his feet, Dungar caught sight of a rope ladder hanging from the side of the coliseum; it must have been how Jimminy made his way inside. He had no idea how he was going to make it up there, but it was his only chance at salvation.

"Sorry 'bout the accommodations, mate. It was too hard to smuggle a real ladder past security!" Jimminy huffed as he helped support his companion's run.

Jimminy raced up the ladder first, his long limbs allowing him to skip rungs with ease. Dungar, in his battered and beaten state, had significant difficulty. It was a bizarre feeling to have one's own body ignore commands from his brain. Slowly, and with great effort, he raised his arms and legs one after the other. His mind went back to lifting the gate, to punching out the second gladiator, to the brutal beating he received from the tall creature, and the world-ending head-butt he dished out in return. He had come much too far now to simply be foiled by a stupid ladder.

"Hurry, mate!" Jimminy called from above, his hand stretched downward to offer assistance. Dungar did not take it though. Petty as it was, he had it in his mind that he was going to get there and he was going to get there on his own. Eventually he felt the hard lip of the railing in his grasp and, with everything he had, he hauled himself over the side of it before flopping onto the hard wooden floor.

"Nap time can come later!" Jimminy insisted as he pulled on Dungar's curly hair. "We've got to get out of here!"

Groaning and growling, Dungar was hauled to his feet once more as the two set off at a slow limp out of the arena. Enraged yells from both Herrow and guards could be heard behind them, motivating Dungar to continue putting one foot in front of the other. They made their way into the town just outside the arena, hoping to lose their pursuers. Dungar's body exhausted quickly and he knew he couldn't carry on this exertion for much longer. At the first empty building he saw, Dungar halted their pace and pushed Jimminy inside before entering himself and closing the door behind him.

They appeared to be in an old storage shed. Packs of grain and flour littered the floor. Dungar's muscles were more than happy to give way and drop his body into them.

"Look alive, mate!" Jimminy admonished Dungar. "If someone were to come through that door how would ya make a quick escape from down there?"

Without even looking up, Dungar drew attention to Jimminy's usual getting comfortable ritual. "Jimmy, you've taken your pants off. You're not going anywhere in a hurry either."

"Ah nonsense!" Jimminy dismissed. "I've been in many a situation where I had to put me pants on and make a speedy exit!"

Dungar grumbled to himself a quiet reminder to punch out Jimminy again in the future, because for now his only priority was not moving a single muscle. He wasn't sure how much of his ordeal Jimminy was privy to, but he must have had some sort of inclination because he sat in silence while Dungar attempted to regain his strength. After a half hour or so, Jimminy clapped his hands and hopped to his feet.

"Alright, mate, the heat should be off! What say we make like me Mum and leave, never to return!"

The last thing Dungar had any desire to do was get up. But he knew the sooner they made it out of town the better. With a low groan and a small heave, Dungar was back on his feet and the duo was out the door. They found themselves in a somewhat crowded marketplace with the coliseum still in full view. There were assorted stands selling a variety of goods like fruits, vegetables, livestock, jewelry, and knickknacks of every kind. Jimminy's desire to run to the hills seemed to have fallen to the wayside in favor of thoroughly inspecting every booth's goods.

Dungar himself couldn't even resist perusing a few goods here and there. Not that he could actually make any purchases though. He didn't know if he had left his house with any money, but even if he had, between the kidnapping, the beatings, and the fact his clothes were torn to shreds, there's no way there would have been any of it left. His attention was immediately diverted when his ears picked up the faint voice of Herrow off in the distance.

"And now, gentleman and ladies, the moment you have all been waiting for! Bring out this year's batch of Blood Bath contestants!"

Dungar's mind immediately went back to the cell where he had been imprisoned with Sir Lee. He had to save him. It was the most irrational thing he had ever contemplated in his life, or at least a close second, but somehow he had to get back into the arena and botch the Blood Bath for a second time.

"Jimmy!" Dungar barked. "I don't have time to explain, but we have to stop the Blood Bath!"

"What's that, mate?"

"I said we need to go back to the arena!"

"Why? Did ya forget something?"

"We need to save the people from Herrow."

"Alrighty."

They moved to head back to the arena, but they did not make it far before Jimminy once again stopped at a booth.

"Jimmy!" Dungar yelled out again. "What are you—"

"Just a moment, mate!" Jimminy cut him off. He then turned to the shopkeeper who had a large assortment of goats on display. "Oh my they all look so wonderful!"

"These be the best goats west of the Demon's Kettle!" The portly salesman encouraged him.

"I want that one right over there!" Jimminy exclaimed, pointing at a goat that stood still right in the middle of the pen. The body of the goat was a creamy brown color with white patches, but its hair got steadily darker as it went up the goat's neck and covered its face. Each of its eyes had a pitch black perfectly circular patch of fur around them, and a matching goatee made out of similar black hairs which would catch the occasional flecks of grass that fell out of the goat's perpetually chewing mouth. Any horns the goat had were also completely hidden underneath the enormous black afro growing out of the top of its head.

"An excellent choice!" The rancher praised. "The most docile one of the pack I'd say, don't never give nothing no trouble, that one! Calm as can be and the least picky eater in all the land. My asking price is—"

"Yeah yeah yeah, I'll take him!" Jimminy cut in, not even waiting for a price. He dropped a purse filled with coins on the counter, leashed the goat's neck, and took it out of the pen.

"Isn't he gorgeous, mista Dungar? I'm going to name him Shaffleton!"

"Where did you get all that money?" A bewildered Dungar inquired.

"I led the local pub in a rousing sing-along after sharing the tale of my daring escape!" Jimminy grinned. "Then when everyone was distracted, I swiped the tip jar."

"Are you done now?" Dungar growled, his patience almost exhausted.

"Yup!"

So off they set, Dungar, Jimminy, and Shaffleton the goat, back towards the arena. The half hour rest Dungar received was hardly adequate for him to regain his strength, but it allotted him the ability to walk and probably at least a few solid punches. Between that, and his posse consisting of a lunatic and a farm animal, this was likely to be a tricky endeavor.

As they reached the arena, a short and chubby guard stopped them at the door.

"Hang on there, gentleman and animal. The show's only for paying customers." He addressed them in his best tough guy voice.

Dungar nudged Jimminy. "Don't suppose you have any more money on you?"

Before Jimminy could respond, the guard cut in.

"Wait a minute! You're the convict who escaped!" He declared, fumbling for his sword.

Dungar braced himself for a fight, but it was over before it could begin when Jimminy picked up a nearby rock on the ground and clubbed the guard over the head with it. Afterwards, he stuffed the aforementioned rock down his pants.

"Like I said, mate" Jimminy chuckled. "Never know when ya might need one!"

The salesman's pitch about Shaffleton's docility seemed to hold true, the goat didn't appear spooked by the altercation in the slightest. It simply remained where it stood, continuing to munch noisily on nothing.

They made their way into the arena lobby, which was completely empty. Herrow's voice could be heard reverberating off the walls, listing the various false crimes that the people in the arena allegedly committed.

Dungar, in a frenzy, began searching the area for anything that could be used in his favor. The halls did not have much to offer. The lobby was a large, circular room with hallways leading around the arena on each side, as well as the entrance to the stadium and the arena exit. On the left side of the arena entrance was a concession stand of sorts that appeared to sell various kinds of cooked meat. It was closed though, the operator likely in the stands with everyone else.

Herrow finished listing the crimes committed, and after the jeers and heckling died down she continued. "And here to put an end to these horrible people's criminal careers are two majestic and ferocious beasts that we had imported from the far away Tyiri Jungle. Put your hands together, unless you are using them to cover your children's eyes, for a pair of the infamous Tyiri Leolos!"

Leolo. Dungar was by no means an expert on the animal kingdom, but everyone knew what a leolo was. They were the largest cats in the world. They were furry quadrupedal hulks with enormous tusks jutting from their cheeks and a thick mane of quills behind their heads and on the tips of their tales. Leolos were the primary reason the jungle ecosystem over in the land of Tyiri was endangered. They had a tendency to breathe fire whenever they're angry or agitated, resulting in their jungle homes being steadily burned to the ground.

Dungar was frantic now; he was running out of time. He raced down the hallway as fast as his exhausted legs could take him, throwing open every door he could find along the way and rifling through the contents of the room. Brooms, mops, spices, meat sauces, extra sword handles, sharpening stones, spear heads, gun powder barrels, helmets, gloves, wait . . . gunpowder barrels?

Dungar shoved a shelf of various armors out of the way and lumbered over to the pile of barrels and popped one open. Sure enough, it was completely full of the black powder. Grabbing some flint and steel off a nearby shelf, Dungar lit the fuse one of them and tossed it down the hallway. The resulting explosion left a gaping hole in the floor as well as a large pile of debris on either side. Satisfied that his handiwork would keep any guards at bay, Dungar hastily began throwing the enormous stockpile of barrels out into the hallway, setting up the foundation for what would likely result in an enormous blast. After he had emptied the storeroom, he grabbed as many as he could carry and proceeded to roll one with his foot out the door and back towards the lobby, leaving a trail of the powder to the main cache.

"Jimmy!" Dungar yelled as he made it back to the lobby. "There's a room just down the hall there, I need you to—"

Dungar's voice trailed off as he rounded the corner and saw Jimminy. The man had broken into the food stand and was drizzling every kind of meat sauce and marinade he could find onto the goat.

"What are you doing?!" Dungar demanded.

"Why, I'm prepping Mista Shaffleton, here!" Jimminy responded matter-of-factly.

"For what?!" The still thoroughly confused Dungar asked desperately as Jimminy took the goat by its leash and headed for the stadium door.

Jimminy strode through the door with Dungar hot on his heels. They reached the edge of the bleachers and looked over the railing into the stadium. The bodies of Dungar's opponents were all gone, but their blood still remained. The arena was now filled with a crowd of terrified men and women all huddled together desperately trying to stay away from two massive leolos who were prowling menacingly around the stadium, eyeing up the prey that lay before them.

"I'm prepping him for his big moment, mate!" Jimminy vaguely explained before he picked up the goat and, ignoring the creature's bleats of protest, calmly hoisted it over the railing and into the arena.

Dungar had no words. He just opened and closed his mouth several times, unsure how to voice his opposition to Jimminy's indecipherable logic. Before he managed to form the words, Jimminy spoke first.

"Relax, mate. That's a Farrawee fighting goat. Those leolos don't stand a chance."

"What?!"

Jimminy didn't respond; he just watched Shaffleton down in the arena. After he got to his feet, the goat once again stood completely still, its jaws absentmindedly chewing up and down on nothing. The leolos immediately picked up the scent of the various sauces that Shaffleton was currently marinating in, and they both turned towards the tantalizing meal on display.

Seeing that the leolos had taken his bait nicely, Jimminy produced the same rope ladder they initially escaped with and once more threw it over the side of the arena, using gravity to uncoil it. Immediately the crowd of people all made a rush for the ladder and one by one they slowly began to work their way up it.

"That better be one bloody chewy goat, or those people aren't going to have enough time to escape." Dungar pointed out.

As soon as the words left his mouth, the entire arena was shaken by a tremendous deep, bassy roar. Confused, Dungar looked at Jimminy who in turn was eagerly staring down at Shaffleton. Dungar turned his attention towards the goat just in time for it to emit another incredible roar. Dungar would never have expected such a noise from the creature. The sound could easily be repurposed as a foghorn. Each time the leolos went to make a move towards Shaffleton, the goat would frighten them with the noise. However, it became less and less effective as the leolos slowly started to get braver.

As the first hostage made his way over the railing, Dungar got an idea. If Herrow thought he ruined her livelihood the first time, then she hasn't seen anything yet. He took a barrel of gunpowder and handed it to the man, ordering him to spread it everywhere before he ran away. He did the same with every new individual that made their way over the railing. There was plenty of gunpowder to go around. Dungar had no idea what they had stockpiled so much of the stuff for, but he felt it was a prudent course of action to teach the arena proprietors the downside of possessing such an obvious fire hazard.

The goat roars were starting to get more frequent now, indicating the leolos were setting upon Shaffleton more often. Eventually they grew immune to the noise, and one of them pounced in for the kill. Soon as the cat became airborne, Shaffleton jumped into the air and did a 180 degree turn before delivering a double hind leg kick right into the leolo's face. Moments after the first cat set in, the second also began bearing down on Shaffleton. After the goat landed from its first attack, it immediately jumped back into the air and sent another spinning kick into the second leolo's ribs.

The battle became quite the spectacle as Shaffleton the goat lay an increasingly vicious beating on these two exotic beasts. The cats were helpless against the goat's speed and agility. Every swipe of their paws or swing of their tails was easily dodged by Shaffleton and promptly countered with a punishing kick from his hooves. The goat also utilized its afro in combat. The afro was apparently much more solid than initial impressions may have implied. All attacks seemed to bounce off of it, and the goat would occasionally swing it like a wrecking ball. Guards began to spill into the arena attempting to halt the hostage's escape. However as soon as they set foot inside, Shaffleton would powderize their ribcages with his mighty hooves.

The fight quickly became a losing battle for the leolos. Even their attempts to breathe fire at the goat were promptly dodged. Unfortunately, one of the hostages still in the arena was not as quick. His clothes caught fire and he began to go into a violent panic. He then cut in front of one of the hostages and made a frantic climb of the rope ladder.

Fearing for the gunpowder that the stadium was now thoroughly coated in, Dungar halted the man at the top of the ladder and proceeded to rip any burning clothes off of him. It was one of the more uncomfortable things Dungar ever found himself being forced to do, but they were all dead men if he didn't. The man was oddly reluctant to lose his clothes for a man who was on fire; probably because once he did he was revealed to apparently have a liking for ladies' underwear. Nonetheless, he too was handed a barrel of gunpowder and sent on his way.

Dungar had managed to save the gunpowder, but during the burning man's ascent the fire from his clothing managed to spread to the rope ladder, which then spread to the thick coating of fresh lacquer on the wooden railing surrounding the spectator's stand. Panicked, Dungar quickly began sweeping his gunpowder trail away from the railings as the fire spread around the circular arena and into the bleachers, his efforts unintentionally aided by the terrified event attendees as they fled from their booths towards the entrance. He shot them death glares as they departed, briefly considering trying to stop them, but had to begrudgingly acknowledge to himself that being unsympathetic jerks didn't mean they deserved to burn to death. Besides, the ensuing chaos from their retreat was helpful to keep encroaching guards at bay.

When he turned back to the arena he felt fortunate to find there were only three hostages left down in the arena. However he felt unfortunate to find the second to last one to leave was, well, a very large man of prodigious girth. The singed rope ladder was hopeless at supporting his weight, and he only made it up about four or five steps before the ropes snapped.

"Cod dangit, fat boy! If yer brains were dynamite you wouldn't even have enough to blow yer nose!" Dungar heard a familiar voice holler from down in the arena. Sure enough, the only two hostages left down in the pit were the large gentleman and Sir Lee.

"Lee!" Dungar yelled. "Hang on! We're going to get you out of there!"

"Are you off yer mental reservation, boy?!" The knight bellowed back. "The cod dang architecture is a-blazin'! Unless you wanna be a lit shuck, I suggest you make like a bird and get the flock outta here!"

"And just what in the blazes do you intend to do then?" Dungar retorted.

"I ain't no hard case hillbilly with a snoot full of honey bees! I got a plan, now git! You and yer uglier-than-a-burnt-steer's-hindquarters friend!"

Dungar looked around helplessly. The ever-spreading fire was quickly making its way around the building and would undoubtedly soon be finding the gunpowder that was spread everywhere. Even Herrow had vacated her vantage point as the flames encroached upon it. The whole coliseum was going to go up at any minute; he had no choice but to get out of there. Jimminy, on the other hand, didn't seem to realize this because he was too busy dwelling on Lee's parting comment.

"And just wot did you mean by that?!" He hollered down into the arena.

"Yer ugly enough to back a buzzard off a gut wagon, son."

"Jimmy we need to go. Now." Dungar ordered, prying Jimminy away from the railing.

"Now just a moment, mate, I haven't adequately ascertained the implications of that gent's—"

Given its effectiveness in the past, Dungar elected to employ yet another stiff backhand to snap Jimminy out of his fixation and return him to reality. Once again, it proved effective.

"Well come on, mista Dungar, we need to go. Now!"

At a full-on sprint, the duo rushed through the lobby and out the exit of the arena. The ordeal had done nothing to stem Dungar's mounting exhaustion, so once he was fifty paces or so away from the arena he had to stop. They looked back at the Vthnnqouayey arena, the blacksmith hoping it would be the last time he or anyone would ever lay eyes upon it. Thick plumes of smoke began to rise from the coliseum now; the ravenous flames making quick work of grossly over-glossed stadium as final stragglers streamed through the entrance. The air grew tenser with every detonation-free second.

Finally the sound of an explosion was heard. It was smaller than Dungar had thought and hoped it would be, only ripping a rather large chunk of the arena wall above the entrance that fell and sealed the doorway closed behind it. There was no fire, just a large pile of debris.

"YEEEEEEEEEEEEHAWWWWWWWWW!"

Suddenly Sir Lee came bursting through the smoky hole above the entrance, riding on a large brown Farrawee fighting goat. With one hand he held its scruffy afro, while the other was wildly waving a big floppy hat. No sooner had they cleared the building than did another more enormous explosion erupt from the top of the arena, sending most of the walls tumbling down and causing some of the closer onlookers to clutch their ears and flinch away from the blast of heat. Even a hundred feet or so back, Dungar marveled at the mushroom cloud and debris that rained from the sky, knowing it was an image he would never forget until the end of his days.

"Howdy there, soldiers!" Sir Lee greeted them triumphantly from Shaffleton's back. "I reckon anyone who's against bein' irresponsible with explosives will be whistlin' a different tune after that display!"

"Don't suppose you know what happened to the other guy who was left in there with you?" Dungar asked.

"I'd wager he's about 350 pounds o' cooked bacon by now."

Sir Lee let out a boisterous laugh, an amusement neither Dungar nor Jimminy shared as evidenced by their awkward looks. They weren't exactly sensitive people, but it wasn't remiss to have at least slight empathy for the deaths of innocents. "Oh unhobble yer lips, fellers! Now what say we go kill ourselves a queen?"

"Say what now?!" A shocked Jimminy asked.

TWELVE

SEA YOU LATER

Dungar had never figured out when or how he was going to tell Jimminy the true intentions of his trip to Jenair. He wasn't even sure why he kept it from the man in the first place. Was it actually due to a lack of trust? Or was he just worried it would sound too ridiculous when he said it out loud? It didn't matter now though, because there it was out there for Jimminy to take in.

Even as the three men made it to the trees outside of town, the cool breeze that rustled the nearby leaves also carried the final floating smoldering bits of Dungar's handiwork. The now distant arena appeared to be little more than a pile of charred rubble, and as he looked back at it Dungar couldn't help but wonder if Herrow or any of her cronies managed to escape like most of the crowd did. Jimminy, on the other hand, was eyeing Sir Lee with a quizzical expression on his face.

"Did ya hear that, mate?" He asked Dungar. "This bloke purports to bury your bride-to-be!"

"What in tarnation!" Lee interrupted, turning to Dungar. "I didn't figure you to be between hay and grass on this issue, son. You still intending to wed the tramp?"

"Everybody shut up!" Dungar ordered.

Lee and Jimminy both fell to silence as they awaited Dungar's response. Dungar turned to Jimminy. He still had no idea what to tell his faithful sidekick who had proven to be startlingly useful over the last few days. But the cat was out of the bag, so to speak. Best to just lay it out there and hope he was still receptive to the idea.

"Listen, Jimmy, I haven't been completely honest with you . . ."

"You mean we actually are going to kill the queen?"

"Well, yes. You see—"

"Alrighty."

Dungar had no idea what to say. Did that really just happen that easily?

"You . . . You understand, Jimmy?"

"Sure, mate." Jimminy smiled. "March into the castle and assassinate the most powerful woman in all the land. Should be a blast."

"BULLY!" Lee announced. "Now let's quit boshin' and get to ambulatin'!"

As the trio, and Shaffleton, set off at a nice, brisk walk northward, Dungar still couldn't get over Jimminy's willingness to help.

"Jimmy you do realize this is going to be incredibly dangerous, right?"

"Oh, Mista Dungar!" Jimminy praised, putting his arm around Dungar. "Are you worried about poor li'l me?"

"I'm just trying to warn you!" Dungar growled as he gave Jimminy a shove.

Jimminy's eyes remained as optimistic and carefree as ever. The change of mission objective did not seem to have impacted him in the slightest. He gave Dungar a knowing smile.

"Well wot else am I gonna do with me time, mate? Committing high treason or just helping me pal grope n' poke his way onto the throne is all the same to me! Can't just sit and kill time or time will just kill me, mate."

"HAH." Lee cackled from behind them. "Yer an ugly feller and yer voice sounds like an ungreased wagon, but you talk some good wisdom, son."

"Thank you for your backhanded compliments, person-who-I-have-no-idea-who-you-are!"

"No problem, boy." Lee grunted before horking and spitting into some bushes. "I'd advise ye to not abandon yer initial intentions though. That feller over there seems like he could certainly use him a good horizontal hoedown."

"Enough, both of you!" Dungar barked.

"Wuh oh." Lee blurted, his grey eyes making contact with Dungar's. "We got 'im lookin' madder than an acocked coon!"

"Just duck if he takes a swing at ya, mate."

Sir Lee put up his fists and began jokingly dancing around Dungar like a boxer.

"I ain't fraid of no hopped up buster! I'd clean his plough if he—"

His voice trailed off as Dungar gave him a one-armed shove down a nearby hill.

"That gent's got a rather bizarre way of speaking." Jimminy pointed out as the two kept walking.

"I don't particularly care a continental fer yer attitude, boy!" Lee hollered from the bottom of the hill. "But jokes on you! I was goin' in this direction anyway."

". . . But god help me if I don't love it." Jimminy smiled.

"We should probably go find him before he gets lost just to spite me." Dungar sighed.

They made their way down the hill into a thicker part of the woods. Shrubs and brush covered the ground, impeding their vision of anything below their waists. Slowly and carefully they waded through the bushes, trying to avoid getting tripped up on anything.

"I don't see him anywhere, Jimmy."

"Perhaps he encountered a 'posse' of 'outlaws' and has now found himself to be 'pushing up daisies?'" Jimminy suggested sarcastically.

Dungar had to admit, given the man's temperament, he wouldn't be surprised if that was indeed the situation, but opted to keep looking anyway. They exited the tree cover and found themselves on the beach of a gigantic lake. The water was a rich blue and had an oddly inky consistency to it. However, it shimmered in the daylight nonetheless as it stretched far into the horizon, farther than the eye could see.

"Ah the balmy shores of Deeplu Lake." Jimminy mused as he inhaled deeply. "You know, mate, if we found a way across it would really cut down on our travel time to Jenair."

"Blech! Y'all would be right smart to not tread into that mockered death trap." Lee called out, emerging from the woods behind them.

"What's that supposed to mean?" Dungar asked.

"It means that any odd stick who sails them there waters is off his chump!"

"Why?"

"IT AIN'T MY DUTY TO EDUCATE YOU, BOY!" Lee bellowed, causing Jimminy to jump. He cleared his throat and regained his composure before he continued. "The notion of bein' on them waters makes me more nervous than a long-tailed hound in a room fulla rocking chairs."

Dungar weighed his options. He was so sure that Sir Lee would be an asset to his quest, given his similar motives and apparent former knighthood. However, in the brief period that Dungar has gotten to know him, his cold callousness as well as over-inflated sense of his abilities had proven to be worrisome. Dungar was fine to simply overlook such drawbacks in exchange for the man's aid, but his seemingly irrational aversion to crossing the lake would cost them precious time that they couldn't afford to lose. His mind made up, Dungar addressed Sir Lee again.

"Well, sir, it looks like this is where we'll part ways then."

"Yer leavin' me to go lone star are ya, son?"

"You can come with us, but we're going by boat. No two ways about it. We need to shave time however we can."

"So be it, boy. If ya live, then best of luck. But you probably won't, so don't worry, I'll bury the bitch when I get there."

Without so much as another word, Sir Lee strode back into the forest and vanished amongst the trees.

"Wot about you then, gorgeous?" Jimminy asked Shaffleton. "Ready to try your sea legs?"

Shaffleton stopped his chewing and looked at Jimminy. He then spit out his mouthful of cud and galloped away into the forest as well, ignoring Jimminy's calls after him.

"Blimey. Maybe he gets seasick."

"Jimmy" Dungar asked cautiously "Is there something I need to know about this lake?"

"Not at all, mate!" Jimminy answered confidently. "Now c'mon, let's go charter us a ride."

They set off down the beach towards a dock off in the distance. Dungar still couldn't shake his growing uneasy feeling towards the lake. He was sure Jimminy was holding back some kind of information. However he had committed to this course of action now, there was no going back. Jimminy, on the other hand, carried on careless as usual. Given the man's propensity to brazenly disregard danger though, it was difficult to discern any sort of comfort from his nonchalance.

"So tell me, mate, why exactly are we going to murder missus queen lady?"

"Long story short, Jimmy, she's going to murder all of us."

"Well that's not very nice of her."

". . . No, I guess it isn't."

"I haven't even met the lady! Why would she want to murder me?"

Dungar sighed at such a stupid question. "I don't think it's some kind of personal vendetta. Some people are just evil, and some of them are able to use their power to hurt people. Look at Herrow."

"I'm not sure I agree with that, mate. If folks do bad things it doesn't make them bad people. I think Miss Herrow is just a bit misguided."

"She tried to have us brutally killed in order to line her pockets."

"Maybe her mum is really sick?"

Dungar slapped his palm to his face. He couldn't help but feel a shred of admiration for the man's optimism, even though it transcended the bounds of simple positivism and encroached well into the endless field of naiveté. At least in Dungar's not-so-humble opinion, anyway.

"So wait, why are you willing to help me kill the queen then?"

"Well you said it yourself, mate. She's going to murder me."

"Well what if she has her own 'misguided' reasons for doing so?" Dungar asked sarcastically.

"Perhaps she does, mate! That's okay. I guess it's just a matter of who murders who first then."

Dungar was starting to find Jimminy's rationale very intriguing. He was tempted to grill him some more on it, but that would have to wait until later. They had reached the dock now, and a much more pressing issue had occurred to Dungar. They didn't have a copper between the two of them; how were they going to buy a ride? A similar notion must have occurred to Jimminy, because he addressed Dungar with his usual famous last words.

"Relax, mate. I'll handle this."

Dungar waited outside as Jimminy confidently strolled into the nearby shack. A shrill scream was heard, followed by Jimminy's voice.

"Terribly sorry, madam! I thought this was the ticket booth!"

The door swung open and a very large woman with a robe wrapped around her threw Jimminy back outside by his hair.

"You're very pretty, by the way!" He offered sheepishly before the door was slammed in his face. He turned back to Dungar. "Apparently it's next door." He chuckled. Still laughing to himself, he strode over to the next building and walked inside. Dungar shook his head and turned back to the tree line. He spotted some berry bushes and was instantly reminded how ravenous he was. During his imprisonment he had received occasional rations of bread and water, but it was hardly more than enough to stave off death.

Trying to distract himself, he turned back towards the lake. There was only one ship docked there, a triple-masted vessel painted a deep forest green. Having lived in a desert all his life, Dungar knew next to nothing about boats. All he could tell was that it was big with a spacious lower deck and had a rather large amount of sails affixed to each other in a very intricate fashion. He figured it was likely a supply boat, mostly because he couldn't imagine what else a ship of that size would be used for on a lake like this.

"I told ya, mate!"

Dungar turned to see Jimminy walking out of the building towards him.

"How did it go in there?" Dungar asked him.

"Swimmingly!" Jimminy insisted, walking right past Dungar and towards the boat. "Yup, I worked me charm on the nice gent and, sure enough, he said it was no problem!"

Dungar followed after him.

"Seriously? What did you say to him?"

"Oh you know." Jimminy mused as he carefully walked up the gangplank. "Just that we were hopeless wanderers who had fallen onto some hard times and could use a break and all that rubbish." He paused as he reached the deck of the ship and quickly scanned around before carrying on.

Dungar paused as he reached the deck too, but not to scan around. While no one could possibly plot out the twisted, nonsensical depths of Jimminy's mind, Dungar was beginning to grasp some of the finer details; such as when all was not as Jimminy would have it appear to be. As such, Dungar had a bad feeling that they may not indeed be as welcome on this ship as his partner would have him believe. However, Jimminy had already disappeared below deck and Dungar wasn't about to strand him on this boat alone. He followed Jimminy down the stairs and watched as the man turned to the left and crouched behind a stack of barrels.

"What are you doing, Jimmy?"

"Oh, uh, I think I forgot something down here."

". . . We just got on this boat less than thirty seconds ago."

"Hah. You said it, mate. Say, I think you forgot something over there behind these crates."

The sound of footsteps on the deck above caused Dungar to think that perhaps he did indeed forget something behind that stack of crates. He moved over towards them and sat on the ground on the corner where he was obscured; settling in for what was likely to be a long and uncomfortable journey.

The room was very dimly lit by whatever sunlight could make it through cracks in the deck and bulkheads; it reminded Dungar of his cell back at the arena. The room was certainly large enough for them to hide in. It spanned the entire width of the ship and was loaded with assorted barrels, crates, and sacks. It smelled of fish, wine, and, oddly enough, gunpowder. As he listened to the flapping of the sails and the creaking of the mast, Dungar traced his finger along the floor. It was coated with a layer of a dark and greasy substance which clung to his finger and stained his clothes.

"Jimmy!" Dungar hissed. "I thought you said it was no problem."

"That's my mistake, mate. What I meant to say was that it may actually be a slight problem."

Dungar clenched his teeth and shook his head. He decided this is really his own fault for gambling on Jimminy's schemes.

"So what happens if they find us?"

"Well it depends. They could either let us stay, or they could throw us overboard. It's anyone's guess, really."

Dungar sighed. Jimminy clearly had no answers to give him, and he had no energy left to drag them out even if the man did. The day had been long and arduous, and the only thing on his mind was getting some sleep. If they ended up getting discovered then he would just have to deal with it then.

The two men were awoken when the silhouettes of a number of individuals all came bursting into the room carrying sacks and crates of unknown contents. At a very speedy and efficient pace they tossed whatever they were carrying into the room and hurried out to make room for the seemingly endless line of people behind them. After a few minutes the bustling finally died down and Jimminy and Dungar were once again left alone in the room, which was now stacked deck to overhead with assorted kinds of cargo. Within moments of the crew's exit, Dungar felt the ship lurch as it began to depart.

"That was impressively efficient." Dungar pointed out.

"Indeed. This definitely isn't a ship from the Jenair navy." Jimminy deduced. "They're the laziest buggers you'll ever meet."

"So who are they then? Private cargo shippers?"

"Probably. Although there is one other possibility."

"What's that?"

Before Jimminy could answer all the boxes and crates they were hidden behind were tossed aside to reveal five men. One of them was holding a torch while the other four had their cutlasses drawn and pointed at the stowaways. They wore white linen shirts with assorted golden adornments that sparkled as they reflected the flame's light. The four swordsmen also wore eye patches, although it was hard to tell as they were mostly hidden behind the black braids spilling down in front of their faces.

"Well" Jimminy acknowledged. "I was going to say it could also be a cruise ship. But I suppose this being a pirate ship is also a feasible circumstance."

They were ushered up the stairs at sword point until they reached the main deck where a crowd had gathered. Dungar surveyed the assortment of faces that lay their eyes upon him, each meaner looking than the last. Skins of every hue and bodies of every size were represented by the crew. Despite being a well varied company of gentlemen, Dungar got the sinking feeling that they did not take kindly to uninvited guests. Suddenly a body came falling from up above, landing gracefully on its feet before Dungar and Jimminy.

"Yahaharrr!! What have we here, me hearties?!"

He was a tall and incredibly handsome middle-aged man. As he straightened up, he swept his smooth, jet black hair behind his ears as he sized up his captors with his confident and charismatic green eyes. His lips were curled into a smile that enhanced the deeply ingrained laugh lines on his face, which was completely clean shaven, save for his magnificent mutton chops.

"Ahoy, me bilge rat beauties!" He addressed them in a voice every bit at confident and charismatic as the eyes that gazed at them. "You are here to join me crew, no? Because surely none would dare be so foolish to try and steal passage aboard the intimidating vessel of Captain Nobeard the fierce! Isn't that right, boys?!"

A chorus of "Arrrr"s erupted from the crew.

"As a matter of fact, wouldn't you believe it, we actually were here to do such a thing!" Jimminy insisted.

Nobeard began to pace quickly in circles around the pair, his long legs taking lengthy strides at a fast pace. Jimminy tried to spin in tandem with the captain while Dungar elected to not bother and simply stand still.

The captain was clearly an energetic man. He wore a long black overcoat with golden trim that flapped behind him as he continued his circular pacing. He then broke into a run towards a nearby rope which he used to swing up to the next level of the deck next to the helm.

"Do ye know what it means to be a pirate?!" He called down to them.

"Pillaging, plundering, rifling, and looting!" Jimminy called back.

"Shut up!" Nobeard ordered him without missing a beat. He struck an epic pose with his hands on his hips, looking stoically off into the distance.

"Me hearties, I stand before ye a true pirate to my core! I have indeed stolen and pillaged before. But that is not all there is to we! We fine family who sail this sea! We do our due diligence to share all our wealth. We promote unity and peace and good health!" He paused briefly for a moment to turn back to Dungar and Jimminy. "We steal from the rich and give to the poor is really what I'm trying to say here."

From somewhere within the crowd an accordion and drum began playing. With hoots and yells of approval, the entirely crowd on deck burst into a drunken and uncoordinated dance session. Jimminy was all too happy to immediately join in and link arms with the nearest scurvy dog.

"Yar har fiddle de dee, being a pirate is alright with me! I've always wanted to swashbuckle."

"We still from the rich and give to the poor." Nobeard repeated as he too began to sway in tune with the music. "But we be more than your commoner altruistic outlaw! We are the very image of that which is not changeable, we are experts in every theft tactic that is stageable, we carry out our deeds to keep the wealth all rearrangeable, despite the occupational hazards being quite unassuageable!" He paused briefly yet again and turned back to Dungar. "Really what I'm trying to say here is that in matters profitable, cartable, and sinkable, I am the very model of a modern mighty liberal!"

Uncomfortable to the point of physical pain, Dungar gritted his teeth and slowly tried to back away below deck. But the captain was there blocking his path in a flash.

"Buck up, ye scallywag! Where be yer piratin' spirit?" He grinned, clasping a hand onto Dungar's shoulder.

"I left it below deck." Dungar replied as he tried to push past the man's arm. Captain Nobeard, however, moved about as much as a tree.

Hand still on Dungar's shoulder; Nobeard leaned in closer so he could lower his voice.

"I am no fool, me lad. Ye be needing thicker wool if ye intend to pull it over these eyes."

Dungar kept quiet, trying to figure out exactly what this meant for his fate.

"Fear not yet, lad, I am not in the business of keelhauling every unfamiliar sea rover aboard this vessel. However, this be no charity liner either. Okay well that's not entirely true, we do the whole steal from the rich and give to the poor thing, but not the type of charity ye be expectin'!"

"So what do you want then?" Dungar asked. "If you expect me to sing and dance then you may as well just kill me now."

"Step into me captain's quarters, ye drivelswigger. I'll give ye the skinny."

They maneuvered through the crowd, still in full swing of the impromptu dance-a-thon, and into the room located beneath the helm of the ship. As they stepped inside, Dungar was floored by the interior which was nothing like he was expecting. It was a small and cramped room; however the walls were completely covered by exquisite paintings in very expensive looking frames. Arranged among the paintings on the wall was also an impressive collection of intricate looking clocks. There was also a desk against the wall which was likely where future excursions were plotted since it was covered by maps, compasses, and sextants. Most bizarre of all, though, was the big four poster bed in the corner that was adorned with brilliant pink silken sheets.

"What's your name, sea rat?"

"Dungar."

"Dungar what?"

"Dungar Loloth."

"Dungar Loloth what?"

"Dungar Loloth nothing, that's my bloody name."

"No, sailor. I mean ye are to address me as captain when ye speak to me."

"I'm going to assume that is just a suggestion, and I am going to decline."

Captain Nobeard laughed heartily as he opened the drawer of his desk. From the drawer he produced a brown bottle which he uncorked and took a swig from.

"Yer not making yerself easy to work with, mister Loloth."

"I am not your employee, captain Nobeard, I am merely seeking passage to Jenair. If I am to earn my keep then so be it; but I am no pirate, glamorous as you try to make it sound."

Captain Nobeard stepped towards him, the height difference between the two forcing Dungar to crane his neck upward.

"Ye be makin' pretty brazen demands for a soul completely at me mercy." Nobeard acknowledged with a smirk. "But I suppose the life of sweet trade is not for all. If ye can display the same pluck ye show me now, but in a manner that acts in me favor, then perhaps I may have use for yer land lubbin ways after all."

"You're going to ask me to do something dangerous, aren't you?"

"Danger be the spice of life, me boy! Forget anything you've heard about that variety bilge, that be for castle cooks!" Nobeard exclaimed enthusiastically as he hurried over to his desk and began rifling through the maps. "Aha!" he declared as he pulled one out of the stack and drove a dagger through it. "Ye are going to be in the band of buccaneers who rob the Wizard Tree!"

ThIRTEEN

TREE MUGGERS

Dungar hated wizards. Growing up honing your profession to perfection only to have it stripped from you by an arrogant and entitled scumbag of a human being will do that to a person. But while Rainchild had certainly fuelled his distaste for magic, Dungar never even heard of a wizard he liked. Wizards of both good and bad walks of life were often present in the many stories he would hear. But, regardless of their allegiance, they would simply swoop in and cast some spells to solve any problems.

Magic was a funny thing; it didn't seem to play by any particular rules. Some wizards would use it for practical purposes, others for nefarious purposes, and others still for constructive and destructive purposes. It seemed to be completely arbitrary what capabilities each magical creature had, as they seemed to vary wizard to wizard and witch to witch. Dungar wasn't entirely sure if it was they were simply born with an innate catalog of spells to choose from, or rather if it was a skill based around discovery and development.

Regardless of the mechanics of the craft though, Dungar felt magic was nothing more than a lazy way to cheat a leg up on the rest of the less gifted folks as well as a cowardly resource that the weak drew upon to subvert the strong. No matter what tricks Rainchild had up his sleeve, Dungar intended to destroy the man. However, his intentions aside, Dungar couldn't help but feel a twinge of worry regarding the potential powers that Rainchild may very well possess.

As for this "Wizard Tree" that the pirate spoke of, the very first image to enter Dungar's mind was that of a glowing sapling that shot fireballs. Surely that wasn't the case though; it was probably the name of some kind of order or organization.

"Did somebody say the wizard tree?!" Jimminy called out as he burst into the room.

"Aye, your hearing be functional, laddy." Nobeard confirmed as he looked up from the table.

"Do wizards grow there?" Jimminy asked with a laugh.

"I hope so . . ." Dungar said forebodingly.

Nobeard gave Dungar a strange look, and then addressed both him and Jimminy.

"Ye lads never heard of the wizard tree?"

"Nope" The two men answered in unison.

"Aye, sheltered lads eh." Nobeard grunted as he took another swig from his bottle. "In the center of this here sea stands the largest shrub any picaroon ever did see. It be taller than a hundred ship's masts, and wide enough that me own mother could hide behind it! But in a hollowed out nook somewhere high in that tree there lay a plunder so prestigious that a nun would sell out her own lord just to lay claim to it! Any who possess that treasure would be irrefutably the saltiest scurvy shellback to ever sail the single sea!"

"Are there other pirates on this lake?" Dungar asked.

Nobeard stopped short from his spiel. "Well, no. But one day there will be! And when there are, they will know who the saltiest scurv—"

"THAR SHE BLOWS!" Jimminy screamed as he looked out the porthole of the captain's quarters. Nobeard threw him aside, grumbling "That be my line" as he too looked through the nautical window.

Off in the distance, through the dim fog that hovered over the lake, there stood an immense tree protruding from a small island on the water. The trunk had to be at least five or six hundred paces around, and the height of the tree was indeterminable as it stretched high into the sky and disappeared in the clouds. There didn't appear to be much to the rest of the island itself, as the sheer size of the tree appeared to take up all the surface area there was. Aside from the unprecedented size of the plant though, it didn't have any other apparent unique qualities.

"Why is it called the Wizard Tree?" Dungar asked as he gaped at the colossal plant.

"Because it's a wizard, laddy." Nobeard stated matter-of-factly.

"What?"

"It's a wizard. It be a magical organism."

Dungar had no words to respond with; he just turned back to the tree with a sour look on his face. The tree wasn't a person, but he still hated it anyway simply based on principle. He couldn't help but wonder if that made him fair or petty.

Nobeard laughed and put a hand on Dungar's shoulder as they both watched the wizard tree grow larger and larger on the horizon. "Yer quite the green globetrotter aren't ye?"

Dungar turned to Nobeard with an eyebrow raised defensively.

"Thar be no shame, laddy! Yer fair captain shall teach ye the brass tacks." Nobeard insisted, gesturing towards a nearby stool.

Dungar, however, opted to remain standing.

"Fair enough!" Nobeard declared, taking the seat himself. "The ways of wizarding and witching be not exclusive to just people! It be an in-born talent that any living creature may possess. In this land lay magic people, magic dogs, magic snakes, magic redbears, and even magic trees like that great weed ye see out yer window thar!"

"How old is it?" Jimminy cut in.

"Do I look like an encyclopedia, matey? I'm just the pirate that's going to rob it!" Nobeard admonished as he headed out the door and back onto the deck. Dungar and Jimminy followed after him.

"Listen up, me hearties!" Nobeard called to the crew as he made his way out onto the deck. "I want all hands on deck and for the designated boarding party to prepare to . . . well . . . board!"

There was a flurry on the deck of crewmen bustling about to man their stations. Amid the chaos of sailors scurrying about, a small ragtag battalion of pirates had formed along the side of the ship next to the lifeboat.

"Alright, men!" Nobeard called, as he signaled Jimminy and Dungar to follow him to the away team. "Here be the courageous seafarers who are going to be the ill-gotten looters of precious tree plunder."

Dungar sized up the men he would be accompanying. There were seven of them in total, each armed with a cutlass. Now that he was beginning to become desensitized to pirates though, Dungar found himself able to tell just what a group of incompetent looking buffoons they were. None of the group could even maintain a standing at attention pose without falling over due to the rocking of the ship. One of them didn't even have legs, and in their place were two wooden pegs, and another didn't appear to have any eyes. Yet another was morbidly obese, and he stood next to a pirate who appeared to be twice the age of Jitters.

"Alright let us be brief!" Nobeard addressed the party. "Sailors, this here be our new recruits: Dungar and Jumpin' Jimminy the Jaunty."

Tearing his eyes away from the pirates, Dungar very slowly turned his head towards Jimminy whilst wearing a look of absolutely inexorable disgust.

"I'm a pirate now, matey!" Jimminy grinned. "I needed me a pirate name!"

With a heavy sigh, Dungar turned back to the band of bun-gling flunkies with whom he was going to storm a dangerous island. Reading the look on the blacksmith's face, Nobeard offered to reassure him.

"They may not look like much, but they be brave souls that will have yer back and they all be havin' at least some experi-ence in rovin' expeditions!"

Dungar couldn't help but wonder where exactly the line between bravery and stupidity was drawn, or if there even was one. Perhaps the defining point between being brave or being stupid is simply whether or not one succeeds. Regardless, his task has been laid before him and this is who he had to work with, so he could take them or leave them.

"Yarr, soon we man the lifeboat to make our final approach to the island! So let us wrap up these introductions, shall we?" Nobeard announced. "For the sake of brevity, each man's nick-name shall make him easy to remember."

Then, one by one, Nobeard went down the line of pirates with their introductions, giving them each a bonk on the head as he stated their name.

"This here be Finn the Fat, Ozzy the Old, Legless Larry, Shoutin' Shane—"

"AHOY!!!" Shane bellowed at an eardrum-shattering volume.

"Shut up, Shane!" Nobeard hollered back. ". . . Wally the Well-Tanned, Blaine the Blind, and Eye-gougin' Hugo Bonny!"

Dungar gaped at Wally. Given the man's complexion, Dungar had assumed he was simply another race entirely. But after hearing the man's nickname, Dungar realized the true origin of the man's brown and leathery skin. Jimminy, on the other hand, appeared to have a stunned fixation on Blaine; particularly the fact he wore an eye patch over both eyes. Tenta-tively, he leaned over and slowly moved his hand up and down in front of the blind fellow's face.

"Hands to yerself, scallywag." The pirate grunted in a gravelly monotone voice causing Jimminy to jump.

"Enough with your cacklin', lads!" Nobeard ordered. "And into the lifeboat with all of ya. We be makin our final approach soon." He then disappeared beneath the deck as the rest of the team began to file towards the boat in an orderly fashion.

As it was Dungar's turn to climb inside, he glanced over the rail of the ship only to see a craft that looked to be nothing more than a hollowed out chunk of wood. It swung ominously from the two fraying ropes that supported it as it hung suspended over the murky waters of Lake Deeplu. The hull of the lifeboat was weather beaten and faded. Dungar also couldn't tell if it was simply poor craftsmanship or damage from a previous incident, but the front of the boat was significantly warped in a way that likely made the act of driving it straight into a challenging endeavor. Needless to say, the dinghy did not look safe in the slightest.

"What's the hold up, ye yellow-bellied bucko? Afraid?" A nasally voice behind Dungar taunted.

Dungar turned around to see the weasel-ish face of Hugo standing behind him. The man was built just like Jimminy, except even skinnier. Rather than Jimminy's bushy black hair though, this man's was short and very oily causing it to cling to his head. His hideous visage was only exacerbated by his particularly sharp features, notably his pronounced brow, narrow chin, and aquiline nose.

Dungar prodded one finger into the man's chest. "How about you shut your mouth, ya horse-toothed freak show."

Hugo narrowed his beady black eyes and put his face close to Dungar's. "Ye have yerself some pretty deadlights there, laddy. Hopefully nothing will happen to them."

Dungar raised a skeptical eyebrow. "I don't know if you're trying to intimidate me or if you're coming onto me, but either way I'm suggesting you knock it off." Then, without another word, he threw caution to the wind and hopped into the boat next to Finn and Larry, the latter riding on the shoulders of the former.

As the rest of the infiltration team boarded the vessel it quickly became cramped and crowded like a sea-faring clown car. Then, finally, came the captain of the crew, Nobeard himself. Before he too hopped into the boat, he first threw a large and heavy looking sack into the lifeboat that made a loud, metallic clang when it landed. Wordlessly, Nobeard then hopped into the craft himself and cut the supports, sending the entire crew plummeting downward into the sea.

The sudden fall and subsequent impact startled Dungar, but it didn't make him nearly as uncomfortable as feeling the frail and wrinkled body of Ozzy wrapped around him in a tight, fearful bear hug. Even after the boat stopped rocking, Ozzy still had not let go which resulted in an awkward eye contact between the two.

"Ye have a very firm body, sailor." He spoke in a wizened voice as he smiled up at Dungar.

"Get off of me!" Dungar demanded, slightly panicked.

"WHAT'S IN THE BAG, CAPTAIN?" Shane called out.

"I'm glad ye asked, Shane!" Nobeard acknowledged. "I would have preferred a slightly less deafening volume, but I be glad nonetheless. This bag here carries the provisions for our excursion. First thing's first!"

Nobeard reached into the bag and pulled out two red linen shirts and tossed one each to Dungar and Jimminy.

"This here be yer pirate apparel, lads!" Nobeard announced, then he turned to Dungar. "I know ye not be too stoked fer our freebootin' ways, but ye are clearly in need of some new vestments given the tattered state of those on yer back."

The man did have a point. What was left of Dungar's shirt was little more than tattered confetti held together by fraying bits of thread. So, begrudgingly, he donned the pirating garb and settled in for the storming.

"Atta lad." Nobeard praised. "Now as for the rest of ye, this here bag contains a varied assortment of armaments to select from. So choose yer weapon, lads!"

Even amid the crowdedness of the lifeboat, five of the seven pirates dove viciously into the bag, each trying to get their hands on the best weapon first. Finn was the one currently rowing the boat, taking it in the general direction of the wizard tree, and Larry just didn't seem to think fighting for a weapon was worth the effort. Hindered by his blindness, Blaine opted to simply grab everything he could get his hands on while Shane took the opposite approach and tried to grab weapons away from his crewmates rather than from the bag itself.

"Look alive, lads, and hurry up! In a moment it be time to disembark!" Nobeard called out after only about five minutes of rowing

Dungar looked towards the island. The tree was now in full view, gnarled and twisted as it was, but there were still about half a league of sailing distance between the island and their boat.

"What do you mean?" Dungar inquired. "We're not even close to shore yet."

"We're almost within range of the tree's defenses, lad." Nobeard replied.

"The captain is correct." Finn chimed in between his already labored breaths. "A target this size would never make it to the island, we're gonna have to swim it."

"Wot kinda defenses are there?" Jimminy asked.

Nobeard put a hand on Jimminy's shoulder and grinned. "If ye stick around to learn, laddy, ye probably will not live to share with the rest of us."

Dungar watched the pirates as they sheathed their weapons, kicked off their boots, and proceeded to tumble off of the lifeboat and into the water. Then they proceeded to space themselves out and swim towards the island. Even Blaine somehow knew the appropriate direction in which to head.

Before long it was just Dungar, Jimminy, and Larry left. Larry, however, simply was taking a few extra moments to swap out his peg legs for flippers. Then he smiled a toothless grin that was barely visible behind his bushy black beard and bid them farewell before he too disappeared with a splash.

"Well come on then, mista Dungar." Jimminy invited. "Best depart before being made into mush!"

Dungar stared at his reflection in the shimmering water that his crewmates had just disappeared into. It was a surreal feeling to be on such a large body of water like this one. Growing up in the Snake Eye Desert, the only bodies of water he had ever seen were scattered pools within the oasis. As such, he found the sheer size of the lake to be both enthralling and intimidating.

"You go on ahead, Jimmy."

"Wot do you mean?" Jimminy asked, confused. "Wot are you going to do?"

"I'm staying with the boat." Dungar asserted.

"Are you bonkers, mate? I'm not particularly privy to the nature of the tree's defenses meself, but I trust the pirates' judgment that it'll be rather nasty."

"I have no choice, Jimmy!" Dungar insisted. "I can't swim."

fourteen

nature's wrath

Up until this point in his life, Dungar had never regretted not learning to swim. If someone were to tell him even a week ago that he'd be storming a faraway island with a group of pirates then he probably wouldn't have had any idea how to react, but he certainly wouldn't have believed them. He figured most of his neighbors who had also spent their lives in a scorching sea of sand probably couldn't swim either, just as it would be a safe assumption that someone who spent their life confined within city walls wouldn't be able to hunt or fish. Most people opt not to hone skills that do not coincide with their day to day lives.

Unfortunately, like it or not, the skill of swimming would certainly coincide quite well with Dungar's life at this very moment. The bobbing box currently keeping him afloat was the only separation between him and what would almost certainly be a watery grave. Therefore, even if it meant he had to face the ominous defenses of a giant plant, Dungar was staying put no matter what.

"If you can't swim, then wot are you doing on a bloody boat?!" Jimminy asked incredulously.

"You said this was the fastest way to Jenair." Dungar countered. "We didn't have time to waste!"

"Oh you brave foolish bastard, you! Just can't resist going and looking for trouble, eh?!"

Dungar gaped back at him. Their current situation was becoming direr by the second though, so he didn't have time to draw attention to such a hypocritical statement. As the current slowly pulled the bobbing boat in the direction of the island, they appeared to have crossed some sort of invisible threshold that triggered the tree's attention.

In a tremendous flash of light, the top of the tree began to spray out massive plumes of fire in all directions. It was so bright that Dungar and Jimminy were forced to shield their eyes from the visual onslaught. The temperament of the water also began to turn steadily rougher. Before long, both passengers were forced to hold onto something to avoid being tossed overboard.

"Blimey!" Jimminy exclaimed. "Those pirates are sure gonna be mad at us when we see them again."

"Grab an oar, Jimmy! We can't stay here forever." Dungar commanded.

Hastily each man grabbed a paddle and began attempting to row amid the violent thrashing of the boat and steady showers of sea spray. Progress was very slow going as much of the two men's effort was devoted to avoiding being tossed from where they sat.

Dungar blinked furiously against the deluge being blown into his face by the suddenly heavy winds. He could barely see the silhouette of the tree amid the flurries now. His entire body was soaked, his clothing and hair both matted against him. He clung to the oar with desperation, fearing he may lose it all the turmoil.

"It's no good, mate!" He heard Jimminy's voice call out over the howling winds.

"It is good, Jimmy!" Dungar yelled back. "Just keep rowing!"

Eventually they began to adapt to the rhythm of the rocking, and the wind and rain became something they could tune out. Fuelled by desire for survival, the two men rowed against the elements, defying the stormy wrath put upon them.

With a bright flash of light and an enormous splash, the storm suddenly became comprised of more than wind and rain. Dungar averted his attention from the chaos around him and looked skyward where he was greeted with the sight of the plumes of flame bursting into a swarm of fireballs and descending upon them. Soon the roiling sea became even more tumultuous with the immense splashes and sizzling of watermelon sized fireballs landing around them.

"Yup, they're going to be really mad at you." Jimminy repeated again as he too spotted the rain of fire. "Hey, that one right there appears to be headed right for us!"

Jimminy was right; bearing down upon their very position was a sinister fireball that had destruction written all over it. Knowing they had only seconds, Dungar tossed his oar to Jimminy before reaching into the munitions bag and grabbing the first weapon he could get his hands on. As he pulled it out of the sack, Dungar found it to be a large Lucerne hammer. It was old, blunted, weathered, and in some drastic need of some maintenance. However, none of that was relevant at this point in time as Dungar required it for but one purpose.

Gripping the mace tightly, in one swift and powerful movement Dungar spun back towards the descending fireball and, with a mighty upwards swing of the hammer, he shattered the projectile into a million glowing particles that were quickly carried away by the roaring winds. As the vibrant spark show dissipated, he could see that the amount of fireballs overhead that were bearing down on the boat had multiplied.

"I need you to keep rowing, Jimmy!" He called out as he held the hammer ready.

With stunning compliance, Jimminy wordlessly locked both paddles into the oarlocks and began to row for all he was worth. The sea was still mercilessly choppy and the storm was as fierce as ever, but each man carried out his duty with stoic determination.

One by one Dungar smashed the fiery orbs as they reached his miniature vessel, the resulting flares from each destroyed projectile vanishing in the rain with a death rattle-like sizzle. His life of working a forge had rendered him all but immune to the occasional singe from stray flares, and the stormy weather that had turned the sky black and drowned the air around the tree with its torrents helped protect the boat from catching fire.

The shoreline was almost within reach now, thirty paces at most. Dungar smashed one last fireball then dropped his hammer and bent down to assist in rowing with his hands. They were so close to safety. As soon as his hand touched water, however, a large, black slimy hand shot from the lake and grasped his wrist. He immediately tried to pull back, but the hand held him firm. Then, with a hefty jerk, Dungar felt his entire body being pulled from the boat and into the frigid water.

It was a similar slow motion feeling to the one he recalled from the arena. There was no pain this time though, just a paralysis from the icy waters and the chilling fear of being completely submerged in water for the first time in his life. Knowing that a predator dwelled there in the deeps with him did nothing to alleviate his panic either.

The gooey hands continued to grip him, pulling him down into the unknown expanse that was Lake Deeplu. They must have been closer to the shore than he had thought, because within seconds of his submersion Dungar felt his face being pressed against the sandy bottom of the lake. He thrashed around as best he could, all the while clawing at the body of the creature. Large chunks of gunk sloughed off of it with every swipe, but it did nothing to wane the creature's strength.

As he continued to scratch at his attacker, Dungar finally felt what seemed to be the outline of a face of some kind, but it was difficult to tell due to the consistency of the being's body. Nevertheless, he was running out of options fast. In a final stroke of desperation, he plunged his hand into the creature's face, digging his fingers into any orifice he came across: mouth, ear, nose, eye socket, anything. When he had a sufficient grip, he yanked as hard as he could.

He didn't know exactly what happened. All he knew was that he had torn a large chunk of something out of the creature, and as soon as he did there was an eruption of bubbles followed immediately by the pressure pinning his face into the sand being removed. In the last remaining seconds he had of breathlessness, he braced his feet against the lake floor and pushed upwards with all his might.

As soon as his head broke the surface, Dungar filled his lungs with deep breaths of the glorious air that he had so long taken for granted. He then grasped frantically at the side of the lifeboat before he sunk back into the water. Just as he hauled himself back into the boat, another head broke the surface of the water. It appeared to be a human skull, however the eye sockets were hollow and soulless, and the skull itself was thoroughly coated in black gelatinous ooze. The jaw also appeared to have been ripped off.

Despite the grievous bodily harm inflicted upon it, the thing hoisted itself into the boat as well with relative ease and resumed its attempts to repel the island invaders, all the while uttering a gargling growling noise.

"Wot in the chuffing sea breeze is that thing?!" Jimminy called out.

Even if he had an answer to that question, Dungar didn't have time to offer it. Immediately he balled up his fist and drove a heavy haymaker into the side of the creature's head. Once again, large chunks of the slime flew off as the being's body recoiled, but it appeared to have little effect otherwise. Within moments of the blow, a sword blade appeared from its chest, Jimminy having impaled it from behind.

Turning its attention from Dungar, the creature spun around to face Jimminy.

"Erm, sorry mate." Jimminy offered sheepishly. "Would you believe I was just hoping you'd hold that for me?"

The creature snarled again before fastening its hands around Jimminy's neck, lifting the man off the ground as it choked him. Seizing the opportunity, Dungar pulled the sword from the thing's chest and used it to slice its hands off, freeing Jimminy. He then swung the sword once more at the neck of the beast, intending to finish it with a decapitation. The blade, however, became imbedded in some sort of skeletal structure that lay underneath all the ooze that coated the creature. Dungar tried to pull it loose, but the attempt was to no avail.

The being was now having difficulty choosing which of the two men to attack, but ultimately it decided Dungar was the greater threat. It lunged at him, the two nubs at the ends of its arms stretched out with murderous intent. Dungar raised his own arms to keep the creature at bay causing his hands to sink into its body until they reached what he could only assume was the creature's clavicles. As the two grappled, Dungar called out to Jimminy.

"You plan on bloody doing something, Jimmy!?"

"Oh right, hang on, mate!" Jimminy called back.

A second later another sword blade appeared jutting from roughly the same spot as the first one, coming to a stop mere inches before reaching Dungar. Jimminy had retrieved another sword from the bag and run the beast through yet again.

"WHY WOULD YOU STAB HIM AGAIN!?"

"I DON'T KNOW! I'M FREAKING OUT RIGHT NOW!"

Dungar's legs were slowly beginning to buckle as the oozy monster continued to press down on him. Glancing to the sky, he saw that it still continued to assault them with its fiery rain, and just Dungar's luck, there was another fireball heading straight for them. In one movement, he pulled his hands from the fiend's body and ducked. The creature fell forward and found itself draped over his shoulder.

Digging his hands into the monster's body yet again, Dungar felt around until he found some ribs to grab onto. Then, with a loud roar of exertion, he heaved the creature over his head and high into the air. The monster hammered at his head with its blunt arms as he slowly rotated whilst still holding it. Carefully, he lined up the beast to be in the trajectory line of the blazing projectile.

A loud crash followed by a sickening hissing and sputtering indicated the fireball had hit its mark. The force of the impact knocked Dungar backwards and flat onto his back. His clothes were stained black from the remnants of scorched slime, and his hands still clutched onto the charred remains of the monster's ribcage. Any other traces of the creature appeared to have been vaporized.

"Woo, teamwork!" Jimminy laughed as he helped Dungar to his feet.

"Sure, Jimmy, teamwork." Dungar grunted sarcastically.

A scraping sound indicated their lifeboat had finally run aground. Dungar was more than happy to hop out, thankful to have returned to land, yet another lifelong commodity of his that he had taken for granted. He never realized just how much he enjoyed the concept of a still, unmoving ground wherein he had all the space in the world to roam. Though that second part wasn't necessarily true about this island.

Despite the gigantic plant growing out of it, the island itself was little more than a sandy ring that didn't stick out any more than ten paces in any given direction from the tree. There was quite literally nothing to mention in the way of wildlife or other greenery; the island simply consisted of sand and tree. An impressive tree it was, though, naturally it looked even bigger up close.

Dungar and Jimminy tentatively approached the massive shrub. Gnarled branches thicker than barrels jutted out in every direction from it, twisting and winding and turning the space around the tree into a vertical jungle. The tree's bark had an incredibly smooth and glassy consistency to it as well, almost as if every inch had been flawlessly sanded. Dungar wasn't exactly sure where any treasure on this tree would be located, or how to reach it. The surface of the tree was way too smooth to just climb, and there didn't appear to be any notches carved in by climbing equipment. Then again, given the stormy conditions he had created, it is just as likely that none of the pirates survived their swim.

"Hey, mista Dungar." Jimminy called out, motioning Dungar towards him. "Wot do you make of this?"

Curious, Dungar walked over to where Jimminy was gesturing. There appeared to be some sort of symbol etched into the tree by where he was standing.

"Perhaps it is a rune of some sort?" Jimminy offered. "A magic symbol with some kinda mystical power that establishes this tree as a wizard perhaps?"

"I'm pretty sure this is just something that somebody put into the tree, Jimmy." Dungar deduced. "It looks carved, and there's a knife laying on the ground."

"Well blimey, that's even more interesting! Maybe it's an ancient language detailing the rich history of the tree!"

"I think it's just an arrow pointing left."

Jimminy cocked his head to the side as he continued to analyze the symbol. "Oh surely that can't be the case, mate. It's way too simple. I'm thinking it's a puzzle that the tree poses to any who seek the treasure! Hm, perhaps the answer is to shoot it with an arrow . . ."

"I'm going to walk to the left and see what happens, Jimmy."

"Oh that's just plain ridiculous, mate. I'm going to follow you so that when you're proven wrong I will be there to rub it in your face!"

So off they walked into the wild blue left direction. Dungar dragging his shoes in the sand with every step, happy to have the familiar feeling of the grit beneath his feet back. Jimminy also found himself returning to old routines, namely his penchant for breaking into song.

> *Way hey and away we go left*
> *With every intention to commit a theft*
> *We'll only succeed if we are deft*
> *A way hey and away we go left*
> EVERYBODY!

Dungar was all but desensitized to it by this point. It was certainly still annoying, but after all he had been through in the last few days, minor annoyances didn't quite have the same effect on him that they used to. Also, while they sky was still made black from the storm anyway, he was fairly sure that night would be falling soon, if it hadn't already. As they walked for another couple minutes, they eventually saw the unmistakable indication of an opening in the side of the tree.

"Blimey, mate!" Jimminy called out as he began to run to it. "I don't believe it!"

Dungar followed after him as the lanky fellow took off. As they rounded the corner and entered the opening they found the entirety of the interior of the tree to be completely hollow. Vines that emitted an eerie green glow covered the walls as high as the eye could see, filling the room with a dim luminescence that exuded a tone of mysteriousness.

However, in the very center of that mysterious shroud, there was a seated around a fire a group of seven individuals forming a miniature pocket of familiarity. As the two entered the room, a tall, recognizable figure rose from the pack to acknowledge them. Nobeard stepped out of the group and strode towards Dungar and Jimminy with purpose.

"Alright. Which one of ye mateys is responsible for tripping the tree's defenses?"

Dungar studied his face; it didn't require a particularly perceptive individual to determine the level of the man's displeasure. He then glanced at Jimminy, who insistently nodding in his direction with a blatant lack of subtlety.

Nobeard took another step towards Dungar, causing them to be mere inches apart.

"Sailor. Ye set in motion a series of events that not only jeopardized our entire mission, but also resulted in the death of one of my crewmen."

Nobeard gestured towards the fire. There were only six silhouettes seated around it, the slim figure of Hugo Bonny not among them. Dungar begrudgingly had to admit to himself that, among the pirates he was tasked to raid the island with, Hugo was at least the one he was the most alright with inadvertently killing. Frankly the only thing that worried him was how Captain Nobeard was going to react.

". . . and it was AWESOME!!" The deranged pirate added enthusiastically, jumping up and down. "Thar was stormy weather, a raging sea, monsters, and even fire falling from the sky! I didn't even know it was possible fer something to be that marvelous!"

Dungar was struck dumb from a combination of surprise and relief. Jimminy shared his surprised sentiment, but the man was rarely at a loss for words.

"You don't miss your mate, mate?"

"Aye don't get me wrong, laddy, Hugo was a beloved member of me crew. But he knew the risks of this excursion. Besides, it's like I always say to me pirate mateys, a drowning death at sea is nature's way of telling ye that you suck at yer job. Now come warm yerselves by the fire, lads."

The two followed Nobeard as he returned to his original spot among the weary looking pirates. Even amid the exhaustion of their ordeal, the party remained as rambunctious as ever.

"QUIT HOGGING ALL THE RATIONS, FAT BOY!" Shane hollered at Finn.

"Great lord of the sea, would you quit your yelling?" Finn demanded. "And I packed these rations myself, don't be jealous that you didn't think to do the same!"

Ozzy then sidled up next to Shane and put an arm around him. "I have some extra rations that I can share with ye, sailor." He offered with a smile.

"WHY THANK YOU, OZZY, BUT FINN'S RATIONS ARE MORE FILLING. AND HE'S HOGGING THEM ALL. YOU'RE A HOG, FINN!"

"ENOUGH!" Nobeard yelled at the group. Everyone jumped and gave the captain their attention, Wally even put his hand mirror down.

"If ye bilge rats don't start behaving, then I'm going to extinguish this here fire and see how that goes for ya's!"

Fearful looks appeared on the faces of the pirate party, fearful looks that were not mirrored on the faces of Jimminy and Dungar. Nobody was cold or wet anymore, and the interior of the tree appeared to be well lit enough, so Dungar couldn't figure out what the big deal was.

"I don't expect ye lads to understand." Nobeard said to Jimminy and Dungar. "This here fire is the only thing keeping the nymphs at bay."

"Nymphs . . ." Dungar repeated.

"They be the tree's protectors, matey. Pretty and effeminate creatures, but every bit as vicious as that lake out there we just traversed."

Dungar chuckled to himself. He had only just escaped the clutches of an evil and dangerous woman, only to trade just one for an entire battalion of them instead. If these were the type of women that he was destined to meet over the course of his life, then at least he'll have an easy time rationalizing never having been married.

FIFTEEN

NOBODY EVER DID SEE THE BODY

While he was still not quite sold on the pirating lifestyle, Dungar had to admit to himself that the company of the misfit mariners was starting to grow on him. Behind all the quarrels and altercations among the crewmen there was still a homeostasis that managed to be maintained in spite of it all. It was via that equilibrium that even after such a harsh journey the crew was able to come together with their common goal still firmly in place. At least, after they finish having a go at one another.

"WHY DO YOU HAVE SO MANY WEAPONS, BLAINE? IT'S NOT FAIR THAT YOU HAVE SO MANY MORE WEAPONS THAN THE REST OF US." Shane continued to yell to pretty much anyone within earshot, which, at this volume, was probably everyone in the kingdom.

Without even moving his head, the blind pirate gently patted the various weapons strapped to his person. "Finders keepers, matey." He grunted.

"BUT I'M REALLY TIRED FROM THE SWIM." Shane insisted. "I NEED TO BE BETTER ARMED SO I CAN PROTECT MYSELF."

This time Blaine turned his sightless face in Shane's direction. "We all made the swim, ya whiny oaf. We're all tired."

"If I may interject," the pompous and pretentiously accented voice of Wally cut in, "if you are going to be sharing your armaments with the rest of us then that jeweled dagger on your belt would look absolutely darling with my current ensemble."

"Nobody is gettin' any of my weapons!" Blaine growled at the group.

"And we're not all tired either!" Finn added, turning his attention to Larry. "SOME OF US felt that it was an okay course of action to simply ride on the back of one of the more able-bodied individuals making the swim."

"Hah, in what ocean are you considered able-bodied you great hefty mammal of a pirate, you?" Larry bit back. "Besides, I helped ya with the kickin'."

"Speakin' of fellow pirates catchin' rides on their crew-mates . . ." Blaine said, turning towards Ozzy. "What's yer excuse?"

"Well I'm old!" The wizened man insisted with a smile. "And surely a spry young strapping pirate like you could handle a little extra burden!"

"A little extra burden?" Blaine echoed incredulously. "I'm already blind!"

"Are you really though, mate?" Jimminy asked. "I mean seriously, how are you able to do any of this if you can't see anything?"

The entire group around the fire fell to a hushed silence as all heads turned to face Jimminy, many with shocked or displeased looks.

"Wot . . . ?" The shaggy man asked warily.

"Great sea weavin' mermaids, lad!" Nobeard criticized. "Ye can't just ask a man if he's actually blind or not! Have ye no decency?

"Oh my lord, mate!" Jimminy exclaimed. "I am so sorry! You are right, that was very indecent of me!"

At that, all the pirates burst into an uproarious laughter as Jimminy looked around in bewilderment.

"We're pirates, matey." Blaine croaked in between guffaws. "Ye really think we care about common courtesy? Hey Finn, why are ye such a fat lard, huh?"

"I'd have to show ya!" Finn mumbled through a mouthful of bread. Then he pointed at Blaine's face and, with a laugh, shouted "Oh wait, I can't!"

As Dungar and Jimminy sat stone-faced and confused, all the pirates burst into another bout of raucous laughter that lasted a few minutes. Then, after it died down, Blaine turned back to Jimminy.

"Aye, I am indeed blinder than fatty over there is obese. You see, our dearly departed Hugo Bonny, may his soul find rest at the bottom of the sea and may his body be eaten by fishies, had something of what ye might call an anger problem. Anywho, long story short, he caught me cheating in a game of Liar's Dice. Here I thought I game called Liar's Dice would promote cheating, but apparently not. After we had ourselves a heated chat on the matter, he simply said to me: 'Ye have yerself some pretty deadlights there, laddy.' Next thing I knew, he had pulled two knives popped me eyeballs clean outta me skull."

Dungar's mind immediately went back to his short-lived encounter with Hugo. At the time he had no idea what the man was even talking about, he had never heard the term deadlights before. Now to know that he was potentially mere moments away from suffering a similar fate was unnerving to say the least.

"So you never told me how you manage to do everything you do then." Jimminy reminded Blaine.

Quicker than Jimminy could react, Blaine reached over and, with stunning precision, pinched Jimminy's nose between his fingers then wiggled the man's head side to side.

"I couldn't explain it to ye even if I wanted to, matey." The blind pirate boasted with a cocky smile, exposing his yellow teeth.

"Alright enough with yer pissing match, lads." Nobeard ordered as he produced three torches. "It be time to continue. Now which three of ye are to be torch bearers?"

Jimminy enthusiastically jumped to his feet and took a torch from Nobeard. He was then followed by Ozzy and Blaine, respectively. After the torches had been lit, Nobeard poured a nearby bucket of water onto the main fire and confidently set off into the bowels of the arboreal maze.

The interior of the tree was vast and twisted. Even with the lighting from the torches and vines, the party's surroundings were still shrouded in a haze of darkness which caused the copious amount of passageways surrounding them to be barely visible. Each person's foot would make a squelching noise as it sunk into the soggy moss that coated the floor. Even over the rhythmic squishing noises, though, faint whispering sounds could be heard emanating from the assorted openings in the walls. Murmurs from members of the crew indicated it was not only Dungar hearing them, Nobeard insisting to them that it was just the wind. However, there was no breeze to be felt.

"Do not let yerselves be driven crazy, lads." Nobeard advised the crew in a low voice. "This tree be having many tricks up her sleeve."

Dungar focused on each one of his senses: the soft feeling of his feet sinking into the mossy carpeting, the stuffy and earthy smell of the tree's interior, the sight of the confident captain juxtaposed with his increasingly wary crewmen, and the sound of his own breathing in tandem with the squishing of his shoes. Yet even completely focused, the faint sounds of distant murmuring were still registering to him. This was no simple mind game, there were other things lurking deep within these passages. It must be the nymphs the captain mentioned, but the sounds were not what Dungar had in mind.

As the excursion continued, Dungar found himself becoming more and more curious as to the nature of the sounds. They seemed to be some form of communication, but not in an ominous or intimidating manner. Instead they sounded almost fearful, as if they were pleading with the party.

"This is our home."

"Why are you here?"

Dungar jumped as he heard the mysterious voices. They were indeed feminine like he imagined, but they had an air of vulnerability to them that he was not anticipating. The rest of the crewmen surely must have heard them as well, as the pace of the group had slowed significantly as the eyes of the wary crewmen began to wander around worriedly.

"There is something down that passageway!" Finn cried out as he pointed down a nearby opening.

"No, lad, don't!" Nobeard ordered him. But the command fell upon deaf ears as Finn took a deep breath and began to trundle at an awkwardly fast pace into the darkness.

"Really?!" Nobeard yelled after him. Then he turned to the crew. "Does it not go without saying that when you're exploring a magic and hostile tree you don't stupidly run away from the pack? Gahhh."

Nevertheless, Nobeard was not one to abandon members of his team, so he begrudgingly took off down the passage after Finn with the rest of the fellowship following suit. Fortunately, Finn was a rather slow moving man, so Nobeard managed to catch up with him right as they made it into a well let clearing at the end of the passage. There were copious amounts of the light vines on the walls, floor, and ceiling that bathed the room in enough light to showcase the grassy meadow that it was. In the very center of that meadow lay a wide log with a delicious looking buffet laid out on it.

Finn stopped short when he first saw the buffet, momentarily stunned by the sheer appetizing beauty of it. He then made a dash towards it, but didn't make it more than two steps before Nobeard grabbed him by his hair and yanked him backwards causing him to fall on his ass.

Nobeard could not even bring himself to yell at the pirate as he loomed over Finn. He was having difficulty finding the right words to express just how much contempt he had towards the situation. Finally he just screamed.

"HAVE YE LOST YER MIND, BOY!?" He turned to the rest of the crew. "Are you all insane?! Is it not too much to expect for ye all to follow yer captain's orders? And another thing, where in the bloody misty shallows is Larry?"

Dungar looked around. Larry was indeed nowhere to be seen.

"He said running was too hard with his peg legs, mate." Jimminy explained. "So he decided to just wait until we got back."

"Why I oughtta throttle that lazy bastard . . ." Nobeard mumbled to himself as he began to make his way back down the hallway."

"Please. We mean you no harm."

Dungar jumped again as he heard the voice whisper to him.

"You alright, mate?" Jimminy quietly asked.

"Do you hear that, Jimmy?"

"Are you hearing voices too? Why am I the only one not hearing voices for once?"

"I don't know what they want. But I'm starting to get the feeling there's something wrong here."

"Alright Larry, you better have one excellent excuse!" Nobeard yelled out angrily as the group reached the end of the tunnel.

Larry was not the silhouette at the end of the tunnel. As it turned around, it was revealed to be a beautiful female figure. Her nose-less face was as smooth as porcelain, her eyes glowing the same vivid green as the vines on the walls. Her shoulder length hair was also green, a darker forest shade that was slightly bristly. Her arms, chest, and waist were all wrapped in shrouds of leaves and vines that clung to her body as she elegantly moved towards the group.

Nobeard didn't even let her get a word out before he drew one of his long, slightly curved swords, and hacked her head clean from her neck before front kicking her body several feet backwards and into a wall. As he sheathed his sword and turned around, he saw the faces of everybody, including Dungar, gazing upon him with mortified expressions.

"Alright look!" Nobeard attempted to comfort them. "I know this looks bad, but you need to trust me!"

"Nooo! Why are you doing this?"

"What is going on, Nobeard?" Dungar demanded as he stepped towards the pirate captain.

"You know why we're here lad, I didn't lie to ya."

"You didn't tell me we'd be killing innocent creatures in order to get the treasure."

"They aren't innocent creatures!!" Nobeard asserted. "They are NOTHING!"

It was in that moment that Dungar realized just what was happening. The nymphs of the tree weren't the vicious predators here, they were.

"I didn't agree to help you murder helpless creatures. And I certainly am not going to stand idly by while you do so without me." Dungar threatened.

Nobeard drew both his swords. "It's a shame, lad, I thought you were mentally tough enough for this. It appears I was wrong."

"Come on, Jimmy!" Dungar called to his friend before grabbing him and taking off back down the same passageway that Finn did. As they reached the same clearing as before, and took the left fork, Dungar noticed that the buffet table from before had disappeared. He didn't know if Nobeard pursued him or not, but he kept running, picking random passages each time he came across forks until he was hopelessly lost in the labyrinth.

Dungar slowed to a walk as he worked to catch his breath. He looked over his shoulder to see an empty hallway behind him. Nobeard was nowhere to be seen, and neither was Jimminy for that matter. Not that it mattered much anyway; he couldn't expect Jimminy to fight the pirates for him. Going toe to toe with the captain was something he was going to have to do himself.

He studied the passageway he found himself in as he walked. At some point during his escape, the vines on the wall had turned from green to white and the moss had turned to a flower meadow. The new setting had a warm and calming effect on him, but he couldn't help but feel mildly suspicious of it. This entire scenario almost felt as if he was dreaming. He ran his fingers over the light vines and plucked the grass from the ground. The surreality of his situation aside, he was quite confident in his lucidity.

As he stood up, he looked down the hallway and saw another silhouette like the first one. She carefully walked towards him, taking care to not step on any of the flowers that bloomed around her.

"Are you not one of them?" She asked him. Her voice was high, melodic and it seemed to echo through the room as she spoke.

"No." Dungar asserted firmly. "I want no part of what they're doing."

A smile of relief crossed her face as she continued to approach. As she reached him, she ran her hand down his arm. "Will you help us, Dungar? Can you protect us from them?"

Dungar was a little taken aback by the request. He was curious how she suddenly knew his name.

"Do not be afraid, Dungar." She assuaged. "By becoming a guardian of the tree, you have become one with us."

Her hands still on him, she began to guide him down the passageway. As they reached the end, he found himself in a large, rounded room with a high dome ceiling rife with light vines dangling from it like chandeliers. In the room was a crowd of other nymphs who appeared to be gathered to welcome him. They invited him to sit at a table on which an extravagant banquet was laid out. There were wines, ales, exotic fruits, delicious pastries, and roasted meats of every kind.

Dungar was ushered over to a seat at the head of the table as all the nymphs seated themselves to dine. Many took it upon themselves to express gratitude to him for his aid while others took to clinking their goblets and celebrating. He didn't even have to fill his own plate, for a fully dished serving of everything simply materialized before him complete with a golden chalice of his favorite whisky.

"Here's to our champion, Dungar!" One of the nymphs cried, standing from her chair and raising a glass. "The bravest protector we could ever hope for!"

The resulting cheer from the rest of the nymphs gave Dungar a feeling of fulfillment and elation more gratifying than anything he'd ever felt. He was the guest of honor, he was somebody's hero, and he was actually appreciated. It was perfect; so perfect in fact, that it's almost as if it was tailor-made for him in particular. Something was not right.

"Why am I so bloody special?" Dungar demanded, rising from his chair. The celebrating ceased, the room fell silent, and all eyes set themselves upon him. "I haven't done anything for any of you and yet you all praise me as if I were some sort of god."

"You're our champion . . ." One of the nymphs tentatively said. "You are our savior, here to rescue us from those who are here to do us harm."

"I haven't saved any of you from a bloody thing." Dungar scoffed. "You expect me to believe that you, you who can make these maze-like rooms and passageways and can conjure banquets and flowers and fireballs from midair, you really expect me to believe you can't deal with intruders on your own? What are you all playing at?"

He looked around at the beautiful yet horrified faces that stared silently at him from the table. Before him there was delicious food of every variety he could possibly desire, every drink that he would carefully brew in his home, and a pack of gorgeous creatures that looked upon him with such admiration. It was all so impeccable, all the way down to the resulting feelings of purpose, acceptance, and affection. It was a scenario so flawless that it was as if it had pulled right out of Dungar's own head. So flawless that it must have been.

"Nobeard was right." He uttered. "You are all literally nothing."

The golden chalice in his hand suddenly passed through his fingers as if he had turned into a ghost. Some of the nymphs leaped from their seats attempting to reason with him while others tried to appeal to the same subconscious desires that built the entire fabricated scenario.

"Foolish Blacksmith, you're throwing away the only opportunity you'll ever have for happiness." A pompous and familiar voice taunted from behind him.

Dungar turned to see the figure of Rainchild standing with his arms casually behind him, the man's mouth twisted into its usual self-important smirk. He reached out for the man's neck, but his hands passed right through Rainchild's body in a similar manner as the chalice.

"He's right, you know." The squeaky voice of Mayor Walph Dooble called out from Dungar's left. "You always were a black sheep, Mr. Loloth. Why would you do away with the only place that would take you?"

Suddenly he was surrounded by all of his old neighbors from his home all gazing upon him with looks of disdain, contempt, and pity.

"You should have stayed there." One of them called out.

"We don't want you back." Another declared.

Dungar couldn't take it anymore. He spun around and made a dash for the nearest passageway, but stopped short when he found the quivering figure of Jitters blocking his only exit. The frail old man slowly raised his shaky head and stared into Dungar's vibrant blue eyes with his own grey lifeless ones.

"I was your only friend, Dungar, and you were mine. How could you leave me to die all alone in this village?" He besought in a voice every bit as weak and frail as the body it came from. The cane fell from his hands as he collapsed to his knees. "Now you are every bit as alone as me when I lay on my deathbed."

Dungar could only watch helplessly as his oldest friend breathed his last before collapsing at his feet.

"Shame, we could have used him at the new arena." Herrow's voice snidely mused from somewhere nearby. She and Dritungo were the next figures to show up to torment him. She folded her arms complacently as she unsympathetically loomed over Dungar as he knelt by the body of his friend.

"Well maybe not." She continued. "It makes for a better show if the contestants at least run around and scream a little before dying, this pathetic fool here probably would have just had a heart attack. Boring."

"I destroyed your arena." Dungar reminded her. "And you with it."

"Oh is that what you think?" Herrow laughed before raising an eyebrow. "That was indeed quite a show you put on, and it set me back quite a bit in my business endeavors. But you didn't actually see my body, did you?"

Dungar clenched his teeth and fists as he rose to his feet and glared at her.

"Yes yes, you're very scary." Herrow mused in a bored voice. "You can't exactly assault a figment of your imagination though. As for my arena, we can always rebuild bigger and better than ever. It's quite a lucrative business, you know. I certainly have the funds to do it."

Dungar couldn't listen to another second of this. He knew that none of them were real, that they were just manifestations conjured by the tree to torment him. But whether or not it was the actual person standing there saying these things to him didn't mean what they were saying wasn't true.

His own home never really was a home to him, it was simply a residence. He knew he never fit in with the townsfolk, but until now it had never really hit home the way it currently did. Nor had it occurred to him that in all likelihood he was never going to see his friend Jitters again. Even his triumph at the arena was ultimately little more than a minor setback for a much larger issue.

On the other hand, this was probably exactly what he was supposed to be thinking. All these manifestations were meant to mess with his head. They were conjured with the express intention of making him doubt his place in the world and drive him insane. This realization brought him to the conclusion that, completely irrespective of the validity of anything they had to say, he was not in a proper state to confront these issues. The only issue that needed confronting at this point in time was getting out of this bloody tree.

He took off down the nearest passageway, not stopping for any of the new figures that would appear around him. He didn't know where he was going; he just knew he couldn't stay in place. As he rounded another corner, he saw a figure up ahead facing away from him.

"Hey!" Dungar called out as he headed towards them. "Who is that?"

As Dungar got to within a few paces of it, the figure turned around and revealed itself to be none other than Sir Pent.

Dungar groaned when he saw who it was. "Another one of you, eh?" He grumbled.

Sir Pent didn't say a word when he turned to Dungar. He just smiled then balled up one of his gauntlets and cracked him square in the face.

Dungar recoiled, stumbling backwards several steps before falling onto his back. As he clutched his nose, he looked up to see Sir Pent looming over him. The knight wore the same armor as he did in the desert; except it was now encrusted in filth and bore a massive dent right in the center of the chest plate. Eerily, he gazed down at Dungar with a similar set of glowing green eyes as those of the nymphs.

"No, Mister Loloth." Pent stated in a calm, monotone voice. "Unfortunately for you, I am very much real."

SIXTEEN

NEVER WOUND A SNAKE; KILL IT

If it weren't for his throbbing and bloody nose, Dungar would never believe that it was the real Sir Pent looming over him. Yet there he was, plain as day and solid as ever. He appeared to be in perfect health too, despite the massive impact he received when struck by the snake. Looks like Sir Lee may have been right after all. At least about the man's resilience anyway, his parentage was still indeterminable.

The only part about him that was different was his eyes; they were no longer the cold, dark eyes that Dungar remembered, but rather bright, green, and ethereal looking. Clearly there was some more of the tree magic present here, but it still didn't explain why the man was suddenly able to touch him. Physical feedback from his hallucinations seemed to have ceased once he became privy to them, so the only remaining explanation would be that this was somehow the real Sir Pent.

"How in the blazes are you alive?!" Dungar demanded as he got to his feet.

"When the snake hit me, it was with so much force that I did not land until I reached Lake Deeplu." Sir Pent explained as he removed his gauntlets. "I managed to stay alive long enough to wash up on the shore of this island where I was healed by the tree. In return I vowed to protect it for as long as it would sustain me. It also promised me that one day it would deliver you to me, and now it appears that day has finally come!"

As he finished speaking, Pent grabbed each side of the collar of his armor and proceeded tear it in half. A series of metallic grinding and screeching could be heard as the folded metal futilely resisted being ripped apart by the knight's impossibly powerful arms. After he had wrenched the armor from his body, the knight dropped it to the ground where it made a loud crash before he calmly walked towards Dungar.

"Oh that's just not even fair." The blacksmith sighed.

Effortlessly, Pent picked Dungar off the ground by his clothes and hurled him through the wall of the passageway they stood in. He landed in a crumpled heap covered with bark in a grassy meadow on the other side of the wall. Groaning, he slowly hauled himself to his hands and knees and looked around.

If he didn't know better, Dungar would have never believed he was currently inside of a large tree. He could see no ceiling, above him appeared to be just an overcast sky partially obscured by the hundreds of branches from the forest of trees that surrounded him. He looked back to where he came from. He saw no wooden wall, just trees as far as his eye could see, trees and the angry looking visage of the former knight walking briskly towards him.

Before Dungar could react, Pent reared a leg back and delivered a brutal kick right into Dungar's waist. The force from the blow was substantial enough to lift his entire body from the ground briefly before gravity took hold of him once more and dropped him back down onto his back. Between gasps for air, Dungar gritted his teeth and rolled out of the way before he received another. Painstakingly, he hauled himself to his feet just as Sir Pent got to within his reach. With a roar, he straightened up and drove a right hook right into the temple of Pent's head. The blow though, solid as it was, was little more than a mild annoyance that the knight easily shook off.

In retaliation, Pent drove his knee into Dungar's midsection before delivering a hook of his own. Once again, the force from the blow sent Dungar hurtling backwards, this time into a tree. However, rather than hitting the tree, he instead passed right through it. The lack of impact startled him for a moment, but then he remembered the banquet and his run-in with the nymphs. He studied the forest he found himself in, taking in the dim while light being emitted from the pseudo-sky and examining the sturdy looking trees, one of which he passed through like air not even a moment ago.

The situation was finally starting to make sense to Dungar, the bizarre magic of the tree and the arbitrary rules it played by. The entire interior of the wizard tree simply was what it was, an intricate labyrinth of empty rooms and passageways. The tree could conjure whatever it desired within them, but they only truly existed to those who were under the plant's spell. A spell that Sir Pent, with his glowing green eyes and zealot-like devotion, was clearly under.

Dungar glanced at Sir Pent as the knight marched towards him, menacingly raising another fist. As his adversary lurched forward to deliver another brutal blow, Dungar took a quick step backwards into a tree. Effortlessly, the blacksmith's entire body passed through it unimpeded. Sir Pent's fist, however, halted as soon as it collided with the wood, resulting in a massive crack spanning the body of the devastated plant. The entire tree shook from the impact, sending its conjured leaves gently falling down onto the two men.

It was an odd, yet powerful feeling to have gained such control of the situation, and Dungar intended to take full advantage of it. Clenching his fist, he reached right through the ravaged tree and shattered Pent's nose. Just as before, the knight recoiled from the blow very little, but the blood now oozing down his face and around his mouth proved all

Dungar needed to know. The man was still vulnerable, just a little impervious to pain.

Normally Dungar would feel cowardly running away from his opponent and hiding behind trees only to pop out and crack him in the face on occasion. But rules and honor go out the window once his life falls into jeopardy. Also, if the knight intended to use dirty magic to beef himself up and swing the odds in his favor, then Dungar felt completely justified to use any underhanded tactic that came to mind to even the scales.

The scales had not become as even as he had hoped though. The blood trickling from Pent's face seemed to have slowed to a halt, and the man's resolve and endurance had not waned in the slightest. Dungar felt that he was a fairly fit man, but repeated bouts of surprise attacks and running away would start to wear on any non-magically enhanced individual after a while. He was far from exhausted, but his pace had become noticeably slower, and before long he could no longer outmaneuver the knight.

Dungar was attempting to make his way from one tree to another when he felt an iron-like grip take hold of his shirt and pull him sideways before he had his feet kicked out from underneath him. He hopped to his knees as fast as he could, but any attempts to get up were halted by five seemingly unbreakable knuckles.

Holding Dungar by the cuffs of his shirt, Pent lifted the blacksmith to his feet and stared menacingly into his eyes.

"Your cowardly tactics won't work here, you sniveling craven." The enraged knight growled. "Not so tough when there's nothing to save you, hm?"

Pent did not wait for a response. Still holding Dungar with one hand, he took the other and clamped it around Dungar's neck and watched sadistically as he slowly began to choke the life out of his helpless victim.

Dungar tried his very best to pry the man's fingers apart, but it was no use. The knight's hand was like a mechanical vice compressing his neck. Desperate, he pulled at the knight's wrist, clawed at his face, and fell limp in his hands, but none of it was any use. The strong arms of Pent effortlessly supported his weight as his adversary continued the suffocation with his bare hands.

It was while clawing at Pent's face that Dungar inadvertently grabbed a handful of the knight's neatly cropped grey hair. As he grasped Pent's hair, his mind went back to the arena and the similarly hopeless fight against the thin bird creature. Out of options, he decided if it worked once, maybe it will work again.

Gripping Pent's hair with as sturdy a grip he had, Dungar yanked the man's head towards him while simultaneously hurling his own head forward until the two met, Dungar's forehead slamming into the bridge of the knight's nose. As Dungar had hoped, the hand around his neck retreated back towards the knight it belonged to as Pent began to assess the damage on his nose that had now been shattered a second time.

Copious amounts of blood poured from the knight's face, but as usual his resolve had not weakened at all. Gasping to regain his breath, Dungar looked up at the incredibly angered knight with worry. He had hit the knight with everything he had, there was nothing left for him to use.

Dungar hopelessly looked around the forest, desperate for anything he could repurpose as a weapon. No matter what he saw, though, it would be useless anyway, for he would not even be able to touch it. But as he looked upon his adversary, stepping around a tree as he came over to finish the fight, Dungar had the realization that it wasn't him who needed to be able to feel the objects of the magic forest.

Throwing caution to the wind, and using the only remaining play in his book, he took off in the direction of Pent in an all-out sprint. When he reached the knight, he bowed his body forward and drove his shoulder into the man's stomach. He did not stop running though. The momentum from his body was sufficient to lift the knight from the ground as he continued to run, carrying his opponent.

Pent screamed and pounded his fists on Dungar, but he pressed on in spite of them. Each blow sent a shockwave of pain through him, but the adrenaline surging through his body and the desperation surging through his mind was once again enough for him to phase out the pain.

Finally Dungar hit his mark. He went from a full on sprint to a complete stop in no time flat as he ran into Sir Pent's body which had, in turn, collided with a tree. When he had recovered from the shock of the collision, Dungar looked down to see a thick tree branch stabbed right through his chest and coming out the back of him. Carefully, he slowly stepped backwards away from the branch where he was relieved to discover there wasn't so much as a mark on him from it.

Pent, however, was not so lucky. The sheer magnitude of the collision likely obliterated many of his ribs and caused severe internal injuries. But the several inches thick tree branch jutting out from the part of his chest where his heart used to be was certainly the most grievous of the bodily harm he had suffered. The lower half of Pent hung limply as his arms felt around his injury. His breathing was hollow and labored, and gurgled slightly due to the blood seeping from his mouth.

Dungar wasn't feeling too great from the impact either, but it was nothing he couldn't manage. He limped slightly as he strode towards the knight, who looked up at him with an unmistakable look of defeat in his glowing green eyes.

"Some might say this'll be a bit overkill." Dungar explained as he cupped Pent's jaw in his hand. "But I'm not quite sure just what this magic tree is capable of healing you of, so I need to be thorough."

One hand on Pent's jaw, and the other on the back of the knight's head, Dungar began to twist until he heard the tell-tale sickly snap. The hollow breathing ceased and the knight's arms went limp at his sides. As soon as they did, the room returned to the empty spacious circle it truly was. With no tree left to hold him up, the body of Sir Pent dropped to the floor where it lay like a crumpled ragdoll.

"Blimey, Mista Dungar!" Jimminy's voice echoed through the room.

Spinning around, Dungar met the gaze of his faithful companion as the skinny man exited the passageway he came from and jogged towards him. As he reached the center of the room, Jimminy stopped and looked down at the mangled body of Sir Pent, pausing briefly when his eyes located the gaping hole in the man's chest.

"What's going on in here?" The gravelly voice of Blaine called out from a different passageway.

"Mista Dungar killed a guy!" Jimminy enthusiastically called back to him.

"I thought it smelled like dead body in here." Blaine stated as he strolled into the room. "Hope it wasn't one of ours."

Before he reached the pair, Blaine halted mid step and looked at Dungar.

"Wait a minute, ain't he the one that ran off earlier? Check his eyes, Jaunty! Are they green and spooky?"

Obediently, Jimminy put his face right in front of Dungar's and looked deep into his eyes.

"Well they're certainly scary, mate." Jimminy relayed to Blaine. "But they're as blue as ever."

Shoving Jimminy aside, Blaine put his face right where Jimminy's was in front of Dungar, poking his finger into the burly man's chest.

"Did they get to ya, landlubber? Ye didn't drink the qoolide did ya?"

"Enough, Blaine!" The authoritative voice of Nobeard called into the room.

The pirate captain, accompanied by Finn, Ozzy, and Larry, had entered the room during the interrogation. He still wore his exquisite black overcoat; however the garment now bore noticeable blood stains, likely the same blood that now coated his swords.

"Glad ye could make it, matey." Nobeard addressed Dungar. "Ye had me worried that I'd be forced to gut ye."

"Easier said than done." Dungar quipped as he pointed to the mangled remains of Pent.

Nobeard laughed heartily as he put a hand on Dungar's shoulder. "Impressive feat there, lad!" He acknowledged. Then he leaned in close so only Dungar could hear him. "But trust me when I say ye don't scare me. By the way, how did ye get here so fast?"

"I took a shortcut." Dungar explained, pointing at the hole in the wall that he was thrown through.

"Well regardless of how ye made it here, ye be here now. So let us continue with the treasure hunting. We be getting close now."

The party of seven headed set off once more down yet another ominous passageway. Dungar and Nobeard led as Blaine, Finn, Ozzy, Larry, and Jimminy walked together in a group.

"So what happened to the rest of your mateys, mates?" Jimminy questioned the pirates.

"Well after you two left, we real pirates figured it was a better idea to look for Larry." Finn explained as they walked. "We all started to lose it after a while though. By the time we found Larry, who was just laying down in the middle of the floor for some reason, we had already lost Wally, Ozzy, Shane, and Blaine."

"I already told ya that I was laying in a bed!" Larry chastised him. "It was an enormous and comfy bed made entirely out of pillows. It was bliss, I tell ya!"

"And we already told you that it wasn't real!" Ozzy admonished back. "Just like mine wasn't either." He added with a sigh.

"What did you see, mate?" Jimminy asked him.

Ozzy's mouth curled into a satisfied smile as his eyes retreated to their corners and his teeth subtly bit down on his lower lip. Before he could respond, though, Blaine cut in.

"Trust me, lad, I know Ozzy here pretty well. Well enough to know that whatever temptation lured him in is not one you'd be wanting to hear about."

"So what about you then, ya blind knowitall?" Finn mocked. "You can't even see your own ugly mug in a mirror, so what did you feel?"

Blaine smiled to himself as well while the group continued to walk down the windy hallway. "There is no description for what I felt, lads. There be no sights, sounds, or smells which I could convey to ye with a coherent description. But I'll tell ye this, though. I felt powerful."

"This be the place, buccaneers!" Nobeard loudly called to the group, causing everyone's heads to turn forward.

They stood before a large wooden door, heavily adorned with vines and flowers.

"Behind this here door lays the treasure we all seek." Nobeard advised the crew as he gingerly reached into his shirt and produced a golden key. "This key is the only device that is capable of unlocking it. It was swallowed many a decade ago by a sea critter within the lake, and trust me, yer mind would be blown by the amount of days I spent fishing up the little bastards until I found it! All of that work will have paid off when I retrieve the fortune hidden behind this door though."

Slowly he put the key in the lock, but before he turned it he cried out a mighty "Yarrrrr!" and drew both his swords on the party. Shocked and terrified, everyone jumped backwards out of the sharp steel's reach. None of them took an aggressive stance, they all poised themselves to run away if the need to arose. Nobeard howled with enthusiastic laughter as he sheathed his swords.

"Sorry about that, mateys!" He apologized to the group. "If any of ye were going to betray me and take the treasure fer yerselves then that woulda been the perfect opportunity! So I figured I'd get the jump on you first!"

He continued to laugh to himself as he casually turned the key and pushed the door open. Inside was a small room with no floor and instead just a long pole leading into an abyss.

"Now I know what you're thinking, lads." The captain asserted as he grasped the pole. "Jumping into a dark hole while you're exploring a magical hallucinogenic tree is about as ridiculous of an idea as cheating in a game of dice against a pirate with anger problems and a couple screws loose."

Blaine acknowledged the comparison with a grunt of approval.

"But if ye want yerselves a piece of my sweet sweet booty then it be time to throw caution to the wind and plunge deep into this hole!"

And just like that, Nobeard courageously leapt onto the pole and slid down it into the ominous depths. Dungar was a lot less hesitant than he thought he would be. He figured with all the outrageous things he'd been put through today it was best to just not question Nobeard's orders anymore. He had no idea how long he slid, it felt like hours, but he was relieved when his feet finally hit floor. He found himself right in the middle of yet another large circular room. However, this one was not entirely empty. On the far side, just as Nobeard had assured, there was indeed a large treasure chest on a pedestal.

As soon as everyone from the fellowship had made it into the room, a spotlight of sunshine shot from the ceiling and onto the treasure chest while a choir of soprano voices could be heard singing from an unknown location. Each member from the crew, naturally with the exception of Blaine, had their eyes transfixed on the treasure chest, giddy over the idea of what was inside. Nobeard, however, was looking around the room unimpressed.

"Huh." He grunted disapprovingly. "I expected there to be at least some kind of final boss fight or something."

He paused for a moment, hoping that his foreshadowing comment would maybe trigger something. But alas, he was not granted such a boon. With a dejected shrug, he strolled over to the chest and proceeded to open it.

"What do ye reckon is inside here, mateys?" Nobeard asked the crew as he fiddled with the lock. "Gold? Jewels? Weapons? Ah I can't even contain me excitement!"

Before he had the clasps unlatched, though, another pirate fell from the ceiling and joined the crew. That pirate was none other than Eye-gougin' Hugo Bonny.

"I should more than suffice as your 'boss fight,' captain!" He sneered at Nobeard. His features were every bit as sharp, and his hair every bit as oily as it ever was. The only aspect of him that had changed was his eyes which now emitted a sinister green glow.

Unimpressed, Nobeard turned back to him. "Ye timed yer entrance awfully, sailor. I'd already changed the topic since I mentioned that boss fight business, so trying to respond to it that late with a one liner just makes ye sound like a dumbass."

". . . What?" The bewildered Hugo asked.

"I'm just saying, matey, if ye wanted to make a cool entrance with a one-liner then ye gotta be fast enough to respond to the comment that prompts ya."

"I'd trust him, Hugo." Finn added. "He's proven himself to be the most eloquent guy in this room."

"Now hold up there, lads," Blaine weighed in. "I've proven my ability to turn a phrase many a time during our voyages."

"I know you gentlemen haven't been acquainted with me all that long." Jimminy interrupted. "But I think I should be considered as a contender for this particular title too!"

"Shut up, ye stupid little bilge rats! I'm the captain, so I'm automatically the best spoken. End of discussion!"

"ARE YOU GOING TO FIGHT ME OR NOT?!" Hugo screamed.

"Are ye waiting fer my permission or something?" Nobeard chided. "Come at me, ye sissy!"

As Hugo walked briskly towards him, the pirate captain removed his overcoat to reveal the tight pink sleeveless muscle shirt that lay beneath. The black overcoat Nobeard wore certainly did his physique no justice. After the garment was removed, his body was revealed to be something that could only be described as nothing less than hairy and hulking. Tufts of jet black chest hair could be seen sticking out from the top of his shirt as he flexed his pecs and cracked his equally hairy knuckles.

He was impressively agile for his size as well. Hugo lunged at him with a barrage of swings which Nobeard dodged with seemingly little effort before he grabbed the weaselly looking man's arm at the wrist with one hand then used his free arm's elbow to snap Hugo's arm clean in half.

Dungar was mesmerized as he watched Nobeard viciously yet meticulously bash the entranced Hugo into a pulp. There were absolutely no wasted movements in the captain's actions. Every punch, every kick, every blow delivered from each part of his body quickly moved into a follow up strike or a counter or a dodge. After breaking Hugo's arm, Nobeard deftly leaned out of the way of his opponent's frantic uppercut before responding with a right knee to the stomach, left knee to the face, foot stomp, and throat punch before kicking the pirate's legs out from underneath him and punching him square in the nose as he fell sending him spinning to the ground.

The fight was over even faster than the conversation that preceded it. The crewmen gingerly gathered around the pirate captain as he kept Hugo pinned to the ground with his boot. The captain wasn't ready to finish him off quite yet.

"As you know, my dear Hugo," Nobeard mused nonchalantly as Hugo futilely tried to lift the man's boot of his neck. "I'm not one who is quick to kill me own crew. Now I know this here wizard tree, seductive little minx that she is, has managed to worm her way into your brain. But after we take this treasure and get out of this place I promise ye will get better, forget all about her, and return to yer proper pirating ways."

Hugo, like a rabid animal, continued to convulse beneath Nobeard's foot as he gazed up at his former captain with hate in his eyes.

"I am indebted to this tree!" He spat. "It was there to save my life when the rest of you were content to leave me to drown! It has promised me life! And vengeance! Every desire that I could ever seek and that you could never provide!"

Nobeard shrugged. "Well that may be true, but it comes at the cost of yer freedom, lad. Life has itself no satisfaction if everything be given to you for free! Accompany us back to the real world. Everything you could ever desire is out there too, but I won't be serving it to ye on a silver platter. Tis better to dish yer own plate in this life, that way ye won't have to eat any veggies if ye don't wanna."

"My life . . ." Hugo breathed as his resistance began to wane. "Belongs to the wizard tree now! My purpose is to protect it, and die for it if need be!"

As he said those words, Blaine reached over and grabbed both of Nobeard's swords off of his back.

"If dying for this tree is what ye wish, matey, then I'll be happy to oblige ya!" Blaine gibed before the blind pirate stabbed both of the captain's swords through Hugo's eyes.

Nobeard sighed as he turned to Blaine. "Yes yes, through the eyes, how very clever and poetic, sailor. But I was right in the middle of reasoning with the poor, misguided lad."

Blaine drew both swords from the lifeless skull of his former comrade.

"I have no time for poetry or reasoning, captain." He stated coldly in his gravelly voice. After he did so, he then stabbed both of the swords he pilfered from Nobeard into the torso of Ozzy and snapped off both hilts.

The old, quivering man was so shocked that he couldn't even react. He just stared disbelievingly down at the two pieces of folded steel jutting out of his chest. His hands shook and his knees buckled as his body quickly began to fail on him. Ozzy the Old managed one last pleading look to his beloved crew before his deadlights dimmed and his long pirating career reached its tragic end.

The five survivors of the original crew of ten gaped at the scene, mortified by what they had just witnessed.

"Don't be so shocked, captain, you just said it yourself. I'm just dishing up my plate," Blaine mused forebodingly. "And a meal as delicious as this one isn't meant to be shared." He added as he removed both eye patches to reveal a brand new pair of glowing green eyes.

SEVENTEEN

THE BLIND WHO LED THE SIGHTLESS

Everyone stood in stunned silence. Not only had Blaine turned on the remaining crew members, but by taking away Nobeard's swords he had left them completely unarmed as well. The sunlight shining on the treasure chest bathed that side of the room in light while Blaine stood alone in the darker half. He was outnumbered, but he had weapons, magically enhanced strength and fortitude, and a newly restored sense of vision.

Until he saw Blaine's face uninhibited by the eye patches, Dungar had never really noticed what an imposing figure the pirate was. He was slightly shorter and slenderer than Nobeard, but his posture and manner in which he carried himself gave the impression of a man of superb physical condition and solidity. It's remarkable what one can overlook when they're distracted by a man's disability.

"I know this is a really inappropriate time to say this:" Jimminy whispered. "But remember earlier when I was the only one who happened to inquire as to whether or not this fellow was actually blind?"

"Now is not the best time to say 'I told you so', Jimmy!" Dungar exasperatedly whispered back.

"Oh is that so, Mista Dungar? When do you propose would be a better time?"

"Shut up, both of you!" Nobeard hissed.

Clearing his throat, the pirate captain slowly moved towards Blaine, positioning himself between the traitor and the rest of his crew. He took his time as he moved, making each step slow and deliberate as he surveyed his surroundings and sized up the corrupted pirate that was currently staring him down. He was at a significant disadvantage, but one would think he didn't even know it by the way he coolly moved around.

"Are ye sure ye wish to do this laddy?" Nobeard condescended, nodding slightly towards the body of Hugo. "I mean, ye did just see what happened to the last man who tried."

Blaine reached down and produced two long, shiny kukri knives from the scabbards on his belt. He then twirled them around in a series of flashy flourishes, all the while staring down Nobeard with a look of superiority.

"Don't compare me to Hugo, captain. Especially Hugo when he's unarmed and useless."

Nobeard shrugged. "Fair point. But it's like you just heard me say to Hugo, lad, none of—"

"Don't tell me none of this is real!" Blaine cut him off. "You see that treasure over there? You see these eyes on my face? They're real, Nobeard. They're real, and there's no other way to get them without this tree! Not even you can deny that."

Nobeard had no response. He just gazed at Blaine's new green eyes. Dungar waited, hoping the pirate captain could come up with some sort of diplomacy between the two. But there was no reasoning to be had. How could one possibly talk a formerly blind man into giving up a chance to see again?

"Alright, Blaine." Nobeard finally spoke. "Stay here with the tree as its defender if ye must. Let it grant ye all the boons ye could ever desire. But if I be not mistaken, your role as defender is simply to protect the tree from harm and exploitation." Nobeard turned and gestured towards the treasure chest. "This treasure is not of this tree, and fer us to take it would pose no danger to yer precious tree whatsoever. Everybody wins."

Silence. Dungar, Jimminy, Finn, and Larry all waited in bated breath as they watched the standoff between the Nobeard and Blaine. Nobeard stood stone faced as he patiently awaited Blaine's response. Stoic as the man tried to appear, Dungar could see the unmistakable subtle earmarks of worry and uncertainty. If the pirate captain was worried then it was generally a sign that there was something worth worrying about.

"Oh, captain." Blaine smiled. "It's like you just said, nothing this tree can conjure for me is real. So why would I let real treasure slip right through my grasp?"

"Wait, wot does the treasure mean in this metaphor?" Jimminy whispered to Dungar.

"This isn't a metaphor, Jimmy. He said he's going to kill us and take the treasure." Dungar muttered back.

"They aren't talking in metaphors? Then wot was the serving each other supper thing all about?"

Dungar sighed as he put a hand over his face.

"Before you do this then, Blaine, there's one other thing." Nobeard called out. He took another step towards Blaine so he was now almost within the man's reach. "What about all those nights we've had at sea over the last several years?"

Dungar and Jimminy halted their discussion and turned back towards the two pirates.

"I faked it every time." Blaine informed him with a smirk.

"What?!" Dungar and Jimminy blurted out.

"You are one evil, deceitful, corrupt, rapacious son of a bitch!!" Nobeard screamed into his face. Then the pirate captain fell to his knees and his voice began to shake. "But how could you lie to me like that?" He pleaded pitifully to Blaine.

"Oh get up you simpering bastard, you're embarrassing yourself." Blaine condescended as he used one of his knives to tip Nobeard's chin back upwards to him. As soon as he felt the blade touch his skin, Nobeard reacted like lightning. In three swift movements he ripped the knife from Blaine's hand, elbowed him in the ribs, and slashed him across the face with the blade.

As Blaine recoiled backwards, Nobeard hopped to his feet and addressed the remainder of his crew. "Alright, lads, there be some bombs in me coat. While I hold him off, I need ye to blow a hole in the tree wall and get the treasure out of here."

"Captain, we're underground!" Dungar informed him. "Blowing a hole in the wall won't get us anywhere."

"DO AS I TELL YE!" The captain commanded him before he leapt at Blaine.

Dungar could hear the grunts and yells of exertion coming from the two men, as well as the occasional metallic clash, but he paid it no mind. He immediately started to leaf through Nobeard's black overcoat until he found a small bundle of grapefruit sized iron balls.

"How do I light them?!" Dungar called to the captain.

"Just throw them, lad!"

Obediently, Dungar turned and whipped one at the wall of the tree. Sure enough, as soon as it hit its mark, the grenade exploded leaving a small hole in the wood. Oddly enough, daylight seemed to be shining through it. Looking to widen their exit, Dungar hurled more and more at the opening until it was large enough for a person and the treasure chest to pass through.

Soon as the opening was made, Finn and Jimminy grabbed the chest and took off through it, Larry following right behind them. Dungar made a move to the exit too, but he looked back at Nobeard and Blaine who were still locked in combat. Now that he had a weapon of his own, Nobeard stood a fighting chance against his entranced adversary. However the differences in physicality were evident as Nobeard slowly began to tire while Blaine still retained his magically enhanced vigor.

Dungar still held the remaining bombs given to him by Nobeard. Carefully he reared his arm back, ready to throw. But the two combatants where moving very quickly, bobbing side to side and moving up and down as they remained engaged in their duel. He followed Blaine carefully with his eyes. The pirate was incredibly agile; this was going to be a difficult shot. If he missed his mark then he will likely doom both Nobeard and himself. But he couldn't afford to wait too long either, lest he lose his opportunity.

It was now or never. Dungar took a deep breath and fired away. The explosive launched straight and hard towards the two pirates. Dungar grimaced, silently praying to a deity he didn't even believe in for a bit of luck. It was a good shot, straight as an arrow with perfect spin. Unfortunately, while Dungar did throw it straight, he didn't throw it straight at Blaine, but rather straight to Blaine's right. The bomb flew wide right of its target's ribs, underneath his arm, and straight into the groin of Nobeard.

Fortunately for the pirate captain, the impact was soft enough that the explosive was not triggered. Unfortunately for the pirate captain, the impact was hard enough that his limbs crumpled into themselves and he fell to the ground. Tears streaming from his eyes, Nobeard looked up at Dungar and could only manage one word.

"Whyyy . . . !?"

Blaine, upon seeing this, began roaring with laughter so raucous that he too was momentarily out of fighting commission. With just one flick of Dungar's arm, the tense fight to the death between two rivals had turned into a bout of pirates clutching their sides for different reasons. For a brief moment, Dungar was so embarrassed that he forgot to be worried.

Through the great pain coursing through his body, Nobeard still managed to take advantage of the situation. Still on his hands and knees, he raised his knife high over his head and stabbed it through the foot of Blaine and deep into the wooden tree floor before frantically crawling towards Dungar.

Blaine's laughter turned to screams as he tried to pry his foot loose. The knife in the ground effectively pinned him in place. Nobeard still slightly limped when he reached Dungar and got to his feet.

"Gimme those, ye ham-handed buffoon!" Nobeard grunted before he snatched the sack of bombs out of Dungar's hands. He then pulled one out and turned to Blaine. His would-be killer was still pinned to the ground, struggling hopelessly as he only opened the wound in his foot further.

"Avast, ye double-crossing mermaid molester!" Nobeard hollered to him.

Blaine looked up from his foot. His magically induced ethereal green eyes meeting with Nobeard's own naturally green pair.

"Would ye like me to wait a moment so ye can piss yerself?" The captain taunted him. Then he turned to Dungar. "Watch me closely, lad. The key is in the grip and the shoulder rotation."

With excellent form, Nobeard burnt the bomb towards Blaine at breakneck speed. It hit the pirate square between the eyes so fast that he didn't even have time to flinch. After the explosion, all that remained were smoking pairs of arms and legs, one of the latter still nailed to the floor.

"Bah, serves him right." Nobeard declared as he shrugged bitterly. "That bloody limpit broke my swords, did ye see that, matey? Snapped em clean off at the hilt. I loved those bloody things." He paused for a moment, considering the situation. "Oh yeah, and the killin' Ozzy thing was pretty low too. Anyway, we best be gettin' outta here, lad."

They began to walk towards the hole in the wall when the tree began to send out violent tremors.

"Well then. Perhaps we best be gettin' outta here a little faster." Nobeard said casually.

The two men broke into a run, trying to escape the convulsing tree. As they emerged through the hole Dungar created, they found themselves high in the air walking out on a tree branch just below the cloud line. Dungar glanced over the side only to find that he could barely even see the island, he couldn't make out any of the details of the ground. A sea of blue just stretched far into the horizon in every direction.

"How did we get up here?!" He called to Nobeard.

"Magic, lad! Inside the tree up is down and down is up. Probably best for one not to try and understand it. Just run!"

Making one's way across the tree was difficult. The massive plant swayed back and forth causing a ripple effect throughout its limbs. The height they were at only served to impede their escape too. The wind howled as it blew through the immense leaves around them and hindered their balance further. As they made their way across the branch, Dungar and the pirate captain saw the figures of the three other pirates clinging to the tip of the branch, hanging on for dear life.

"Ahoy, mateys!" Jimminy waved to them, grinning.

"Captain! What do we do?" Finn called to them.

Nobeard and Dungar both stopped as they reached the branch edge. They had absolutely nowhere to go. Unless they intended to climb back up the tree, or down it technically, then a thousand foot drop into open water seemed to be their only option.

"Alright, lads, we almost be out of the woods. But we got ourselves one last hurdle to traverse!" Nobeard reassured the party. He stepped out to the tip of the branch and looked off into the distance where the ship could be seen waiting for them. The wind rustled his jet black hair and made his coat flap behind him as he gazed out to sea.

"Do ye trust me, lads?" He asked the crew, wearing his charismatic grin.

He was silently answered by four blank faces, unsure how to respond.

"That's the spirit, mateys! Everybody grab a leaf."

Tentatively but obediently, each of the pirates approached the monstrous leaves and picked one. The leaves were all enormous, at least ten or twelve feet long apiece. Dungar and Jimminy each picked one as well.

"You can't possibly expect us to do what I think you're expecting us to do." Dungar protested.

"Do ye have a better plan, lad?" Nobeard asked rhetorically while grabbing a leaf of his own. "It's easy, just run, jump, and hang on tight til ye get close to the ship. Then swim 'til they pick ye up."

Dungar sighed; he forgot that Nobeard still didn't know.

"I can't swim, captain." He informed the man.

Nobeard stopped short and turned back to Dungar. Then he shrugged. "Guess you'll have to fly all the way to the ship then. It be a big boat, I'm sure you'll be fine."

Dungar looked out into the distance. The enormous pirate ship he rode in on, in all its triple-masted glory, now looked no bigger than a bath toy floating in an ocean. If it weren't for the tremoring tree and wild winds he wouldn't even consider attempting what he was about to attempt.

"It works better if ye take a bit of a run at it." Nobeard reassured him. "Here, watch how your companions do it."

As if on cue, Jimminy, Finn, and Larry all dashed down the length of the tree branch and tossed both caution and their bodies to the wind. It was oddly graceful the way Jimminy and Larry daintily drifted through the air. Finn not so much. Seconds after the chubby pirate took to flight he lost his grip and plummeted downwards into the water, his leaf drifting away in the breeze.

Nobeard, who had been fumbling with the treasure chest trying to affix it to a leaf of its own, stopped after he saw Finn fall.

"Alright, don't do it like him."

Dungar grimaced as he looked out into the horizon. The entire shimmering blue lake may as well have been a pit of lava for all the good landing in it would do for him. He couldn't expect them to sail in and pick him up though, they'd never make it. He briefly considered trying to get back to the life-boat, but he had no way of getting down to it without using the leaf, so there was no point. He couldn't think of any other course of action, this was his only option.

"Hold up, lad!" Nobeard called out.

Dungar turned around to see Nobeard dragging the chest towards him.

"It's no use trying to tie it to its own leaf, lad, it'd never stay. I need yer help carryin' it!"

"You better be kidding with me, captain." Dungar informed him skeptically as he peered at the heavy looking chest. "There's no way we can bring that thing."

Nobeard set the chest down and stared at Dungar with a pleading look in his eyes. "Please, lad . . ." He urged. "This box be the culmination of me livelihood, I can't leave it behind."

Dungar sighed. He had neither the time nor the ability to talk this man out of taking the treasure. He looked down at the box. It was a simple wooden chest with iron trim but, given the captain's difficulty pulling it, it had to have weighed at least three or four hundred pounds.

"Even if I did help you, how could we even do it?"

"Aye, I'm glad ye asked, matey!" Nobeard declared before he hopped up several branches, higher into the tree. After a few moments he jumped back down pulling behind him the largest piece of foliage Dungar had ever seen. The leaf was truly enormous; it looked every bit as big as one of the pirate ship's sails. It made a slight whooshing sound as it gently floated to the ground behind the captain.

"Alright, here's our ride!" Nobeard informed him enthusiastically. "Grab a side of the chest and hang on tight!"

As instructed, Dungar grasped one of the handles on the side of the chest with his left hand while he gripped the tip of the leaf with his right. This entire plan was just plain ridiculous. Nobeard mirrored him on the opposite side of the chest, in both stance and demeanor.

"This plan be totally solid, matey! Are ye ready?"

"Not particularly."

"Here we go!"

They didn't even need to take a run. The sheer size of the leaf caught the first gust of wind that blew by, catapulting Dungar, Nobeard, and the treasure chest off the branch and into the air. The moment Dungar started to move his heart began to pound. He thought he was uncomfortable enough with being on a boat, but it did not hold a candle to being airborne. There was an inherent feeling of exposure and vulnerability to flying, knowing that the slightest mishap meant a long fall to a watery grave.

Breathing did not come easy, especially when he looked down at the passing sea a long way down beneath him. The view clouded his mind and knotted his stomach. The only thing keeping him focused was the stress on his hands. The pressure on his left hand was quite formidable; doubly so on his right hand, but fear itself was enough to keep both his fists clenched every bit as tight as his ass cheeks were.

The ship was getting close now; outlines of sailors aboard it could be seen buzzing about. They were descending awfully quickly though, even if they made it to the pirate ship they were going to be in for a rough landing.

"Hang on tight, lad." Nobeard ordered him. "I be aiming us for the mainsail. It won't be comfy, but we'll live. LOOK OUT BELOWWWWW!"

As soon as they saw the sturdy wood of the ship's deck beneath their feet, both Dungar and Nobeard released the chest and let it plummet into the ship where it smashed a hole through the upper deck and landed in the hull with a loud crash. Mere moments afterward, their leaf wrapped itself around the mast and drove both men face first into the sail affixed to it. As far as landing after a thousand foot drop goes, it certainly could have been worse, but sailcloth is far from being an effective shock absorber.

The initial impact rattled Dungar enough, but it was a slight bump compared to the following tumble down the sail and rough landing onto the deck. After enduring that terrible touchdown, all Dungar could bring himself to do was lie still for a brief period and groan some incoherent obscenities. Thankfully, within seconds of his own difficult disembarkment onto the deck, Nobeard had hopped to his feet and began barking orders to his crew.

"Look alive, mateys! Raise the headsail, secure the boom, and man the cannons!" He then pointed at a nearby crewman who was bustling over to his station. "You, sailor! We lost our helmsman in the giant shrub ye see across the sea. Ye shall be our new helmsman now! Get up there and take us hard to starboard, we be needing to make a speedy exit!"

"But captain, I've never driven the ship before!"

"It be easy, laddy! It practically sails itself. Just don't hit any rocks or I'll kill ye."

"Mista Dungar! You're alive!" Dungar heard Jimminy yell into his ear.

With another groan, Dungar got to his feet and rubbed his head.

"Hello Jimmy." He sighed. "Did you guys have a better landing than us?"

"I'm quite alright, mate, thanks for asking! Larry's in some rough shape though. The bloke broke both his legs!"

"Jimmy, you do know that Larry just has two wooden peg legs right?"

"Oh yeah . . ."

"Oi, landlubbers!" Nobeard yelled at them. "Man a battle station!"

"What do you mean?" Dungar asked as Jimminy scurried away. "Are we not out of danger?"

"Look at the water, lad, that bubblin' be not a good sign."

Curious, Dungar peered over the side of the boat. Sure enough, the deep blue lake water bubbled as if it were boiling. Schools of fish could be seen leaping from the water and mass migrating away from the tree. He had no idea what was going on, but he didn't really want to find out either.

Having reached the helm, the pirate yanked the wheel and the ship veered sharply to the right. Various cargo began to slide across the deck as the ship tilted. Nobeard also fell over as if he wasn't expecting the sudden change in direction.

"Damn it, boy!" Nobeard yelled at his new helmsman. "I said starboard!"

"But captain, starboard is to the righ—"

"IF SOMEONE TRIES TO TELL ME ONE MORE TIME THAT STARBOARD IS RIGHT THEN THEY'RE GOING OVERBOARD."

All the bustling about halted briefly as eyes began to turn to the aggravated mariner.

"Do ye all want to die!? Get back to yer stations!"

"What's going on?" Dungar asked the captain as the rest of the pirates darted away.

"Aye, the tree isn't done with us yet, it seems. I guess it be more attached to the treasure than I initially anticipated."

The words had hardly left his mouth when several long, thin brown tentacle-like objects surfaced from the lake and began to loom dangerously over the vessel.

"What in the blazes are those things?!!" Dungar demanded.

"I've never seen me a creature that possessed appendages like those." Nobeard commented, intrigued. "If I had to place me a wager then I'd reckon those are the roots of the wizard tree, lad. Methinks it wants its treasure back."

Dungar gawked at the tree limbs that now loomed over the boat, swaying and writhing menacingly around them.

"God I hate wizards."

EIGHTEEN

WITHIN THE FATHOMS
OF THE GREAT BIG SEA

At no point in this entire excursion did Dungar feel as attached and protective of the treasure as he did now. It was an interesting feeling of possessiveness. It wasn't that he wanted the treasure, but rather he just didn't want the tree to have it. He didn't know if the feeling stemmed from his prejudices or was just plain pettiness, but it made no difference either way. His patience for magical dealings had long since run out, so he had a very hostile answer in mind for this call from nature.

"Head down to the cargo hold and fetch us some weapons, lad." Nobeard ordered Dungar. "I be about ready to go lumberjack on this wench."

Dungar couldn't have said it any better himself. He pushed his way through the scurrying pirates and towards the door leading to that familiar staircase then through the door and down into the dim and gloomy storage area. Just as he remembered, there was very little light to illuminate the room, the air instead filled with the smell of now decaying fish. But there was no time to be wasted.

Dungar began rifling through boxes looking for any weapons capable of cleaving through any attackers. The available resources were meagre at best. Most of the boxes were filled with assorted produce, raw materials, or petty loot from small-time raids. As he continued to search, Dungar found himself distracted by a faint scraping sound slowly becoming audible over the usual sounds of sailing on the sea. He also noticed the room seemed to be somehow getting even darker.

As he slammed down the lid of the crate he currently rifled through, Dungar looked around the room. The various cracks and holes in the wooden room were still present, just smaller, as if something were plugging parts of them. The scraping sound continued as he tentatively moved towards the wall to inspect it. The openings were still becoming smaller yet, almost like the walls were repairing themselves, but it was impossible to know for sure in the darkness.

"Back away from the bulkheads, lad!" The authoritative voice of Nobeard called out.

Dungar could just barely make out the pirate captain's silhouette in the room with him.

"Hold this." Nobeard ordered once again, handing an unlit torch to Dungar.

With a quick flash from Nobeard's flint and steel, the torch ignited and the cargo hold was illuminated by a faint light. The light, albeit dim, was still enough to make the walls visible. The cracks and holes were still very much present, however any light shining through them was hindered by the hundreds of slim roots forcing their way through like brown worms. They made the eerie scraping noise as they slid against the wooden wall, making their way farther inside the ship and finding things to latch onto.

"It be tryin' to stop us cold in the water!" Nobeard exclaimed.

Thinking on his feet, Dungar took the torch he held and plunged it into the writhing entanglement of the creeping roots. Hisses and sizzles were immediately heard as the plant organs began to wriggle frantically, trying to escape the flames. He continued to stick the torch into each of the entanglements until they had all retreated out of the cargo hold.

"Brilliant, lad!" Nobeard cheered. "I need ye above deck with me though, I'll send some hands down here to keep the bastards out in your stead!"

They hurried back up the stairs and onto the deck where several more of the giant roots had appeared. The entire crew was going crazy as the enormous roots swept across the deck like pendulums. Anything that wasn't affixed to the ship somehow was knocked airborne and likely overboard.

"Arm yerselves, lads!" Nobeard yelled to anyone who would listen. "It just be a tree! Fight back! Fine, don't fight back then! At least get yerselves below deck before—" His voice trailed off as he watched one of the roots wind itself around a crewman's leg, pull him off the deck, and drag him into the water.

"—that happens . . ." Nobeard finished. "Are any of the bloody cannons loaded yet?"

"Yes, captain!" A muffled voice called out through the hole left by the treasure chest.

"Then what are ye waitin' fer, ye flea bitten loon? Fire the blasted thing!"

Seconds later, the thunderous bang of cannon fire rang out from a few decks below. Dungar and Nobeard both watched with a grimace as a large cannonball shot out from beneath them, missing every tree root by at least five paces. Frustrated more than ever, Nobeard ran over to the hole in the deck and screamed into it.

"Is it too much to expect ye to aim the thing before ye fire it?!"

"But captain, you ordered us to—"

"Now I be ordering ye to shut yer flappin' gums! Fire the cannons AT the tentacles before I keelhaul every last one of ye! They be difficult targets, but I believe in ye!"

Breathing heavy from all his yelling, Nobeard got up and hurried back to Dungar.

"Those grog addled milk maids couldn't hit themselves in the face with their own fist. We need to get out of here, matey! Go tell the helmsman to head fer the Northward Passage of Doom!"

Dungar started to head for the helm, but stopped short when he realized just what Nobeard said.

"Uh, the Northward Passage of Doom? What is that?"

"Ah don't worry, lad. It be like any normal northward passage. Just, y'know, doomier."

"But what does tha—"

"No more questions, matey, just go!"

Begrudgingly, Dungar made his way across the hectic deck, ducking under the swinging tree roots and dodging the panicking sailors until he made it to the ladder leading to the helm. He quickly clambered up it and found the quivering pirate at the helm cowering behind the ship's wheel. His knees were shaking so badly that his white knuckled grip on the wheel seemed to be the only thing keeping him on his feet.

"You really don't look like you'll want to hear this," Dungar informed him forebodingly. "But the captain, er, sends orders to, er, navigate the Northward Passage . . ." His voice trailed off as he gazed into the terrified eyes of the frail sailor trembling before him. ". . . of Doom."

"Oh come on!!" The pale pirate protested. "Even a good wheelman couldn't take us through that! Why doesn't he just tell us to get off and swim?"

Dungar shrugged, sympathy had never come easy to him. He hopped back down onto the lower deck and headed back to Nobeard who was darting around the deck flailing an axe.

"Are we on course, lad?" Nobeard asked him as he sliced through a nearby tree root.

"I think so. Your designated driver didn't seem to be a big fan of the idea."

"Ah he just has no faith. The Polina can punch ahead in any gale."

Dungar cocked his head to the side curiously.

"That be the name of this vessel, lad. Did ye need anything else? Now isn't really the ideal time for chitting or chatting."

"I have meself a few questions if you don't mind, mate." Jimminy interjected, emerging from behind a pile of barrels. "Wot's the Northward Passage of Doom?"

Exasperated, Nobeard looked back and forth between Dungar and Jimminy before he sighed and lowered his axe.

"It's a wee little inlet between some sharp rocks where some unfriendly critters live. Most seafarers opt not to traverse it, but we don't have much choice."

"Huh, I see." Jimminy acknowledged. "Alright, next question!"

"WHAT?!!"

"Are you aware there's an angry lookin' beastie attempting to devour your boat, mate?"

Nobeard paused for a moment, contemplating the statement. "Well I am now!"

The captain picked up his axe and the three men hurried to the stern of the ship where, sure enough, a giant sea monster had emerged from the water and was slowly trying to draw the pirate ship into its gaping maw. The dilated pupils of its enormous glowing green bug eyes were transfixed on the vessel as the several rows of razor sharp teeth slowly drew closer. The colossal red fish was even bigger than the pirate ship, and the tough looking scales that coated its body likely rendered it more durable too. Dungar and Nobeard both gaped wide eyed at the creature, but Jimminy remained nonchalant as ever

"Bet you're glad that wasn't the fish that swallowed the key eh, mate?"

"You would be correct, sailor." Nobeard acknowledged, not taking his eyes off of the monster. "Alright, lads! I'm going to need me a hoister!"

Instantly a pair of pirates appeared with a rope which they fastened around the mast and tossed over a high wooden beam jutting out over the rear end of the ship. Nobeard made his way over to his captain's quarters, burst inside, and began rifling through his belongings, Dungar hot on his heels.

"What are you doing, captain?!"

"Somebody needs to tangle with the creature, matey. Otherwise we're all going to be fish chow."

"And how do you intend to do that?"

Triumphantly, Nobeard pulled a pair of bandoliers out of the trunk at the foot of his bed. As he removed his coat and strapped them on, he turned back to Dungar. "There be much debate regarding which is mightier between pens and swords. I meself have always preferred bombs."

Before Dungar could respond, Nobeard had darted out of the room and back to the stern of the ship where his hoisters awaited. Dutifully they fastened the end of the rope through the clasps on the captain's bandoliers, and within seconds he was hoisted in the air, dangling in front of the giant fish and swinging gracefully back and forth.

"It's a good thing ye are a sea dweller, ye slimy wastrel!" Nobeard shouted at the beast as he drew a grenade with each hand. "Because yer gonna be on an all soup diet when I'm done with ye!"

The second he finished his taunt, he hurled both bombs simultaneously into the immense jaws of the sea creature. Each bomb impacted a spot on one of the multiple rows of teeth, resulting in an explosion that splattered pulverized gum and fang in all directions. The monster roared with pain and blood continued to gush from the open wounds, but it spite-fully continued its pursuit. The bubbling water coupled with the waves sent off by the swimming monster had caused the boat to rock even more violently than before. Waves crashed against the ship, showering all occupants with a shower of sea spray as the wind howled around them reducing the air to chilling temperatures.

The Polina now neared the narrow opening of the rocky Northward Passage of Doom. Once inside, they would be out of the tree's reach. The wizard tree was surely aware of this, because the roots were starting to become more aggressive, latching onto the ship and striking crew members more frequently. Seeing the void that needed to be filled, Dungar retrieved Nobeard's axe and picked up where the captain left off; darting about the ship chopping wood like a madman. Finally, a task that he was used to.

The roots were a lot tougher than the logs he was used to splitting. The axe would become lodged in them with each swing, and it took great effort to prevent the weapon from being yanked from his grasp. The recoiling roots didn't make it any easier. Unlike earlier in the trip when he was bludgeoning fireballs, the roots soon learned to avoid him and instead attack other parts and personnel of the ship. The monster continued its pursuit as well, but with every lurch forward the ship made from a wave of water generated by the beast there was a resulting yell and explosion provided by Nobeard to keep the creature at bay.

The entrance to the passage was close now, less than a quarter of a league. The deck also looked rather empty from the crowd of sailors that had been on board when they first returned from the tree. He couldn't help but wonder if they had simply retreated into hiding, or if as many had been wiped out as it appeared.

With a final swing of his axe, and a final end lopped off of a Wizard Tree root, the pirate ship entered the rocky confines of the Northward Passage of Doom. Huffing from the exertion of the trip, Dungar lowered his axe and leaned over the side of the boat to check the status of their pursuers. It appeared Nobeard's efforts were not in vain as the backside of the ship remained uneaten.

The sea monster had pursued them all the way into the passage, but had become wedged in the narrow rocks of the entrance, effectively wedging the roots with it. The beast had almost no teeth left, the entirety of its jaws coated in a disgusting bloody pulp where the intimidating jowls once protruded. Its eyes also appeared to be virtually obliterated. Large black patches from explosions were visible on and around the eyelids that were swollen shut over each oculus. Slowly, the defeated creature sank back beneath the surface and into the lake depths.

Within moments Nobeard descended from his makeshift trapeze and met with Dungar on the deck to offer praise.

"Excellent work, lads!" He cheered at anyone who remained above deck. "We sure gave the bastards what for, eh?"

"Captain, we aren't out of danger yet, are we?" Dungar asked rhetorically.

"Ah you landlubbers are all the same, thinking a passage be dangerous just because the word doom be in the title."

"You told us yourself that it was dangerous . . ."

"Aye but it's not named over that! Y'see, lad, many a year ago when this lake was filled by the tears of the sky, the stalwart Captain Guy Doom was the first to sail its expanse. He would routinely navigate this here passage to get to and from his varying destinations until the tragic day where it is said a giant ferocious fish descended from the sky and scuttled his schooner." He stopped speaking briefly as he cocked his head to the side. "Now that I think about it, it may have been the very beastie we just fought. Hah, small sea eh?"

". . . Is any of that true?" Dungar asked.

"Couldn't tell ye, lad. Frankly I've already forgotten what I just said. The point I be trying to make is that we aren't out of danger yet!"

"What? That was the point that I was trying to make!"

"Mista Dungar," Jimminy interrupted. "Mista beardless here just informed us we're all in danger! Now's not the time to be arguing he said she said they saids!"

Dungar opened his mouth to protest, but stopped when he noticed another tentacle-like object reach over the side of the ship and affix itself to the deck using some sort of suction appendage. Noticing it as well, Nobeard quit his goofing with Dungar and turned serious again.

"They're a-comin', lads."

"Wots a-comin', mate?"

The owner of the tentacle's head now appeared over the railing. It was the most hideous thing Dungar had ever seen in his life, which admittedly wasn't saying much, but there was no other way to describe it. Its face was flat and perfectly circular, its slimy greenish brown skin gleaming in the light. A few dozen black and red eyes littered the creature's face like acne, each of which looking independently in random directions. In addition to the long pale tentacles jutting from the creature, the head also had many long, hairy black feelers that waved creepily around, touching anything within reach. As it slowly moved into the deck, a low bassy rumble could be heard over the sloshing of the creature's body.

Dungar, Jimminy, and the remaining pirate crew stood staring at the creature transfixed and unsure how to proceed. Fortunately Nobeard, always a man of action, leapt forward and booted the disgusting creature with one of his massive feet hard enough to drive it off the boat and into the rocks where gooey yellow blood splattered everywhere.

"That, me hearties, was what is known as a nopefish. They be slow-movin' critters, but they got many tricks up their sleeves. Keep 'em off the boat and whatever ye do, don't slice 'em open."

All hands were on deck now, everyone huddled in the middle tentatively surveying the narrow passage that they slowly drifted through. The Northward Passage seemed to have been carved right into a mountain. It was a narrow channel, only a few paces between the ship and the tall rock wall on each side.

The rock faces flanking them loomed menacingly like prison walls. They were a greyed blue color and had a very smooth and sheer surface, climbing up them would be all but impossible in the event the ship went down.

A thick fog hung in the air like an ominous haze. In the narrow channel wind was almost non-existent and only the current served to push the ship along its route. No one onboard made a sound; the only noises that could be heard in the silence were the labored breaths of terrified sailors and ominous creaking as the boat rocked back and forth. Every bump and jostle from the boat elicited a startled jump from the nerve addled sailors.

Three pairs of the tentacles silently emerged over the rails of the ship. Then another four as more and more fish began to siege the ship. Armed only with fear and whatever they could find, the surviving pirates charged the aquatic interlopers. A rhythm of battle cries and squelching noises could be heard as the sailors employed boxes, paddles, and other assorted pieces of metal and wood to repel the invaders.

Nobeard had disappeared below deck then re-emerged with an armful of cannonballs to throw at the fish, Jimminy wielded a large sea bass in each hand, and Dungar still possessed the axe he used to tangle with the tree roots. It was a grueling process, but their efforts were sufficient to keep the intruders at bay, at least for the time being. However, the nopefish numbers continued to grow. For every pair of tentacles Dungar severed with his axe, two more would appear over the same railing.

The battle of attrition was quite taxing on the pirates. The fish seemed like inherently easy opponents in the beginning, but their seemingly infinite numbers rendered them into a formidable force. Occasionally one of the creatures would make it up the side of the ship and close enough to reach a member of the crew. The sight of what death at the hands of a nopefish looked like is an image that will haunt Dungar for the rest of his days.

The poor sailor didn't even see the creature coming until it was too late. Chef Gurdy was the lone cook aboard the Polina. Armed only with a rolling pin and a frying pan, he gallantly stepped up to the ship's defense with everyone else. He never realized just how much of a mistake that course of action was until he found himself face to face with the red and black eyes of one of the creatures. The movements of a nopefish were slow and sluggish, but the feelers jutting from the beast's face would strike with the swiftness of a snake.

Gurdy couldn't even react as the feelers punctured his skin and bored deep inside him wherever they made contact. His screams and futile twitching as his innards were gutted served to further demoralize his shipmates. They watched in horror, helpless to save their chef lest they become victims themselves.

After the screams had silenced, and its victim fell limp, the nopefish retracted its feelers and let the perforated body of Chef Gurdy flop onto the deck. Slowly it dragged its slimy body across the deck, searching for more prey. Dungar wasn't about to let that happen though. He raised his axe high over his head and rushed at the creature.

"No, lad, don't!!" Nobeard bellowed frantically.

But his words fell upon deaf ears. Dungar was locked in on his target. Soon as he was within range he plunged the business end of his boarding axe into the cylindrical body of the nopefish. The beast immediately flopped onto the deck, dead. He removed his axe and looked around triumphantly at all the naysayers. However, they all remained gazing at him wearing terrified expressions.

". . . What?" Dungar asked tentatively.

"Oh no!" One of the pirates called out. "Not the bees! NOT THE BEES!"

Dungar watched, baffled, as two crewmen sprinted to the nopefish body and attempted to throw it overboard. But before they made it, thousands of bees erupted from the axe wound and proceeded to swarm the deck.

"Everyone into the captain's quarters NOW!" Nobeard commanded as he grabbed the petrified blacksmith by his arm and hauled him away.

The deck of the ship was in chaos as many of the seamen succumbed to panic and began swatting at the bees while others hurried over to the captain's quarters. Everything that happened during these moments was a blur for Dungar. His mind was trapped in a state of horror and bewilderment at the ramifications of his action. If Nobeard hadn't grabbed him he likely would have been left out on the deck where he could hear the cries of others.

Not a word was uttered by the dwellers of the room. The captain's quarters was a small space designed for a maximum of two people to inhabit comfortably, but there was easily ten times that crammed inside now. The sounds of the chaos outside began to die down, leaving a frightening silence as every survivor's mind imagined the scene on the other side of the door.

The defeated faces of his subordinates looked up at Nobeard solemnly. Few of them expressed much hope towards the situation at this point. Their fate was at the mercy of the vessel that housed them, and as such the burden of their salvation fell upon the shoulders of their captain.

"Alright look, lads." Nobeard spoke softly into the room. "I shall be frank with ye. I haven't any notions as to how to eradicate a nopefish infestation."

"Am I the only one wondering how it's anatomically possible to have a beehive in your belly?" Jimminy polled the group.

"Shut up, Jimmy." Everyone in the room answered in unison.

"Wow that was perfectly in sync! Did you practice that just for me?"

"If we live through this, lad, we will have ourselves a discussion on the concept of time and place." Nobeard informed Jimminy. "But fer now, I'm open to suggestions."

Everyone looked around at each other nervously.

"Anyone?"

"I have an idea!" Jimminy announced.

Groans echoed throughout the room, but no one denied him the right to speak.

"Here's wot we do. We construct an elaborate costume to disguise ourselves as being one of them! We then integrate ourselves into their society by setting up a small business to earn their trust. Through that small business we will develop a monopoly on whatever good or service that we provide. Then we will hike the prices to extortionate amounts so that they will be at our mercy! Then when they come to us begging for more manageable prices, we will all jump out and yell 'surprise'! Then beat them to death with boat paddles!"

"Wow." Nobeard commented. "I actually regret inviting outside ideas."

A crash brought the group back into reality as the boat ran into one of the rock walls.

"Who's driving this thing?!" Dungar asked, rubbing his head.

"Aw scallywags." Nobeard said as he made a realization. "I forgot to fetch the helmsman! Welp, he's probably dead now . . ."

"I'm right here." A small voice near the wall called out.

Sure enough, there the frail pirate stood, alive as ever.

"Ye abandoned yer post, sailor?!"

"Can you blame me!?"

"Eh, not really I s'pose. We're gonna need someone up there to take the left stream though."

"Wot happens if you take the right stream?"

"We'll end up sailing through a huge waterfall."

"So?"

"I don't know if you've ever seen what falling water can do to something, matey, but—"

Nobeard's voice cut off as he raised his head and his eyes lit up. "—it just might be enough to work! Dungar, you and Jaunty come with me!

"Aye aye, captain! Where are we going?" Jimminy asked

"To the helm, ye dullard. Now I want the rest of ye to get as far below deck as ye can, otherwise yer in fer the shower of yer life. Now let's get a move on."

Nobeard burst out the door with Dungar and Jimminy on his heels. The deck was infested with nopefish wriggling all over the place. There we so many that some were crawling on top of others. All of their heads turned to the door once it burst open. Nobeard punted the nearest one several feet into the air before addressing his assistants.

"To the helm, mateys!"

Kicking the occasional fish out of the way, the trio weaved their way to the helm ladder and clambered up it faster than they had ever ascended a ladder before. Dungar continued to use the blunt end of his axe to club the creatures out of the way, careful not to repeat the same mistake as last time. Before long they had cleared the helm, but the creatures continued to ascend and the fight turned into a matter of holding them off until they reached the fork in the distance.

Nobeard motioned to Jimminy. "Man the helm, lad, we'll keep the bastards at bay."

With boot and bludgeon, Dungar and Nobeard hammered the nopefishes as they crept over the banisters until the tell-tale sound of crashing water alerted them that their destination was near.

"We're en route to suicide, captain!" Jimminy called out.

"Expert steerin', lad! Let's get outta here, mateys."

After a final swing of his axe, Dungar hopped the rail with Nobeard and they landed back on the deck. They could hear the sound of the crashing falls creeping closer as they raced to the staircase leading to the lower decks below the captain's quarters. Nobeard ripped the trapdoor open so viciously it nearly came off its hinges.

"Come on, Jimmy!" Dungar bellowed to his comrade.

"I'm a-comin, mate!" Jimminy yelled back, hurrying across the deck. Agilely, he zigzagged through the crowd of nopefish, deftly hopping over outstretched tentacles and dodging feelers.

The waterfall was dangerously close now. As the ship hit the churning embroilment where the falls met the channel, brutal vibrations reverberated through the wooden ship, knocking all the men off their feet. Dungar and Nobeard had railings to hang onto, but Jimminy was not so lucky. Soon as the tremors hit the ship, his body hit the deck. He had just enough time to groan, roll over, and look up at the cascade bearing down on him.

Dungar was frozen in place as he watched it all unfold. He could see what was coming, but was powerless to stop it. The last thing he heard before the destruction hit was the sound of Jimminy's voice.

"Oh, blimey . . ."

Mere moments after the man uttered the words, a devastating torrent of water smashed onto the deck and obliterated all in its path. Dungar and Jimminy caught one last glimpse of each other before everything left above deck was crushed by the rapids.

nineteen

we'll meet again in another life ... if you believe that sort of thing

Dungar lay deep within the bowels of the ship, a half drowned mess covered in debris. Miraculously, he and Nobeard had survived however many thousands of pounds of force the waterfall delivered into their ship. If it weren't for the captain's quarters being directly above them, they likely would have been pulverized under the immense water pressure. He was rather envious of the rest of the crew, for he knew they had to have fared better than him, Nobeard, or Jimminy.

Jimminy. Of all the awful sights Dungar had seen within the last day, the image of his only friend crushed under a waterfall before his very eyes was certainly the most haunting. The phrase "no one could have survived that" was well known to be considered an example of famous last words; but much as he would like to believe Jimminy awaited him up there on that deck, Dungar knew that there was indeed no way that anyone could have survived that.

What remained of the ship was in tatters. There was a gaping hole in the main deck where Jimminy had been laying before the destruction occurred. The gap in the deck allowed the cargo deck to be flooded with light, revealing that it was now also flooded with a foot high layer of water. Assorted scrap piles of wood and shattered planks could be seen sticking out of the makeshift reservoir.

Soaked to the skin, Dungar rose from the water and ascended the staircase. The wreckage in the cargo hold paled in comparison to that of the main deck. All three masts had been torn from the ship and were long gone, as well as any sails. Both the captain's quarters and the helm too had been utterly destroyed, few traces of either remained. The bowsprit at the front was also gone, likely the first thing destroyed by the waterfall. With no sails for propulsion, and no manner with which to steer, the ship was little more than a block of wood adrift at sea.

But the damage made no difference to Dungar; it was for the pirates to worry about. His mind would not be focused on anything besides Jimminy's fate. There was no trace of him above deck or in the cargo hold. Even if by some miracle he had managed to survive the torrent, he would have been washed overboard to content with the legions of nopefish.

Nobeard was the next to surface above deck, followed shortly by whatever remained of the crew. They too surveyed the carnage with hearts as broken as their beloved vessel. The pirate captain put a hand on Dungar's shoulder as they solemnly continued to inspect the scene.

"There be no greater honor fer our kind than a death at sea, lad. Whether it be yer dear matey, or my beloved Polina. He may not have been a pirate in the strictest sense of the word, but damn if he didn't have the spirit of one. I liked that lad, and we'll all miss him too."

The words, kind as they were, offered little consolation to Dungar. His lonesome life had resulted in him cultivating his own appropriate methods of coping with loss. Those methods involved solitude and introspection, neither of which he would find aboard a vessel of post-traumatic pirates.

"I need to get off this boat. Sooner rather than later."

Nobeard was surprisingly accommodating to the notion. "I understand, lad. With the ship being the way she is, we cannot steer her to any docks. But within her lower portions there be an old lifeboat that I can row ye to shore with."

"Much obliged, captain." Dungar thanked him with the faintest sheepish smile he could muster.

Nobeard retreated into the bowels of the ship and emerged shortly afterward single-handedly carrying a small dinghy. The rails of the ship were also destroyed in the deluge, so the small lifeboat was easy to drop over the side.

"We be lackin' any lowering apparatus, matey." Nobeard explained as he handed a length of rope to some pirates. "So you'll have to trust some of the laddies to lower ye down."

Nobeard was the first to jump ship, hardly even slowing during his descent. Dungar was much more careful and meticulous about it. He'd gotten wet enough that day and would be content to avoid water for the next little while. When the two men were settled, Nobeard locked in the oars and began to row.

"Best get comfortable, matey, this will not be a short voyage."

Night had fallen by this point, and the exhaustion from the day finally started to hit Dungar. He couldn't even remember the last time he slept. He knew for certain that he hadn't gotten a full night's sleep since this whole misadventure had begun. The gentle rocking of the lifeboat and the smooth, rhythmic sounds of the paddles were starting to make him drowsy, but he wouldn't allow himself to sleep while Nobeard was rowing him somewhere.

"How're you feeling, laddy?" The pirate captain asked in a gentle tone.

"Tired." Dungar mumbled. "And rather confused about a lot of things now that you mention it."

"Well perhaps I can try to cure yer confusion?"

Dungar straightened up and faced Nobeard. The more he tried to wrap his head around the events of the day, the more questions he found himself asking. Nobeard was likely just as able as anyone else to potentially answer them.

"What exactly were the nymphs?"

"Well I already told ye. They were nothing, just figments of yer imagination."

"But if they only existed in my imagination, then how did you know about them? Everyone can't imagine the same thing."

"You would be correct, lad." Nobeard agreed. He paused for a few moments, trying to work out an explanation in his mind. "As I'm sure ye have deduced, that was not me first excursion to the Wizard Tree. I have had many. Each time one goes, they learn things. The tree, she hordes herself protectors, you see. There be many out there who seek her fer nefarious purposes. As such, she reaches into yer mind and offers you what it is ye desire most, in exchange fer fealty. Many men find beautiful women offering them naughty favors to be particularly compelling. I meself do not see the nymphs per se, but rather a different variety more to me . . . tastes if you will. As such, I figured it was a safe assumption that you would see the nymphs. Was I right?"

The blacksmith briefly pondered the question as he recalled the experience in his mind.

"Not entirely. I was greeted by the nymphs, but there were no 'favors' being offered. They offered me a banquet and hailed me as some sort of hero . . ."

At that, Nobeard began to laugh to himself. "Ah so that's yer game, ye egotistical bastard. Got yerself a hero complex. Watch out, they often lead themselves to recklessness."

"I don't know if that's really what it was, though." Dungar insisted. His voice grew softer as he struggled to find the words to express what he experienced. "It was more personal than that. They didn't just want a hero, they wanted . . . me."

Nobeard stopped his chuckling and looked at Dungar again with his cocky smile.

"Look at you eh, matey? Didn't think ye were even capable of opening up. Makes me ol' heart happy to get a glimpse at the teddy within ye."

He hadn't even realized just how much he had been sharing until Nobeard laid it out for him like that. Accusations of being a teddy were about as vile as any insult could be.

"Hardly." Dungar growled at the captain.

"Aw no need to be like that, lad. Everyone wants to be loved. Even big tough bastards like you who would never admit it. Don't worry, matey, I promise I won't think you're any less stiff and scary."

If Dungar had to listen to one more second of this he may actually consider jumping into the water and swimming for it.

"Where did the treasure come from?"

"Oh right, I never did explain that did I? Well, not that I really have all the answers anyway. The legend goes that many years ago, before Lake Deeplu even existed, the Wizard Tree stood proud at the top of a hill, just minding its own business doing tree stuff. But there was a wizard in those days that prided himself as the mightiest wizard in all the land. He made a point to challenge all other magical beings to prove his superiority. No matter how many of his thaumaturgic foes he bested though, all anyone could speak of was the insurmountable prowess of the wizard tree. So he tracked it down, not that it was particularly hard to find, and made it a point to somehow best the tree in some sort of competition. However the tree, as ye have seen, be just a tree. It is not susceptible to such mortal desires as materialistic greed or reputation and social status. As such, the wizard found himself at a loss for ways to coerce the tree into competition. For a brief time he considered simply destroying the plant, but he was just an egoist, not a savage. Finally, he settled upon a course of action. He gathered together all of his prizes and awards, every valuable artefact he possessed, and made his way deep into the twisted labyrinth of the tree. He braved all of the hazards that the plant could throw at him until he made it into the very room where we found that box. Only instead of there being a chest to take, he had brought with him a chest to leave. And he left that chest there as an open challenge to all the other wizards in the land to prove their mettle. He felt that not only had he beaten the tree by bypassing all of its defenses, but also that until his treasure was retrieved by another, he would stand as the most formidable mage in all the land."

The two men drifted in silence for a few minutes after that, each contemplating the nature of the story, trying to determine if there was even a moral to be found.

"The funny part is:" Nobeard finally spoke. "That his legacy and even his name were completely forgotten anyway, and his treasure was retrieved by a ragtag buncha dimwits using nothing but a pocket full of bombs and a reckless disregard for personal safety."

They both got a good chuckle out of that.

"That was quite the explanation." Dungar pointed out. "I thought you said you weren't an encyclopedia?"

"Aye, I am not. But I love stories. There be few things as enthralling as a tale regarding the marvelous things beyond yer imagination that lay out there in the world. How could ye not want to explore and adventure when ye are privy to the possibilities that await ye? The treasure be a perfect example. But even if ye tread out into the great wilds and come up empty handed, I challenge ye to have such an adventure where ye don't emerge enriched by the mere experience."

Nobeard smiled at him again as he finished.

"I haven't known ye long, mister Dungar. But, whether ye believe me or not, even I've seen changes in ye just within the span of our own miniature excursion together."

Introspection was much less effective when a third party is doing it for you. Dungar knew pondering any insights Nobeard had to offer while the man was still talking would be fruitless. Tuning the captain out, he looked up into the night sky and let his mind wander to how he would continue his quest without Jimminy. Whether or not the clown was still with him was only of partial consequence anyway.

He had been so preoccupied with other pressing matters throughout this trip that he still hadn't taken the time to consider just how he intended to kill the queen. According to word he had heard, the Koey making public appearances was quite rare. And even when she did, she was always surrounded by guards. It wasn't just the act of killing he needed to concern himself with either; he also had to consider the aftermath. If he were to assassinate the queen in front of a crowd of people then he would undoubtedly be thrown in a cell to rot, that is, if he wasn't executed on the spot.

He had come no closer to formulating a plan by the time he succumbed to the gentle rocking of the boat and drifted off to sleep.

"Wakey wakey, lad." The soft voice of Nobeard roused him. "Land ho."

Startled, Dungar twitched awake. The sky was still dark, but traces of dawning light could be seen creeping over the horizon. Their little dinghy was beached on a narrow sandy stretch adjacent to a sparse looking forest. A look back to the lake indicated that the pirate ship was nowhere in sight. His chauffeur must have rowed for a long time.

Wasting no time, Dungar hopped out of the boat and onto the comfortably solid and secure land where he could walk with perfect balance and not have to worry about fish sneaking up on him. He was on his own now, the reigns of his journey placed firmly into his hands. The pressure of the excursion felt even greater than ever now, no one to share the burden. Unless, of course, he could recruit someone.

"You're welcome to come along. If you want."

"Hah, oh I am, am I?" Nobeard laughed. "'Fraid not, laddy. I don't know where yer goin or why yer goin there, but my place is aboard the Polina with me crew. Them maroons would be lost without me anyway, they don't even know the difference between port and starboard!"

Dungar laughed. He didn't know the difference between them either, but it was slightly less relevant for him.

"I guess this is where we part ways then. Farewell, captain. Good luck with your, uh, boat."

"This not be a privilege I grant to many, laddy. But call me Lukey. Ye have earned it." Eyes gleaming, Nobeard tossed Dungar his flint then triumphantly stared out into the water. "And fear not, matey. For as long as there be wind on our quarter and sails flowing free then there be no finer vessel to sail this gorgeous sea!" He paused for a moment then turned back to Dungar. "Of course, the sails be currently out of commission, so catching up shan't be too difficult! Well, lad, until we sail again, fair winds to ye!"

On that, Captain Nobeard, the fearless captain of what remained of the mighty Polina, shoved off the beach and, with several mighty oar strokes, drifted off into the sunrise.

For the first time during his entire adventure, Dungar was truly on his own. His newfound independence, despite being somewhat daunting, actually felt quite comfortable to him. The decisions now fell to him, such as what route to take and pretty much nothing else. As he trudged up the hill and into the forest, he lamented to himself how overrated the concept of being the leader was if there was no one but one's self on the journey. Fortunately, his isolation was eliminated almost immediately when he reached the crest of the hill and found himself face to face with a crowd of identically dressed individuals.

As the twig underneath Dungar's foot snapped, all heads in the congregation turned and faced him. Everyone in the crowd sported a blood red robe and wore it with the hood up. In the center of the group was a large stone statue of some sort of angry looking theological creature that they appeared to be worshipping. Everyone was still for a few moments during the stare down before the mass of individuals stood up and turned to face Dungar.

"Uh . . ." Dungar began uncertainly. "I don't suppose you lot are one of them friendly groups of cultists?"

"*Jum, Jum, Jum, Jum!*" The group began to chant in deep voices.

"Uh . . . I don't suppose that means yes?"

"*Jum! Jum! Jum! Jum!*"

"Didn't think so."

The blacksmith was helpless as the horde rushed towards him, his strong arms futile against the combined might of the crowd. His struggles and kicks did little to impede his kidnapping.

"Gahhhhh!" Dungar yelled as he attempted to fight off his abductors. "Doesn't anyone in this bloody land have the decency to just leave travelers unmolested!?"

His protestations fell upon deaf ears as he was pulled away by the group. His feet dragged limply against the ground as he was hauled off to yet another unknown destination. He elected to no offer resistance this time, deciding he'd rather save his strength to crack skulls as soon as someone was foolish enough to let go of him.

None of the cultists seemed to pay him much mind. They all just marched purposefully forward, continuing their "Jum! Jum! Jum!" chant. Their feet hit the ground in unison as their robes flapped behind them. Dungar hoped against hope that it wasn't some more ridiculous magic business. He'd certainly dealt with enough of that lately.

They reached the crest of the hill they were scaling to find a small clearing filled with tents surrounding a large tree. In the tree was a shack of sorts that appeared to have been hastily built. Dungar was forced to his knees in front of it as the chants changed to "Immolate! Immolate! Immolate!"

Suddenly magic didn't seem like an inferior course of action.

Immediately a robed figure emerged from the tree house and hurried down a convenient sliding pole. The golden embroidery on his similar red robes and his prestigious abode indicated he was likely some sort of authority among these people. The chanting stopped and a hush fell over the congregation as their leader made his descent. Soon as his feet touched the ground, the man bustled over towards Dungar and the group.

"Hello, gents! Much as I have assured you I appreciate your delightful sentiments, you really don't need to kill every passer-by that we encounter!"

The cult leader's loud and cheerful voice alone would have been enough to arouse Dungar's suspicions, but the familiar uncharacteristically posh accent left little doubt in his mind. He tilted his neck upwards to find himself face to face with the patchy black goatee and beady brown eyes of his deceased sidekick.

"Oh hello, Mista Dungar! Fancy meeting you here, mate."

As was often the case when dealing with Jimminy Appaya, Dungar had no words. There were so many questions and so many conflicting emotions welling up in his throat, but so few ways to verbally convey them.

"WHAT?!?!–" was the best he could manage.

Immediately one of the cultists smacked him over the head. "Speak only when spoken to!"

"He was speaking to me!"

The cultist slapped him again.

"I said speak only when spoken to!"

". . . but you just spoke to me!!"

The same cultist backhanded him yet again then leaned in close.

"Don't make me tell you again."

Dungar looked helplessly back at Jimminy who was failing to stifle his giggling underneath his hood.

"Alright, mate, that's enough. You can leave him with me and get back to your culty business."

In an instant, Dungar was dropped to the ground and the entire herd of cultists set off back towards the statue as if nothing had happened. He growled under his breath as he got to his feet and watched the robed men unapologetically leave. But Jimminy was much more important now. The man who he had seen die before his very eyes now stood before him as solid and whimsical as ever.

"Erm. Wot are you looking at, mate?"

"What do you think I'm looking at!?!? You're dead!"

"Oh my god, I am?! Does that mean you are too? Is this the afterlife? A lot more servants than I would have reckoned to expect . . ."

Well if it wasn't Jimminy then it was certainly a convincing impression. Dungar still couldn't believe it. He had Jimminy back. The bumbling idiot had somehow resurrected himself and came back to him. Foreign feelings of relief and gratitude floated through his mind. He could feel the uncomfortable desire to hug the fellow, or shake his hand, or at least crack a bloody genuine smile.

"Just when I thought I was rid of ya." Dungar grunted with a slight frown. "I suppose you still want to come along."

Jimminy laughed as he followed Dungar northward. "I'm like herpes, mate. I may go away for a while, but you're never rid of me!"

Dungar did not respond. He just walked in silence for a few minutes hoping that Jimminy would take it upon himself to explain, well, everything. Unfortunately his cohort did not seem to consider any explanation necessary. When the man spoke it was to simply address his usual random thoughts. However rather than sigh or silence him, Dungar found himself quite content to take part in the small talk session.

"Those blokes seemed rather fond of me, I wonder if I should have at least said goodbye or something. Perhaps farewell, it seems more formal. Though, they didn't seem to have a particular affinity for formalities. Come to think of it, all they really seemed to care for was lighting blokes on fire. Boy, what an awful way to go that would be, eh? I meself was engulfed in flames once. Don't worry though, mate, I lived. I was rather thoroughly barbecued though. Slap some sauce on me and I reckon I woulda been delicious! You hungry, Mista Dungar?"

"Uh. Yeah, I suppose I could eat."

"I'd think so, big fella like you and all! Blimey, look at ya. Bet you put food away like a redbear! Curious creatures they are, redbears. I remember the first time I saw one I was all like 'whoa! That looks nothing like how I pictured it!' Right? I mean you'd think with the name redbear they'd be more . . . Ah wot am I even saying, you know what a redbear looks like. I'm a bit hungry too, mate. Those blokes loved their food stockpile, but all they ate was raw birdies. Wot kinda meal would you go for if you had a pick?"

"Hmm." Dungar grumbled as he briefly pondered the question. "Well, I suppose it's been awhile since I've had a good venison—"

"Deer meat eh! Have yourself quite the refined palette don'tcha? I tangled with the stuff once, didn't work out well. I was laid up in the infirmary for weeks!"

"Huh, is that right? It give you a parasite or something?"

217

"Well no. It beat me up and kicked me down a hill. They're some vicious buggers!"

They both laughed at that as they kept walking. The already thin forest was beginning to completely dissipate as the cultist compound disappeared behind them and out of view, yet Jimminy continued to wear the robes he was outfitted in.

"Why are you still wearing that thing?" Dungar asked him.

"It's called a diro, mate. Big shot blokes of the Dynamism religion are supposed to wear em. Er, I'm also totally naked underneath."

"Wait. You're religious?"

"Well, not particularly. But I woke up in their wee compound completely nude sometime last night and they put these robes on me and started calling me 'messiah,' whatever that means! Anyway, once you get used to them, they're quite nice company. They built me that adorable tree house, lit every poor sod we came across on fire, then you showed up! Hello!"

"Messiah . . . Jimmy, they think you're some sort of manifestation of their god!"

"Oh nonsense. They worship some horned guy named Dynam. There was a statue of him around there somewhere."

"It explains everything though." Dungar insisted. "Well, except how you ended up there in the first place. But they gave you fancy clothes and built you a bloody house, Jimmy. Why would they do that?"

"Well. Perhaps they're gracious and accommodating to weary travelers?"

Dungar stared at him blankly.

"When they found me they kidnapped me and tried to light me on fire on your behalf!"

"Perhaps you need to work on your first impressions, mate?"

"JIMMY!!!"

Things went quiet for a moment as Jimminy took a moment to actually ponder Dungar's claims. Surely even he could figure out there was something quite off about his situation.

The two men had finally cleared the sparse forest and had emerged into an immense hilly field stretching far into the distance. The bright blue cloudless sky contrasted beautifully with the verdant countryside. Copious rocky outcroppings jutted from the lush green grass and exotic flora that painted the ground vibrant colors as a cool breeze blew what almost sounded like music through the rocky formations. As Dungar took it all in, Jimminy appeared to have reached a conclusion to his conundrum.

"You know, now that you mention it, mate, there was that weird business when I was in the service."

"What's that?"

"Well, while I was in Nom I got mixed up with some rather shady characters if you will. Me and some of me mates went out one night and got throshed and sloshed. Long story short, while we were out on the town, some snooker loopy looking gent offered me three coppers to hang onto some demon soul thingy or whatever for him while he cleaned its jar or something. It's all a bit fuzzy, really. But I assure you it was nothing, mate. I do remember that there wasn't even anything in the jar. Easy three coppers for me!"

Dungar opened his mouth to respond, but then closed it and looked away instead. He realized he wasn't too sure what to believe. He couldn't decide which was a more ridiculous notion: Jimminy leaving that exchange completely unscathed, or Jimminy being possessed by evil spirits and not even knowing it.

"Er, Mista Dungar, could you perhaps grant me a favor?" Jimminy asked, snapping the blacksmith out of his train of thought.

"Will it involve getting us almost killed?"

"Most likely not."

"What is it?"

"Well, I was hoping we could make a quick pit stop before making our final push into Jenair. I'm sure your missus can wait a little while longer."

"You want to make a pit stop? Where? For what?"

"Well, you see, mate, there's a little town just a teeny tad bit out of the way." Jimminy explained as he gazed into its direction. Then he turned back to Dungar, eyes gleaming. "It's the residence of me one that got away."

TWENTY

WOMENFESTATION

It had been a long and twisted journey. Dungar had seen many sights that he could have never even fathomed. From dodging enormous snakes to escaping fire breathing cats to going on a voyage with a band of gay pirates, he had found himself enriched with all the wondrous sights and experiences that had lay beyond his comfortable home his entire life. But, even with his freshly opened mind, he could not even begin to envision the kind of woman that Jimminy would covet.

He had also never really considered his faithful sidekick in that light either. Thinking back to when they first met Herrow, Dungar didn't really notice any changes in the man's behavior. Even in the presence of a beautiful woman he continued with his shamelessly nonsensical ways without so much as an attempt to impress. This lady that he had waiting wherever they were going must be quite a catch.

"Just remember we're on a schedule, Jimmy." Dungar reminded him as they strode through the rainbow meadow. "We can't stay long."

"Of course, mate! I just wanted to say me hellos. Blimey it's been so long since I've seen me beloved. I hope she's well."

Dungar couldn't resist. He was too curious. "What did you mean by she got away?"

Jimminy sighed and stayed quiet for a few moments before responding. "A guy like me couldn't hang on to a woman like that, mate. How could a bloke like meself possibly contend with the hordes of fellows who wanted her? She would remind me all the time too just how lucky I was to have her too. Every day she'd come home to me over all the other mates she had pawing at her. Silly me had to blow it all. I hope she can forgive me."

"That's . . . actually kinda sad, Jimmy."

"Ah like I said, mate, it's me own fault. Couldn't expect a lady like her to stay with a man who wasn't good 'nuff for her. But we'll see about that once I go see about her!"

Dungar regretted asking. With all of Jimminy's wacky antics and his eccentric approach to the world, he had expected a rather unorthodox story rather than an answer that was so . . . human.

The wind continued to whistle its soothing melody through the rock formations as the two men wandered their way through the rocky fields. But it was more than a gentle nature sound. Each rock seemed to tune the breeze to different notes, turning each gust into true music.

"Do you hear that, Jimmy?" He asked his friend. He didn't actually care about the answer, he just wanted to change the subject.

"Course I do, Mista Dungar, it's the windsong of the Star Fields."

"Star Fields?"

"Yeah, this here grassy and flowery business that you're tromping with your big ol' tootsies!"

". . . What?!"

". . . The field that we are currently walking in is called the Star Field, mate. And blimey you have big feet for a short fella!"

"Oh. I see."

"Yup! Y'see, it is said that the goddess Suola has taken this here land as her personal garden. She used her goddess-y magic to keep the baddies out and tended it into this pretty meadow. And at night all the flowers glow a reflection of the constellations so she can see what her home looks like."

"Hm. How poetic." Dungar grunted uninterestedly.

"And did you know the song actually has lyrics?"

"Is there any possible way I can get you to not sing them?"

But there was not. Completely ignoring Dungar's protest, Jimminy began to belt out in his tone deaf voice his familiar tune that was not even close to the rhythm of the windsong.

> *Way hey and away we explore*
> *Gonna see the woman I adore*
> *Then we'll find the queen and give her what for!*
> *A way hey and away we explore!*

A small walled community could be seen in the distance now, maybe a ten minute walk away. It was a scenic looking community with cobblestone streets that matched the walls and overlooked the colorful meadows. From its idyllic appearance, and the faint smell of freshly baked bread that wafted from it, the town gave off a very peaceful feel.

"Behold, mista Dungar, the town of South Redspring Starmoor. Or SRS for short."

Thunder crashed somewhere in the distance as he said that, even though the sky was cloudless.

The two men's feet left the soft mushy meadow ground for the hard stone paving as they entered the town. There appeared to be one main road that carved right down the middle with occasional side alleys jutting out of it. The neat cobblestone paving wasn't the only stark difference between this place and Woodwall. Unlike Dungar's home town where all buildings were the same shade of palm tree wood, each building in the town was expertly painted beautifully contrasting colors with great attention to detail. In fact, attention to aesthetic was evident all over. From the hand painted signs of the shops to the neatly swept sidewalks, this was a very pretty place.

"Excuse me, m'dear!" Jimminy called out to a portly yet pleasant enough looking middle aged woman who had just stepped out of the bakery. She hadn't noticed them during her exit, so Jimminy reached over and tapped her shoulder before she could walk away. "'Tis a bit of a longshot, but do you perhaps know a—"

His inquiry was cut off when the woman turned around and, upon seeing the two men, screeched an ear shattering scream loud enough to drop Dungar into the fetal position.

"Blimey. That was quite a sound you made just now—"

He was cut off yet again by another banshee wail from the woman.

"JIMMY! WHATEVER YOU'RE SAYING, STOP SAYING IT!" Dungar yelled through plugged ears.

"I DON'T KNOW WOT I'M SAYING!!" He screamed back, hands now over his ears.

"AMBASSSADORS OF THE PATRIARCHY ARE HERE TO RAPE AND OPPRESS US!!!" The woman yelled at the top of her lungs.

At that moment, Dungar and Jimminy realized something about the people moving about the street. There was not a single man among them. Immediately similar shrieking and cries for guards echoed through the streets. Within moments a detachment of women armed with swords and chain mail tore around a corner and confronted the duo. Immediately the bewildered men raised their hands high over their heads.

"Er . . ." Jimminy stuttered to the intimidating looking ladies. "I don't suppose any of you know a—"

This time he was silenced by a metal clad fist cracking him in the face. The guards did not say a word to either one of them. Instead they silently ushered them at sword point towards a brick building at the far end of one of the alleys.

As the party stepped inside, the building was revealed to be none other than a makeshift prison. There was a small cell tucked in the corner that contained nothing but a canvas bed-roll and a shallow hole in the ground. The rest of the building was empty save for the decrepit table and stool where a guard likely sat. Due to the lack of maintenance present, it was likely a safe assumption this room didn't often have inhabitants.

As Dungar and Jimminy were ushered into the cell, one of the guards turned to the others to give instructions.

"Check the perimeter for any others, and notify Lady Dubya to come immediately. Tell her that we have . . . guests."

Wasting no time, the entire detachment hurried out the door to carry out their assigned duties, leaving Dungar and Jimminy alone in jail. Again.

"Blimey!" Jimminy called out. "That's her!"

"Come again?"

"They said Lady Dubya, mate! That's her last name! Don't worry, mista Dungar, once she comes down here I'll get this all straightened out!"

Despite Jimminy's assurances, none of this sat well with Dungar. He couldn't even figure out why they had been locked up in the first place. The other times he was taken against his will were by corrupt individuals, but this time it was as if he had broken some sort of law. He had been in the town less than thirty seconds, so the question became what could they possibly think he had done?

Jimminy was in a great mood now that he knew his beloved was on the way.

> *Way hey and away we're jailed*
> *Our crucial quest briefly derailed*
> *Here we'll sit 'til we are bailed*

A way hey and away we're jailed.
EVERYBODY!

A few minutes later, some guards reappeared and unlocked the cell.

"The Lady is on her way as we speak. Out, both of you."

Happy that time wasn't being wasted; Dungar obligingly got to his feet with his cellmate and strode out the door at the behest of the guards. Outside there were at least ten more of the armor clad women waiting for them. The formed a semi-circle around the two prisoners before forcing them to their knees.

"Hands on your heads, dicks!" One of them called out. "If you make a move I will not hesitate to cut you down! Stay still, quiet, and wait for the Lady to come."

With no alternate options, the men complied with the orders given and obediently waited. In a town as small as this, surely it couldn't take more than a few minutes to arrive no matter where one started from.

Time began to stretch and the minutes began to multiply as they knelt there. Occasional coughs could be heard from the guard detachment, but not a sound was made by anyone including Jimminy. The man likely did not want to do anything that could jeopardize his reunion. Impatience within the group began to mount as well, as occasional confused murmurs and sighs indicated Dungar was not the only one experiencing it.

After almost an hour and a half had passed, although it was difficult to be sure in their position, something caught their attention. The ground began to shake. Terrified flocks of birds burst from the trees and dark brooding clouds rolled menacingly over the skies as an amorphous mountain of flesh slowly trundled towards them. It's perfectly spherical body heaved up and down in tandem with its labored breaths, and every few feet it had to pause for a short rest supported by the unfortunate souls tasked with escorting it. Whoever it was, they were truly enormous. And having lived his life with emdeema addicts, Dungar knew truly enormous. Or at least he thought he did before today. Packing on some pounds was one thing, but this person was inhuman.

After several more painstaking minutes of repeating that process, the beast had finally reached her destination and Dungar could get a better look at this overlord. Her eyes could not be seen from under the fatty folds dangling over them. All that could be seen of her face under her greasy brown hime cut and excessive overhanging adipose tissue was a gaping mouth noisily sloshing up and down as she crudely ingested the massive turkey leg in her hand.

At this point Dungar realized why they were taken outside to meet her. There was no way she could have fit through the doorway into the prison. What she wore could only be described as a royal sized table cloth draped carefully over her globular girth and affixed in place by a worn looking belt that was hanging on for dear life. The bright white color of her chosen attire did not flatter her in the slightest.

"Bibi, my darling!" Jimminy exclaimed, hopping to his feet. The guards reacted like lightning to subdue him.

Bibi drew in a long breath, swallowed the massive amount of food in her mouth, then sneered in a hoarse, nasally voice. "What do you want?!"

The smell hit Dungar before the words had time to register. A putrescent mix of curdled milk and rancid chicken wafted from her mouth and sent him into a fit of dry heaves. Jimminy, however, seemed completed unfazed.

"Don't you remember me, my dear? We lived together!"

Bibi's chins quivered as she conversed disinterestedly with her prisoner.

"Uh. Yeah . . . Jerry, or something."

"It's Jimmy, actually!" The ecstatic Jimminy corrected, happy to be making headway. "I was in the neighborhood and I just wanted to see you!"

"What did you bring me?"

Jimminy paused briefly, a little confused by the question.

"Er, nothing. I didn't have anything to bring. Oh blimey, Bibi, I'm so sorry! How could I be so thoughtless."

"I'm a lady, Jummy!" Bibi shamelessly admonished him as she removed an entire pie from a flap in her dress and began eating chunks of it with her hands. "You ain't gonna win over a real woman like me if yuh don't even get her no gift!"

"Of- of course not!" Jimminy stammered, looking around nervously. "If you give me just a few moments I can go pick your loveliness a lovely bouquet of flowers from the Star Field!"

"FLOWERS!" The incredulous blob screamed. "Oh, because I'm girl you think you can just tide me over with flowers! How dare you make assumptions about me based on my gender!"

Dungar couldn't take anymore. He did not care how much misplaced affection Jimminy had for this woman, her mere presence made his skin crawl.

"You threw us in jail for nothing more than being men!" He snapped.

The beating he received for his words was well worth enduring.

"That's different!" Bibi snapped right back. Slowly, both for the pause in conversation and due to her being unable to move any faster, the hefty woman waddled towards him and sized him up with a pronounced lower lip. "By being a man you are a potential rapist and murderer and I need to protect my girls!"

The blacksmith was struck dumb by the accusation, for he was amazed that such ridiculous claims had been made with such fervor.

"You . . . You can't be serious . . . There are people that actually think that?"

"You bet your ugly beard I do!" The town Lady snarled. "We're strong independent women who don't need no men strutting around thinking they can snu-snu as they please!"

The combination of eating the pie and giving the speech had caused her to start sweating and breathing heavily, so she paused for a moment to catch her breath and scarf down the remainder of the pie. As she finished, she threw down the pie tin and screamed.

"GO GET ME FLOWERS, JERRY!"

Instantly Jimminy jumped to his feet and tore in the direction of the flower fields. Dungar immediately took off after him, unwilling to remain in the hands of the psychotic women any longer. He caught up to his frail friend just as they made it to the town entrance.

"What in the blazes was that?!?!" Dungar demanded as soon as they slowed.

"I have no idea wot I was thinking, mate!" Jimminy insisted. "Why would I tell her to call me Jimmy? I hate being called Jimmy. But I can't ask her to stop now!"

"What?! No, not tha—never mind. Let's get out of here."

"Wot do you mean, mate? I gotta pick her some flowers."

"Wait, you're actually doing that? Why?!"

"Because she wants flowers!"

Dungar opened and closed his mouth several times before he thought better of trying to reason with him. Jimminy on a normal day was nonsensical enough, this love-struck persona of his made him doubly hard to deal with.

Whistling to himself as he labored for his love, Jimminy dove enthusiastically into the flower fields and began putting together as varied and colorful a bouquet as he could manage. Meanwhile, Dungar paced idly through the field trying to decide on a course of action. He wanted nothing more than to simply take off and make for Jenair, it was so close now, but his partner insisted on staying put until further notice.

He furled his brow as he glanced back to Jimminy. Dungar was no genius in the ways of love, but even he could see what was happening here. His distaste towards his friend's taste in women didn't stem from aesthetics, much as his personal preferences certainly differed, but rather the clear abusive implications from their short introduction. If his skinny friend puts himself forth as a willing manservant, then she will undoubtedly take him in to squander his affection as she pleases until she gets bored of him. Unfortunately, they didn't have that kind of time.

'There we are!' Jimminy called out as he straightened up with a fist full of flowers. "Wot do you think, mista Dungar? A classy corsage if I ever did see one!"

"Looks like a handful of flowers, Jimmy." Dungar dismissed disinterestedly, head still deep in thought.

"Well, back to town, then! My dear Bibi is gonna love this!"

Begrudgingly, Dungar followed his friend back into town. Naturally, the town Lady and her ensemble hadn't moved far in their absence.

"Jimmy!" The woman called out excitedly, struggling to spin her enormous frame in his direction. "There you are! You know I didn't mean anything I said earlier. Teehee, you know I get moody when my blood sugar is low!"

"Of course, darling!" The poor whipped fellow conceded. "Here's your flowers, my dear. As you can see, I made sure to fill it with your favorite colors! See, there's purple and blue and—"

"Yeah yeah that's wonderful." Bibi acknowledged dismissively. "Say, you should come see where I'm living now! Maybe I'll even give you the exclusive tour. Teehee. Nothing but the best for little old me."

Dungar snorted at the proposition. This woman was about as little as Jimminy was mentally sound.

"I would love that, dear!" Jimminy exclaimed, wrapping his bony arm around her bulging, inflated limb.

"And YOU!" She snapped at Dungar before the left. "You can wander free. But my girls got their eyes on you! We know all your tricks!"

She turned back to Jimminy the duo toddled slowly down the road towards the biggest house on the block, leaving the carefully picked bouquet sloppily strewn all over the street. A few of the guards offered the blacksmith sheepishly sympathetic looks, but all went their separate ways as soon as the town head departed.

Dungar weighed his options. He briefly entertained the idea of putting the large lady out of her misery, but that would just create more problems than it would solve. Not to mention being entitled and bigoted wasn't quite grounds for committing murder. This left him with plan B, finding a place to get a drink.

The town of South Red whatever was far from big. However there was little aid in terms of navigation. Most of the residents probably knew the town backwards and forwards, and, due to their less than stellar policy regarding visitors, it was safe to assume that the town did not pride itself on being foreigner friendly. Still, a town populated exclusively by women was an interesting notion to Dungar. So while he waited out the current fiasco unfolding, he may as well have a look around.

The landscaping in town was immaculate. There were flower beds everywhere, each one densely filled with a plethora of pink flowers and no weeds in sight. Many of the buildings also had pink paneling, as well as pink lettering in their signs. There was pink all over. In addition to the pink saturation, all buildings seemed to be equipped with small mirrors that were always at head level for some reason.

The most prevalent aspect of the town did not become apparent until after Dungar began to inspect the buildings themselves. There were bathrooms absolutely everywhere. There did not seem to be a single spot within the city limits where one was not within ten paces of a lavatory. Not only was every shop equipped with one, but there was also at least one stand-alone bathroom building on every block. They were the fanciest lavatories he had ever seen as well. Having no notion of the concept of plumbing, the elaborate and intelligent system that the women had designed to eliminate waste was so intricate that he just assumed magic was involved.

When he finally endeavored to explore the shops, he had the jarring realization as to just how far out of his comfort zone he was. He was no stranger to intoxication, but the aromas that assaulted the senses each time he dared enter one of the forsaken buildings was like nothing he had ever experienced. Once he finally managed to peel open his watery eyes, he found it was filled to the brim by what could only be described as girly things. Bath salts, purses, perfumes, nail polish, make-up, jewelry, and bizarre torturous devices apparently intended to be worn on one's feet; there were so many different kinds.

There were also scented candles, scented soaps, scented tissues, scented towels, scented inks, even scented paper, which the women seemed to have invented a neat liquid form of. Virtually any everyday object that one could think of they managed to reproduce and sell with a funky bouquet. Ironically, the only thing that didn't seem to come scented in this town was their other chief export, clothing. Having never even heard of the concept of fashion, he entered and subsequently left a number of effeminate yet potentially bar sounding names like "Vicky's Mystery," "Cocoa's," and "Lilylimes." When he saw a building labelled "haute couture" he thought perhaps he at least found somewhere that'd serve coffee, but left disappointed yet again upon realizing it was just another girl word for clothes. However, willing to give credit where credit was due, he had to admit that the paper bags they provided to transport purchases were a pretty neat invention.

With only one building left on his current block, he figured he'd might as well check it out. As he gingerly poked his head through the door, hand on nose and eyes narrowed, he found the building to be stocked not with feminine wares, but shelves and shelves of books. He lowered his hand and straightened up to look around. Books had never been a favorite pastime of his, but even he could find something inherently magical about so many stories available in such close quarters. He wished he could show Nobeard.

"Hey!" A perky voice called out from somewhere in the room.

"Please don't start screaming." Dungar muttered with a sigh as he searched for the voice.

"You're that man guy that everyone's talking about!"

The voice came from a young lady sitting at a table who looked to be in her mid-twenties. She had long flowing brown hair held in place by a thin gold headband that gave her a rather angelic appearance. Her bright eyes were such a light blue that they almost looked white like her pale skin that contrasted felicitously with her bright red smiling lips. She appeared to be friendly enough, but appearances have been known to deceive.

"Well, you're not wrong." Dungar acknowledged, still looking around. "What is this place?"

The girl appeared to be confused by the question.

"Uh. It's a library . . . ?"

"I'm not familiar with that lingo."

"You don't know what a library is?"

"No."

She seemed to find the notion to be absolutely bewildering.

"It's a place where books are kept!" She informed him enthusiastically, getting up from the table. She was a lot taller than he had expected, taller than him in fact. Her slender build and long legs served to enhance it further. As she made it over to him, she studied him with palpable curiosity.

"That thing on your face . . . Is that a beard?"

". . . Is that some kind of trick question?"

"No no. I've just never seen one before. I've read about them in books, I just pictured them to be much . . . er . . . uglier."

Dungar raised an uncomfortable eyebrow then turned his attention back to the shelves.

"This is where books are kept . . . These are all your books?"

"No no." She said with a laugh. "These aren't mine. They're, well, everyone's."

"You mean anyone can just walk in here and take these?"

"Well, yeah."

Her initial curiosity began to fade into mild trepidation. Sensing this, Dungar opted to change the subject before he alienated yet another resident.

"Why did people in town lose their minds when they saw Jimmy and me?"

"Well most of us haven't ever really met men before. And we've heard, er, bad things."

Dungar furled his brow and clenched his fists. He felt he had a fairly good idea as to who these bad things were heard from. The girl grimaced and sneakily backed away in reaction to the blacksmith's change in demeanor.

"What are you doing?" He asked, confused.

"Uhh, I remember reading somewhere that when encountering an aggressive animal one should bare their teeth, maintain eye contact, and back away slowly?"

Dungar sighed.

"Look." He said in as calm and friendly a voice as he could manage, which still wasn't particularly calm or friendly. "I don't know what you think you know, but don't believe everything you hear. I don't know if you're familiar with it, but there's this thing people do called lying—"

"I know what lying is!" She interrupted. She continued to smile at him in spite of his condescension. "But I don't know what I think I know though. Whoa, that kinda rhymed! I've spotted quite a bit of conflicting information between what I've been told and what I've read." She began rummaging through the massive pile of books on her table, muttering to herself about testosterone and beards.

"Ah, here it is! Says here that you're typically taller, more muscular, have larger hands and feet, and have deeper voices than women." She looked him up and down studiously. "Well, seems like you are most of that."

Dungar had no response; he just stared at her with a mostly expressionless face.

"You have very crazy eyes . . ." She added uncomfortably in a soft voice.

"So I've been told." He agreed, returning to his pacing. "And I'm more interested in what you've been told. Clearly the popular opinion on men around here didn't come out of that book in your hand."

"Oh. No it did not."

The room went quiet for a moment. Dungar stopped his pacing and looked back towards the table. The girl's eyes were still transfixed on him, but she didn't seem to want to answer the question.

"Okay look I get it, men are bad. Or something." He grunted, running a hand through his beard."

"Well you can't be all bad!" She offered quickly. "I mean hey! You've been in here almost ten minutes and you haven't raped me!"

Dungar turned back to her with another raised eyebrow.

". . . yet?" She added, smile weakening.

"I'm not a bloody rapist!"

"Oh. Well that's good."

The blacksmith let out another exasperated sigh as he slumped into a chair at a table of his own and put his face in his hand.

"My name's Rose!" The girl informed him happily in her perky voice. She flipped open another book and began turning pages. "I looked it up a while back. It means pretty flower!"

"A rose is a kind of flower . . ." Dungar mumbled into his hand, not looking up.

"Really? Oh Suola that makes so much more sense!"

He mumbled something incoherent as acknowledgement, clearly not interested. Rose continued to look at him curiously while twiddling her thumbs and making popping noises with her mouth before piping up yet again.

"What's your name? Men have names right?"

"Dungar."

"Dungar . . . Dungar . . . You ever fight marbalts?"

He perked up at the remark, but before he could respond the door to the library burst open and two guards came in.

"You! Prisoner! The town Lady has demanded your presence. Come with us now."

"Damn it, Jimmy . . ."

TWENTY ONE

IT AIN'T OVER 'TIL THE FAT LADY CRIES

Dungar, unsurprisingly, was not much of a ladies man. He had always been content enough with his reclusive lifestyle that he'd never really needed to mingle with the creatures much. Still, even in lieu of receiving much affection from them, he never harbored prejudice. Regardless of age, weight, or gender, he lived by his stalwart "live, leave me alone, and let live" policy, even having no real opinion on those with radical views so long as they didn't endanger or impose them upon him. However, despite his penchant for neutrality, he couldn't help but notice dealings with women hadn't been working out for him very well lately.

He couldn't even fathom how Bibi managed to become the leader of this town in the first place, let alone why the rest of the residents put up with it. The town seemed to function well enough and perhaps even thrive under her sweaty rippling tutelage. However it was unclear if such prosperity was achieved because of her or in spite of her.

Regardless, her lemming guards appeared more than willing to carry out her wishes and now he was stuck being forced into an audience with her. Wordlessly, Dungar complied with their instructions and accompanied the guards out of the library while Rose silently watched. Most of the trip to the queen bee's house was rather uneventful. No friendly banter was shared between any members of the party. It was only when another voice was heard that things got a little more interesting.

"SPIDER!!!" A voice shrieked off in the distance at a volume somewhere between deafen and kill.

Immediately every single woman on the street erupted into a full blown panic attack. Arms went into the air and screeches were screeched as everyone lacking a Y chromosome began scanning the ground in a terrified hurry to locate the creature and avoid encountering it. Eventually a void had formed in the horrified mob, a perfect circle of ladies yelling, pointing, and hopping up and down hysterically as the tiny bewildered arachnid slowly inched in Dungar's direction.

As the miniscule creature reached him, Dungar shrugged and stomped it with his boot. Immediately the panic and fear turned to mirth and celebration as all the women cheered then proceeded to pick up any dropped or thrown items and carry on with their business as if nothing had happened. The guards seemed a little embarrassed as they slowly returned to their escorting duties. From her pocket, one of them produced two gold coins and handed them to the blacksmith.

"Here."

"What are these for?" He asked curiously before he'd take them.

"It is protocol to reward anyone who kills a spider in our town."

Dungar was struck dumb by the statement. Two pieces of gold for the life of one measly spider that posed a threat to nobody. If this town was more male-friendly he would seriously consider relocating here. He could make a killing doing pest removal.

Eventually they made it to what he could only assume was Bibi's house. There was an absolutely enormous doorway, the likes of which Dungar had only ever seen on a barn. What the house lacked in height it certainly made up for in width, not unlike the individual housed inside. It appeared to be the equivalent to a three story building if each floor was removed and placed on ground level next to each other. He couldn't imagine how she utilized all that space.

"Alright, she is waiting for you inside." One of the guards instructed as she and her partner stationed themselves at the entrance.

"How can she afford a place like this?!" He inquired, flabbergasted.

"Her parents left it to her." She explained nonchalantly. "They left her the whole town. The Dubya family has run the town of SRS for generations."

"Generations? How can you have more than one generation if the town is all women?"

"It hasn't always been this way. The town has always been predominantly women. But when she took over about fifteen years or so ago, Lady Dubya ordered the execution of her THREE rapists." She glared at Dungar as she looked him up and down. "Since then we haven't allowed you savages within our walls. Now go, our lady is waiting."

"Can't wait." Dungar mumbled as he pushed open one of the double wide doors and lumbered into the lair. Immediately his nostrils were assaulted by the putrid aroma of mold. From floor to ceiling the room he entered was piled with what could only be described as junk. The stacks of broken chairs, albeit fitting, could not be judged as they reminded him of home. However the furniture heaps were interlaced with old rotten food, dirty dishes, dirty clothing, rat droppings, and, most of all, dust. There was a thick coat of dust on everything in sight as if the room had not been cleaned since its construction.

Clearing his throat so he could breathe through his mouth, Dungar followed the pathway that was helpfully carved in the detritus. It was a shot in the dark, but seemed to be his best bet to locate her. Entering the next room, he found it to be filled not only with more of the same rubbish and filth but also the sound of movement, indicating there was something else in there with him.

"Oh hello, mista Dungar!" Jimminy greeted, emerging from a part of the pathway that was blocked by a garbage hill. "Wot brings you to our neck of the woods?"

"Your girlfriend wanted to see me." Dungar informed him worriedly.

"Oh is that right? That's good. I was hoping you two would get along! I meself was just off to the Star Fields. Me sweet Bibi said she loved me last bouquet and wanted another."

"Jimmy, she didn't even take the last one you gave her. She left it behind when you two walked away."

"Well then that's probably why she wanted another! You're a clever bloke, mista Dungar."

"That's not what I'm saying at all!"

They stood in silence for a moment just staring at one another. Jimminy's usual optimistic smile had weakened a bit as he read the visible distress on the blacksmith's face. Dungar inhaled deeply, coughing a bit on the smell, before he resumed trying to reason in a calmer voice.

"Look, Jimmy, I know she has the troubled past and I guess that might help to explain why she is the way she is. But don't you at least think it's possible that she's just using you? I mean I don't give a damn who you love or if you want to get hurt or anything. It's just . . . Y'know, the mission. I don't want you to get needlessly side-tracked."

Jimminy silently mulled over Dungar's statement as he thoughtfully ran his hand over his goatee. It seemed like an eternity before he finally spoke again.

"Mista Dungar, I know that Bibi can seem a little rough around the edges. And perhaps I'm just blinded by how unbelievably hot she is, but I cannot help how I feel for her. I'm happy just to be around her, I'm made happy by how sure I am that deep down she feels the same way about me, and I can't remember the last time I met anyone else that made me feel this way. I know that not everyone will see her in the same light that I do, but I'm sure even a great bloke like yourself is disliked by some. I hope you can bring yourself to understand."

Dungar stood silently taking in everything his friend just said. He had no response, he wasn't even sure what he thought anymore. He knew how he felt and he knew how he should be feeling, and mediating between the two was never easy. Fortunately Jimminy did not wait for a response.

"Anyway, mate. I should go pick some lovelies for me lovely. Be back in a jiff!"

Familiar cheeky smile back on his face, Jimminy strode past him and off towards the entrance, agilely hopping over piles of trash.

Now alone in the room, Dungar tried to collect his thoughts. He still couldn't bring himself to eliminate any of his contempt for Lady Dubya, but, painful as it was to admit, his friend did raise a valid point. Whether or not she truly was wicked, as long as she made Jimminy happy then maybe it was no one's business besides the two of theirs.

He wasn't sure why he resumed delving deeper into the disgusting den after that. Perhaps something subconscious drove him to, or perhaps he never took the second to think better of it, but before long he found himself walking into the room at the end of the wretched passage. As he opened the door he discovered the origin of the offensive odor.

The stench permeating the room was positively fetid. Even breathing through his mouth couldn't keep him from doubling over. Nothing could have possibly prepared him for what lay inside. There were food remnants absolutely everywhere one could look. Some of it was still its original color, much of it was not. There was no attempt at cleanliness or organization either. The entire layout appeared to have resulted from lefto-vers simply being tossed to the side and left to go rancid. The sound of tiny scurrying paws indicated the local vermin had decided to capitalize on this horrific squalor shrine.

But then there was the elephant in the room, and the fact she had squeezed her enormous body into what appeared to be a teddy, although much of it was hidden beneath rolls of doughy flesh. Cottage cheese could not even begin to describe her complexion. The parts of her that weren't covered in sauce so white and lumpy it almost looked like she had melted into place while striking her unnerving attempt at a provocative pose.

"Hey there, big boy. Your turn." She cooed at the black-smith who was now frozen in place.

Dungar had found himself at a loss for words many times over the course of this adventure, but in this particular situa-tion he was so surprised, confused, and revolted that he may have actually blacked out for a moment. A brief muffled chok-ing sound was all he could muster.

"I'm glad you could accept my invitation for some alone time." She spoke seductively, rolling over flat onto her back.

Dungar remained motionless. His mind was blank, his body was fixed, and his senses had shut down to protect them-selves from further harm. Bibi did not seem to register his reluctance and continued with her efforts to entice.

"Come here, mister manly man." She whispered, using one of her swollen sausage-like fingers to beckon him while wiggling her tongue around.

Dungar's mind had now come back online, and the first thing he noticed was his eyes had glazed over. He quickly shook his head and refocused his attention before she mistook them for doughnuts and attacked. Reeling from her audacity, he briefly fantasized about how one flick of his flint and steel could turn her into a raging grease fire before he retorted.

"Are you out of your mind?"

The shocked stack of cellulite displayed impressive physical strength when she hauled her rippling self upright in the bed. Clearly she had not been expecting this response.

"I SAW YOU LOOKIN' AT MY CURVES!" She screamed back, her mighty mane of blubber wobbling as she yelled.

"You're mistaken." He informed her in a calmer tone, regaining his composure. On that, he turned to leave the room, but the Lady was not done with him yet.

"If you don't make love to me I'll have you executed!"

He froze in the doorway then slowly turned around.

"That's right." She informed smugly, casually inspecting her nails with a malicious smile on her face. "Don't think I won't. I already have a buncha times, and it has been awhile since I reminded my girls about the dangers of men. Fear helps keep them in line, y'know?"

Just like that he had the chilling answer to all the questions floating around in his mind. He could only wonder how many men had been scared into stiffness from this tactic of hers. But before he got to weigh his options he had a realization that made the decision quite easy.

"I'd rather die."

"YOU'RE NOT A REAL MAN! REAL MEN LIKE GIRLS WITH CURVES! REAL MEN KNOW THAT REAL BEAUTY IS BURIED INSIDE! YOU'RE JUST A SHAL-LOW BASTARD WHO ONLY LIKES SKINNY BITCHES! YOU JUST HATE ME BECAUSE I'M FAT! YOU'RE NOT A REAL MAN LIKE JIMMY! HE KNOWS HOW TO TREAT A PROPER LADY LIKE ME RIGHT! HE'LL DO ANYTHING I WANT."

Turning back around, Dungar stomped over to the bed and used one of his monstrous hands to grab her jiggling jaw as he roared:

"HIS NAME IS JIMMINY!"

Now it was Bibi who was frozen in place. Her eyes were so wide that they could actually be seen under their fat folds, and they were fearfully frozen in Dungar's commanding gaze. Using all of his strength, he threw her back down into the bed then leaned in close while pointing a menacing finger at her.

"Now I was content to let him be happy with whoever he wanted, but seeing the kind of vile human being that you are I now know that could never happen with you. He has thrown himself at your feet and you're comfortable to just kick him around until he outlives his usefulness, knowing all the while he will just blame himself for everything like he did last time. I don't hate you because you're two tons worth of lard, I hate you because you are a selfish, entitled, manipulative, and evil woman, and anyone who might have ever loved you was wrong. I am not letting my friend spend another second here with you even if it means I have to drag him out of here against his will."

In all his life, Dungar had never said anything that awful to another person, and the greasy tears welling up in her eye sockets indicated his words had hit home. But there had been many firsts on this trip, and he had never met anyone more deserving of those words than Lady Bibi Dubya. In fact, he decided while he was at it he may as well go for broke.

"And even if I did want to find this beauty that you claim is buried deep down, I'd need an excavation team and about six lifetimes' worth of digging."

At that, the sobbing began. But frankly Dungar had felt worse for the bed than for the blubbering woman lying in it. He had never felt less sympathy for anything else. Bad idea as it was to say, he had meant every word. Maintaining tact and rationale in the face of threats was a skill he needed significantly more practice in. Calmly, he stood up and proceeded for the door. He was then stopped one last time by one last yell amid the sniffling.

"I'M BIG BONED!"

"BONES DON'T JIGGLE!" He fired back over his shoulder.

As he rounded the corner, he stepped up to a much brisker pace. He knew there were definitely going to be ramifications for the events that had just transpired, but if he was quick enough he may be able to make it out of town before they were upon him. An ear piercing shriek from the bedroom determined that he would have no such luck.

Within seconds he found himself tackled to the ground by his armor-clad escorts. One held him at sword point while the other quickly ran to check on Bibi.

"HE . . . HE RAPED MUH!" The ham planet managed to blurt out amid the tears and sobbing. Her freshly shattered emotions helped make her lie more convincing. This was certainly not good; the fiery eyes of the guard looming over him indicated they bought every word of the sniffling lady's story.

As the other guard returned, Dungar was hauled to his feet and his wrists shackled. Shortly afterward, his rotund accuser emerged from the bedroom wearing a tent-sized robe. Her thick painted-on makeup was now running down her cheeks with her oily tears. The look she was currently giving him was a clear sign that her brief spell of sadness had made the transition to anger.

"Take him to the Den of Disposal!" She snapped, smearing her makeup further as she tried to wipe it.

Obedient as ever, the guards ushered Dungar out the door, onto the street, and down another avenue towards a town hall of some sort. If it weren't for the sharp metal objects they carried, Dungar would have considered tossing both guards and making a run for it. However, at the rate word spread around town, he'd probably have an entire barricade waiting for him by the time he made it to the gate anyway.

It hadn't even been five minutes since he was arrested for his alleged crime and already a crowd was beginning to form at this ominously named Den of Disposal. He gaped at the glaring women that filed into the city center after him. He was familiar with the concept of gossip getting word out quickly, but the rate of information transfer in this town was inhuman.

Inside the town hall was a large square room that contained an absolutely enormous padded throne with a podium surrounded by bleachers. The walls were also lined with extra chairs. Assorted pots of flowers hung from the ceiling and each wall had murals of hearts, flowers, or beautiful landscapes painted on it. It vaguely reminded Dungar of the town square in his home town where his town meetings were conducted. If he were not in such a serious situation, he would have taken more time to admire the aesthetics.

"Stand there and do not move a single muscle." One of the guards ordered, pointing next to the podium. As the blacksmith took his position, the crowd efficiently filed into the bleachers while the guards pulled up chairs beside him. Soon the buzz of crowd chatter filled the room as everyone shared theories and individual versions of the rumor they heard while they all presumably waited for their fair Lady to make her inevitable appearance. It was never a good sign when everyone was convinced of the defendant's guilt before the trial had even begun.

As time ticked by, more women would occasionally drift into the room, having been informed of recent events, but Bibi still had not shown. It wasn't entirely surprising. The hall was at least a hundred paces away from her house, so they'd be lucky to see her before nightfall.

Reflecting on his actions, Dungar recalled her promise to execute him and he found himself wondering if he would indeed rather die. He had stared death in the face enough times as of late that the experience was almost starting to become mundane, but being executed for a crime as heinous and ridiculous as this was certainly not the legacy he wanted to leave. He vowed not to make any rash decisions just yet, but he was fully prepared to give these women a fight if events came to it.

Finally a familiar rumbling was heard from outside. The window panes began to vibrate and Dungar swore he could hear small children screaming somewhere in the distance as the thuds began to grow more and more violent until some of the women in chairs had to hang on to avoid tipping over. Then the double wide doors flew open and in walked Jimminy bearing a silver platter that held an overflowing smorgasbord. Following a short ways behind him was the alleged victim herself. She was so slow coming through the doorway that a line of women had formed behind her like a clogged artery.

Eventually she managed to ooze her way through the doorway and into the hall. The moment she set foot inside, every single chair snapped under the mere prospect of encountering her pulchritudinous curves. Slowly but surely, Bibi waddled over to her throne, collapsing into it like she had just run a marathon. Mighty waterfalls of sweat cascaded down her face, ruining her freshly reapplied makeup. She had also swapped her tent-sized robe for a bright pink blouse that, despite its equally enormous size, was stretched so tight that if the buttons popped then someone was getting hurt. Perhaps that's how they intended to execute him.

After stuffing her face with several handfuls of food from Jimminy's platter, Bibi turned to the accused and immediately started bawling again, much to his disgust.

"You see what happens!?" She called out to the audience, hoping to incite sympathy. "You see what happens when you let an animal like a man into our town?!"

Sympathetic murmurs echoed from the bleachers while Dungar just gaped in awe. Strange how she could be so convinced men were dangerous enemies while simultaneously letting one hand feed her.

"I should have known when I saw how he was looking at me! Looking at me like I was a piece of meat. But, being the good soul that I am, I gave him the benefit of the doubt! And this is the payment I get for my actions."

The rest of her sanctimonious speech became unintelligible over her wails and blubbering. A short middle aged lady in a black pantsuit emerged from the crowd to comfort her while everyone else stared daggers at Dungar, who was just shaking his head.

"I can't look at him anymore!" Bibi declared, dramatically covering her eyes and leaning away. "Throw him into the puppy pit!"

"The what?!" Dungar and Jimminy both rang out simultaneously.

The lady comforting Bibi stood up and addressed the crowd. "It is the decree of Lady Dubya that, for the crime of rape, the prisoner is to be subjected to the canines of the puppy pit!" She then turned to Dungar. "Here in the city of SRS, we have a supply of puppies that we keep sufficiently starved until they are aggressive enough to eat people. Dying is really gross, so the puppies offset the grossness with their cuteness so we can watch long enough to make sure you're actually dead. And there's no clean-up!"

As soon as she finished speaking, a lever was pulled and the floor opened up to reveal a pit filled with emaciated puppies of every breed. As soon as they saw the light above, they began yipping frantically and pawing at the walls. It was morbidly adorable.

"Do you have any final requests, prisoner?" The pantsuit lady inquired.

Dungar thought for a moment. If there was any time to not be aggressive, it was while asserting your innocence in regards to a heinous crime like rape. But if he even hoped to successfully assert that then he needed to buy more time.

"Surely I should be allowed one last drink."

"NO!" Bibi shrieked. "Throw him in already!"

"With all due respect, dear Lady," the woman in black interjected. "We are not savages. It is our custom to grant a final request. Very well, male, what beverage do you desire?"

"Scotch. A lot of it."

"Ew. We don't have that."

"Any kind of whisky then."

"We don't have that."

"Well what in the blazes do you have then?"

"The only alcoholic beverages we have available are apple-tinis, cosmos, daiquiris, mojitos, fuzzy navels, pink ladies, and bellinis."

"Alright, I'm ready to die now."

Pantsuit lady shrugged and took her seat. Dungar's two guards both stood up and guided him over to the lip of the pit. At the sight of the blacksmith, all the puppies gazed up at him with voracious looks of hunger that were quite reminiscent of another nearby consumption machine. The moment the two gloved hands were placed on his back, he called out once more.

"Okay, hang on a second!"

The confused guards froze as all murmuring stopped. All eyes were on Dungar, who decided to take advantage of the attention and plead his case.

"Of all the women in this town, why would I rape YOU?!" He asked desperately, nodding towards Bibi.

"How should I know how your twisted mind works?!" She snapped back. "Maybe you thought I was an easy target because of my size and that's why you snuck into my house and attacked me!"

"Snuck into your house?! You sent armed guards to escort me there."

"Nuh uh!" Bibi denied, a faint smug smirk on her face.

Dungar looked frantically at the two guards, hoping against hope they would validate his story. They just exchanged guilty looks with each other before looking at him and shaking their heads.

"It's true!!" Rose's voice rang out from the doorway.

All eyes turned to her standing in the doorway, bent over and taking heaving breaths.

"Man, I need to work on my cardio . . ." She soliloquized to herself. Then, noticing the attention from everyone, she straightened back up. "Er, yes! I was there when the guards came for . . . Uh, I'm really sorry but what's your name again?"

"OH I SEE HOW IT IS!" Bibi shrieked, pounding her beefy paws against the arm rests of her throne. "YOU THINK YOU'RE TOO GOOD FOR ME BECAUSE YOU'VE BEEN BANGING THIS SKINNY WHORE, HAVEN'T YOU?!"

"What?!" Rose and Dungar exclaimed in unison.

"THROW HER IN THE PIT TOO!"

Bibi folded her arms defiantly and sat pouting in her chair as a pair of guards grabbed Rose by the arms and hauled her over to the pit next to Dungar. Worried looks were starting to spread over members of the audience, as well as the pantsuit woman, but no one said a word in protest.

"Oh, Rosie . . ." The lady whispered mournfully, putting a hand on Rose's shoulder. "It is the decree of Lady Dubya that, for the crime of, er . . ." She looked over at Bibi confusedly.

"BEING AN UGLY HARLOT!" Bibi screeched.

". . . You are to be thrown into the puppy pit." She finished with a sigh. "Do you have any final requests?"

"I request to not be executed!" Rose declared.

The pantsuit woman looked back at Bibi hopefully, as if the request had a chance of being honored.

"NO!" Bibi denied vehemently, mouth full of hors d'oeuvres. "THROW THEM IN ALREADY!"

As the guards grabbed them once more, Dungar reared back, ready to start throwing head-butts. But, almost as if on cue, another voice rang out in the room.

"THAT IS ENOUGH!"

It was a woman's voice, the most confident and imposing he had ever heard. It came from one of the guards from the line had broken rank and stepped out onto the floor. As she walked, she removed her helmet revealing her youthful face and blonde pixie cut. She was tall for a woman, almost the same height as Rose, and she carried herself in a very digni-fied manner and with an air of stoicism that intensified as she unflinchingly stared down Bibi with her azure eyes.

"With all due respect, Lady, Rose has done no wrong. Do whatever you wish with the male, but one of our citizens can-not be executed on such a whim. It would be unforgivable. I urge you not to resort to the same savage tactics that you con-demn men for."

All in the hall fell silent. Even though it wasn't his life the woman was trying to save, Dungar hoped the message she preached would be enough to rouse the Lady to reason and mercy. As all attention turned to her, Bibi continued to slump in her chair, apparently deep in thought. She could feel the penetrating stares of her audience pressuring her to a decision. It seemed unlikely that she of all people would be able to assess a situation with any amount of rationality or compassion, but stranger things have happened. Eventually her head rose and she met the defiant guard's gaze.

"I don't like you." She stated with a frown. "THROW HER IN THE PIT TOO!"

TWENTY TWO

PINT-SIZE ALLIES

The hall was filled with stunned silence once more in the wake of Lady Dubya's power play. Even Dungar found himself shocked by just how little concern she had for the welfare of everyone in her life. Putting three people to death didn't faze her in the slightest. In fact, the look on her face implied a level of macabre enjoyment.

Rose, by contrast, now wore a look of unbridled despair. She had gone limp in the arms of the guards as she shot pleading looks at anyone who could bring themselves to make eye contact with her. She then turned to the other prisoner.

"Please!" She begged. "Please, you have to do something!"

The blonde guard just stared at the ground solemnly. "You know I cannot harm the innocent, Rose." She reminded her soberly.

"But they're not innocent! They're going to kill us!"

"They are but faithful servants, not unlike myself."

"Gilly, we're going to die!"

Gilly looked up at Rose, her blue eyes welling with tears.

"Rosie, you know I'd do anything to protect you. I love you more than anything in this world. But I cannot break my vows to Suola!"

"WHY HAVEN'T THEY BEEN THROWN IN THE PIT YET!?" Bibi shrilly interjected.

"Bibi, my darling perhaps maybe you should perchance—" Jimminy attempted to reason with her.

"GO GET ME MORE FOOD, JIMMY!" The dictator screamed, dumping the remnants of the platter into her lap then handing it to Jimminy.

As he stared down at the dish, Jimminy's hands began to shake. First they shook in small vibrations, then in full blown tremors as he looked up at his beloved with a quivering lower lip. Then, without warning, he hurled the empty silver platter at the ceiling hard enough that it punched a hole clean through.

"YOU'RE NOT A VERY NICE LADY!"

It was difficult to tell who between Dungar and Bibi was more shocked by Jimminy's sudden growth of a spine. But after her brief stint of shock, Bibi huffed loudly and motioned for the guards to take him away as well.

"Don't even bother!" Jimminy snapped at the approaching women. "I'll throw meself into the pit!"

Without so much as a pause to reconsider, he marched right over to the pit where Dungar and the women stood, gave a slight bow, and hopped into it. The moment the thud of his feet against the ground was heard he began screaming.

"OH BLIMEY, THIS WAS A VERY BAD IDEA! OW! OW! THEY'RE SO BITEY!"

Immediately his hands reappeared above the pit as hastily tried to climb out. Screams erupted from the audience as some covered their eyes while others craned their necks for a better look. One of the guards ran over to stomp his hands and prevent his escape. However, before she could reach him a spider dropped out of the hole and the ceiling and landed on her face. She froze immediately and the screams began.

"SPIDER!!!!!!!!!"

She began running around flailing her arms wildly while the audience struggled to decide which commotion was preferable to watch. Taking action, another guard ran up and slapped the first right across the face where the spider crawled.

"Hey!" The first guard screeched. "I just had my makeup professionally done this morning!" She then slapped her slapper. Her slapper did not take kindly to this and gave her a shove backwards whilst shouting at her.

"Then get a hold of yourself and bloody well do your job! It's just a spider for god sakes."

The moment she uttered the words, a virtual waterfall of tiny black spiders came pouring out of the hole in the ceiling and quickly began filling the room. The guard was thoroughly covered with them within a matter of seconds, and immediately fainted.

No coherent words or sounds could have been heard over the terrified wails that ensued. Women abandoned the bleachers and guards abandoned their posts faster than they would have if the building was engulfed in flames. No longer held at sword point, the four prisoners took the opportunity to make their escape as well, slipping out a back door. Once they were outside, though, Jimminy stopped them.

"Wait, mista Dungar! What about Bibi?"

"What about her?! You can't possibly want to go back and save her!"

"I can't let her die, mate! Sure she's not a nice lady, but she doesn't deserve to die if those spiders are poisonous!"

Dungar had no response because he couldn't immediately decide if he agreed with that or not.

"Um, the spiders aren't venomous." Rose interrupted.

Stopping their bickering, the two men looked at Rose who was standing with her hands behind her back and a guilty look on her face.

"Rosie . . ." Gilly prompted her. "What did you do?"

"I . . ." Rose began with a grimace. "May have read a book about spiders then started secretly breeding them in the attic of the town hall so I could kill them for the bounty?" Her voice trailed off as she looked out at the growing carpet of black insects that was making its way through the town. ". . . And it may have gotten just a little out of hand."

"Hah!" Dungar laughed while Jimminy and Gilly both looked at her incredulously.

"Don't look at me like that! I told you they weren't venomous!"

"EEEEEEEEEEKKKK!" Bibi screamed from inside.

Immediately Jimminy bolted back into the hall, forcing Dungar to begrudgingly follow. The interior was still crawling with spiders, many continued to spill from the hole in the ceiling as well. Their bloated would-be executor had not moved from her throne. Spiders were crawling all over her, making her spasm and flail, but she continued trying to inhale the remaining food in her lap. Her strongest instinct was neither fight nor flight, but rather consume.

"GIT EM OFF ME, GIT EM OFF ME!" She howled incessantly between bites.

"Bibi we need to get out of here!" Jimminy insisted, pulling at her greasy arms.

"GIT EM OFF MEEEEE!!!"

Disregarding his animosity momentarily, Dungar joined in the hoisting efforts as well, but even with his added might, the large slimy creature could not be budged. Her limbs continued to flail increasingly violently, and her words were no longer coherent, just a medley of screams and syllables. Then, out of nowhere, she lost all consciousness. Her screams fell silent, her flailing limbs went limp, and her grinding jaws halted.

"Oh blimey, mista Dungar, she's unconscious! We're going to have to carry her out!"

"Jimmy we can't even move her! And I think she's dead."

"No no, she's just unconscious! Quickly now, if we find a doctor then she'll be okay!"

Bibi's body then spontaneously combusted.

"Does anybody have any water handy?" Jimminy yelled into the empty room.

"Jimmy . . ."

"Why is she on fire?"

"I don't know. Look, we should probably get out of here before she explodes."

"People don't do that, mate."

An ominous rumbling sound then came from within the deceased woman's bulky burning body.

"Er, let's go outside for a completely unrelated reason, mate."

Nodding, Dungar led the defeated Jimminy out of the burning spider-infested building to where Rose and Gilly still stood.

"What happened in there?" Rose asked.

"And where is Lady Dubya?" Gilly added.

Before the blacksmith could respond, an explosion blew a gaping hole in the side of the building and the air became filled with the sickening stench of burning fat. Dungar and Gilly both grimaced, Rose immediately vomited, and Jimminy breathed the air deeply, basking in the final putrescent odor his lost love would bestow upon the world.

They all stood in silence for a few moments, allowing the surprising turn of events to sink in. Jimminy mourned Bibi in silence, Dungar debated internally how long to give him, and Rose and Gilly tearfully hugged one another, thankful to be alive. As usual, Jimminy was the first to break the silence.

"Alright, mista Dungar, I guess it's back to the quest!"

The blacksmith responded by punching him square in the face. Gilly and Rose both gasped as Jimminy's limp body fell over.

"He said this detour wouldn't involve us almost getting killed." Dungar explained nonchalantly as he picked up his friend's limp body and tossed it over his shoulder. "Well ladies, I'd say it was a pleasure . . . but it wasn't. Good luck with your pest control."

"Wait!" Rose called out. "What is this quest you're on?"

"Something dangerous, illegal, and I probably shouldn't even have told you anything."

"I want to come with you!"

"Are you crazy?" Gilly reprimanded her. "You don't even know this man, and he just told you it's dangerous. Absolutely not, Rose. Your place is here."

"What do you mean my place is here? Gilly, I've spent my whole life here. Every day I read stories about adventures and quests and the wonders that await me out in the world. Now I finally have a chance to have an adventure of my own." She stared at Gilly pleadingly. "I can't stay here anymore."

"Rose, you're all I have. I can't risk losing you."

"Hey!" Dungar cut in. "I didn't even invite you!"

"I can only spend so long whiling away my time in a library." Rose continued, ignoring him. "I want to do something with my life. I don't want to just know about the world, I want to experience it! A life spent in safety is a life devoid of fulfilment, that's what Thathery always said."

"Very well . . ." Gilly conceded.

"No!" Dungar demanded.

Raising a finger to silence the blacksmith, Gilly continued. "If you are to tread into danger, then I shall accompany you. I could never forgive myself if anything were to happen to you."

Rose squealed with excitement. "YAY! Let me go pack some things quickly!"

As she ran off, Gilly turned to Dungar. "I do not wish to infringe upon your quest, but I thank you for allowing us to accompany you."

"Look." Dungar stated firmly, dropping Jimminy to the ground. "If she wants to go out into the world on a quest then that is her business. But if you fear danger then you should not be coming with us."

"If we are to encounter danger then I assure you that I am more than equipped to deal with it."

"Not the kind of danger that we are up against."

"And what kind of danger is that?"

Dungar sighed. Reasoning with people was a lot harder than he thought.

"I have not ever dealt with men before." Gilly informed him. "But I am familiar with your penchant for bravado. I am not sure how little you think of me as combatant, but I promise you that anything you can handle I will be able to as well."

"And what if I told you that I don't know if I will be able to handle this?"

She paused for a moment, considering his response. Apparently she was not expecting any level of humility.

"Why would you attempt such a quest then?"

"Because someone has to." He grunted, picking up Jimminy again. "Give my regards to Rose. And if you love her, then you will not come with us."

Gilly had no response as he walked away carrying Jimminy. It was much easier to simply decline their help rather than attempt to convince them to kill the most powerful woman in all the land. The fact that they had come from a town comprised solely of women and had been propagated to distrust men would only serve to impede further.

As he reached the town gates he breathed a sigh of relief and continued his trek north. They were so close now. He couldn't see the capital yet, but he knew enough to continue heading north. Given the sun's spot in the sky, he only had about an hour of travel time before it would be dark. That would be ample time to put some distance between them and the town before setting up camp.

Walking in silence like this was quite comforting. He found himself wondering why he didn't think to knock Jimminy out more often. He was slightly cumbersome to carry, but it was a fair trade off. In light of recent events, Dungar had to admit his growing attachment to the man. He had gone from having one friend who couldn't speak to having one friend who spoke far too often, and it was slightly more bearable than he would have figured. Still, silence was nice, especially when it didn't involve coping with death. All was well for now.

As the sun began to slump and the flowery fields became bathed in the warm glow of twilight, Dungar began to wonder what the queen was like. He had heard tales of her beauty so larger than life that it seemed almost impossible she could live up to expectations. But any talk regarding her personality was all but non-existent. It seemed unlikely she would be boisterous and insufferable like Bibi given her reputation for reclusiveness. He imagined her more like a femme fatale, coolly stalking her prey and ensnaring them with her charms. But none of that explained how or why she kills. He had a bad feeling that somehow magic was involved, especially if Sir Lee was to be believed.

The sun had now almost vanished beneath the cover of the horizon and Jimminy was finally starting to feel a little bit heavy, so Dungar decided to set camp for the night. The temperature was perfect as the faint Star Field windsong could be heard whistling around him. Trees weren't exactly numerous in these parts, but they were populous enough for him to steal a few branches here and there to get a fire going. He laid Jimminy in a particularly fluffy looking patch of grass as he produced Nobeard's flint from his pocket and arranged a rock formation for a campfire. It had been a long and quite unsettling day, and he was so happy to be at rest that he drifted off to sleep almost immediately.

"WAKEY WAKEY, EGGS AND BAKEY!"

Dungar sat bolt upright. He had slept clear through the night and well into the morning given how high the sun was. But the sun wasn't the only thing above him. The perky grin of Rose also loomed overhead.

"Morning! Just so you know I don't actually have eggs or bacon." She informed him. "I just like saying that. Oh! I do have some bread though. Here!" Without waiting for a response, she shoved half a loaf of bread into the face of the groggy blacksmith, who quickly swatted it away as he tried to grasp the situation.

"Morning, mate!" Jimminy called to him as he sat next to Gilly at the fire. "You didn't tell me you invited the ladies. Look at you being all social! I'm proud of ya."

Still drowsy from his sudden awakening, and acclimating to the situation, Dungar just pointed at Gilly and grunted.

"You. Me. Words."

Nodding, Gilly set her bread aside and excused herself from the campfire as the blacksmith hauled himself to his feet. He didn't even know what he was going to say to her as they made their way behind a nearby outcrop. Casually, he leaned against the rocks while his new companion maintained her perfect posture with hands behind her back. They spent a moment simply looking at each other before Dungar finally spoke.

"Are you going to make me actually ask what you know I'm going to ask?"

"Fair enough." Gilly agreed. "After discussing what you said with Rose, we came to the conclusion that you would not be risking your life without confidence in your abilities on an endeavor unless the circumstances were dire. Therefore, I felt honor bound to provide you with my assistance."

"Ah c'mon, mate." Jimminy's voice called out from the other side of the rock. "More the merrier!"

"Jimmy! Privacy!"

"Wots that?"

"It means he doesn't want us listening." Rose's voice informed him.

Dungar put his face in his palm, defeated. "Fine." He relented, throwing his hands in the air. "You want to come that bad? Come then."

"Yay!" Rose exclaimed, leaping behind the rock and giving Gilly a big hug.

The blacksmith glowered at Jimminy as he too emerged from behind the boulder, cheeky grin firmly in place.

"Grab your things." Dungar ordered the group. "We're leaving now."

Without waiting for them, he set off in Jenair's general direction. He knew they would have no trouble catching up, so his early departure left him a few moments to grumble in peace. Sure enough, before he had made it too far the trio were hot on his heels.

Gilly, in addition to the armor and sword she wore, carried several skins of water as well as a large pouch containing various breads and produce. Rose, on the other hand, had bogged herself down with several bags all filled with books and clothes. She resembled a pack mule the way she had herself all laced up. However, her bogged down body bore no infringement upon her spirit as she was clearly elated to finally be under way. Sharing her spirit, Jimminy was once again compelled to burst into song.

> Way hey and away we go
> To the castle to vanquish our foe
> Now we got two ladies in tow
> Way hey and away we go.
> EVERYBODY!

Up until this point in the adventure, all of Jimminy's breaks into song would end at that. He would belt out his piece and be done with it. But not on this day. Rose's eyes lit up after the first verse, and by the time it was over she was completely captivated.

"That was amazing!" She praised. "Did you just make that up?!"

"'Tis to the tune of our old marching song from the foreign legion." Jimminy proudly informed her. "We always used to make up lyrics. But no one was better than me!"

At that, they began singing it together repeatedly and enthusiastically, swaying to the rhythm as the marched confidently out of the Star Field and into a thicket.

"Sing with us, Gilly!" Rose called out amid laughs as she grabbed the woman's hands and began dancing in a circle with her. Although she did not sing, the innocent smile on the former guard's face marked her reluctant playful enjoyment.

The mirth began to die down as the group entered the thicket and treaded onto the marked path to Jenair. The bright rays of sunlight shining from above grew dim as they became eclipsed behind the leafy canopy. The dirt path was well travel worn and packed down hard by the soles of a hundred thousand boots.

Dungar hoped the city wasn't too much farther away. The day's trip had been short thus far, but already his patience was beginning to wear thin. Fortunately, the rest of the party was all but oblivious to his souring state of mind.

"So wot's the deal with you two ladies anyway?" Jimminy asked the girls.

"What do you mean?" Gilly responded.

"Well are you two . . . Er, well, y'know . . ." He stammered, moving his hands in the air as he struggled to come up with words or gestures.

". . . Sisters?" Rose finished with a very confused look on her face.

"YES!" He exclaimed quickly. "Yes, sisters! Yup, that is exactly the word I was looking for. I like words. Don't you like words, mista Dungar?"

"No."

"Is he always in such a good mood?" Rose asked.

"Mista Dungar? He's a delight!"

"Shh!" Gilly interjected, motioning for the group to stop. "There's something here."

Everyone came to a halt and peered cautiously at their surroundings. Gilly moved Rose behind her into the center of the group as she felt at her sword while Dungar just glared at both sides of the trail with fists clenched just begging for something to try his patience. Several paces ahead of them, four figures stood up from their bushy cover and strutted onto the path. They were identically dressed in hooded green tunics that blended perfectly with their surroundings.

"Those are quite the senses you've got yourself, blondie!" One of them called has he removed his hood. He was a handsome man, a little bit older than Dungar, with short black hair and a winning smile vaguely reminiscent of Rainchild's.

"Hello!" Jimminy called to them, unruffled by the situation as ever.

"HEY! THAT'S OUR WORD!" The man screamed back, causing everyone to jump. All eyes wide and staring at him, he quickly cleared his throat and the sly smile appeared again.

"Alright so here's how this works! You relinquish all of your worldly goods to yours truly and in return I will refrain from shivving you in the nether regions with this here pointy object!" He pulled out a small knife and held it up for them to see. "That's right folks, this is a stick up!"

He sauntered over to the group, one hand open to receive goods while the other brandished the knife rather half-heartedly. Gilly was the first he approached, and she looked him up and down with a raised eyebrow.

"C'mon there, pretty eyes." He smooth talked her whilst raising the knife to her neck. "Anything you donate goes to the poor."

"And what poor is that?" She quipped, totally unfazed.

"Well, mostly ourselves really. We're very poor, you see."

She continued to meet his gaze unflinchingly for a few more moments before shrugging and handing him her bags. Rose followed suit with hers as well while Jimminy removed the rock from his pants and handed it over. The man looked at it confusedly before looking back up at Jimminy.

"It's all I got, mate."

Between Jimminy's stained and ripped clothing and a funk that was now beginning to emanate from him, it wasn't a difficult claim to believe. So the man tossed the rock into one of the bags and moved on to Dungar.

"What about you there, smiley?" He gibed.

Very calmly, the blacksmith reached up and grabbed the hand that held the knife to him. The bandit's eyes immediately went wide as he listened to the sound of his fracturing carpals. Dungar then used his other hand to grab all the bags before driving his knee into his robber's stomach hard enough to lift him off the ground.

"I'm poor too." He growled flippantly at the mugger who was now wheezing in the fetal position.

At the sight of their fallen comrade, the other three bandits removed their hoods and cracked their knuckles.

"You want these!?!" Dungar yelled to them as he threw the bags to the ground and put up his fists. "Then come and get em!!!"

Surprisingly, the three highwaymen actually did charge at him. Secretly pleased to have willing individuals on whom to work out his frustration, Dungar rushed the trio and simultaneously tackled all three of them. It quickly devolved into a flail fest wherein all participants would blindly swing their fists, hoping to connect with something. Outnumbered but not outmatched, Dungar shrugged off all their paltry blows as he tirelessly continued to lay into the three of them, even grabbing and throwing one.

During all the fighting, Jimminy and Gilly took to picking up all their belongings and then carefully helping Rose lace her cargo up again. Afterwards, Gilly offered them each some rations to munch on as they casually watched the unfolding violence, none of them feeling an inclination to jump in.

Eventually, with a busted lip and several new tears in his clothes, Dungar was the last fighter still on his feet. Two of the bandits lay in crumpled heaps on the ground while the other had been put into a tree at some point. Feeling better but still a bit agitated, Dungar looked back at his allies who stood in the same spot. Rose and Jimminy both wore big grins as they clapped a polite applause while Gilly studied Dungar curiously with her arms folded and head cocked to the side.

"You're welcome." He redundantly grunted at the group before they resumed making their way down the path.

"Why did you do that?" Gilly inquired curiously.

Dungar gave her a strange look, hoping she was kidding. Her facial expression indicated otherwise.

"Did you miss the part where they were going to steal our stuff?"

"I did not. I surrendered my belongings as requested."

"Well I didn't feel like surrendering my stuff. I like my stuff. He would have put me down for it, and if I am going to go down then I will go down fighting."

"An honorable notion, perhaps. But does one retain their valor if they go down fighting a fight that need not be fought?"

Dungar had no response to that. Fortunately, they had now emerged from the thicket and onto the manicured rolling green hills of the plains of Jenair. They could see the city now. The tall stone spires of the castle, the firm ivy-covered walls, and the ominous looking plume of black smoke that appeared to be billowing from within.

TWENTY THREE

JOIN THE FIGHT THAT'LL GIVE YOU THE RIGHT TO BE FREE

Granted there had been many a hiccup during their journey, but Stranger's story made it seem like they had more time. They couldn't be too late already. Royal weddings were supposed to last for a week or more, and the whole city was supposed to be drunk and partying the whole time. Now that he thought of it, wedding week would have been the perfect time for a royal assassination. But nothing ever seemed to go according to plan anyway.

Ominous smoky plumes aside, the city of Jenair appeared to be a scenic and tranquil place to live. The white stone walls capped with red contrasted beautifully with the vibrant green fields of the countryside giving the capital a rather fairytale appearance. The city's location was advantageous militarily as well. It had a perfect view of the wide open fields that surrounded it from the hilltop on which it sat. None could approach without being seen. Fortunately, their small group did not present a threatening appearance.

"It looks just like the illustrations!" Rose gushed, awestruck.

"Why is smoke billowing from it?" Gilly asked.

"Alright listen to me very carefully because I'm only going to explain this once and it will be very quick." Dungar informed the girls. "The 'queen' isn't actually a queen she's some woman from a faraway place who has already destroyed

Farrawee, probably other places too, and she's now moved on to ours so we're here to kill her and I thought we had more time but we don't so let's get moving, ok? Ok." Without waiting for a response, he began hurrying towards the capital.

"So wait, she destroys cities and kills people?" Rose asked, struggling to keep up with him. ". . . Is it bad that I think that's actually kind of awesome?"

"Yes."

"Do we even have a plan, mate?"

"No."

"We're infiltrating a city for the purposes of using violence to influence its politics." Gilly pointed out. "Doesn't that technically make us terrorists?"

". . . Technically yes I guess." Dungar acknowledged. "Look, everybody stop talking!"

They clambered up the hill until they reached the city to find it completely deserted. Upturned carts of fruit and goods littered the streets of what appeared to be the remains of a marketplace. A commotion could be heard off in the distance, but besides the debris the only thing remaining at the city entrance was some rushed graffiti on a nearby wall. "*Law Resistonce*" was painted on the tavern exterior in big red litters.

"Law resist . . . ons?" Jimminy read confusedly. "Wot does that mean, mate?"

"It means someone doesn't know how to spell resistance." Rose surmised.

"Not quite, my lady!" A young man called out from inside. The door burst open to reveal a young man with curly blonde hair and a bright red vest. "Law Resistonce is the name of our revolutionary group that is totally gonna overthrow this fascist regime! Because in order to revolt you have to resist the law and if you do it right then you only have to do it once! Law Resistonce!"

"Oh I get it!" Jimminy exclaimed. "Resist the law! Clever, mate!"

"So what say you, fair travelers? Will you join in our plight that'll make all the knights go and flee?"

A wave of relief washed over Dungar after this explanation. Not only had the queen not yet enacted her plans, but there was also widespread social unrest that would make for the perfect distraction.

"We would be happy to aid in your liberation!" Dungar exclaimed, clasping a large hand on the boy's shoulder.

"Wonderful! If you need supplies we have a small cache here in the tavern. From there, just follow the noise!"

Curious, the group stepped into the tavern to find it rife with tools and goods from seemingly every store on the street. Dungar immediately ran to the blacksmithing pile to choose his weapon. There were handmade armaments of every kind ranging from sharp to blunt. However, Dungar knew his craft, and he knew to go with what felt comfortable in his hands. So he ignored the conventional swords, maces, and axes and instead selected from the tool section.

The chisels were tempting, but he had his eyes on something a little more his speed. A perfect pair of double faced lump hammers, ideal for all situations where use of force was the answer. They were untarnished with brand new leather grips and they were heavy too, at least five pounds apiece.

Turning back to his accomplices, he found none of them to be considering the violent implications of embarking into a riot. Gilly was already armed with her sword and armor, but Jimminy and Rose were exploring some of the more pacifistic sections of goods, namely the clothing and herb sections respectively.

"Are you ready to leave?" He asked them, hoping to draw them away from indulging their hobbies.

"Yup!" They all announced in unison.

". . . Seriously? You do know it's going to be a warzone out there."

"Those blokes won't be able to touch me, mate!" Jimminy informed enthusiastically, kissing one of his biceps then slipping on a pair of pants under his robe.

With a sigh, the blacksmith lead the fearless foursome out the back door and into another empty street. Smoke filled the air of the narrow alleyway as they made their way down the cobblestone path towards the shouting. Rounding the corner they found themselves in the town square before the castle, or what remained rather. The entire scene was a roiling pit of angry citizens swinging anything they could get their hands on. All wooden structures burned the bright red glow of the revolution banner as the rebels continued their onslaught on the town guard.

Rose's jaw dropped and even Dungar's fervor waned when they saw the stage that had been set up. Law enforcement officials were executing captured revolutionaries on display to set an example for the rest. The rioters, however, were undeterred. They continued to push the knights slowly backward towards the city hall. Participants from both sides yelled resounding battle cries as they fought. Jimminy found himself swept up in the moment and before long had torn his robe off and leapt into the fray mimicking the rebel yells.

Dungar felt apt to do the same. However before he did he noticed a pair of side doors to the castle that were free from any attack whatsoever. The three guards stationed near the entrance could only watch the chaos that unfolded around them, duty bound to protect their post, their oddly sparkling swords remaining at their side.

"Don't suppose you'd be willing to help me fight them?" Dungar mumbled to Gilly, pointing to the guards stationed at the wall near the castle gate.

"You know I cannot, Dungar." She mumbled back.

"Yeah yeah, the innocent, I remember."

"I have an idea!" Rose exclaimed.

Confidently, she strutted up to the guards with Dungar and Gilly following her warily. Gilly attempted to stop her, but the blacksmith held her back until they could see what she was up to.

"Hi there, fellas!" Rose greeted the guards sweetly.

"Miss, in case you haven't noticed, there is a riot going on." One of the guards informed her snidely. "If you think we're going to let you into the castle then you're even stupider than you look."

"But I absolutely must see the queen! It's urgent!" She insisted, doing her best at puppy dog eyes.

"Oh? What's the trouble, miss?" A different one asked her, seemingly taken in by her façade.

"Uh . . . She has evil magical powers and needs to be stopped before she kills us all?"

At that, all three guards burst into raucous laughter as Rose's smile slowly weakened. After he finished laughing, the first guard gave her a shove.

"Look, miss. Our guard is stretched as thin as it can get right now. There are fires in the streets and I haven't even got to have my lunch. I got 99 problems, but I can assure you, a witch ain't one."

Defeated, Rose slinked away and regrouped with her bewildered friends.

"Rosie, what was that all about?" Gilly asked.

"You can't have honestly thought that would work." Dungar added.

"Oh, I would have been shocked if it did." Rose agreed. "I just needed to keep them focused on me while I sprinkled binding powder on their boots."

She put on a very satisfied smile as the guards began to yell from behind her.

"Hey! My feet are stuck to the ground!"

"Oh god, mine too!"

"Alchemy 101!" Rose chirped, patting her book bag. "We should probably get inside before they learn all they need to do is spit on them to get free."

The trio quickly hurried past the helplessly snared guards, Dungar pausing briefly to get another look. "Clever girl . . ." He mumbled to himself before following the women inside through the large red double doors.

As he stepped inside, his draw dropped at the sheer enormity of the castle interior. The entrance hall was a colossal circular room with at least a fifty foot radius. Elaborate tapestries and exquisite paintings hung from the walls and large marble columns jutted from floor to ceiling, each engraved with unique flowery designs. In typical castle fashion, there was a grand staircase which forked midway up as it led to the second floor, and there was also a maidservant dusting one of the marble columns who gave the group a funny look when they walked in.

Rose was in awe. She stared wondrously around, hardly able to contain herself as she flitted from tapestry to painting, gushing over each one, unable to keep still. Gilly, however, was sizing up the maid who had still not taken her eyes off them. After she managed to get a hold of herself, Rose noticed her as well.

"Hello." Rose called to her nervously. "Uhm. Nice place you got here?"

The maid remained still for a moment, then dropped her feather duster and began sprinting up the stairs rather quickly for a middle aged woman. Dungar immediately gave chase as fast as his short legs could allow.

"What are you doing?" Gilly demanded, taking off after him.

"She's going to call the guards!" The blacksmith reasoned.

"And so what are you going to do!?"

"Keep that from happening."

"I cannot allow you to hurt this woman, Dungar."

"I'm not going to hurt her, dammit!"

As they continued to follow the maid, Dungar and Gilly had broken into a shoving match of sorts while Rose brought up the rear, yelling at them both to calm down. Amid the commotion, they had rounded several corners and become hopelessly lost within the bowels of the castle. Slowly the group came to a halt, trying to get their bearings.

Dungar furled his brow and grumbled at Gilly. "I swear if the guards catch us and kill us then I am going to kill you."

"Then may Suola have mercy on your soul." Gilly replied, unfazed.

Somewhere up ahead, the sound of a door being slammed and locked was heard, prompting the group to quit their bickering and investigate. Around the corner was a long corridor with a few rooms on each side and one lone door at the end. Slowly, the group followed the red and gold rug, stopping at each door to try them. Every room alongside the hallway was unlocked and empty except for the final door on the end. Dungar went to move towards it, but was stopped by Gilly's hand on his shoulder.

"You promised you would inflict no harm."

"And I meant it!"

"Then why are you bringing those hammers with you?"

Dungar looked down at the tools he still clutched in his hands. Despite being instruments for creation, they were certainly every bit as capable of causing destruction. Given the implications that them being in his hands presented, he considered putting them down to placate his female accomplice. However, he then decided against it.

"I might need to hammer some nails." He dismissed, once again stepping towards the door.

In a flash, Gilly stepped between him and the door, meeting his stern gaze just as hard.

"In the interest of avoiding confrontation, I would insist you let me make an attempt at diplomacy." She calmly but intently instructed him.

With a sigh and a shrug, Dungar waved his hand towards the door then folded his arms. With a satisfied smile, Gilly lightly knocked on the door.

"Excuse me, miss? We did not mean to frighten you. However, we do need to speak with you before you take any rash actions. Would you please open the door?"

One second later, a mighty blow from a size thirteen boot tore the door off its hinges. Appalled, Gilly shot Dungar an incredulously dirty look.

"See? My way gets results." He said with a satisfied smile of his own.

"You didn't even give her a chance to respond!"

"Oh please, did you honestly think she'd open the door for a group of armed strangers?"

"If we were friendly then maybe!"

Dungar shook his head as he ignored her and walked inside.

"Look, miss, perhaps we got off on the wrong foot." He called into the room. "I assure you we mean no harm . . . to you . . . We're here for completely morally justifiable reasons. They may sound a bit crazy when we say them, but if you just give us a chance to explain . . ."

His voice trailed off when he looked into the corner of the room and saw the chambermaid brandishing a letter opener threateningly. But it was the beautiful blonde woman dressed in a very fancy looking shiny blue gown that caught his attention. Her long flowing golden hair seemed to fill the room with light as her radiant blue eyes froze Dungar in place. For a brief moment, the only coherent thought in his mind was one involving taking her to the bed and thoroughly disappointing her.

Queen Koey. Finally in the flesh. Surprisingly, she looked almost exactly how he imagined. From her pouty ruby lips to her sexy swinging hips, it was easy to tell why every man in the kingdom had his eyes on the prize of her thighs. She was a truly breathtaking sight to behold.

"Who are you?" She demanded. "Revolutionaries here to depose me?"

Her voice was smooth and sultry with a slight hint of a rasp to it. Her words had a refined inflection to them, indicative of royalty.

Gilly motioned for Rose to stay back as she clutched her sword while Dungar continued to menacingly move towards her holding his hammers ready.

"Oh it won't be that easy, because I know who you really are . . ." He informed her threateningly. ". . . Witch."

Her eyes went wide. "Witch . . ." She repeated as the imposing blacksmith continued his advance. "I WISH I WAS A WITCH!"

Dungar froze again.

"Uh . . . What?"

"Do you have any idea how much easier it would be to keep the citizens in line?!" She raved. "I can barely wrangle the guards to carry out orders if their lives aren't in danger. Nobody has taken me seriously since I've assumed power! All they want to do is have me marry some man so he can make all the decisions!"

He was amazed by this response; it was the last thing he had expected. He almost wished she had just reacted and attacked him because it would have made his job so much easier. Instead she spoke with so much conviction that he was very tempted to believe her. However, the words of Stranger and Lee still rang in his mind loud as ever. Two men who had no contact whatsoever telling virtually the same tale, it couldn't just be a mere coincidence. Perhaps she was using some sort of enchantment to weaken his resolve.

"No one is buying your story." He growled. "I met a survivor from Farrawee that you overlooked during your killing spree, as well as a former knight that you would have had executed. There is no hiding your past crimes."

"If you're talking about Sir Lee, that knight was clearly deranged and made an attempt on my life!" She countered. "He spied in on me administering medicine to my ailing father and then flew off the handle, accused me of trying to kill him via witchcraft, despite my father already being sick. He was clearly unhinged and unfit for duty and any self-respecting monarch would have reacted the same. I don't know where you got the notion of execution from. He is lucky I only dismissed him from duty rather than charging him with anything. As for your accusation about Farrawee, I am familiar with the recent genocide that occurred there, but I will hardly accept responsibility for the tragedies of a location I've never even been to!"

"He witnessed it all happen!" The blacksmith insisted with utter conviction. "And he saw you there! Now let's face it, '*your highness*,' you have a rather unforgettable look to you, especially when someone watches their home crumble around you. And I'm not the type of man who just takes a witch on her word."

"I already told you I'm not a witch!"

Dungar opened his mouth to yell back, but he found himself forced to stop when he realized that he was about to say "That's something a witch would say." It was such a ridiculous statement he couldn't even justify it in his head. The confliction building inside his mind was becoming harder to bear. He finally had his opportunity to finish her like he had planned, but he couldn't seem to find any justification to do so now. However, he'd never forgive himself if he let her get away only to find he'd been tricked. At a loss, he turned to Rose and Gilly.

"I know how to prove if she's a witch!" Rose declared, rifling through her book bag. "Does anyone have a duck?"

"Stop! All of you!" The maidservant called out. "Please! She's telling the truth!"

"She's fooled a lot of people, lady." Dungar said. "Most of them aren't here to talk about it."

"But I can vouch for everything she's said."

"With all due respect, ma'am." Gilly stepped in. "As a humble servant of sorts myself, I can understand your conviction to defend your mistress. However, these are serious crimes we're dealing with. A mere servant couldn't have the intimate knowledge necessary to truly vouch for the events in her mistress's life."

"First of all, I don't know who or where you serve, girl. But you underestimate the servants around here. Secondly, I am not her servant. I am her mother."

Rose gasped as Dungar stared disbelievingly. If this was true then it changed absolutely everything. He felt like such a fool, having been taken in so readily by the testimonies of past acquaintances. Now he didn't know what to believe, and consequently didn't want to believe anyone anymore.

"I was a servant to King Ik when our affair began." Koey's mother explained, slowly lowering her weapon. "When he learned of our child he planned on taking us public even though I was a mere commoner. He never had much patience for royal etiquette or traditions. Unfortunately, when he discovered his child was a daughter he no longer possessed the same pride and confidence. He was the first Theik in the history of the royal bloodline to not produce a son, and it weighed on him. Only in his final days did he finally become able to embrace us as his family and heirs. He wanted to present us both, but for the sake of Koey, I insisted that I never be revealed as her mother in hopes she would be accepted by the people. As you have seen, it did not work. But the point is, dear intruders, I have cared for this girl for her entire life. She has never left the kingdom, nor has she displayed any aptitude for witchcraft."

"That's so sad." Rose said solemnly, small tears welling up in the corners of her eyes. "It's so unfair how undervalued women are everywhere else."

Dungar still wore a frown. He believed the lady's story, and he even saw the mother daughter resemblance. But something wasn't adding up. In spite of the conflicting information he was provided, he still believed Stranger's account. Koey confirmed herself that a genocide did indeed happen, and Stranger insists that it was someone who looked identical to the queen who caused it.

"Do you have any sisters?" He asked the queen. "Perhaps even a twin?"

"No." Her mother answered for her.

"Even dead ones. At this point I'm not ruling anything out."

"There was only ever one child."

"Well this doesn't make any bloody sense!" Dungar declared, exasperated.

"I share your worry about the genocide, stranger." Queen Koey acknowledged. "But I cannot hope to defend my kingdom against an unknown threat when I cannot even unify my own citizens."

"You could start by not having your guards publicly putting revolutionaries to death." Gilly interjected. "It only serves to rile them even more."

"What are you talking about?" Koey asked, confused. "I gave no such order."

"Well your wardens are outside executing revolutionaries as we speak."

"What?! That is unacceptable!"

Shoving Dungar out of the way, Koey raced out the door and out the hall towards the courtyard, ignoring pleading protests from her mother not to go out there. Dungar, Rose and Gilly chased her down the hallway, through the portrait-lined passages and down the grand staircase until eventually they had followed her all the way out into the town square. The screaming citizens and burning buildings did little to faze Jenair's queen as she pushed her way through the crowds and knights and onto the stage where the executioner continued to work.

"OH NO!!" Rose screamed as she too made it to the stage, but was held back by guardsmen. Jimminy lay shirtless as ever on the stage, head pinned against a chopping block that was stained with the blood of many before. A hooded man with a large gleaming axe stood next to him, ready to strike.

After grabbing and tossing Rose to the side, Dungar grabbed a fiery market cart and smashed it into the two guardsmen blocking the stage before pushing his way onto it. He nearly made it to the executioner before himself tackled to the ground by more guardsmen who were barely able to keep him pinned.

"Nice of you to show up, mista Dungar!" Jimminy greeted. "It appears you're here just in the nick of time!"

A scraping sound of a sharpening stone being used by the executioner was heard behind him.

"Erm. Maybe not."

"Relax, Jimmy." Dungar insisted, wriggling against the guards. "We're getting you out of this."

"WHAT IS THE MEANING OF THIS?!" Koey screeched at the guardsmen on the stage as she gestured around. "I demand you put a stop to all this right now! Who authorized you to do this!?"

Ignoring her inquiry, the guard captain instead turned to the enraged crowd. "Your benevolent queen is here, ladies and gentlemen!" He called out as he gestured towards her. "We must all bow before our beloved ruler!" He then ceremoniously knelt before her.

Shocked and appalled, Koey stared out into the crowd as their screams and threats grew even louder. They thought she was responsible for all this, and the guards shifting blame only confirmed their suspicions. Her shouts and gestures of denial were drowned out by the crowd's yells of protest.

Returning to his feet, the guard captain continued his address. "It is our duty as sworn servants of the crown to inform you that any who oppose the divine regime of Queen Theik will be subject to the highest of punishment!" As he finished he nodded to the executioner who then raised his large diamond axe high over his head.

"Stop this!" Koey shrieked desperately. "I command you!"

Dungar craned his neck upwards at his friend. Jimminy's familiar cheeky grin was gone, in its place was a look of worry.

"Jimmy . . ." Dungar breathed between gasps for air as he fruitlessly struggled against the guards. "I . . . Just, hang in there . . ."

"I had the time of me life, mate." Jimminy said softly, a weak forced smile on his face. "And the life of me time."

Dungar tried to yell, but no sound came out. Rose painfully shrieking "JIMMINY!!!" could be heard from behind him while Koey futilely continued to try and assert her power. However, none of it was to any avail. Words and screams could do nothing to hinder the trajectory of the axe as it swung downward into its target. All sound cut out for a brief moment when the thud was heard.

TWENTY FOUR

HITTING THE FAN

Dungar watched horrified as the disembodied head of Jimminy Appaya sickeningly fell from the block and rolled off the stage. The surprise and fear was still present on his face, though lacking the life and luster usually present in his brown eyes. Members of the crowd screamed and jumped backwards as it came towards them before the angry yells resumed. Then, from somewhere within the mob, the chant began.

"Burn the witch whore. Burn the witch whore! BURN THE WITCH WHORE!"

It spread quickly through their ranks until the whole horde had taken up the mantra. The guardsmen shot each other worried looks as the swarm's vitality began to remerge, stronger than ever.

None of these events had registered to Dungar yet. All of his attention was focused on one thing, and one thing alone. For the second time in just a few days he had watched his best friend die right in front of him. But this time it was different. This time it was intentional, this time it could have been prevented, and this time there were blameworthy individuals.

The first stage of grief was entirely non-existent to the blacksmith as the situation sunk in. The surge of adrenaline that now coursed through his body was wholly derived from him skipping straight to the second stage of unbridled rage. Seemingly effortlessly, he threw the two guardsmen from his back before driving his elbow right between the executioner mask's eyeholes, snatching his gleaming diamond axe, and burying it deep into the chest cavity of the guard captain.

The mass chanting of the crowd continued to reverberate off the stone walls of the buildings surrounding the square as the rioters redoubled their efforts to attack the queen. The guards also seemed to put up very little of a fight as the radicals steadily began to filter through their blockade. Fortunately, Gilly was one of the first onto the stage. With one of her hands she was pulling Rose while the other reached out and grasped the wrist of Queen Koey as she attempted to pull them both to safety.

After grabbing the executioner and throwing him to the mercy of the crowd to buy time, Dungar retrieved his hammers from the ground and brought up the rear all the while viciously pummeling any protester or guardsman that came within his reach. He didn't know which side to be on, he didn't care to consider which side to be on. He just knew he was mad and someone was going to get hurt.

With a mob of enraged civilians hot on their heels, the fleeing foursome raced back to the castle, abandoning any bags they were carrying. When they reached the entranceway, Gilly shoulder checked the doors open and ushered everyone inside before slamming them behind her and jamming her sword between the handles. Immediately the door began to pound and rattle from the outside, but the affixed sword held firm.

Safe for the moment, she slumped against the wall to catch her breath. Rose did the same, sobbing between her labored breaths. Tears in her eyes and hands shaking, she addressed nobody in particular.

"Oh my god . . . They killed Jimmy . . ."

"Those bastards!" Koey yelled, pacing back and forth. "This is treason! How dare they sell out their queen! And for what?! And wait, did you tell them I was a witch?"

The sound of rock being smashed drew the attention of the girls who looked over to see Dungar bashing chunks out of one of the marble columns with his hammer.

"Hey!!" Koey yelled at him. "Those are hand chiseled and hundreds of years old!"

"Do I look like I give a damn?!" He yelled back.

"Everybody calm down!" Gilly called to the group, kneeling next to Rose and trying to console her. "None of us told anyone out there about any accusations of witchcraft. And we are still in danger so we need to find another way out."

"There's only three doors to the castle unless you count the one to the courtyard." Koey offered. "But the rioters are probably on their way to the other two doors by now, and the courtyard is surrounded by twenty foot high walls."

"There's a panic room with an escape route hidden in the dungeons." Rose quietly informed them from her spot on the floor.

"How could you possibly know that?" The queen demanded.

"It doesn't matter." Gilly interjected. "She probably read it somewhere. If you want to live, m'lady, then I suggest we get going."

She pulled Rose to her feet then motioned for Koey to lead them to the dungeons. Dungar, body on autopilot while his mind was elsewhere, followed suit. He had no idea how to go about anything anymore. It was difficult enough to choose a course of action before the events of the town square. He still wasn't sure what to make of Queen Koey and as such did not want her to escape. However, there was no visible reason that she was anything but a mere victim of circumstances. If she truly was the conniving villain from Stranger's story then surely she wouldn't be in the position she's in. There were too many variables to be sure.

No one spoke as the group wound their way down staircases deeper into the bowels of the castle. Torches lined the walls and the smell of mildew hung in the air as they made their way down the narrow stone hallway into the dungeons. Once they encountered the cells, Koey slowed to a stop and turned back to Rose.

"Alright we're in the dungeons. Where is this panic room you speak of?"

"Er . . ." Rose mumbled, trying to remember. "For times of crisis when danger is great, the king had issued a crucial mandate, to always keep cell number twenty eight, completely free of any inmate."

Her three companions all stared at her curiously.

"What? It was a children's book . . ."

"We're trusting our lives to information from a children's book . . ." The exasperated queen sighed.

"It'll work!" She insisted, making her way deeper into the dungeon. "Where is cell twenty eight?"

"It's farther in the back, close to the . . . oh no."

"What . . . ?"

"That's the cell where we keep the marbalt."

Rose stopped mid step then looked at Gilly worryingly. Gilly returned the same look back at her before glancing back towards Koey, hoping she was wrong. Koey couldn't decide which one of the sisters to look at so she just grimaced, hoping one of them would come up with an idea. Then, simultaneously, all three women turned to Dungar who hadn't even been paying attention.

". . . What's going on?"

"You're going to need those." Koey informed him matter-of-factly, pointing to an armor rack. On the top shelf was a regular town guard's helmet, but on the middle shelf was a pair of thick steel gauntlets with large, pronounced knuckles that had to be several inches thick.

"What are those for?" He asked tentatively as the each girl handed him a piece of equipment.

"You'll see." Rose informed him uneasily.

Mildly worried, Dungar allowed himself to be guided down the hallway and to the left. Many of the cells were empty, but occasional inmates would clang against the bars or shout obscenities at them. He couldn't help but wonder how long some of them had been there for, and how many, if any, were given to Herrow for her blood sports. However, he didn't have long for such thoughts because his attention was immediately grabbed when the party came to a halt in front of what one could only assume was cell number twenty eight.

"What in the bloody blazes is that thing!?!" He demanded alarmedly.

"That's a marbalt." Rose informed him nonchalantly.

At a glance, the creature in the cell appeared to be nothing more than a bizarre statue. Until it moved. It was roughly the same height as Dungar, and walked bipedally. However, that was where any similarities ended. What he could only assume was the head of the creature was a perfect cube that had no facial features whatsoever, but rather six completely smooth sides. The body of the creature had a more weathered texture to it, and appeared to be slightly porous, but was solid rock nonetheless. Four stony arms protruded from the torso, each with a massive four-fingered hand on the end and every bit as smooth as the cubical head. It walked slightly hunched over, occasionally grabbing at the bars and walls, but as soon as the group appeared it stopped any activity and turned to face them.

"Sorry." Dungar apologized to the girls. "I have a rule. I don't fight anything without a face."

"In the event we survive this, I will see to it that your courage is adequately compensated!" Koey offered. "I'll even grant you honorary knight status."

"Look, 'princess,' 'queen,' 'whatever,' I haven't even decided whether or not I'm going to kill you!"

"Please, mister Dungar!" Rose urged as she looked up at him with the same puppy dog eyes she gave the guards. "You're our only hope!"

"Put that face away, dammit. It doesn't work."

"Look, Dungar," Gilly interjected. "We have nothing to bribe you with. But we're trapped in this castle and sooner or later we are going to be found. We may not have been considered enemies of the revolution before, but now that we are harboring the queen I can assure you they will not grant us a warm welcome. This cell is our only escape. Now if you don't have it in you to confront the creature, then give me the gauntlets."

Dungar growled to himself after she finished speaking. Like it or not, she was right. Someone had to go in there, and whether it was due to being inspired by her, or for the sake of spiting her, he wasn't letting Gilly go in instead of him. He closed his eyes and took a deep breath.

"Just open the bloody door already . . ."

Wordlessly, Koey produced a key on a necklace and unlocked the cell door. After the blacksmith walked inside, she closed it behind him.

"I am sorry, brave sir." She informed him regretfully. "But for the sake of our safety I need to lock this behind you."

He sighed. It made sense, but still didn't bode well for him.

"That was really brave of you to offer to go in his place." Dungar overheard Rose quietly say to Gilly.

"Not really." Her sister responded. "I just knew there was no way he'd let himself be showed up by a woman."

Once he entered its domain, the marbalt stood up straight and spread its arms almost in a wrestling stance, continuing to face him as he slowly circled it. He couldn't be sure due to its lack of facial features, but he was pretty sure the creature was sizing him up.

Hoping to catch it off guard, he reared back and threw his iron hammer directly at its head. Almost lazily, the creature deftly caught the hammer. It examined the tool for a moment before its face split in half and ate it whole. Dungar stared at the creature, mouth agape, before turning back to the women.

"Try not to hit it in the face!" Rose called to him. "Its jaws can crush steel!"

"Where am I supposed to hit it then?!"

"Focus on the torso!" She pointed to her midsection. "It's hollow and comprised of a more brittle mineral than the head and limbs!"

He turned away from her back to the marbalt. The torso did appear to be more weathered looking, and after seeing a solid iron hammer crushed so easily he didn't feel comfortable putting his fists anywhere near the creature's block of a head.

Heart beginning to beat faster, and breaths becoming more frequent, Dungar slowly inched towards his opponent with his hands at the ready. The marbalt's arms swung ominously back and forth seemingly ready to strike at a moment's notice. The cold, faceless head eerily watched him as he stepped side to side, psyching himself up to strike.

"Just do it . . ." He grunted to himself. "Just do it . . ."

Bending his knees and leaning forward, Dungar threw a jab towards the dead center of the marbalt's torso. Two stony arms immediately swung forward and deflected his arm while another gave him a hard slap to the side of his helmet. A loud clang rang out in the cell causing the spectators to grimace and the blacksmith to stagger sideways, ears ringing. Once he regained his footing, he returned a blind wild haymaker to the side of his opponent's square head. The blow did negligible damage, but sufficiently upset the marbalt's balance giving Dungar enough time to regain his equilibrium.

Once he was righted, he once again went for the punch to the midsection. And once again found his arm deftly deflected and a loud bang inches away from his right ear. Every reach of his within the creature's range was fruitless; there were simply too many arms to contend with. Having only two of his own, even fake swings weren't enough of a distraction to create a suitable opening.

Soon the heavy iron gauntlets began to weigh on his arms. His swings became even slower and more sluggish than before. He may as well have been moving in slow motion for how easily his opponent could counter his shots.

"Mister Dungar!" Rose hissed to him, touching his shoulder through the bars. "Have you ever read the *Chronicles of Gundar Stoneslayer?*"

"Of course I haven—" Dungar began. "Wait, who?"

"Gundar Stoneslayer! He was a famous marbalt boxer. When I first heard your name I thought you were him because your names are kinda similar. Anyway, in this book it is said—"

After hearing the name Gundar Stoneslayer, anything else Rose had to say did not reach the blacksmith. He never knew much about his father's past, never really cared either. However, he did always wonder how the man managed to own such a large building and well equipped smithy. Gundar Loloth was the most hardened man he had ever known, his handshake was so firm it killed a guy once, he wouldn't be surprised if the man did used to kill these beasts for sport. If that was indeed the case, then he wasn't going to let himself be beaten down by one.

". . . and then after he did that apparently it would leave their defenses open enough to strike." Rose finished. "Did you get all that? Did it help?"

"Sure."

With gritted teeth and cracked knuckles, Dungar approached the marbalt once more. He opened with a fake left jab. The creature took the bait and went for the counter swing. He then reared back for a right cross. He then stopped short once more as he watched another wild counter swing drift through the air. Knowing it was coming, he then ducked under the inevitable slap that had gotten him so many times before. Now was his time to strike. With a deep breath, he lunged forward to drive an uppercut into his opponent's chest. However once again he found his arm swatted away and another slap colliding with his head.

Dungar lay on the ground and groaned for a moment before getting back to his feet. His ears were ringing and he was having a bit of trouble focusing his eyes. His helmet looked pretty worse for wear too. Even through the persistent tinnitus, he could hear the even more persistent voice of Rose trying to inform him of one thing or another.

"No no, mister Dungar, you forgot there part where he—"

"I DON'T CARE IF MY DAD WAS A BOXER!"

"Uh . . . what?"

With a roar of rage, he ripped off the gauntlet on his right hand and hurled it at the marbalt. Once again the creature caught it and ate it, pausing briefly as it slowly managed to crush the thick knuckled part. During the chewing he charged at the creature, dropping to his knees and sliding under the swinging arms. Once he made contact, he wrapped his arms around its thin rocky thighs then used his own to lift it off the floor and high into the air. Small chunks of debris from his ground up glove trickled down onto his face as he spun around, still holding his heavy encumbrance. Now facing the center of the room, he took one last deep breath then power-bombed the heavy hunk of slag into the ground where its torso shattered into a million tiny pieces of rubble.

Gasps and declarations of surprise were heard from outside the cell. Pieces of the powderized marbalt wriggled their last as the cell door clicked and screeched its way open. Hiding the key necklace back in her cleavage, Koey rushed to Dungar's side to help him up.

"That was quite an interesting tactic." Rose mused as she stepped into the cell. "But props for effectiveness!"

"We can celebrate later." Gilly interrupted. "We're in the cell now, Rosie. Where's the exit?"

"Ok ok hold on." Rose waved her off as she put two fingers to her forehead, trying to recall the next verse. "Uhm . . . When filled with dread, hop into bed, then pull the thread, to not be dead."

". . . That's a pretty dark children's book." Koey pointed out as she walked over and climbed into the bed. "Where's this thread it's talking about?"

"I'm not sure." Rose admitted as she joined her. "Stupid book, sacrificing coherent instructions for the sake of rhyming!"

"Maybe it's not actually on the bed itself." Gilly offered, climbing in next to them. "I think I see something on the ceiling up here."

Dungar didn't even bother searching as the three girls tore the bed apart in their own way. The term bed was a very loose description for the particular piece of furniture they were in. It seemed to resemble a coffin more than anything else. It had wooden sides all the way around and the inside contained nothing but straw that Koey ripped apart during her search for a thread.

Leaning on the foot of the bed watching the mayhem, Dungar noticed a nearly invisible strand of fishing line affixed to the corner of the box. Feeling it with his fingers, he looked around to see identical strands at each corner of the bed as if it were being suspended in midair. He then looked back to Gilly, who was balanced on the side of the bed reaching as high as she could for a small metal hook that dangled from the ceiling.

"Uhh . . ." He began, but not quickly enough. Before he could form a sentence, Gilly grasped the hook and pulled. Immediately, the four wires severed and the bed plunged into a pit that had been hidden beneath it. The sudden fall sent both her and Dungar tumbling into the box, knocking down the other two girls as well. Upon landing, they were a heap of tangled bodies groaning and attempting to wriggle free.

"Get your foot out of my face, Dungar!"

"How do you know that's my foot?"

"Because your shoe is bigger than my head!"

"Uh, guys? Are we moving?"

Everyone stopped for a moment, then began to wriggle even harder so they could see what was going on. Dungar braced his feet against the bottom of the box and pushed himself into a standing position, letting everyone else fall away around him. Once he was upright, he felt something smack him in the fore-head. Crouching and rubbing his face, he looked overhead to see ceiling beams flying by him. Turning his head forward, he felt a cool breeze on his face as the former bed of cell number twenty eight now rolled through a small tunnel down a rail-road track steadily picking up pace.

"Cool!" The voice of Rose called out, having surfaced from the dogpile. "This is completely safe, right?"

"I have no idea." Koey grumbled, rubbing her face. "What did your children's book have to say about it?" She added sarcastically.

"Actually now that you mention it, the next verse does make more sense now. 'Rather than hide, keep hands inside, go for a ride, murder denied.'"

"These tracks don't look like they've been very well main-tained." Gilly pointed out.

Barely clinging to the tracks as it raced around corners, the bed cart shook violently on the bumpy and unkempt terrain. Rose and Koey wrapped themselves around Dungar's body as the blacksmith clung to the sides for dear life.

"Slow it down!" Koey screamed, eyes closed tight as she clung to Dungar.

"How in the blazes do you expect me to do that?!"

"I don't know, just do it!"

He looked around wildly. The tunnel they currently raced through was almost pitch black. All he could make out was the faint blur of the walls as they flew past him in a blur. Even if he could manage to grab something it would probably tear his arms off. They air that blew into his face was thick and stuffy, and occasional dust piles falling from the ceiling kept hitting him in the face. All he could do was bow his head and raise his arms to protect himself and the girls.

"Rosie!" The scared voice of Gilly called out in the darkness. "Do you know where this is taking us?"

"No!" Rose called back. "The next verse just goes 'roll down the line, compress your spine, exit the mine, close to the shrine.'"

"The mine close to the shrine!?" Koey jumped in. "That's probably the Alka Mine near the shrine to my grandfather. But that was boarded up decades ago."

"And what does compress your spine mean?" Gilly added.

"DUCK!!!" Dungar yelled as he saw the obscured light at the end of the tunnel.

At the behest of the blacksmith, all four hit the deck in the fetal position. Even through their closed eyes their vision became flooded with daylight as the mine cart smashed into the wooden barricade. Broken chunks of plank shot in all directions as the wrecked cart flew off the rails and began tumbling down the dirt hill in front of the mine entrance, ejecting its four passengers.

Fortunately for Dungar and the ladies, the ground they became forcefully acquainted with was relatively soft topsoil that absorbed much of their impact. However, the hill was steep and their momentum was great. Each one of them did several flips and somersaults before inevitably coming to a stop in the meadow at the bottom.

"That was awesome!" Rose's voice rang out somewhere nearby. "I bet you we could sell tickets to that and make a fortune!"

"Oh, Rosie . . ." Her sister chuckled.

"Oh hello, Queen Koey." A foreign voice greeted. "I figured you would be showing up sooner or later."

Dungar pulled his face from the dirt and pried his body from the ground, curious to see who would be that nonchalant about seeing the most powerful woman in all the land come crashing out of a hole in it.

Sitting in the middle of the meadow in a large chair, holding a goblet of wine and lazily reading *Gloating Effectively for Dummies*, was the familiar long scraggly brown hair and smug chiseled face of Rainchild Earthumper.

CWENCY FIVE

ANAGNORISIS

Even after running into the manifestation of Rainchild in the wizard tree, Dungar hadn't really given the man much thought in the last few days. When confronted with real problems he found that petty rivalries and trivial interpersonal issues often fell to the wayside. However, to see the man sitting there, allegedly having anticipated their arrival, resulted in an influx of old grudges so potent he could barely restrain himself long enough to let the important questions be asked.

The wizard didn't appear to recognize him underneath his battered helmet. Since coming into contact with the group, all of his attention had been focused on the queen, although he did shoot a few confused glances at Rose. Dungar and Gilly's attire probably gave them the impression of being guards, albeit ill-equipped ones. If so, that fact may prove useful in the event that Rainchild was hoping to maintain a guise of anonymity.

There were still the pertinent questions pertaining to subjects such as how he knew they were going to end up here, why he was here waiting for them, and why he wasn't moving a muscle to help the queen to her feet. Such lack of action was not indicative of a man hoping to marry her.

"Rainchild!" Koey exclaimed. "What are you doing here?!"

"Why, I'm here to defeat you!" He responded coolly as he flipped his book shut and got to his feet. Hands casually behind his back, he slowly paced around. "The evil witch Koey. Terror of the west, destroyer of cities!" He paused for a moment before looking back to her with narrow eyes. "Usurper of the throne."

"Are you addled?!" Koey yelled out incredulously as she got to her feet. She looked around wildly from Rainchild to her companions. "I'm serious! Are you all positively insane, or is this just the worst bachelorette party prank in the history of the kingdom?"

Rainchild opened his mouth to speak, but Koey sharply cut him off as she pointed a finger towards him menacingly.

"I don't care how long you were an advisor to my father, wizard! You are going to knock off this absurdity right now. You cannot possibly believe that I destroyed Farrawee."

"You don't give me orders, girl!!" The wizard barked as he shoved Koey backwards into the arms of Gilly. "And of course a pathetic and incompetent child such as yourself didn't destroy Farrawee. You're not even well enough equipped to govern a city, let alone overthrow one! To accomplish such a feat would take an individual who was a master of strategy, deception, and manipulation. An individual who was abundant in political savvy, ingenuity, and ruthlessness. An individual who- Oh for god sakes it was me. I did it."

"You monster!" Rose yelled at him.

"Look, girl, I don't know who you are or why you're here, but I'm trying to relish my moment of victory. So shut up."

"Why does everyone think it was me then?" Koey demanded.

"Why? Because it WAS you, Queen Koey!"

Before she could respond, Rainchild's body began to mutate. He began to grow shorter and slenderer as his body appeared to fold into itself. His long scraggly brown hair became silky and golden, and his deep brown eyes changed to the rich blue hue of the Jenair heir. A perfect mirror image of

Queen Koey now stood before her wearing the malicious smile that only Rainchild could muster.

"And man, these were fun to play with." Rainchild added, absentmindedly squeezing at his chest.

"HEY!" The now enraged ruler shrieked as she swatted the wizard's hands. "Those are mine!"

"Yes yes. Well anyway." Rainchild dismissed as he produced a large bowie knife. "Now that that's cleared up, down to business."

Dungar now knew everything he needed to know. He still didn't have his head completely wrapped around the entire plot, but there would be time for questions after the cowardly hippie has been pummeled to a point of being barely able to answer them. Marbalt glove still on his left hand, he clenched his fist and slugged Koey's doppelgänger right in the mouth sending him stumbling backwards onto his currently perfectly proportioned ass.

"HOW DARE YOU!" Rainchild screamed, spitting out blood and broken teeth. "I'll have your head for this when I am king!" He then pointed at Gilly. "YOU! Arrest your partner!"

With a slight frown, Gilly delivered a perfectly placed kick right into the perfectly placed cheekbone of the Koey clone.

Face sufficiently shattered, the wizard reverted back to his original form where he could be injury free. His agitation, however, did not wane.

"What is the meaning of this?! We had a deal!"

"What deal?" Gilly asked, genuinely interested.

At that moment, something in Dungar's head clicked. His mind went back to the execution block in the town square, and the solid diamond axe that the executioner wielded. Focusing on memories of earlier, he could also recall the strangely sparkling weapons of the guards Rose rooted.

"He supplied the town guard with diamond weaponry."

"How could you know that?" Gilly asked. "And how is that even possible?"

"His body isn't the only thing he can transform. I've seen him do the diamond magic before."

"Hate to interrupt!" Rainchild sarcastically butted in as he got to his feet. "But you clearly aren't Jenair city guards. Admittedly I probably should have realized that sooner, but regardless it begs the question: who are you?"

Wordlessly, Dungar removed his dented and dirt encrusted helmet to reveal his glowering crazy blue eyes and a scowl hard enough to shatter stone.

". . . Blacksmith!?" The wizard exclaimed after taking a moment to recognize him. "Well this is certainly unexpected."

All five stood in silence for a few moments, waiting to see how events proceeded.

"Oh well, always fun to see a familiar face." Rainchild finally spoke. "But if you'll excuse me I'll have to be carrying on with my master plan."

"Do you honestly expect us to just leave you to continue your evil?!" Gilly called out incredulously, putting herself between Rainchild and Koey. "Witchcraft alone is an abomination, and you have also admitted to the most serious of crimes!"

"You're not going anywhere." Dungar growled as he too stepped between the wizard and the queen.

Rainchild smirked as he looked his old neighbor up and down. Despite being outnumbered, he remained calm and composed as if he didn't perceive them as a threat. "Oh is that right? You intend to stop me?"

Teeth clenched and lips pursed, Dungar scowled at his old nemesis. He then turned to the woman-at-arms next to him.

"We do."

Gilly's frown faded for a brief moment at the acknowledgement. She then mirrored Dungar's expression towards the wizard.

"You and your foul magic are to be banish—"

Her voice trailed off mid-sentence as once again their opponent began to transform before their eyes. His body and limbs stretched as his shoulders and chest widened. When the metamorphosis finished, the wizard had become a giant bald headed humanoid creature with sparse patches of brown fur tufting from various spots. Its legs were short for its eight foot stature, causing the beast to naturally lean forward and brace part of its body weight on a pair of enormous hands attached to gigantic forearms. Black animalistic eyes stared down at them as an upturned gorilla-like nose snuffled loudly and a gaping half-toothless mouth snarled strands of saliva everywhere.

"Rosie! What is this thing!?"

"How should I know!? I'm not a bestiary!"

"Well, blacksmith!?" The monster roared in a deep breathy voice as his bulging eyes turned to him. "You told me to face you like a man. What are you waiting for?!"

Dungar's legs were frozen beneath him. His arms were at the ready, but he had no idea how to proceed. His mind went back to the arena. The pain of battle, the helplessness of debilitation. Looking into the face of yet another monster sapped any fervor he had going into this confrontation, instead reminding him of hopeless battles past, knowing that he couldn't expect someone to jump in and save him again.

"Aw. So much for being a big man." Rainchild taunted him before a using a mighty backswing to knock him several paces backwards. Gilly ducked his other arm before she received the same treatment. She then shoved Koey backwards out of his reach before grabbing a nearby rock with which to distract the monster. The wizard attempted to give chase to the queen, but the barrage of stones hurled by Gilly effectively diverted his attention for the time being.

"Mister Dungar!" The panicked voice of Rose shouted as she shook him. "This is bad, this is bad!"

Groaning, Dungar slowly hauled himself upright before looking at Rose, who was wildly looking back and forth between him and her sister.

"What are we going to do?!"

"I don't know, Rose." He acknowledged quietly as he rubbed his chest where he'd been hit. "Don't suppose your books have some way of dealing with this?"

"This is nothing like my books." She swallowed nervously as she looked back at him with worry in her eyes. "The good guys aren't supposed to die. They're supposed to have heroes that are stronger and smarter than the villain. They're supposed to defeat him and save the day."

They both turned back to the fighting. Tired and outmatched as she was, Gilly continued to protect the queen one way or another. As Dungar watched, he could see her weakening throws and dodging of blows became steadily less effective as the conflict wore on and the monster slowly began to gain the upper hand. He could empathize all too well with the feeling. However, grim as it was, the day was not yet totally lost.

"We're not stronger or smarter than this thing." He said as he brushed Rose's hands away and got to his feet. "But," he added, turning back to her, "For better or for worse, *we* are the heroes of this story."

A faint sick smile twisted onto his stubbly face as he looked down the meadow towards Rainchild. It was in those short moments where the true meaning of being a hero crystallized inside his mind. A hero wasn't the toughest, noblest, most untouchable, and most admirable person on the battlefield. A hero didn't even have to win. A hero was just someone who did what needed to be done. True or not, it was a satisfying enough notion for him at that particular moment.

He gritted his teeth and charged the beast. Still distracted by Gilly, Rainchild didn't know he was coming until he felt the full force of the blacksmith slamming into his ribcage.

In spite of the size difference, the lunging tackle struck with enough force that both man and monster were sent tumbling down another nearby hill. Quickly rolling to his feet, Dungar paused for a moment to glance back to his friends.

"RUN!!!!" He roared before returning his sights to the wizard.

As the sound of racing footsteps rustling the bushes faded away, Dungar hopped onto the downed body of his enemy before he could get up and proceeded to relentlessly pound away at his head. His fists, gloved or not, seemed to have little effect on the giant creature. Each blow caused its recipient to recoil slightly, but he only got five or six hits in before Rainchild swatted him off and hopped to his feet.

His attacker appeared to be the least of the wizard's worries as he wildly scanned around looking for Koey. Within moments, the blacksmith was on him again repeatedly dishing a futile assault. Offensively ineffective as it was, the persistent onslaught was sufficient at drawing the beast's attention. Dungar resorted to every underhanded tactic he could think of. He stomped Rainchild's enormous feet, he gouged at the man's eyes, he kicked him in the groin several times.

"ENOUGH!" The monster roared, covering his small aggressor with a huge gob of slobber.

Balancing on his giant knuckles, he swung forward and drove his feet into Dungar's chest hard enough to send him into a series of backflips. He then wasted no more time before beginning his pursuit of the women, leaving Dungar behind in a crumpled heap.

Struggling to catch his breath, the wounded warrior slowly got to an upright seated position. He silently cursed himself for a few moments for not being able to distract Rainchild for longer. Rose and Koey were not fast runners, particularly not in Koey's dress, and Gilly would never leave them behind. Unless they found a place to hide, they would never outrun their pursuer.

With a deep breath and a grunt, Dungar was back on his feet and lumbering behind them. He couldn't see where anyone had gone as the forest area around the meadow grew dense quickly. Drained but driven, he slogged through the thick underbrush slowly picking up pace. He paid no mind to the fact he had no idea where he was or where he was going, he didn't even realize how hopelessly lost in a foreign land he was, his mind was completely focused on his wooded surroundings and those who dwelled within.

He looked around wildly as he ran, scanning for any signs of movement or tracks or any indication whatsoever of recent passersby. Eventually an external sound entered his ear, the sound of snapping twigs and breaking branches. Something large was tearing through these woods near his position, and he hoped it was Rainchild because the last thing he felt he needed to do was pick a fight with another large woodland creature.

The shapeshifted wizard galloped through the woods on all fours in pursuit of his prey. His flattened snout snuffled at the air as he continued to zero in. He began to slow down and paw at nearby bushes as if he knew the women to be near. Concealed beneath the long and flat rock he currently stood on was a small cave. The entrance was just wide enough that three young women were able to crawl inside one at a time in attempt to outwit their hunter.

At the sound of large feet thudding overheard, three hands clasped over three mouths and terrified expressions were shared. Suddenly a colossal hand reached through the opening, frantically swiping at the air.

"Hello, girls."

The low breathy rumble filled their small crawlspace as a one of the large coal black eyes peered in at them.

"Room for one more?"

He retracted his arm and grasped the boulder with both hands as he tried to lift it off of them. Slowly light began to peek inside as the rock was slowly pulled free from the binds of nature.

"Rosie, listen to me!" Gilly spoke urgently as dust trickled onto her face from above. She grasped her hyperventilating sister by the shoulder to assure her attention. "As soon as the way is clear, I need you to take the queen and run. Do not look back, just get her far away from here."

"No . . . No, I can't!"

"Yes you can! There is no other option."

"Gilly, I can't do this! I'm not brave like you and Dungar. I wish I was fearless like you. I wish I wasn't scared. I wish I could beat up bad guys. But I'm not! And I can't . . ."

"You know I'd never leave you unless I absolutely had to!"

Gilly glanced over her shoulder worriedly as Rainchild's figure became slowly more visible. Turning back to her sister, she could now see her fearful face in the dim light. "What do you think being brave is, Rose? If one is not scared then one is not brave, for fear is a necessity to courage."

The sound of snapping roots and displaced ground cut off any part of her speech that may have remained. Their cozy cave had been reduced to a simple indent in the landscape as the wizard finally hoisted the rock away, bathing them all in sunlight.

"I believe in you, Rosie! Go now!"

Grabbing two handfuls of dirt from the ground, Gilly charged towards the monster, jumped as high as she could, and plunged the small piles of the damp soil into his eyes. Immediately he recoiled, thrashing around wildly while furiously trying to rub at his eyes. After a quick scan of her surroundings revealed all she had at her disposal were rocks, she grabbed the largest one she could wield one handed and began clubbing Rainchild in the mouth with it, attempting to knock his teeth out once again.

Bits of pulverized oral flesh were leaking from his mouth by the time the monster regained his eyesight. Enraged, he grabbed Gilly by her swinging arm and lifted her off the ground by it. Using his free hand, he grasped her by the shoulder and began to pull her arm clean off. Before he could do so, a grass stained, dirt encrusted, and incredibly pissed off bearded blacksmith leapt down from the top of a nearby rock face, grabbed Rainchild's monster form's mane of fur, and used his own body weight to pull the wizard off his feet and to the ground.

A loud thud rang out through the forest as Gilly landed on Rainchild who, in turn, landed on Dungar, knocking the wind out of him once more. Immobilized and gasping for air, Dungar saw only one viable course of action. He wrapped his hairy, steely arms around the beast's neck as he had done for many of his patrons before. However, this time he squeezed for all he was worth.

Rainchild began to thrash around, mouth wide open gasping for air while his dirty thick, pipe-like fingers furiously clawed at his choker's arms. With narrowed eyes, Gilly got to her knees while still the wizard's chest and shoved her arm into Rainchild's now toothless mouth then retracted it quickly, his freshly ripped off uvula squished in her fist.

The ensuing roar of pain echoed through the forest, reverberating off of trees and frightening flocks of birds. The pain of the injury caused the wizard to contort so violently that he managed to break the blacksmith's grip.

"Dayum, that was loud!"

"It came from over there!"

Dungar and Gilly looked off into the woods towards the voices while Rainchild reverted back to his human form, a look of relief spreading over his face as the pain in his throat vanished. Three armor clad men emerged hurriedly from the trees to investigate the scene of the scuffle

"What's goin on here?!" One of them demanded. "What are you lot doing to that man?!"

"This man is a murderer and a sorcerer—" Gilly began

"KNIGHTS!" Rainchild cut her off as he threw his arms up. "Thank Suola you're here! I finally had the Queen but then these two thugs attacked me!"

"How dare you mention Suola, you vile—"

"Unhand that man immediately!" The knight commanded, drawing his steel.

Begrudgingly, Gilly and Dungar raised their hands submissively and inched away from Rainchild, who quickly hopped to his feet and dusted himself off.

"Thank you, sir knight! I don't know what I would have done if—"

"Where is the queen?!" A different knight demanded. "Is she far?"

"Not at all! Just keep these two away from me and we will track them down!"

Held at sword point and forced to follow the man who was at his mercy mere moments before, Dungar glanced over to Gilly who appeared to share his attitude towards the situation. Unarmed and outnumbered, obeying commands and quietly hoping they don't find Rose or Koey seemed to be the best course of action for the time being.

Something about the situation felt rather peculiar. The three men certainly appeared to be guards from the castle, likely searching the forest to see if Rainchild succeeded. However, while two of them possessed the diamond swords symbolizing the wizard's corruption, the third carried a regular sword of folded steel. Naturally that could mean a number of things, or indeed nothing at all, but it was odd to Dungar nonetheless.

Things were tense as they made their way through the forest. The four other men were intently scanning their surroundings and jumping at any seemingly foreign sound. He considered making a run for it a few times, but he wasn't sure it was a good idea to test shady law enforcers on their reflexes. Consequently he bit his tongue and bided his time until a sound was heard that made his heart sink and regret his decision.

"There they are!"

Sure enough, down at the foot of a small bank were the two young ladies in tattered clothing hoofing it through the thick underbrush as best they could. Abandoning chaperoning the prisoners, the three knights sheathed their weapons and took off after the girls. Not content to wait and see what would happen, Dungar and Gilly chased the chasers.

The pressure of pursuit was not handled well by Rose who stumbled almost immediately upon feeling it. Koey stopped to help her to her feet, but the damage was done. In an instant the guards were upon them and their retreat terminated. The girls became separated and all weapons were immediately drawn. Rainchild slowed to a walk as he composed himself to gloat once again.

"My my, dear Queen, you gave us quite a scare there. However, now that all that business is over, it is going to be my distinct pleasure to—"

"HOLD IT RIGHT THERE!"

All heads turned to the knight with the steel sword who had drawn his weapon and held it to Rose's throat from behind.

"ROSIE!" Gilly screamed, taking a step forward.

"You best hold your pretty little self right there, missy!" The guard grunted warningly. "Or I'ma slice this damsel here worse'n a grouchhawk guts a codfish."

Dungar stared at the knight wide-eyed.

"Now you lot here listen up and you listen yerselves good!" He continued. "Yer gonna surrender that there queen into my charge whereupon I will commence the bringing of justice down upon her!"

Rainchild stared at him incredulously, mouth twisted into an expression of thorough confusion.

"Who is this guy!?" He demanded of the other knights.

With his free hand, the knight removed his helmet and tossed it to the ground.

"I am Sir Lee, the only remaining true knight of this here glorious kingdom and all her freedoms! And I am here to honorably execute lady whatever-the-tit-her-real-name-is for the crimes of murder, treason, and impersonating a royal official!"

"YOU IDIOT!" Rainchild loudly berated him. "WE'RE here to kill the queen!" He added, gesturing to himself and the other two guards.

Lee's eyes went wide and he lowered his sword. "Well shoot! If I knew we were all here to kill the queen then that woulda saved me one whole of a lotta trouble reenlisting in the town guard and whatnot."

"Only WE are here to carry out an execution." Rainchild corrected him, once again gesturing to himself and the guards. He then gestured to Dungar and Gilly. "THEY are the ones who would have our efforts thwarted."

"Naw naw, you got it all wrong, son! That there bearded feller is Doonger. He saved my bacon a few sun-ups past. He's got it in fer the queen too. We're all on the same team!"

"Well if it weren't for mister 'Doonger,' as he is referred, the queen would be dead already and we could all be carrying on with our lives."

"Aw well, it's fer the best anyhow! I wanted to be the one to do it anyway."

"Well that is absolutely out of the question, you drawling inbred. The people promised to elect me monarch once *I* ridded them of their evil overlord, as I convinced them only *I* could."

"Now YOU listen to ME, you fancy talkin' flower fondler! I don't care what kinda deal you made with what kinda people. I'll be the one taking that lady's head and I'll be doing with it whatever I see fit!" He then grabbed a fistful of Rose's hair and pulled her towards him. "Even if I gotta resort to giving some undeserved treatment to some undeserving people to get my way!"

As Rainchild opened his mouth to rebut, Gilly reached over and stole one of the other guard's diamond swords right from its scabbard then sliced off the hand that held Rose's hair at the wrist so fast that Lee didn't even have time to react. Her precision was perfect as the hand fell to the ground without a single hair being severed. She then pulled her sister to her side as Lee fell to his knees gaping at the bloody stump at the end of his arm.

"My wise and faithful watcher above." Gilly quietly recited to herself as she closed her eyes and held her free hand to her chest. "I pray forgiveness for I have broken my seventh vow by harming one who had not caused harm unto me or my faith."

"DANGIT, YOU GUTLESS WENCH!" Lee screamed into the forest as he raised his sword once more. "Yer gonna pay for that!"

Paying him no mind, Gilly's eyes remained closed and her oration continued.

"I pray you can understand my actions of harm were perpetrated only with the intent of preventing greater harm."

The disarmed knight drew a long, thin knife from his ankle scabbard while his partner unsheathed his own diamond armament. Rage in his eyes, Lee took another step closer to Gilly, brandishing his sword menacingly.

"ARE YOU LISTENING TO ME, GIRL?!"

"Furthermore, I pray that you take mercy upon the three souls that will soon be joining you in your garden of stars."

Paying no attention to her words, Lee lunged forward with a wild swing of his sword. Eyes suddenly open wide, Gilly gave Rose a harsh shove that knocked her to the ground before agilely rolling under Lee's swipe. Now in front of the two guards, she transitioned directly from her roll to a spinning leap into the air during which she roundhouse kicked the sword guard in the face with her metal greaves.

Her combat style was elegant and flowing like a dance. She drifted around her opponents with ease as if not encumbered by her heavy armor at all. Even though he watched the entire thing happen, Dungar was unable to pinpoint the exact moment wherein the sword wounds from which the deceased guards now bled were inflicted. By the time Sir Lee had spun around from his wild swing, he was the only armed man left standing.

Gilly stood before him, eyes closed once more. Her feet were placed together in a strange T shape and although she did not look towards her opponent, her sword was aimed directly at him. With a guttural cry of barbarism, the doomed knight raised his sword again. The moment he did so, Gilly's eyes opened and she began to spin once more. On her first rotation, her swinging sword severed the man's remaining hand in the exact same spot as the first one. It was on her second spin that she lopped the man's head clean from his shoulders.

Rose and Koey were mortified at the carnage that now surrounded them, leaving them unable to so much as gasp. Even Dungar found himself looking back and forth between Gilly and her handiwork wide-eyed. Before long, however, both fighters had turned their attention back to Rainchild, who was inspecting the bloodshed with a pronounced lower lip. Seeing the eyes of hatred upon him, he simply shrugged.

"Oh, is this where I'm supposed to cower in fear?" He threw up his hands and contorted his face into a faux look of terror. "You two don't scare me!"

Dungar and Gilly shared a confused look briefly before they began towards the wizard.

"Allow me to amend that statement!" Rainchild added quickly, causing a pause in their advance. He pointed to a particularly tall tree nearby that, at some point during the commotion, had been turned into a solid diamond pillar that caught the setting sun's light and brilliantly shone like a beacon, lighting up the forest around them and even the sky itself. Smug smile on his face, he continued. "What I meant to say was: you two wouldn't scare me . . . even if I didn't just alert the entire Jenair military to my current position. In fact either that's a funny looking cloud or that's them on the horizon right now!"

Sure enough, at the crest of the hill the sun was currently setting behind, was the unmistakable silhouette of an amassing army. Teeth clenched into a grimace, Gilly turned and faced them stoically with her sword, momentarily unaware that Rainchild had reached over and turned it into cheese while she was distracted.

"You know, I totally could have killed you both right there." The wizard chuckled as he leaned against his diamond tree. "But I'd rather sit and watch how this unfolds. How is it the kids say it these days? Oh right. 'Dis gon b gud!'"

TWENTY SIX

NO FEAR CAVALIER

Every knight in the kingdom had to be on that ridge. With a missing ruler and zero law enforcement, Dungar figured the city itself was likely in a state of anarchy by this point. Though it was still probably more peaceful than it was when the guards were there.

The sinking sun stretched the soldiers' shadows spookily down the slope. Their diamond blades glowed ethereally as they reflected the bright star's light. To the sound of a distant drum beat, they all began to march in step down the horizon. As soon as the infantry began their approach, Rose rushed over to the body of Sir Lee and retrieved his steel sword.

"Here!" She called to Gilly, taking the dairy blade from her and handing over the real weapon.

Rainchild snorted loudly behind them during the exchange. "Oh you think that will help you, girl? Diamond is the hardest material in the world. Simple folded steel will be no match."

"I'm afraid he's right, Rosie." Gilly sheepishly admitted as she pushed the metal blade away and moved towards the other diamond sword. But Rose leapt in front of her, blocking her path.

"Don't any of you know anything?!" She lectured them urgently. "Do you even know what hardness means?!"

Everyone shared uneasy looks with one another before turning back to Rose looking mildly embarrassed.

She sighed and smacked her forehead. "The covalent crystalline structure of diamond minerals results in a rigidity that eliminates any capacity for flexion!!"

Her audience stared at her completely blank faced.

"THEY WILL SHATTER WHEN YOU SMACK THEM!"

Her three allies all glanced back to Rainchild. Although the wizard attempted to hide his consternation, the faint frown on his face indicated he had not considered that tidbit of information.

"I love having a brilliant little sister!" Gilly exclaimed triumphantly, grinning ear to ear as she took the steel sword from Rose.

"You're still hopelessly outnumbered!" The wizard snarled. "Even with weapons you don't stand a chance!"

Koey retrieved the other diamond sword from the ground and dug the point of it into his chest.

"For your own sake you had better hope you're wrong, you treasonous malefactor!" She threatened him as she slowly applied more force to the blade boring into him. "For if we do not survive this battle, then I will personally see to it that you do not either!"

Dungar grabbed one of the knight's helmets from the ground and put his hand inside it. He still had the marbalt glove on his left, now he also had protection for his right. If what Rose said was true, then armor clad hands would be more than a match for flimsy weapons. If it wasn't, then he'd have a lot more to worry about than some digital lacerations.

"Are you ready, Dungar?" Gilly asked him as she defiantly stared down the approaching horde.

"That's kind of a pointless question, don't you think? I don't imagine they intend to wait if I'm not."

"Now is a poor time to be difficult, blacksmith."

"Well it might be the last time I get to be."

"Not on this day." She lowered her sword and turned to her ally. "I can feel a presence watching over us. If your cause is just and your actions valiant, then Suola will always—"

"DUCK, GILLY!"

Diamond sword raised aggressively, the soldier at the head of the pack was nearly upon her. As he began to bring his blade down, Gilly swung her heavy steel sword upwards causing the two weapons to powerfully crash together. True to Rose's word, the air became filled with a flurry of fragmented shining shards as the knight's weapon exploded on contact with the steel blade.

He froze in place as he stared down at the stump of a weapon he now held in his hand. As soon as he became disarmed, Gilly ceased in her attack and readopted her odd fighting stance, prompting Dungar to take matters into his own fists and finish the soldier off with an uppercut.

Seeing the fate of the fighter before them, the swarm of Jenair guardsmen came to a sliding halt as they began inspecting their own swords. Soon the air was filled with the sounds of metallic clangs and shattering blades as sword after sword was subjected to, and subsequently failed, every test of tensile strength the soldiers tried. Before long, they had all thrown the remains of their weapons to the ground and proceeded in their march unarmed.

Gilly lowered her own sword as well, much to Dungar's dismay.

"Don't tell me they're now innocent just because they're unarmed!"

"It is a tenet of my faith that I may not apply greater force than is applied towards me."

"Then drop the sword and start cracking skulls!"

Obediently, she discarded her weapon and raised her hands, palms facing the chargers. Dungar too raised his hands, balled into the tightest fists he could muster. His whole body shook from adrenaline as he was bore down upon.

Finally the remaining attackers reached them. The blacksmith reared back then swung as hard as he could towards the first in line, a move that was completely useless as the sheer number of men in the army immediately overwhelmed him and Gilly. They were both instantly knocked to the ground and force to curl up as an innumerable amount of punches and kicks were laid into them.

Rose watched the ordeal in horror, eyes wide and both hands covering her mouth. Koey pushed the sword even harder into Rainchild.

"Order them to stop!"

"Well you're their queen. Why don't you do it?"

"I am not jesting, wizard!"

"You know, my dear Koey, if you start running right now then I could probably still get the public's favor on the grounds of having simply driven you away. That way you don't have to die. It would be less fun, sure, but I'll make that sacrifice just for you."

"I AM WARNING YOU!"

A booming roar suddenly swept over the forest, shaking the trees and stopping the skirmish. The Jenair guards looked wildly around at the forest and each other, searching for the source of the sound. Then it came again, louder this time. Dungar and Gilly hurriedly crawled away in the shower of falling leaves as several guards were forced to their knees with their hands on their ears.

"THERE!" A guard shouted, pointing behind everyone. "On the horizon! What is that thing?!"

Bathed in the dimming rays of the nearly set sun was the silhouette, complete with unmistakable enormous afro, of Shaffleton the Farrawee fighting goat. The soldiers watched in awe as the graceful creature began its charge down the hill towards them. A path was efficiently cleared in the crowd as guards either dove out of the way or were effortlessly knocked aside.

Dungar's jaw dropped at the display. Not only had Shaffleton returned to help them in their time of need, but mounted upon the formidable fighting goat, pale frail body clad only in a pair of tighty whities as his mighty mane of bushy black hair flowed majestically behind him, was Jimminy Appaya.

"Good evening, mates!" He announced triumphantly as Shaffleton kicked in the faceplate of a nearby guard. "And mate-ettes!" He added with a nod at the girls.

"Who is this guy?" Koey inquired.

"How are you alive?!" Dungar demanded, ignoring her.

"How did you find us?!" Gilly added.

"Where did you get that katana?!" Rose jumped in, pointing at his weapon.

"Why are you all standing there and letting them have this conversation?!" Rainchild screamed at his henchmen.

"All will be answered in good time!" Jimminy insisted. "But first, would any of you lovely lads or ladies care to inform me of the current events?"

"Oh god where to begin?!" Rose exclaimed exasperatedly. "So we managed to get into the castle, and then—"

"QUEEN GOOD, KNIGHTS BAD!" Dungar screamingly interjected.

"Thanks, mate!" Jimminy grinned and winked at him. He then turned back to the soldiers and yelled into the distance. "GET THE SHINY ONES, MATES!"

The guards once again found themselves looking around confusedly, clearly having no idea what was going on anymore. What happened next certainly only served to exacerbate their bewilderment, for yet another strange noise came rolling in from beyond the horizon.

"*Jum! Jum! Jum! Jum! Jum!*"

Like an army of fire ants, the robed red army swarmed over the hill and converged upon the unsuspecting soldier battalion. With neither party having weapons, the conflict quickly devolved into a massive bout of fisticuffs. However, the cultists were both outnumbered and outmatched by the impressive Jenair military.

"Er, Jimmy, your 'friends' are getting the snot beaten out of them." Dungar pointed out uneasily.

"That is quite a keen observation, mate!" Jimminy acknowledged, not taking his eyes from the fight. "They're not the greatest fighting blokes out there, but once a fellow pledges himself to Dynam and goes through initiation to become a Dynamite, upon death he will—"

His explanation was cut short by a large explosion that sent dismembered pieces of former guards in all directions. The blast then triggered the rest of the cultists, resulting in a domino effect of exploding people and mutilated military personnel. When the smoke finally cleared, roughly a quarter of the original guard population remained as well as a few scant surviving Dynamites.

Of the remaining guardsmen, many decided they could take no more and fled into the woods leaving roughly twenty or so remaining in fighting spirits. Dungar and Gilly reassumed their fighting stances while Jimminy tightened his grip on Shaffleton's afro. Not a sound was uttered from anyone as the two sides stared each other down, waiting for a member of the other to make the first move.

"Oh right!" Jimminy suddenly exclaimed, smacking his forehead and causing everyone to jump. "I forgot about the other friends I ran into along the way!"

Everyone looked back to the hill where the Dynamites came from, expecting to see another pack on the horizon. However the hill remained empty, the woods remained still, and the air remained soundless yet rife with palpable tension.

Jimminy cleared his throat with a loud harrumph, then announced again. "I SAID I FORGOT ABOUT THE OTHER FRIENDS I—"

"AVAST, YE CUTLASS FLAPPING, RUM SWIGGING RASCALS!" Nobeard yelled as he came crashing down from a nearby tree. Suddenly all the trees began to shake as a slew of pirates descended from them with knives in their teeth. Dungar looked around in amazement, now realizing the true reason the trees shook during the roaring cries of Shaffleton.

"This was supposed to be a bit more coordinated of an effort." Jimminy explained, attempting to demonstrate with his hands. "But SOMEBODY felt they had to make a show of their arrival!"

"In entrances piratical, atypical and impractical I am the very pinnacle of appearances theatrical!" Nobeard exclaimed enthusiastically, waving his sword in time with his words.

Rainchild watched the whole exchange with a contorted pained expression on his face while Rose stared in Nobeard in awe, grinning ear to ear. Jimminy shared a similar sentiment.

"Oh blimey, how could I possibly be mad at someone as glorious as you, mate?!"

"Let's kick some asses, Jaunty!"

At that, every man, and Gilly, rushed into battle. Nobeard was the first to strike, driving a front kick into a knight so hard that the man's chest plate caved in and he was hurled backwards into two of his comrades. The armor they wore was no match for the force behind his swinging cutlass as the weapon effortlessly cleaved limb from body and head from neck.

Shaffleton the goat flailed around violently, delivering kicks left and right while Jimminy's body flailed in tandem. Although it appeared he was barely capable of even hanging on, his long thin blade continued to cut down his adversaries in spite of it.

Gilly resumed her strange circular approach to battle. Constantly spinning one way or the other, she opted to somehow dodge every swing directed at her rather than counter or parry. She almost appeared to possess a level of clairvoyance the way she was able to anticipate when to evade and when to strike with her surgeon-like accuracy and efficiency. Even without a sword, larger and more armored men dropped around her like the novices they were in comparison.

Lacking any formal training whatsoever, Dungar leapt into the fray relying on nothing more than the skills he acquired via bar brawls. Of all the conflicts he had engaged in throughout this adventure, it was in this one that he felt truly in his element. Countless angry men, double that amount of swinging fists, one oddly tough woman, and a confused and aggressive wild animal. This felt just like home.

The scene was chaos from its inception. Even if he had tried, Dungar couldn't have counted the number of blows he received in the carnage. All sorts of limbs and body parts, not all of which were still attached to their bodies of origin, made violent contact with him during the scuffle. He knew it was going to happen, and that mere knowledge somehow helped make it bearable. Lacking any sort of strategy of his own, the most prudent course of action in his mind was to slug the nearest individual in sight with his armored hands. He was pretty sure he punched Nobeard in the face at some point, but in the midst of the chaos it was hard to know for certain.

The only thing anyone felt they could be certain of was that if they dared fall down they were not getting back up. As soon as a body hit the ground it was immediately besought upon by the merciless boots of both friend and foe. Significantly more unfortunate individuals found themselves simply stomped to death in the heat of battle than those who were done in by a calculated blow.

The combined might of the good guys was superior to that of their adversaries, but the true edge in the battle was allotted to them by way of being in the company of pirates that happened to be armed with sharp objects facing opponents who mostly had fists, having previously discarded their diamond swords. However it did not render the conflict completely one-sided. By the time the crowd thinned, there were only five standing combatants left. Conveniently, they were Dungar, Gilly, Nobeard, Shaffleton the goat, and one random Dynamite that managed to finish the fight unexploded.

Weary from battle and breathing heavily, they all turned to face Rainchild who was wearing a facial expression that indicated he had absolutely no idea what to make of the events that had just transpired before his eyes. Before anyone could address him, however, the frantic voice of Rose called out.

"OH MY GOD! JIMMINY!"

Whipping back around to the pile of bodies, Dungar saw Jimminy laying among them, somehow having managed to get several different knives jammed into his chest. Immediately the blacksmith rushed to him and knelt by his side, cupping his head as he coughed feebly at the brink of death.

"Damn it, Jimmy!" Dungar scolded the fellow, half pained, half exasperated. "Will you stop bloody dying already!"

"Wa thi . . . mate . . ." Jimminy struggled to speak as he clutched Dungar's shirt. "I gunb . . . cul . . ."

"Jimmy I don't . . . I don't understand you . . ."

Hacking violently and spitting out the blood from his mouth, Jimminy pulled him closer and whispered into his ear.

Before Dungar could respond, a final death rattle rasped from the man's mouth and his body fell limp in the blacksmith's arms. Nobeard bowed his head and put his hand over his heart while Rose clung to her sister, weeping as her eyes remained transfixed on Jimminy. Dungar, however, simply looked around confusedly.

"Did anyone else hear what he just said to me?"

"No." Gilly replied. "What did he say?"

"He said 'watch this, mate, it's gonna be cool' . . ."

"GRRRRRRRAAAAAAAAAHHHHHHHHHHHHH-
HHH!!!!!"

Everyone jumped backwards at the sudden booming roar
that the lone Dynamite was hollering. His eyes had begun
glowing a bright neon red and his voice had changed to a bar-
itone demonic pitch that was clearly not his own.

"ONE STEP CLOSER TO RELEASE FROM THIS MOR-
TAL COIL!" he yelled.

He then exploded in a shower of guts and body parts.

When the gang lowered their arms that had been raised to
protect them from said shower, Jimminy Appaya stood once
again good as new in the center of a blood splatter that looked
oddly like a smiley face.

"Wasn't that awesome, mates?!" He exclaimed giddily,
jumping up and down. "That happens to the one nearest to
me every time I die. Apparently I'm possessed by Dynam or
something!"

"Don't look at me, guys, I'm not familiar with this religion
at all." Rose dismissed the confused looks she was getting.

"If you are all quite finished." The smooth voice of Rainchild cut in. "We still have the matter of me to deal with."

Tentatively, the group surrounded him, unsure how to proceed. Koey lowered the sword and backed away to join them
in their scrutiny.

"I suppose locking him in the dungeons is out of the question." She proposed.

"Absolutely." Gilly confirmed. "With his transmutation
powers, no cell could hold him."

"We could donate him to scientific research on magic!"
Rose suggested hopefully.

"Or maybe just use his magic powers for diamond manu-
facturing." Koey offered.

"Typical." Rainchild scoffed at them. "I knew none of you
would have the guts to kill me. It's why you're weak in terms

of ruling, 'queen.' How do you think I got your subjects to turn on you so easily? The people love being told who to hate! Nothing unites them more. You think you can govern through benevolence? I can help you. Like it or not, people crave to be ruled by a commanding individual! An iron fist if you wi—"

He was unable to finish the sentence as Dungar silently retrieved the cheese sword during the sanctimonious spiel and then proceeded to cram the entire thing into the wizard's mouth.

"Eat it! Eat it!! EAT IT, YOU COWARDLY VEGAN WORM!!!"

Choking and sputtering out chunks of cheese, Rainchild found himself helplessly pinned against his diamond tree as Dungar relentlessly crammed the entire length of the conjured coagulated dairy product down his throat. After the whole thing had disappeared into the wizard's gullet, Dungar began to viciously bash Rainchild's face in with his gloved hand all the while screaming "I'LL SHOW YOU A REAL IRON FIST!"

Jimminy and the women grimaced with distaste as Rain-child's face was turned into mush before their very eyes. Nobeard merely cocked his head to the side and studied the unhinged brutality with a slight level of respect.

With revenge in his eyes and fire in his veins, Dungar had lost all touch with the situation and self-awareness. All rationality fell to the wayside as his arm and fist became an outlet or every frustration that had built up inside him over the course of the trip, and at that particular moment the only respite he could imagine came from turning the face of the catalyst into a bloody pulp.

During his blind barrage of blows, the blacksmith didn't even notice the battered face of the wizard slump to the ground. He continued his furious swings, his iron knuckles knocking chunks of diamond out of the tree for several more seconds before he finally relented. Shoulders heaving up and down, Dungar turned back to his friends to find them gazing at him, mortified. A few moments of silence passed before Rose finally spoke.

"Er, mister Dungar . . . Do you need help working out your anger issues . . . ?"

"Nope." The blacksmith answered flatly. "I just did."

"You blithering idiots just don't get it, do you?!" The voice of Rainchild piped up behind them. Whirling around, Dungar now saw the form of a new man wearing Rainchild's blood stained clothing.

"I'm all but invincible to you meddling worms!" He continued. "By merely mumbling a word or two I can simply change into another form before you can kill me! I mean you did just shatter the jaw of my main form so now I need to start cultivating my social ties all over again, but the fact still remains I am far from beaten!"

He began to pace and murmur to himself, causing his body to morph once more. This time it settled in the form of Dungar, complete with narrowed eyes and bared teeth.

"Rawr, me smash everything!" He mockingly impersonated the blacksmith. "I'm incapable of doing anything else!"

The true Dungar reacted by throwing a wild haymaker at his reflection. However, Rainchild ducked the swing and threw a right cross in retaliation, causing Dungar to feel what it was like to be hit by one of his fists. It was not pleasant. He staggered backwards rubbing at his face yet feeling oddly proud to know his swings hurt that much.

"Ye may find yerself having a wee bit o' difficulty trying to speak—" Nobeard began, drawing his sword. "—without a head."

Mumbling to himself once more, Rainchild strode casually over to the pirate. By the end of his short walk, his form had changed yet again into that of a marbalt.

"Yarrr, matey!" He taunted in a bizarre gravelly voice, head split in half and looking like a puppet. "And how do ye propose to dislodge me cranium?"

Nobeard grimaced at the rocky creature before him, clearly not aware of what he was looking at. At the lack of response, Rainchild shrugged and then ate the blade of the sword pointed at him.

"Whoa." Rose exclaimed. "I didn't know marbalts were able to talk."

"Well there's a lot you don't know, you naïve little wench!" Rainchild declared as he spun around to face her, taking her form as well. "In fact you're probably the most useless member of this ragtag group of misfits. Why are you even here? Do you think some ability to recall factoids from library books makes you useful? Do you think it makes you intelligent? My god, girl, it's clear as day to everyone here that you're nothing more than dead weight with a penchant for trivia."

"Wizard!" Gilly yelled at him as she drew her sword. "I'll have you know that I am still armed and able to lop off your head faster than you can mumble your magic words."

"And yet you still haven't!" Rainchild snapped back at her. Gilly pointed her sword at him threateningly, but he was completely unfazed by it as he changed shape once again. Gilly watched powerlessly as a perfect replica of herself casually walked towards her and slowly pushed her sword away.

"Pathetic slaves to faith like yourself are the easiest to deal with of all." Rainchild scoffed as he looked her up and down. "You're all completely devoid of individuality. I've memorized all the tenets of your adorable faith, all the obligations you must uphold to pay lip service to your precious goddess. So long as I'm not a direct threat to you, you are even less of a threat to me than your crying counterpart that I just tore to pieces."

He paused briefly to glance back at Rose who was futilely trying to disguise her crushed self-esteem. Satisfied that his harsh words had hit home, he turned back to Gilly to finish his bullying rhetoric.

"It's always a shame when you come across a scenario that your precious book of values doesn't tell you how to resolve isn't it?"

Gilly looked at him with clenched teeth but ultimately lowered her sword. Instead, she moved to go console her sister.

"Oooh, do me next! Do me next!" Jimminy insisted, bouncing up and down excitedly.

Trading Gilly's bright blue eyes and short blonde hair for Jimminy's beady brown optical organs and long black bushy locks, Rainchild strutted over to his next victim.

"Oh blimey, mista mate!" He exclaimed, waving his arms and parodying Jimminy's accent. "There's not a whole lot I can say to tear down someone who is completely devoid of respectability to begin with. Out of all the deserving individuals who could capitalize on immortality and an army of servants, it is truly depressing such a boon was wasted upon a dim-witted imbecile like yourself."

"Blimey I'm handsome." Jimminy smiled to himself, looking his reflection up and down. "I missed wot you said, mate. I was lost in me eyes."

Futilely attempting to contort Jimminy's naturally cheerful face into a frown, Rainchild opened his mouth to speak. However, all that came out was a muffled "Hurk—"

Everyone watched in bewilderment as the wizard's eyes began to bulge and his boney fingers grasped at his throat. His face quickly became flushed as muffled choking sounds began to emanate from his mouth. Within seconds he had fallen to his knees, his eyes and lips swollen and his arms flailing around.

"What in the six crystals is going on?!" Koey exclaimed. "Who did this to him?!"

"He's the only wizard here!" Dungar fired back. "None of us could do this to him."

"I don't think this is magic." Rose offered urgently. "I think he's in anaphylaxis!"

"ENGLISH, ROSE!"

"I . . . uh . . . he's . . . choking?!"

"On what?!" Koey demanded.

"Well no . . . It's . . . His body reacting to something!"

By this point Rainchild had fallen to the ground, tongue protruding from his mouth. Everyone stared open mouthed at his now motionless body.

"Huh." Jimminy mused. "So that's wot I look like dying."

"What did you do to him, Jimmy?"

"I don't know, mate. I just said I wasn't even paying attention."

"Rosie, what just happened to him?" Gilly grilled her sister.

"I . . . I don't know!" She stammered. "Maybe something stung him? That usually only happens when something your body can't handle is introduced to your system. Remember what happened to that lady that ate the peanuts?"

"But he didn't eat any peanuts, Rosie."

"He ate cheese." Dungar stated, staring down at the body.

Everyone stopped for a moment to look at the body, then back to Rose.

"Uh. Maybe? I've read about people having bad reactions to lactose."

"Are you serious?!" Koey exclaimed incredulously. "After everything we just went through, all of his scheming and evil powers we had to overcome, and he died from lactose intolerance?!"

"Well technically it would be an allergy, not an intolerance." Rose clarified. "But it does appear that way, yes."

"I say." Jimminy mused. "That was statistically improbable."

"Wait." Koey interjected. "Why did it just kill him now then!?"

"Well, I have no idea how the inner workings of a shape-shifter . . . well . . . work." Rose began tentatively. She then looked at Jimminy. "If you're allergic to dairy products then he probably reacted to the cheese that was already inside him when he turned into you."

"Oh right, I am allergic to that cow business." Jimminy exclaimed, smacking himself in the head. "Never liked the way it tasted anyway."

"This is the dumbest thing I've ever heard." Koey grumbled, folding her arms and looking away.

"Aye. And yet here it be." Nobeard affirmed with a shrug.

"Cut his head off just to make sure." Koey ordered Gilly.

"Without just cause I cannot bring myself to deface a corpse." She informed the queen gravely.

"I'll do it!" Jimminy excitedly offered, decapitating the body with his katana before anyone gave a response. Sickeningly, the head rolled away from its body just as it did the first time Jimminy was beheaded. He eagerly chased after his head as the rest of the company looked on in disgust.

"I look so surprised!" He exclaimed as he poked the head's swollen face. "Can I keep it?!" He asked the group.

Koey sighed. "I still can't believe any of this, but I don't have time to dwell on it. I still have the matter of my treasonous subjects to deal with."

Without another word, she began making her way through the dark forest back to the castle, the rest of the party following suit. No one had anything left to say; all that was left was to let the situation sink in.

Dungar looked over to Jimminy who was having difficulty trying to determine the proper etiquette for carrying a dismembered head. Eventually he pulled all the hair back into a pony tail and used it like a handle. He found himself sharing a similar sentiment as his friend towards Rainchild's body. The thought of a dismembered corpse of the wizard was so satisfying he wished he could have it taxidermized so he could carry it around and use it as a stress reliever.

Stuffed or not, the death of Rainchild was an enormous load off of his mind. He agreed with Koey that the nature of the man's death was one of the dumbest things he'd ever witnessed. However, dumb as the death was, it had been a pretty dumb day and a pretty dumb trip and it was oddly satisfying to see it all wrapped up in one big fat fittingly dumb conclusion.

TWENTY SEVEN

RESOLVING, ABSOLVING, AND EVOLVING

By the time they had cleared the forest a clear night sky loomed over them. As he looked up at the stars, Dungar couldn't help but wonder if they were indeed the garden of lights of lore. Looking at Gilly, it was clear there was no question of the sort in her mind as she too gazed skyward. He found himself ever so slightly jealous of her surety.

Despite his many brushes with it, he had never really given death much thought. He had always assumed it would simply happen when it happened and there would be nothing he could do about it anyway. However the world was no longer as simple to approach as he once found it to be. It was a sprawling place filled with things beyond his imagination that no story had ever done justice. After experiencing such a small part of it he found himself compelled to wonder what may lay in the rest of it, let alone beyond. Now he knew how Rose felt.

"It's interesting, you know!" Rose thought out loud, breaking the silence of the group. She looked around expectantly, hoping someone would ask her what was. But no one bothered, they just looked at her and waited for her to carry on of her own accord.

"I know this is real life." She continued. "But it played out just like my favorite stories! The good guys rallied together to defeat the big evil wizard guy even after he tried to overpower them and divide them! It's just like a fairy tale!"

Everyone looked at her curiously before dispersing confused glances amongst themselves.

"Alright well . . ." Rose qualified hastily. "Yeah there was no mystical prophecy, or prince charming, or wise old wizard, or romance . . ." She glanced shyly at Nobeard before continuing. "But still—"

"Let us not disregard the fact my kingdom was still pushed to the verge of collapse." Koey interjected. "My entire town guard was massacred and my subjects are all against me."

"And my original plan was to kill the queen, not save her." Dungar added.

"And our salvation only resulted from our savior having uncontrollable anger issues." Gilly also added as she nodded sheepishly towards Dungar.

"And Jaunty died like five times!" Nobeard pointed out.

"Nah, three, mate!" Jimminy corrected with a grin as he booped his severed head's nose. ". . . That I'm aware of." He then added as he looked up thoughtfully.

"But you guys are all missing the point!" Rose insisted. "Rainchild failed because he was so busy pointing out the flaws in all of us that he failed to see his own! He saw himself as a perfect mastermind who was impervious to defeat while we knowingly embraced ourselves as flawed people, using both our flaws and our strengths to overcome his adversity. That is why we triumphed and he failed!"

Everyone stopped for a moment to let her words sink in and be considered. The faint sounds of wildlife were all that was heard as each surviving member of the fellowship considered their role in the preceding plot. Dungar quite liked the notion as it was presented, though he wasn't quite sure if he bought it or not. The brief period of reflection was cut short by Jimminy's penchant for silence shattering.

"I'm pretty sure he failed because he died, mate."

"And one should not be obliged to take credit when they may not be privy to all the unseen forces that may have come to their aid." Gilly added.

"Oh you guys are hopeless." Rose sighed. "Whatever. I finally have a story of my own to write! But I'll have to get a bit of background somehow. Like how he managed to overthrow Farrawee."

"Well I can tell you that." Dungar grunted, thinking back to his conversation with Stranger. "He posed as the queen in order to lure the king's attention and then probably used some of his stupid magic to put the king under his spell to do his bidding."

Koey nodded with pursed lips, looking down at the ground.

"See that's the thing, though." Rose mused. "Rainchild was a shapeshifter, his only magic consisted of changing the makeups of his body or things around him. So if he influenced the king to do his bidding somehow then it couldn't have involved magic."

"Perhaps he transformed into the king?" Nobeard offered.

"No no, that can't be right." Koey cut in. "The intent of his exploits in Farrawee was to frame me, so he had to have been very public that I was manipulating the strings somehow. I'm not sure how he managed to accomplish that. King Sheen was not a dumb man, in fact the only thing he was really known for was . . ."

Her voice trailed off as a look of pure unbridled horror spread across her face. Dungar grimaced as he put it together and arrived at the same conclusion. Everyone else, however, continued to look on in confusion.

". . . What?" Rose finally asked.

"OH MY GOD HE MADE ME A WHORE!!!!" The queen shrieked into the night.

"Blimey." Jimminy exclaimed. "Perhaps we oughtta call him Rainchild Kinghumper, eh, mate?" He chuckled and nudged

Dungar as he said it. His laughter was cut short by a sharp look from Koey.

"Erm..." He stammered. "Or we could never talk about it ever again?"

"See to it that you don't."

"For wot it's with, me lady, everyone else who knew is probably dead!"

His grin weakened as he surveyed the uncomfortable expressions around him.

"Oh right, people are dead now . . ."

"I'm so confused!" Rose proclaimed loudly.

"Ye best leave it alone, lass." Nobeard advised her. "I don't think any of yer stories would have covered anything like this."

No other conversation was had as they climbed the torch lit hill towards the familiar castle gate and made their way into the confines of the walls. Eerily, the main entrance was just as empty as it was when they first arrived, even with no commotion left taking place. The "Law Resistonce" graffiti was now crossed out and underneath it now read "Law Resisted!" However the latter graffiti also had a line through it and underneath it, in different writing, read "Please stop painting on my wall."

The group made their way down the charred streets and into the main square where the riot had taken place several hours before. Much to their amazement, the crowd was still there. In the wake of the chaos, after the guards left, they appeared to have banded together and taken it upon themselves to clean up the mess that was made. The burnt carts were now all neatly stacked in a bonfire that lit the area as detachments of citizens swept away debris and cleaned up blood. However, at first sight of their queen, all carried items were immediately dropped.

"The witch whore has returned!!"

"She must have defeated Rainchild!"

"Burn her in the bonfire!"

"People please!" Koey yelled to them as she hopped on the remnants of the stage and raised her arms. "Before you take up your arms I beg for your ears!"

Grumbles of disdain echoed from the crowd as citizens as they gathered menacingly around her. But they stayed their advance, even if only temporarily.

"I do not wish to presume upon your intelligence!" The would-be deposed queen insisted, struggling to reason with her subjects. "However there has been much trickery afoot in recent days! I understand your scorn for witchcraft; therefore I must inform you that the man to whom you entrusted the task of vanquishing me was a practitioner himself."

"We know!" One of the citizens called out. "That's why we needed him to kill you."

"Wh- What?" Koey stammered in bewilderment. "You're permissive of magic? Then why did you want me killed?!"

"Because you're a witch!" The crowd roared unanimously. "So is he!"

A low buzzing swept over the crowd as they debated with themselves.

"No, he's a wizard." One of them eventually called out. "There's a difference. Wizards are good and witches are bad!"

"They're the same thing!" Koey insisted.

The crowd buzzed amongst themselves once more.

"Alright then!" Somebody shouted. "Burn the witch . . . AND THE WIZARD!"

"BURN THE WITCH AND THE WIZARD! BURN THE WITCH AND THE WIZARD!"

"The wizard's already dead, mates!" Jimminy called to the group as he too jumped on the stage. "I got his head right here!"

"Hey they saved us from the wizard! They're alright after all!"

"Elect them our new king and queen!"

"But the princess is still a witch!"

"Oh yeah . . ."

"Burn the witch! Burn the witch!"

"Is that guy holding his own head?"

"Listen to me!" Koey yelled once more, stepping in front of Jimminy. "Do not use your hatreds to unite yourselves! It only leads to dissention and downfall! This was a thriving city under the regime of my father, and he never resorted to such underhanded tactics. He governed by way of freedom and fairness. There was no thought policing or mandatory opinions enforced by royal decree! As your ruler I will support the rights of the individual to form their own impressions! Under my command there will also be freedom of religion, and no taxation without representation, and—"

Her voice eventually became drowned out by the rising roar of the crowd.

"Didn't King Ik teach us to hate Nonamay?"

"And redbears!"

"GOD I HATE REDBEARS!"

"Me too!!"

Koey stared disbelievingly out into the crowd as her hands slowly fell to her side.

"Hello!?" She called into the crowd. "I'm offering you freedoms . . . and options for representation . . . These are good things, why don't you want them . . . ? ALRIGHT FINE THEN!!!!" She bellowed at the top of her lungs.

The crowd quieted down as curious eyes turned back to Koey.

"If you accept my reinstatement as queen then my first official act will be to declare tomorrow to be Everyone Go Out Into the Forest and Kill Redbears . . . AGAIN day!"

At that, the entire crowd threw their tools in the air whilst cheering. Chants of "All Hail Princess Koey!" broke out amongst the masses.

"For the love of Suola it's 'Queen' not 'Princess.'" Koey corrected exasperatedly.

Still rife with mirth, the crowd began to disperse back to their self-prescribed duties while the new queen returned to her friends. Upon seeing the looks on some of their faces, she felt compelled to explain herself.

"I know what you're thinking, and it pained me to have to do that." She insisted to Rose's dissatisfied facial expression. "I share my father's contempt for political games and ploys, however it is a sad truth that, pretty or not, there seems to be no way around them."

"Ye landlubbers be a strange bunch." Nobeard mused.

"Well in my books the benevolent princesses always . . ." Rose began. However she was cut off by Koey before she could finish.

"I would love to hear about all your stories, Rose. But let us make our way to the castle before we begin our discussion of such things. You all have been invaluable assets to the crown and the kingdom and I would be thoughtless if I did not find a way to reward each of you. So if you would allow me the pleasure of your company for a little while longer, we shall take up such conversation in the banquet hall. Follow me please."

The once beautiful blue gown Koey wore was now stained and tattered from her time in the forest. However the elegance and regality she effortlessly exuded couldn't be stifled even if she were clad in no more than a potato sack. Gracefully she led everyone in the party away from the stage and into the castle. Everyone in the party except for Dungar, that is.

Part of him did indeed want to accompany the group and receive a reward for the ordeal, but a larger part compelled him to stay behind and let them go. They had all been forever bound together by the adventure, and the memories will stay with them for the rest of their lives.

However, in his heart of hearts he knew that the adventure was the only thing that bound them together. Now that it was at an end they all once again became normal people, normal people with nothing left keeping them together who would inevitably go their separate ways.

"Taking an early leave are ye, laddy?"

Whirling around, Dungar saw Nobeard casually leaning against the wall of a building behind him.

"Uh huh." The blacksmith replied flippantly. "I need to be on my way."

"After all that eh? I don't know everything ye folks have been through, but I think it be fair to say it be quite a lot to just simply walk away from."

"Don't gimme that. They're good people, but you and I both know it wouldn't work out."

"Ye don't know yerself a bloody thing, lad. Ye can justify yer actions to yerself all ye like, but the fact of the matter is, ye be the one leaving. Not them. And if yer still leaving at this age, then I'd be willing to bet ye always have been the one who left. Because if ye'd ever tried sticking around then ye'd be privy to the merits if ye catch me drift."

"Oh you think I'm always the one to leave? I have a window that says otherwise." He retorted proudly. "And what about you then? I don't see you going with them."

"Aye, because I'm here saying me goodbyes to you, lad! I can always say me goodbyes to Jaunty later, or I could just wait til the next time he dies and shows up on me shoreline. But fer now I just had to get away from the lady folk. I could see the googly eyes that the young brunette be giving me, and I didn't want to give her the difficult explanation that she ain't me preferred holster fer me captain's log."

He paused to give Dungar time to blink several times and let the words sink in before he continued.

"Ye life is yers to live, mister Dungar, don't let anybody stop ye from doing so. I imagine ye will be going through some ideological changes in the wake of yer recent exploits. But whether or not they be formed in unconventional circumstances, true friendships be more valuable than anything I ever fished out of a fishy's belly. I advise ye to think long and hard before making or breaking any commitments."

"You are a very strange pirate." Dungar said flatly.

"Aye I be. But what are ye gonna do?" From his coat he produced a small bag of what Dungar assumed to be coins which he put into that blacksmith's hand. "Get yerself some rest, lad. Wise men don't make decisions when they're weary from a long day."

Wordlessly, Dungar accepted the gift. Once he did so, the pirate began to back away down the street.

"Wait." The blacksmith called out, one last thing popping into his mind.

Nobeard stopped his departure and looked back.

"What was in the chest?"

At that, the pirate captain chuckled to himself, much to Dungar's confusion.

"I wouldn't know, laddy! I never opened it."

Dungar's mouth fell open. After all that effort, risking life and limb and lung to rob the most powerful plant in the land when it clearly didn't feel like being robbed, all the while listening to Nobeard insist that this was the pinnacle achievement he could ever aspire to, and he didn't even open the bloody thing? His face must have conveyed all of that because the snickering pirate opted to answer all those questions before Dungar could even ask them.

"What do ye think be in there, laddy? Gold? Jewels? Dirty pictures? It's the treasure I want, not any of those things. If I open the chest then it just becomes a box that holds assorted items of varying value. But if it stays closed then it remains the treasure of the wizard tree, and that be worth more to me than any material good that might be inside."

In a strange way, that kind of made sense to Dungar. But he was really tired and had taken many blows to the head today, so what did he know?

"Farewell, mister Dungar." Nobeard bid him one last time with his pearly pirate smile. "May the wind always be at yer stern."

"Uh, you too. Whatever that means."

As the mighty Captain Lukey Nobeard disappeared once more, Dungar looked down to the coin purse in his hand and felt a wave of tiredness wash over him. Wearily, he traced back through the streets until he found the familiar defaced "Law Resistonce" building which he remembered to be a tavern.

Absentmindedly, he shoulder checked the door open and ambled over to the counter where the blonde boy from earlier froze midway through polishing a glass in reaction to his sur-prise visitor. The blacksmith slumped heavily onto the counter and looked the unnerved young man in the eyes.

"I need a room." He grunted.

"This tavern doesn't support lodging, sir." The boy offered uneasily. "We're only equipped to serve food and drink, which I would be happy to provide."

Dungar blinked several times, struggling to compute the information just provided to him. He then dropped the sack of coins Nobeard had just given him onto the counter.

"I'll be taking the keeper's suite tonight then. Goodnight." He grumbled as he walked away. As he made his way up the stairs he heard a faint rustling followed by the boy's voice.

"Sir, this is just a bag of rocks . . ."

"Son, I just killed this town's entire guard regiment with my fists. The next word out of your mouth better be goodnight."

"Goodnight."

The moment Dungar collapsed into the small cot that was so reminiscent of his own at home he was immediately whisked off into the most restful dreamless sleep he had ever had in his life.

"WAKEY WAKEY EGGS AND BAKEY!"

Dungar shot bolt upright in his bed, head butting Jimminy in the face and causing him to spill his plates of eggs and bacon everywhere. The two men sat in shock for a moment, each rubbing their faces.

"Well I probably should have seen that coming." Jimminy lamented to himself as he began picking strips of bacon off the floor. He was wearing fancy new clothing and carried with him a handsome looking leather bag.

Dungar had no idea how long he had slept for. Blinking in the sunlight and rubbing his face, he looked out the window to find the sun was well into the sky and the town was in full swing.

"The ladies were wondering wot happened to ya, mate." Jimminy informed him as he set a plate full of floor food into his lap. "And you missed out on presents!"

"There's nothing she could give me anyway." The blacksmith mumbled as he devoured the contents of his plate.

"Don't be so sure about that, mate. She's quite creative, the queen, and she makes the best sandwiches!"

Dungar raised an eyebrow. "Is that right?"

"Sure is, mate. She appointed Rose as the new curator of the kingdom's library and offered Gilly the spot as captain of the new town guard. Oh, and she also had her canonized!"

"Really?"

"Yeah! We did it down at the church this morning. She's now known as Gilly, the patron saint of badasses. The queen also tried to arrange an exorcism for me but the priest kept telling her that if it was a legitimate possession the body has ways to try and shut that whole thing down."

The two men ate in silence for a few moments after that, reflecting on their journey and the wide open aftermath they now found themselves in. Dungar figured thiswas likely a familiar feeling for his friend, adventure seemed to be something of a routine for the man. However he found a strange sentiment towards the notion of adventure in his own mind.

He had always thought when the trip finally came to a close, and he wasn't in jail or dead, he would want to return home to his simple life where he was most comfortable. But now having experiences under his belt, and new knowledge in his head, he found a strange thirst for adventure inside himself that had never been present before. A simple life of modest means no longer appealed to him. The world was too vast, too compelling to be neglected.

"Where do they brew the best ale in all the land, Jimmy?" Dungar smirked under his scruffy beard as he got out of bed.

"Well they usually decide that at the ale competition held at the base of the Demon's Kettle every year." Jimminy smiled as he too got to his feet.

"Demon's Kettle?"

"Yeah. It's a volcano, mate."

"Sounds dangerous."

"It's been known to be hot headed once in a while."

"Well I don't know about you, Jimmy, but after all this business I reckon I could use a drink."

"Why now that you mention it, mate, I have a bit of a hankering meself."

As they strode out of the bedroom and towards the stairs, a question popped into Dungar's mind.

"How did you know I was in here anyway?"

"You're not a hard man to track, mista Dungar."

They made their way down the stairs to find the door to the tavern knocked clean off its hinges and chairs strewn all over the floor with a very noticeable wake carved through them.

"Blimey, mate. You're like a bloody redbear!"

"I'll be honest with you, Jimmy. I have no idea what a red-bear is."

Jimminy turned to his friend, head cocked to the side as they exited the tavern into the street.

". . . Honestly, mate. Me either. I always hear people talk about them though so I didn't want to seem out of the loop."

Dungar snorted loudly and Jimminy began to laugh as they made their way back out of the castle gates and into the wide open green fields of Jenair. The world stretched out around them in infinite directions, beckoning them to limitless locations. The blacksmith's body felt light, as if uplifted by the freedom to explore. He breathed the fresh air in deeply and then turned to Jimminy.

"Alright, Jimmy. Where's this drinking competition?"

"Far to the east!" The shaggy fellow replied enthusiastically. "Over ranges and rivers, lies a land that changes and shivers! If you reach said land, you've gone too far. The demon's kettle is just a little ways that way." He pointed with a grin.

Confidently, they made the first step of their new journey into the world. Then the second, then the third, then Dungar stopped counting. His mind drifted back to the girls and how he never did say goodbye to them. But it was too late now. Besides, they were probably too happy with their new appointments to give him any thought anyway. That thought, however, did spawn a question in his mind. A question he would regret asking immediately after doing so.

"You know, Jimmy, you never did tell me what your reward from the queen was."

"Oh blimey, thanks for reminding me!"

Gleefully he reached into his new leather bag and produced from it a shiny new flute carved out of solid diamond.

"Oh god, no . . ."

"Gorgeous, isn't it?! She had the finest woodwind crafts-men at her disposal retrieve a branch off the diamond tree last night so they could have this ready for me by morning! It sounds amazing too! Want to hear?"

"Jimmy you know I—"

"A one two three four!"

Keeping in step with his rhythm, Jimminy Appaya began to play the all too familiar melody of his favorite tune. Dungar briefly considered shattering the thing on the nearest tree, but instead he found his own head bobbing along ever so slightly to the beat.

"I saw that, mate! You have to sing with me now."

"Not in a million years, Jimmy."

"EVERYBODY!"

> *Way hey and away we slink*
> *Off to the kettle to get a drink*
> *Where the men are fat and their bodies stink*
> *We'll raise our glasses and make them clink*
> *That journey went by in just a blink*
> *We're going to need a sequel I think!*

ABOUT THE AUTHOR

Logan J. Hunder is a 23 year old humanoid creature that records his rambling in text until he has enough to print in book form. A seasoned thinker, he's been having thoughts about things for over two decades. Born in Victoria, Canada, he attended college for subjects completely unrelated to heroing and witch slaying but didn't let that stop him from concocting wacky adventures, with only limited help from mind altering substances. In his spare time he enjoys watching movies, repurposing things as balancing beams, and giving inspiring pep talks to himself in the mirror. *Witches Be Crazy* is his first novel.